KT-500-279

THE WORLD'S CLASSICS

THE MASTER OF BALLANTRAE

ROBERT LOUIS STEVENSON, only child of Thomas Stevenson, engineer and lighthouse keeper, and Margaret Balfour, daughter of a Scots minister, was born in Edinburgh in 1850. In 1871 he exchanged the study of engineering for the law. From 1876 he pursued a full-time literary career, beginning as an essayist and travel writer with the publication of *An Inland Voyage* (1878), *Edinburgh: Picturesque Notes* (1878), *Travels with a Donkey in the Cévennes* (1879), and *Virginibus Puerisque* (1881). He is probably best known for *Treasure Island* (1883), *Kidnapped* (1886), and *Dr. Jekyll and Mr. Hyde* (1886). Ill health prompted Stevenson to travel widely on the Continent and in the South Seas, where he settled in 1889–90 until his death in Samoa on 3 December 1894.

EMMA LETLEY has spent several years teaching Literature at the University of Hong Kong and is currently lecturing at the Roehampton Institute. She has edited Stevenson's *Treasure Island*, *Kidnapped* and *Catriona*, and *Dr Jekyll and Mr Hyde* and *Weir of Hermiston* for the World's Classics.

THE WORLD'S CLASSICS

ROBERT LOUIS STEVENSON

The Master of Ballantrae
A Winter's Tale

Edited with an Introduction by
EMMA LETLEY

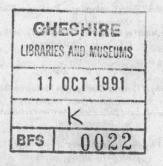
Oxford   New York
OXFORD UNIVERSITY PRESS

Oxford University Press, Walton Street, Oxford OX2 6DP

Oxford New York Toronto
Delhi Bombay Calcutta Madras Karachi
Petaling Jaya Singapore Hong Kong Tokyo
Nairobi Dar es Salaam Cape Town
Melbourne Auckland
and associated companies in
Berlin Ibadan

This edition first published 1983 as a World's Classics paperback
Reprinted 1988, 1990

British Library Cataloguing in Publication Data

Stevenson, Robert Louis
The Master of Ballantrae.—(The World's classics)
I. Title   II. Letley, Emma
823'.[F]   PR5484.M2
ISBN 0-19-281635-7

Library of Congress Cataloging in Publication Data

Stevenson, Robert Louis, 1850-1894.
The Master of Ballantrae. (The World's classics)
Bibliography: p.
I. Letley, Emma   II. Title.
PR5484.M2 1983   823'.8   82-22325
ISBN 0-19-281635-7 (pbk.)

Printed in Great Britain by
BPCC Hazell Books
Aylesbury, Bucks

CONTENTS

CONTENTS

INTRODUCTION

But the intensest throb of my literary life, as that of many others, has been *The Master of Ballantrae*—a pure hard crystal, my boy, a work of ineffable and exquisite art. It makes us all as proud of you as you can possibly be of *it*.[1]

I have an impression that I didn't make copious or clear to you in my last what a grand literary life your *Master of B*. has been leading here. Somehow, a miracle has been wrought for you (for you they are,) and the fine old featherbed of English taste *has* thrilled with preternatural recognitions. The most unlikely number of people *have* discerned that *The Master* is "well written." . . . It's "fate," my dear fellow, has been glittering glory—simply: and I ween—that is I hope—you will find the glitter has chinked as well.[2]

Henry James's comments on *The Master* show how this novel reclaimed Stevenson's reputation. The four works published since *Kidnapped* (1886) had been disappointingly received: *The Wrong Box* (1889), a collaborative effort with his step-son, Lloyd Osbourne, had been particularly savaged, calling forth the worst critical reaction of Stevenson's literary career. A novel was needed to revive the acclaim he had received with *Treasure Island* (1883) and the *Strange Case of Dr. Jekyll and Mr. Hyde* (1886). As Henry James's second comment suggests, *The Master* was that novel. Praised by contemporary reviewers for its tragic power, its characterization, and its visual force, the novel takes up

[1] Letter to Robert Louis Stevenson, 21 March 1890, in *Henry James and Robert Louis Stevenson*, ed. J. Adam Smith (1948), p. 185.
[2] Letter to Robert Louis Stevenson, 28 April 1890 in Smith, op. cit., pp. 188–9.

once more that Scots background which Stevenson had employed to such powerful effect in earlier fiction such as *Kidnapped*, "Thrawn Janet" and "The Merry Men", and was to exploit again in *Catriona* (the sequel to *Kidnapped* published in 1893) and the unfinished *Weir of Hermiston* (published posthumously in 1896).

Stevenson was born in Edinburgh in 1850, the son of Thomas Stevenson, a well-off harbour and lighthouse engineer, and was educated at the Edinburgh Academy and University. Even in his early years he suffered from that ill-health (respiratory disorders) which was to trouble him throughout his life. Initially he intended to follow his father's profession and study engineering, but then he decided to read for the Bar and was admitted in 1875. He did not, however, practise as a barrister but rather kept to his decision, made in 1871, to pursue a literary career. In spite of the widespread success of *Treasure Island* and *Jekyll and Hyde*, Stevenson was not, as a full-time writer, financially independent until he received an inheritance on Thomas Stevenson's death in 1887. His poor health prompted him to travel widely: in 1879 he went to the United States, married Fanny Osbourne, and spent many of the following years at Davos in Switzerland and by the Mediterranean, returning to Scotland at intervals to see his family. After his father's death, Stevenson left Edinburgh and travelled with his mother and Fanny. They made a trip to the United States in 1887 (much of *The Master* was written at Lake Saranac, New York), and then cruised around the Pacific. Stevenson settled for his last years at Vailima in Samoa, the place of his death in 1894. Although he never returned to Scotland after 1887, its influence was an inherent part of his literary personality and it is in his Scots stories, particularly *The Master* (1889), that his genius is most fully realized.

What kind of novel is it that aroused the "glittering glory" to which Henry James refers and which caused a renaissance in Stevenson's reputation? In December 1887 he writes to Sidney Colvin, his friend and literary agent, that he has "fallen head over heels into a new tale". This is how he describes it:

It is to me a most seizing tale: there are some fantastic elements; the most is a dead human problem—human tragedy, I should say rather . . . I have done most of the big work, the quarrel, duel between the brothers, and announcement of the death to Clementina [Alison] and my lord—Clementina, Henry, and Mackellar (nicknamed Square-toes) are really very fine fellows; the Master is all I know of the Devil. I have known hints of him, in the world, but always cowards; he is as bold as a lion, but with the same deadly, causeless duplicity I have watched with so much surprise in my two cowards . . .

In March 1888, writing to Henry James, Stevenson expands on the nature of the Master's devilry and encapsulates the novel's story:

The elder brother is an INCUBUS: supposed to be killed at Culloden, he turns up again and bleeds the family of money; on that stopping he comes and lives with them, whence flows the real tragedy, the nocturnal duel of the brothers (very naturally, and indeed, I think, inevitably arising), and second supposed death of the elder. Husband and wife now really make up, and then the cloven hoof appears. For the third supposed death and the manner of the third reappearance is steep; steep, sir . . . it leads up to the death of the elder brother at the hands of the younger in a perfectly cold-blooded murder, of which I wish (and mean) the reader to approve.

The emphases of the novel in these quotations are corroborated by the alternative titles and sub-titles considered by Stevenson in the course of writing *The Master*. He mentions both "The Familiar Incubus" and "Brothers" in his working outlines as possible titles: these were eventually rejected in favour of *The Master of Ballantrae*. He also thought about different sub-titles ("A Romantic Tale", "A Fantastic Tale" and "A Fantasy") before settling on its final sub-title, "A Winter's Tale", with its echoes of

Scots fire-side tales as well as its appropriate atmospheric
suggestion. Both the American and the British first editions
of *The Master* include this sub-title although it has tended
to be omitted from some more modern editions.

In view of recent critical comments on *The Master*,[3]
which tend to stress the ambiguity of the younger brother's
character to the point of underplaying the rightness of his
"murder" of the Master, Stevenson's comments should be
invoked to understand the inherent, and brilliantly portrayed, devilry of the elder brother, James Durie, Master
of Ballantrae.

There are to be found in *The Master* literary parallels in
earlier and subsequent Scots fiction: the nature of evil and
those divisions caused by the vexed question of inheritance
are central concerns of John Galt's most powerful tragic
novel, *The Entail* (1823); the portrayal of the diabolic is
similar to that found in James Hogg's *Confessions of a
Justified Sinner* (1824);[4] but most influential, in Stevenson's
conception of *The Master*, was Captain Marryat's *Phantom
Ship* (1839). He had been re-reading this story during his
stay at Lake Saranac, New York, in October 1887 and it
had provided him with just that impetus he needed for his
new novel. Looking back on this time at Saranac, Stevenson
writes in "A Note to the Master of Ballantrae":

I reminded myself that it was a long time since I had cast a
plot . . . and determined to design one there and then; this was
to be a story on a great canvas; it was to cover many years, so
that I might draw my characters in the growth and the decay
of life; and many lands, so that I might display them in changing and incongruous surroundings. Above all, it was to be such
as should present the large, conspicuous features of incident,

---

[3] For a representative selection of recent critical work on Stevenson's Scots fiction see *Stevenson and Victorian Scotland*, ed. Jenni
Calder (1981).

[4] For a fuller treatment of the relationship of *The Master* and Scots
fiction, see Douglas Gifford, "Stevenson and Scottish Fiction", in
Calder op. cit., pp. 62–87.

and might be treated in the summary, elliptic method of the book I had been reading.[5]

Set in seventeenth-century Holland, *The Phantom Ship* shares with Stevenson's *Master* a carefully exploited historical background, a wide variety of setting, the theme of family division caused by a wrong deed, supernatural intervention and a highly-wrought sense of suspense. Philip Vanderdecken, Marryat's hero, learns from his dying mother that his father is not, as he has believed all his life, dead but is "In Living Judgment", a half-alive spirit who has once returned to see his wife. After his mother's death, Philip discovers that his father can only be released from his doom (that is, to wander the seas in the "Flying Dutchman") by re-possession of the relic on which he made his fatal, God-defying vow. Philip's task is to find him and hand over the relic. *The Phantom Ship*, a tale incorporating elements of the Wandering Jew and the Flying Dutchman legends, is the story of this quest. The novel is firmly set within a Christian framework: Philip's task is seen as a Christian duty to release the father from torment; the diabolic one-eyed spirit, Schriften, who thwarts the son's efforts, is portrayed ultimately as an agent in the divine, providential scheme; and Amine, the "white witch" heroine, is seen as a wronged martyr of the Inquisition. Neither Schriften nor the haunted father are, in the true sense, incubuses—the first is an agent of Providence, the second a suffering, but redeemable spirit. As Marryat takes his heroine to Goa during the time of the Inquisition, India becomes not the place of the strange and the uncanny (the appropriate spiritual home of Stevenson's Secundra Dass) but rather the centre of trading opportunity and religious persecution.

Like that of Marryat's novel, the action of *The Master* is precisely located in a certain historical epoch, the period following the Jacobite Rebellion of 1745 until 1764. The

[5] Unpublished section of "Note", as quoted in Roger G. Swearingen, *The Prose Writings of Robert Louis Stevenson* (1980), p. 120.

news of Bonnie Prince Charlie's landing in Scotland comes to the Durie family. Like a number of Scots families of the period, they decide to ensure the preservation of their landed interests in the event of either a Royalist or a Jacobite victory: one brother is to follow Prince Charlie, the other to support King George. This historical background, employed also in *Kidnapped* and *Catriona*, enables Stevenson to give a far-reaching context to his theme of division in *The Master*: divisions in one family mirror divisions in Scottish society that had existed since the sixteenth century and continued after the Union of 1707. For a modern reader, the novel provides a gloss on those divisions, of language and of political allegiance, which persist today.

The decisive Jacobite defeat at the Battle of Culloden (1746) gives Stevenson the opportunity to make the disappearance of the Master coincide with the defeat of the romantic (i.e. Jacobite) cause and thus, indirectly, to make the reader consider the relationship between *The Master* and romance.[6] The incorporation of the Battle of Culloden enables Stevenson plausibly to remove his hero, supposedly a Jacobite rebel, to foreign places and thus extend the "canvas" of his narrative. Stevenson's second narrator, the Irish Francis Burke, is richly characterized by his allegiance to Jacobitism as a man of uncontrolled romantic instincts; and the manner in which Stevenson treats him casts an ironic glance at the romantic spirit and literary romance. Further, in a novel where family splits play a crucial part, and, in particular, threaten the inheritance of the next generation, the possibility of Jacobite pardons (p. 211) is transmuted into an additional danger for Henry Durie and his son.

The way Stevenson handles his diabolic material and portrays James Durie, immediately shows his superiority to his source, *The Phantom Ship*. Whereas Marryat employs a simple, third-person narration, Stevenson filters his "world-wide" events through two (three if we include

[6] See F. R. Hart, *The Scottish Novel* (1978), pp. 162–4.

Mountain's contribution to Mackellar's narrative) main narrators. The method is masterly not only in the variety of pace it affords but also in convincing the reader of the complexities of the incubus's character. First, there is Mackellar, an old servant of the Durie family and a participant in the main incidents of the Master's "returns" and key events during his voyage to, and travels in, America. Presenting himself as a conscientious witness and reliable historian, Mackellar appears to give a trustworthy report of the schisms within the Durie family; but, often, his reliability is undermined by his partisanship, by his intense commitment to upholding the Durie family name, and by his cowardice. His pedantic attention to detail and fussy footnoting of the text give the illusion of integrity as well as a bona fide contract between first-person narrator and reader. This is deceptive. Although he is most conscientious about verifiable facts, such as the relationship between Teach and the notorious Blackbeard (p. 55), on more important matters he is less reliable. On occasion, Mackellar is so unsure about his own material, his own reaction to events, and his ability as a reporter that we have considerable doubts about taking him on absolute trust. These doubts lead the reader to a right apprehension of the ambiguities of Stevenson's characters. The night duel, when Henry apparently kills his brother (Chapter V), is a case in point: Mackellar's narrative is dubious and fissured with uncertainties. His own fear prevents him from taking an objective view. Did James act in a cowardly, underhand way and thus justify Henry's action? Was James ever even apparently dead? Mackellar is so circumspect and halting in his report that we are never quite sure. We are not meant to be; and, in this, lies much of the subtlety of Stevenson's narrative method.[7]

In the earlier sections of the novel, Mackellar fulfils the function of witness, with varying degrees of unreliability,

[7] See Gifford, op. cit.; James F. Kilroy, "Narrative Techniques in *The Master of Ballantrae*", in *Studies in Scottish Literature*, 5–6 (October 1967), pp. 98–106

without problem. The final two chapters of *The Master* were
more difficult for Stevenson. Here he has to deal with the
darkest material in the novel. He reports that, in the course
of writing these episodes "In the Wilderness", he felt his
cautious, prevaricating Scotsman would not do:

How, with a narrator like Mackellar, should I transact the
melodrama in the wilderness? How with his style, so full of
disabilities, attack a passage which must be either altogether
seizing or altogether silly and absurd?[8]

He was anxious also about how "the pen of Mackellar was
to relate a series of incidents so highly coloured, so excessive, and so tragic?" He solves the problem eventually by
having his cautious Scot re-construct the events in the
Wilderness from information given to him by the Indian
trader named Mountain and conversations with Secundra
Dass (p. 223). Their narrative, passed on to and assimilated
by Mackellar, makes plausible material which might otherwise seem an impossibly out-of-character report by the
Steward of Durrisdeer. Stevenson also intentionally makes
Mackellar only partially aware of the events he describes.
He is more aware, because of his active part in the Duries'
family history, than the English pioneer, Sir William
Johnson but he is not in possession of the total significance.
In this, he is comparable to narrators like Lockwood in
Emily Bronte's *Wuthering Heights* (1847) who are called
upon to report events outside their customary, rational
frame of reference and, in so doing, underline the wider
implications of the experiences narrated. The omissions in
the narrator's understanding encourage the reader to take
a more comprehensive view. Mackellar's style further aids
his credibility as narrator of "highly coloured", "excessive" and "tragic" matter: his "disabled" manner, with its
fussy pedantry, latinate constructions and obstruse use of
archaic terms, together with his Scots expressions, produces

[8] "A note to the Master of Ballantrae", Tusitala Edition, X,
p. 239.

a counter-balance to the fantastic events he is called upon
to describe: as, indeed, does his very character.

Francis Burke is similarly unreliable by virtue of his
personality. What prompted Stevenson to choose one of
Prince Charlie's Irishmen for this task? He tells us that his
tale was "world wide enough" with Scotland, India and
America all naturally included in the canvas; but there was
a problem: Stevenson had only the most cursory knowledge
of things Indian. He realized that he "should have to get
into India and out of it again upon a foot of fairy lightness".
One might ask why he wanted to "get into" India at all in
The Master: from the early nineteenth-century, Anglo-
Indian characters had appeared in fiction in the form of
returning nabobs—John Galt's Mr. Rupees, in *The Last of
the Lairds* (1826), and Mr. Jobbry in *The Member* (1832)
are examples from earlier Scots fiction; Indian servants
appear in mid-nineteenth-century novels, for example, Jos
Sedley's servant in *Vanity Fair* (1848); the Indian as
evocative of mystery, the uncanny and unfamiliar is exploited in Wilkie Collins's *The Moonstone* (1868); while the
publication of Kipling's *Plain Tales from the Hills* in 1888
further intensified the trend of literary fascination with
India and the Indian. In relation to these antecedents,
Stevenson makes some slight use of the French Indies as
the site of the Master's commercial hopes; but he is closer
to Collins, rather than Galt, in his use of the Indian to
signify strangeness and, specifically, in *The Master*, a non-
Christian culture of which Secundra Dass, and his alien
burial practices are the products.

It was at this point of considering the inclusion of India
in *The Master* that Stevenson arrived at the idea of Burke
for his second narrator. At first he had intended that this
narrator should, like Mackellar, be a Scot; but his own *oeuvre*
posed a problem. In this case, might not the second reporter
be considered merely the "degraded shadow" of Alan
Breck, *Kidnapped*'s romantic, Jacobite hero? Burke's role
then takes shape:

Presently, however, it began to occur to me it would be like my Master to curry favour with the Prince's Irishmen; and that an Irish refugee would have a particular reason to find himself in India with his countryman, the unfortunate Lally.[9]

Still there was a problem, another shadow: Barry Lyndon, the bad Irishman of Thackeray's novel (1852–3). Although Stevenson realized that he could well make use of such a character, and indeed make his literary antecedent unrecognizable even to Lyndon's creator, he was still unconvinced of such a choice:

And then of a sudden there came to me memories of a young Irishman, with whom I was once intimate, and had spent long nights walking and talking with, upon a very desolate coast in a bleak autumn: I recalled him as a youth of *an extraordinary moral simplicity—almost vacancy; plastic to any influence, the creature of his admirations*: and putting such a youth in fancy into the career of a soldier of fortune, it occurred to me that he would serve my turn as well as Mr Lyndon, and in place of entering into competition with the Master, would afford a slight though a distinct relief. (Italics mine.)[10]

In Burke's first narrative in Chapter III, the narrator's character as a youthful, foolish romantic means he does more than just provide some "relief": he throws *into* relief James Durie's diabolic nature as he exhibits signs of the Master's influence on his personality. James Durie decides whether he and Burke should be friends or enemies not, as in a morally-ordered world, on the basis of inherent conviction or affinity, but merely by the tossing of a coin: this is a repeated motif in the novel, both invoking traditional associations of the diabolic and stressing the arbitrary way in which potentially moral issues are decided in the House of the Duries. Burke, the "creature of his admirations", does not realize the implications of this appeal to a coin, seeing it only as "too highly chivalrous not to take [his] fancy" and as an attractive "romantic circumstance". He

[9] "The Genesis of *The Master of Ballantrae*", Tusitala, X, p. xxv.
[10] Ibid., pp. xxv–vi.

likes to see James and himself as "a pair of ancient paladins"; and his concentration on heroic posturing obscures
for him the Master's essentially evil nature, stressing early
on in the novel James Durie's malevolent duplicity. Burke
insists on perceiving the Master as "that original genius":
the projection of a romantic image blinds him to the impli
cations of James's murderous actions on the pirate ship, his
chilling dispatch of all those not immediately necessary to
his schemes.

Just as Mackellar's trustworthiness is called into question
in *his* narrative, so Burke's authenticity is modified not only
by the nature of his pliant personality but also by the
alternative interpretations given in the text: at the point
when the Master and Burke quarrel and separate, Mackellar
makes his intervention (p. 69); in drawing attention to
Burke's "simplicity", Mackellar warns us that we should
not take his childish enthusiasm for the Master without
reservation. More importantly, he suppresses certain parts
of the Irishman's narrative, and, in so doing, asks the reader
to consider his own perceptions of the Master. Mackellar
states that Burke's "version of the quarrel is really more
than I can reproduce; for I knew the Master myself, and a
man more insusceptible of fear is not conceivable". This
follows Mackellar's reference to Burke's "simplicity": it is
also shortly after Burke has portrayed James's cowardice
when he believes himself near death. Which narrator should
we trust? The alternative versions of James's cowardice/
fearlessness by their presence in the text make the point
that the reader cannot fail to take: that neither narrator is
without bias and the truth about the Master is extremely
complex. The fact that he can arouse such varying, and
apparently contradictory, responses is the mark of his
duplicity. In the final sections of the novel, there is a further
complication in that Mackellar's compilation relies on two
potentially biased sources: Mountain, the Indian trader,
and Secundra Dass. By involving us in the process of *not
knowing*, and of being rightly confused by differing responses

and interventions betraying inconsistencies, Stevenson insists that we appreciate the complexities of James Durie's incubus nature and try to come to an understanding of his machinations.

A reviewer, E. T. Cook, in the *Athenaeum* of 19 October 1889, suggests that Stevenson's "great gift lies in the power of inventing and thoroughly grasping all the possibilities of his original and ingenious design." This "gift" is, of course, seen in the narrative techniques of *The Master*; but it can, perhaps, most interestingly be considered in the light of the novel's linguistic variation. Mackellar's "stylistic disabilities" have, in themselves, a dramatic role; similarly, the whole issue of language in *The Master* is crucial to its total design. At its simplest, language competence is a plot crux in terms of Secundra Dass's ability to understand English; but language and attitudes to language are much more than a convenient plot device. In India, in the second of Burke's narratives (Chapter VII), the Master refuses to speak to the Irishman insisting, in the most reductive manner, that he is only able to speak Hindustani. His assumed muteness is a denial of ordinary humanity, a rejection of any relationship with Burke, a man who was once his friend. It is also a way of stressing the fact that Burke cannot, in any profound sense, understand him: the refusal of a shared language indicates this. This limitation of understanding is an essential part of the thematic function of the Indian section, a chapter which is important in ways other than making the reader aware that Dass does, in fact, understand and speak English. In the episode in India, the Master and Dass speak a' tongue which means nothing to Burke: he is debarred from understanding except when Dass gives him an attenuated, translated version. On the Master's "return" from India, Mackellar hears strange voices in the Duries' house:

I drew nearer, and stood like a man dreaming. Here was certainly a human voice, and that in my own master's house, and yet I knew it not; certainly human speech, and that in my

native land; and yet listen as I pleased, I could not catch one
syllable. An old tale started up in my mind of a fairy wife (or
perhaps only a wandering stranger), that came to the place of
my fathers some generations back, and stayed the matter of a
week, *talking often in a tongue that signified nothing to the hearers*;
and went again, as she had come, under cloud of night, leaving
not so much as a name behind her. (pp. 152–3, Italics mine.)

Mackellar here cannot understand what he hears just as
Francis Burke could not understand the Master's and
Secundra Dass's speech in India. Secundra's speech at
Durrisdeer means nothing to his listeners apart from the
Master: *their* shared speech suggests a spiritual connection,
making the point that, as in the Indian section, they are
united in their foreign tongue as alien, black spirits, as
Master and Familiar. It is a bond that James Durie might
well wish to deny and yet his adoption of Secundra's
language makes it very clear indeed. Similarly, the Master's
manipulation of his native Scots dialect, on those rare but
significant occasions when he employs it, are self-revelatory
in a way in which he clearly would not intend. James *uses*
his dialect as part of the mechanics of his charm: he says he
has never failed to charm anyone he wished. His nature as
incubus means that he draws life from those whose lives he
disrupts or destroys; and the way he inveigles himself into
the favour of his family on his "returns" is shown by his
manipulation of broad Scots and the associations this has
for his listeners—he assumes that they will connect his use
of dialect with a warm, friendly and affectionate disposition.
The way Scots is used in the novel draws attention to one
of its most crucial themes: the manner in which the younger
brother, Henry, is infected by the incubus. This is shown
by Henry's equivocal employment of the dialect of his
childhood. There is more affinity between he and James than
Henry would willingly allow: he unwittingly underlines
their similarity by a use of Scots as spurious, in some cases,
as James's. At the same time, Henry's Scots, unlike James's,
is linked with his position as victim of a malevolent spirit;

and the fact that he has *more* Scots speech than the diabolic
Master makes a distinction between them which is important
in vindicating Henry's actions in the closing sections of the
novel.

After he is supposed dead at Culloden, James arrives on
the shores of Scotland speaking "in the English accent" and
saying that he wishes thereafter to be known by an alias,
"Mr. Bally" since this is how he has "curtailed" his own
name. The Master has rejected his Scots name of Ballantrae
and his Scots accent (we know that he *has* spoken with
such an accent from Burke's earlier comment on its "barbarous and disgusting" quality); but he is prepared to
return to the dialect for special and insidious purposes. In
Chapter IV (p. 85), James begins by taunting his brother
with the name of Jacob, the younger brother who has
usurped the elder son's place and privileges. But then, there
is a subtle change in his assumed personality as he takes up
the part of returned prodigal, loyal son and dutiful brother.
Mackellar is partly taken in: "He [James] had laid aside
even his cutting English accent, and spoke with the kindly
Scots tongue, that set a value on affectionate words" (p. 86).
Should we be in any doubt as to the duplicity involved in
this dialectal manipulation, we should note that Stevenson
has already clarified James's underlying denigration of the
Scots language in his comment to Mackellar that the term
"sneck up" is a "common" phrase (p. 85). James's scornful
attitude towards Scots, often the mark of a character of
dubious moral status in Scots fiction, shows us that his
move away from "cutting English" to warm Scots is merely
a change of form not a change of heart. In fact, the
transition is linked, in Mackellar's words, with James's
"diabolical amusement" and the "diabolical acts" of an "insidious devil". James's is a divisive influence and he employs
Scots here only in a public context as part of his performance: contrast his public "broad accent" in addressing his
brother as *"Hairry lad"* (p. 88), as part of an effort at
persuasion and dissimulation, with his use, in private with

Henry, of an anglicized style interlarded with French phrases which he assumes his less cultivated brother will not understand (p. 106). The adoption of Scots is thus part of the incubus's ability to transform himself, and the "return" to the dialect signifies an affected resumption of loyalties he has long since abandoned or, perhaps, never truly espoused.

Henry is united with James by a comparable use of Scots. Upon receiving a satisfactorily incriminating reply to a request for information about James's political status, he responds, with some glee, that he can now give his brother a "shog" (p. 99). The fact that he uses this one Scots word in a negative context when his scheming is redolent of James's own, and that this follows on from James's accentual manipulation, suggests that Henry shares something of his brother's duplicity. At the climax of the novel, the duel between the two brothers in Chapter V, this similarity is reinforced. Henry believes he has killed James: using Scots words, he begs his father's and his wife's forgiveness (p. 122). This is linked with his fear and is, in one sense, the natural register for a moment of horror and apprehension; but there is also something ignoble about this retreat into the language of childhood for special, and, in the circumstances, unreasonable pleading. How could his father forgive Henry for killing his favourite son? There is little doubt that, despite his lack of James's charm and Satanic grandeur, Henry is the more sympathetic of the brothers; but, to some extent, he shares his brother's equivocation, and the similarity of their uses of Scots makes this point. But Stevenson is too intelligent and humane a writer to leave this matter as it stands: there is further ambiguity in the relation of Henry to his brother and, again, the language provides a key.

With James's second disappearance, the indications that Henry has been infected increase. The younger brother becomes arid, mercenary and cruel, unjustly beats a servant, and tries to instil a hatred of James in the young Alexander. Mackellar challenges him on this point. Seized with a kind

of fit, Henry uses Scots to the narrator (p. 145); here the
dialect signifies a change of heart, a change in Henry's
mental state and a partial return to equilibrium and his
original, softer character. There is still some ambiguity,
however, in the fact that his return to dialect expresses a
weakened mental condition and an effort to persuade
Mackellar that he is harmless. He is, indeed, harmless to the
narrator but he is certainly not harmless to his brother. As
Henry is undermined by James's arrival in New York and
declining into drunkenness, he again uses Scots to Mackellar,
and this contrasts with James's now consistent Standard
English. Henry speaks of a place in Scotland, "where the
burn runs very deep" and says, "I mind being there when
I was a lad—dear, it comes over me like an old song! I was
after the fishing, and I made a bonny cast" (p. 216). The
Scots here, in contrast to James's cold, diabolic English, is
associated with Henry's humanity and with a certain
sympathy which we feel for him on his brother's appearance
in New York. But, at the same time, the nostalgic reference
to the "old song",[11] echoes *James*'s use of a sentimental
ballad, when he sings the "Exile's Song" after his return
from Culloden, as a way of manoeuvering himself back into
his sister-in-law's affections (p. 95). In a psychologically
accurate way, the dialect is also linked here with Henry's
childish mental state; and this is combined, in the subsequent scene, with the darker side of his sentimentality as
he is heard unmusically crooning two lines from the old
ballad, "The Twa Corbies" (p. 218):

[11] "An Old Song", with its suggestion, as here, of a recurrent
theme, is the title of Stevenson's first published story, which appeared
anonymously in *London* in 1877; at the time of going to press, this
has been published for the first time since then, as *An Old Song and
Edifying Letters of The Rutherford Family*, ed. Roger G. Swearingen
(1982). In some ways a forerunner of *The Master*, "An Old Song"
shares with this novel the themes of family division and duality; two
cousins vie for the affections of the same girl; the elder, more attractive cousin is banished and "returns" to disrupt the domestic har-
mony of his rival-cousin's life.

> And over his banes when they are bare
> The wind sall blaw for evermair!

These Scots lines emphasize the bleak tenor of Henry's mind and his brooding desire for revenge on James; in this, they foreshadow James's death and initiate the Scots speech of the denouement. It is in one of the final scenes that we find the strongest coincidence of a use of Scots and the essentially problematic nature of the incubus. The trader, Mountain, insists that James is dead; but Henry cannot believe this to be the case. Sir William Johnson tries to understand:

> My lord caught Sir William by the coat with a hooked hand. "This man has the name of my brother," says he, "but it's well understood that he was never *canny*."
>
> "*Canny?*" says Sir William. "What is that?"
>
> "He's not of this world," whispered my lord, "neither he nor the black *deil* that serves him. I have struck my sword through his vitals," he cried; "I have felt the hilt dirl [ring] on his breastbone, and the hot blood spirt in my very face, time and again, time and again!" he repeated, with a gesture indescribable. "But he was never dead for that," said he, and sighed aloud. "Why should I think he was dead now? No, not till I see him rotting," says he. (p. 241, Italics mine.)

Sir William, understandably bewildered by this outburst and unable to account for it rationally, cannot comprehend Henry's comments at all; nor is he able to appreciate the significance of not being "canny", the idea that James Durie is not natural and must be understood in terms of the supernatural. Johnson's anglicized response is an incomplete one and the Scots–English tension points this fact. The English-speaker does not know the literal meaning of not being "canny" (i.e. not natural) because he does not know Scots, and he has not had the experience of the Master's *un*canny nature during his "returns" to Scotland. The reader, however, recalls these together with the fact that the Master's diabolic nature has, earlier in the novel, been expressed through the medium of Scots. This recall helps him to accept James's death as right and inevitable. The Scots of the final scenes echoes linguistically, in particular, the description in Chapter II of James's "murder" of Willy White, the Weaver, a miniature version of the main action of *The Master*, and a forerunner of the Count and Baron tale in Chapter IX. The expression of the Willy White story in Scots, emphasizing the link between James Durie and "Auld Hornie" (Satan) of folk-tale tradition, helps convince the reader of the Master's evil power. Partly as a result of its presence early on in *The Master*, the exploitation of Scots in the closing scenes, subtly stresses James's devilry and gives a different perspective on his death than that put forward by Sir William Johnson. The Scots asks the reader to include, in his understanding of James Durie, an appreciation of the unnatural, even extra-terrestrial, aspects of this incubus; and it reminds us that all Stevenson knows of the Devil cannot be contained within a rational, and Standard English, frame of reference:

"No," says my lord, "It's not to be supposed that he would understand me. Mackellar does, for he *kens* all, and has seen him buried before now. This is a very good servant to me, Sir William, this man Mackellar; he buried him with his own hands —he and my father—by the light of two *siller* candlesticks. The other man is a familiar spirit; he brought him from Coromandel. I would have told *ye* this *long syne*, Sir William, only it was in the family," (p. 241, Italics mine.)

Mackellar *kens* all: the Scots word stresses not only the speaker's and the narrator's national origins but also the part Mackellar has had in the affairs in the Duries—only one who has been a participant in the events at Durrisdeer can grasp the implications of what Henry has said. Mackellar may not understand James's nature but he does understand the implications of Henry's comments and, in this case, has a first-hand relationship to them. Henry's Scots is further significant in showing that he is speaking from his deepest feelings: his overlay of anglicized speech has gone as the Scots leads up to the moment of his death in terror at what he sees.

In writing to the French translator, Marcel Schwob, Stevenson warned him of "Scotticisms used deliberately" in *The Master*[12]: and it is in this novel that the Scots language is most skilfully and accessibly employed to explore one of Stevenson's most important preoccupations—the ambiguities of man's nature, his essential duality; in *Jekyll and Hyde* he investigates its complexities; in tales, such as "Thrawn Janet" and "The Merry Men" he introduces the linguistic dimension of Scots in contrast with rational Standard English to articulate his theme; and in the "Tod Lapraik" tale in the later novel, *Catriona*, he shows how a tale of possession not only admits, but requires Scots for its expression; but it is in *The Master* that the theme finds its fullest literary expression and its complexities are most fully articulated through a use of Scots. At the end of the story, the uncertainties remain, those uncertainties that perhaps prompted Stevenson to sub-title his novel, at one stage, "A Fantasy" and, indeed, to describe it as "A *Winter*'s Tale"; and what we could call the linguistic plot of *The Master* ensures that, whilst not forgetting Stevenson's own assertion as to the rightness of Henry's actions, we also appreciate the dualities and ambiguities involved. Indeed, we too should ask as does the Master at the end of *his* tale of the Count and the Baron:

". . . And now, was that a murder?" (p. 187)

[12] *Letters*, Swanston Edition, XXV, p. 52.

NOTE ON THE TEXT

The text is reproduced from the Swanston Edition (1912) of
The Master of Ballantrae: this has been checked with both the
First and the Edinburgh Editions of the novel. In the main,
the Swanston text follows that of the Edinburgh Edition. On
the basis of Sidney Colvin's assurance that the E.E. volume of
The Master, "follows a copy of the first edition corrected by the
author before his death", minor amendments to spelling and
punctuation have been made to conform with this edition.
However, in some few cases where there is evidence to doubt
Colvin's editing (for example, in the matter of Scots spellings),
I have restored the readings of the First Edition. Such instances
are indicated in the Explanatory Notes, as are details of the
occasional major divergences between these different editions.
The Preface included here was part of Stevenson's "original
plan" of *The Master*, and intended to give his friend, Charles
Baxter, "another corner" in the "lofty monument" of the
Edinburgh Edition.

The existence of an explanatory note is indicated in the text
with an asterisk.

/

SELECT BIBLIOGRAPHY

(Place of publication London unless otherwise stated)

BIBLIOGRAPHY

George H. Ford (ed.), *Victorian Fiction: A Second Guide to Research*, Cambridge, Mass., 1978 (includes a chapter on RLS by Robert Kiely)

George L. McKay, *The Stevenson Library of Edwin J. Beinecke*, 6 vols., New Haven, 1958

W. F. Prideaux, *Bibliography of Robert Louis Stevenson*, 1903; revised 1917

Roger G. Swearingen, *The Prose Writings of Robert Louis Stevenson: A Guide*, 1980

EDITIONS

Collected Editions of the Works of R. L. Stevenson include:

The Edinburgh Edition, ed. Sidney Colvin, 1894–8

The Pentland Edition, with Bibliographical Notes by Edmund Gosse, 1906–7

The Swanston Edition, with an Introduction by Andrew Lang, 1911–12

The Vailima Edition, ed. Lloyd Osbourne, with Prefatory Notes by Fanny van de Grift Stevenson, 1922–3

The Tusitala Edition, 1923–4

LETTERS

Vailima Letters, 1895

The Letters of Robert Louis Stevenson to His Family and Friends, ed. Sidney Colvin, 1899; new edition 1911

Henry James and Robert Louis Stevenson: A Record of Friendship and Criticism, ed. Janet Adam Smith, 1948

RLS: Stevenson's Letters to Charles Baxter, ed. De Lancey Ferguson and Marshall Waingrow, New Haven, 1956

BIOGRAPHY

Graham Balfour, *The Life of Robert Louis Stevenson*, 1901

Jenni Calder, *RLS: A Life Study*, 1980

Elsie Noble Caldwell, *Last Witness for Robert Louis Stevenson*, Norman, Oklahoma, 1960

David Daiches, *Robert Louis Stevenson and His World*, 1973

J. C. Furnas, *Voyage to Windward*, 1951

J. A. Hammerton, *Stevensoniana: an Anecdotal Life and Appreciation of Robert Louis Stevenson*, Edinburgh, revised ed. 1910

James Pope Hennessy, *Robert Louis Stevenson*, 1974

CRITICISM

Robert E. Bonds, "The Mystery of *The Master of Ballantrae*", *English Literature in Transition*, Purdue University, Lafayette, Indiana, 1964, pp. 8–11

Jenni Calder (ed.), *Stevenson and Victorian Scotland*, Edinburgh, 1981

David Daiches, *Robert Louis Stevenson*, Glasgow, 1947
Stevenson and the Art of Fiction, New York, 1951

Joseph E. Egan, "From History to Myth: A Symbolic Reading of *The Master of Ballantrae*", *Studies in English Literature 1500–1900*, VIII, Rice Univ., Houston, 1968, pp. 699–710

Edwin M. Eigner, *Robert Louis Stevenson and Romantic Tradition*, Princeton, 1965

Nathaniel Elliott, "Robert Louis Stevenson and Scottish Literature", *English Literature in Transition*, XII, De Kalb, Illinois, 1969, pp. 79–85

Francis R. Hart, *The Scottish Novel: A Critical Survey*, 1978

Robert Kiely, *Robert Louis Stevenson and the Fiction of Adventure*, Cambridge, Mass., 1964

James F. Kilroy, "Narrative Techniques in *The Master of Ballantrae*", *Studies in Scottish Literature*, V, Lubbock, Texas, 1969, pp. 98–106

Maurice Lindsay, *History of Scottish Literature*, 1977

Paul Maixner (ed.), *Robert Louis Stevenson: The Critical Heritage*, 1981

MISCELLANEOUS

George L. McKay, *Some Notes on Robert Louis Stevenson, His Finances and His Agents and Publishers*, New Haven, 1958

A CHRONOLOGY OF
ROBERT LOUIS STEVENSON

1850   Born in Edinburgh, 13 November.

1862-3 Excursions with his parents to Germany, the Riviera and Italy.

1867   Enters Edinburgh University to study engineering.

1871   Decides to abandon engineering for the Law.

1872   Passes preliminary examinations for the Scottish Bar.

1873   Crisis with his father over his agnosticism; following this, and a bout of ill health, goes to Suffolk to stay with his Balfour cousins. Meets Frances Sitwell, one of the most important influences on his life until his marriage. Beginning of friendship with Sidney Colvin. Further ill health sends R.L.S. south to France at the end of the year.

1874   At Menton in France. Returns to Edinburgh in May and resumes reading for the Bar. Contributes to the *Cornhill Magazine*.

1875   Meets W. E. Henley in Edinburgh. Called to the Scottish Bar but does not practise as a barrister. Visits France and joins his cousin, Bob Stevenson, at the artists' colony at Barbizon, Fontainebleau, 1875-6; contributes to *Vanity Fair* and the *Academy*.

1876   Makes a canoe trip around the canals of northern France, later to be recorded in *An Inland Voyage*. Meets Fanny Osbourne, a married woman with two children, from Indiana.

1877   Divides year between Edinburgh, London and Fontainbleau. "An Old Song" is published in *London*.

1878   Fanny returns to her husband in California and, eventually, divorce proceedings begin. R.L.S. goes on travels with his donkey, Modestine, in the Cévennes. Publication of *An Inland Voyage* and *Edinburgh: Picturesque Notes*.

1879   Divides time between London, Scotland and France. Very ill in March and April. Sets off on journey to join Fanny in America. *Travels With a Donkey* published.

1880   Marries Fanny in San Francisco in May. They stay in the Californian mountains and then return to Scotland. Publication of *Deacon Brodie*, R.L.S.'s first play written in collaboration with W. E. Henley.

1881   Visits Davos in Switzerland. Publication of *Virginibus Puerisque*.

1882   At Davos, then R.L.S. and Fanny move to Hyères, France, their main home from March 1883–July 1884. Publication of *Familiar Studies of Men and Books* and *New Arabian Nights*.

1883   Publication of *The Silverado Squatters* and *Treasure Island*.

1884   Illness at Nice in January and further serious ill health in May. The Stevensons return to England at about the same time as an outbreak of cholera at Hyères. They go to Bournemouth, their home from September of this year until August, 1887. Publication of *Austin Guinea* and *Beau Austin*, both in collaboration with W. E. Henley.

1885   Moves to "Skerryvore", Bournemouth (the house was a wedding present from Thomas Stevenson to his daughter-in-law). Henry James spends long visit in Bournemouth. Publication of *A Child's Garden of Verses*; *Prince Otto*; *More New Arabian Nights*; *The Dynamiter*, with Fanny Stevenson; and *Macaire*, with W. E. Henley.

1886   Publication of *The Strange Case of Dr. Jekyll and Mr. Hyde*, Stevenson's first large-scale British and American success, and *Kidnapped*.

1887   Thomas Stevenson dies in May. In August, R.L.S. sails for America with his mother, Fanny and her son, Lloyd Osbourne. For health reasons, stays at Saranac in the Adirondack Mountains and there works on *The Master of Ballantrae*. Publication of *The Merry Men and Other Tales and Fables*; *Underwoods*; *Memories and Portraits* and *A Memoir of Fleeming Jenkin*.

1888   Scribner's, Stevenson's American publishers, commission a volume on the South Seas. Voyage on the yacht *Casco* (June 1888–January 1889) to the Marquesas, the Paumotus, Tahiti and then to Hawaii. Further work on *The Master*. Publication of *The Black Arrow* and *The Misadventures of John Nicholson*.

1889   Mrs. Thomas Stevenson returns to Scotland. Stevenson, Fanny and Lloyd remain in Honolulu. Voyage on the trading schooner, *Equator*, to the Gilbert Islands and then to Samoa (June to December). Buys estate at Opolu, Samoa. Publication of *The Wrong Box*, with Lloyd Osbourne, and *The Master of Ballantrae* (completed earlier this year at Waikiki).

THE MASTER OF BALLANTRAE

A Winter's Tale

CONTENTS

THE MASTER OF BALLANTRAE

PREFACE

ALTHOUGH an old, consistent exile, the editor of the following pages revisits now and again the city of which he exults to be a native ; and there are few things more strange, more painful, or more salutary, than such revisitations. Outside, in foreign spots, he comes by surprise and awakens more attention than he had expected ; in his own city, the relation is reversed, and he stands amazed to be so little recollected. Elsewhere he is refreshed to see attractive faces, to remark possible friends ; there he scouts the long streets, with a pang at heart, for the faces and friends that are no more. Elsewhere he is delighted with the presence of what is new, there tormented by the absence of what is old. Elsewhere he is content to be his present self ; there he is smitten with an equal regret for what he once was and for what he once hoped to be.

He was feeling all this dimly, as he drove from the station, on his last visit ; he was feeling it still as he alighted at the door of his friend Mr. Johnstone Thomson, W.S., with whom he was to stay. A hearty welcome, a face not altogether changed, a few words that sounded of old days, a laugh provoked and shared, a glimpse in passing of the snowy cloth and bright decanters and the Piranesis on the dining-room wall, brought him to his bed-room with a somewhat lightened cheer, and when he and Mr. Thomson sat down a few minutes later, cheek by jowl, and pledged the past in a preliminary bumper, he was already almost consoled, he had already almost forgiven himself his two unpardonable errors, that he should ever have left his native city, or ever returned to it.

"I have something quite in your way," said Mr. Thomson. "I wished to do honour to your arrival; because, my dear fellow, it is my own youth that comes back along with you; in a very tattered and withered state, to be sure, but—well!—all that's left of it."

"A great deal better than nothing," said the editor. "But what is this which is quite in my way?"

"I was coming to that," said Mr. Thomson: "Fate has put it in my power to honour your arrival with something really original by way of dessert. A mystery."

"A mystery?" I repeated.

"Yes," said his friend, "a mystery. It may prove to be nothing, and it may prove to be a great deal. But in the meanwhile it is truly mysterious, no eye having looked on it for near a hundred years; it is highly genteel, for it treats of a titled family; and it ought to be melodramatic, for (according to the superscription) it is concerned with death."

"I think I rarely heard a more obscure or a more promising annunciation," the other remarked. "But what is It?"

"You remember my predecessor's, old Peter M'Brair's business?"

"I remember him acutely; he could not look at me without a pang of reprobation, and he could not feel the pang without betraying it. He was to me a man of a great historical interest, but the interest was not returned."

"Ah well, we go beyond him," said Mr. Thomson. "I daresay old Peter knew as little about this as I do. You see, I succeeded to a prodigious accumulation of old law-papers and old tin boxes, some of them of Peter's hoarding, some of his father's, John, first of the dynasty, a great man in his day. Among other collections, were all the papers of the Durrisdeers."

"The Durrisdeers!" cried I. "My dear fellow, these may be of the greatest interest. One of them was out in the 'Forty-five; one had some strange passages with the devil—you will find a note of it in Law's 'Memorials,' I

think ; and there was an unexplained tragedy, I know not
what, much later, about a hundred years ago——"

"More than a hundred years ago," said Mr. Thomson.
"In 1783."*

"How do you know that ? I mean some death."

"Yes, the lamentable deaths of my Lord Durrisdeer and
his brother, the Master of Ballantrae (attainted in the
troubles)," said Mr. Thomson with something the tone of
a man quoting. "Is that it ? "

"To say truth," said I, "I have only seen some dim
reference to the things in memoirs ; and heard some
traditions dimmer still, through my uncle (whom I think
you knew). My uncle lived when he was a boy in the
neighbourhood of St. Bride's ; he has often told me of the
avenue closed up and grown over with grass, the great gates
never opened, the last lord and his old maid sister who
lived in the back parts of the house, a quiet, plain, poor,
humdrum couple it would seem—but pathetic too, as the
last of that stirring and brave house—and, to the country
folk, faintly terrible from some deformed traditions."

"Yes," said Mr. Thomson. "Henry Graeme Durie, the
last lord, died in 1820 ; his sister, the Honourable Miss
Katharine Durie, in 'Twenty-seven ; so much I know ; and
by what I have been going over the last few days, they were
what you say, decent, quiet people, and not rich. To say
truth, it was a letter of my lord's that put me on the search
for the packet we are going to open this evening. Some
papers could not be found ; and he wrote to Jack M'Brair
suggesting they might be among those sealed up by a Mr.
Mackellar. M'Brair answered, that the papers in question
were all in Mackellar's own hand, all (as the writer understood) of a purely narrative character ; and besides, said he,
' I am not bound to open them before the year 1889.' You
may fancy if these words struck me : I instituted a hunt
through all the M'Brair repositories ; and at last hit upon
that packet which (if you have had enough wine) I propose
to show you at once."

In the smoking-room, to which my host now led me, was
a packet, fastened with many seals and enclosed in a single
sheet of strong paper thus endorsed :

Papers relating to the lives and lamentable deaths of the late
Lord Durisdeer, and his elder brother James, commonly called
Master of Ballantrae, attainted in the troubles : entrusted into the
hands of John M'Brair in the Lawnmarket of Edinburgh, W.S. ;
this 20th day of September Anno Domini 1789 ; by him to be kept
secret until the revolution of one hundred years complete, or until
the 20th day of September 1889 : the same compiled and written
by me,

EPHRAIM MACKELLAR,

*For near forty years Land Steward on the
estates of his Lordship.*

As Mr. Thomson is a married man, I will not say what
hour had struck when we laid down the last of the following
pages ; but I will give a few words of what ensued.

" Here," said Mr. Thomson, " is a novel ready to your
hand : all you have to do is to work up the scenery, develop
the characters, and improve the style."

" My dear fellow," said I, " they are just the three things
that I would rather die than set my hand to.   It shall be
published as it stands."

" But it's so bald," objected Mr. Thomson.

" I believe there is nothing so noble as baldness," replied
I, " and I am sure there is nothing so interesting.   I would
have all literature bald, and all authors (if you like) but
one."

" Well, well," said Mr. Thomson, " we shall see."

[*" Johnstone Thomson, W.S.," is Mr. C. Baxter, W.S. (afterwards the author's executor), with whom, as " Thomson
Johnstone," Stevenson frequently corresponded in the
broadest of broad Scots.—The scene is laid in Mr.
Baxter's house, 7 Rothesay Place, Edinburgh.*] *

THE MASTER OF BALLANTRAE

CHAPTER I

SUMMARY OF EVENTS DURING THE MASTER'S WANDERINGS

THE full truth of this odd matter is what the world has long been looking for, and public curiosity is sure to welcome. It so befell that I was intimately mingled with the last years and history of the house; and there does not live one man so able as myself to make these matters plain, or so desirous to narrate them faithfully. I knew the Master; on many secret steps of his career I have an authentic memoir in my hand; I sailed with him on his last voyage almost alone; I made one upon that winter's journey of which so many tales have gone abroad; and I was there at the man's death. As for my late Lord Durrisdeer, I served him and loved him near twenty years; and thought more of him the more I knew of him. Altogether, I think it not fit that so much evidence should perish; the truth is a debt I owe my lord's memory; and I think my old years will flow more smoothly, and my white hair lie quieter on the pillow, when the debt is paid.

The Duries of Durrisdeer and Ballantrae were a strong family in the south-west from the days of David First.* A rhyme still current in the countryside—

> " Kittle folk are the Durrisdeers,
> They ride wi' ower mony spears "—

bears the mark of its antiquity; and the name appears in another, which common report attributes to Thomas of Ercildoune himself—I cannot say how truly, and which some have applied—I dare not say with how much justice —to the events of this narration :

> " Twa Duries in Durrisdeer,
>   Ane to tie and ane to ride.
>   An ill day for the groom
>   And a waur day for the bride."

Authentic history besides is filled with their exploits, which (to our modern eyes) seem not very commendable : and the family suffered its full share of those ups and downs to which the great houses of Scotland have been ever liable. But all these I pass over, to come to that memorable year 1745, when the foundations of this tragedy were laid.

At that time there dwelt a family of four persons in the house of Durrisdeer, near St. Bride's, on the Solway shore ; a chief hold of their race since the Reformation. My old lord, eighth of the name, was not old in years, but he suffered prematurely from the disabilities of age ; his place was at the chimney side ; there he sat reading, in a lined gown, with few words for any man, and wry words for none : the model of an old retired housekeeper ; and yet his mind very well nourished with study, and reputed in the country to be more cunning than he seemed. The Master of Ballantrae, James in baptism, took from his father the love of serious reading ; some of his tact, perhaps, as well; but that which was only policy in the father became black dissimulation in the son. The face of his behaviour was merely popular and wild : he sat late at wine, later at the cards ; had the name in the country of " an unco man for the lasses " ; and was ever in the front of broils. But for all he was the first to go in, yet it was observed he was invariably the best to come off ; and his partners in mischief were usually alone to pay the piper. This luck or dexterity got him several ill-wishers, but with the rest of the country enhanced his reputation ; so that great things were looked for in his future, when he should have gained

more gravity. One very black mark he had to his name ;
but the matter was hushed up at the time, and so defaced
by legends before I came into these parts that I scruple
to set it down. If it was true, it was a horrid fact
in one so young; and if false, it was a horrid calumny.
I think it notable that he had always vaunted himself
quite implacable, and was taken at his word ; so that he
had the addition among his neighbours of " an ill man to
cross." Here was altogether a young nobleman (not yet
twenty-four in the year 'Forty-five) who had made a figure
in the country beyond his time of life. The less marvel
if there were little heard of the second son, Mr. Henry
(my late Lord Durrisdeer), who was neither very bad nor
yet very able, but an honest, solid sort of lad, like many
of his neighbours. Little heard, I say ; but indeed it was
a case of little spoken. He was known among the salmon
fishers in the firth, for that was a sport that he assiduously
followed ; he was an excellent good horse-doctor besides ;
and took a chief hand, almost from a boy, in the manage-
ment of the estates. How hard a part that was, in the
situation of that family, none knows better than myself ;
nor yet with how little colour of justice a man may there
acquire the reputation of a tyrant and a miser. The fourth
person in the house was Miss Alison Graeme, a near kins-
woman, an orphan, and the heir to a considerable fortune
which her father had acquired in trade. This money was
loudly called for by my lord's necessities ; indeed, the land
was deeply mortgaged ; and Miss Alison was designed
accordingly to be the Master's wife, gladly enough on her
side ; with how much good-will on his is another matter.
She was a comely girl, and in those days very spirited and
self-willed ; for the old lord having no daughter of his own,
and my lady being long dead, she had grown up as best
she might.

To these four came the news of Prince Charlie's landing,*
and set them presently by the ears. My lord, like the
chimney-keeper that he was, was all for temporising.

Miss Alison held the other side, because it appeared romanti-
cal ; and the Master (though I have heard they did not agree
often) was for this once of her opinion. The adventure
tempted him, as I conceive ; he was tempted by the opportunity to raise the fortunes of the house, and not less by
the hope of paying off his private liabilities, which were
heavy beyond all opinion. As for Mr. Henry, it appears he
said little enough at first ; his part came later on. It took
the three a whole day's disputation before they agreed to
steer a middle course, one son going forth to strike a blow
for King James, my lord and the other staying at home to
keep in favour with King George.* Doubtless this was
my lord's decision ; and, as is well known, it was the part
played by many considerable families. But the one dispute
settled, another opened. For my lord, Miss Alison, and
Mr. Henry all held the one view : that it was the cadet's
part to go out ; and the Master, what with restlessness and
vanity, would at no rate consent to stay at home. My
lord pleaded, Miss Alison wept, Mr. Henry was very plain
spoken : all was of no avail.

" It is the direct heir of Durrisdeer that should ride by
his King's bridle," says the Master.

" If we were playing a manly part," says Mr. Henry,
" there might be sense in such talk. But what are we
doing ?   Cheating at cards ! "

" We are saving the house of Durrisdeer, Henry," his
father said.

" And see, James," said Mr. Henry, " if I go, and the
Prince has the upper hand, it will be easy to make your
peace with King James. But if you go, and the expedition
fails, we divide the right and the title. And what shall I
be then ? "

" You will be Lord Durrisdeer," said the Master. " I
put all I have upon the table."

" I play at no such game," cries Mr. Henry. " I shall
be left in such a situation as no man of sense and honour
could endure. I shall be neither fish nor flesh ! " he

cried. And a little after he had another expression, plainer perhaps than he intended. " It is your duty to be here with my father," said he. " You know well enough you are the favourite."

" Ay ? " said the Master. " And there spoke Envy ! Would you trip up my heels—Jacob ? " said he, and dwelled upon the name maliciously.

Mr. Henry went and walked at the low end of the hall without reply ; for he had an excellent gift of silence. Presently he came back.

" I am the cadet, and I *should* go," said he. " And my lord here is the master, and he says I *shall* go. What say ye to that, my brother ? "

" I say this, Harry," returned the Master, " that when very obstinate folk are met, there are only two ways out : Blows—and I think none of us could care to go so far ; or the arbitrament of chance—and here is a guinea piece. Will you stand by the toss of the coin ? "

" I will stand and fall by it," said Mr. Henry. " Heads, I go ; shield, I stay."

The coin was spun, and it fell shield. " So there is a lesson for Jacob," says the Master.

" We shall live to repent of this," says Mr. Henry, and flung out of the hall.

As for Miss Alison, she caught up that piece of gold which had just sent her lover to the wars, and flung it clean through the family shield in the great painted window.

" If you loved me as well as I love you, you would have stayed," cried she.

" ' I could not love you, dear, so well, loved I not honour more,' "*sang the Master.

" O ! " she cried, " you have no heart—I hope you may be killed ! " and she ran from the room, and in tears, to her own chamber.

It seems the Master turned to my lord with his most comical manner, and says he, " This looks like a devil of a wife."

"I think you are a devil of a son to me," cried his father, "you that have always been the favourite, to my shame be it spoken. Never a good hour have I gotten of you since you were born ; no, never one good hour," and repeated it again the third time. Whether it was the Master's levity, or his insubordination, or Mr. Henry's word about the favourite son, that had so much disturbed my lord, I do not know : but I incline to think it was the last, for I have it by all accounts that Mr. Henry was more made up to from that hour.

Altogether it was in pretty ill blood with his family that the Master rode to the North ; which was the more sorrowful for others to remember when it seemed too late. By fear and favour he had scraped together near upon a dozen men, principally tenants' sons ; they were all pretty full when they set forth, and rode up the hill by the old abbey, roaring and singing, the white cockade in every hat. It was a desperate venture for so small a company to cross the most of Scotland unsupported ; and (what made folk think so the more) even as that poor dozen was clattering up the hill, a great ship of the King's navy, that could have brought them under with a single boat, lay with her broad ensign streaming in the bay. The next afternoon, having given the Master a fair start, it was Mr. Henry's turn ; and he rode off, all by himself, to offer his sword and carry letters from his father to King George's Government. Miss Alison was shut in her room, and did little but weep, till both were gone ; only she stitched the cockade upon the Master's hat, and (as John Paul told me) it was wetted with tears when he carried it down to him.

In all that followed, Mr. Henry and my old lord were true to their bargain. That ever they accomplished anything is more than I could learn ; and that they were anyway strong on the King's side, more than I believe. But they kept the letter of loyalty, corresponded with my Lord President, sat still at home, and had little or no commerce with the Master while that business lasted.

Nor was he, on his side, more communicative. Miss Alison,
indeed, was always sending him expresses, but I do not know
if she had many answers. Macconochie rode for her once,
and found the Highlanders before Carlisle, and the Master
riding by the Prince's side in high favour ; he took the letter
(so Macconochie tells), opened it, glanced it through with
a mouth like a man whistling, and stuck it in his belt,
whence, on his horse passageing, it fell unregarded to
the ground. It was Macconochie who picked it up ; and
he still kept it, and indeed I have seen it in his hands.
News came to Durrisdeer of course, by the common report,
as it goes travelling through a country, a thing always
wonderful to me. By that means the family learned
more of the Master's favour with the Prince, and the
ground it was said to stand on : for by a strange condescension in a man so proud—only that he was a man still
more ambitious—he was said to have crept into notability
by truckling to the Irish. Sir Thomas Sullivan, Colonel
Burke, and the rest, were his daily comrades, by which
course he withdrew himself from his own country-folk.
All the small intrigues he had a hand in fomenting ; thwarted
my Lord George* upon a thousand points ; was always for
the advice that seemed palatable to the Prince, no matter
if it was good or bad ; and seems upon the whole (like the
gambler he was all through life) to have had less regard
to the chances of the campaign than to the greatness of
favour he might aspire to, if, by any luck, it should succeed.
For the rest, he did very well in the field ; no one questioned
that : for he was no coward.

The next was the news of Culloden, which was brought
to Durrisdeer by one of the tenants' sons—the only survivor,
he declared, of all those that had gone singing up the hill.
By an unfortunate chance John Paul and Macconochie
had that very morning found the guinea piece—which was
the root of all the evil—sticking in a holly bush ; they had
been " up the gait," as the servants say at Durrisdeer, to
the change-house ; and if they had little left of the guinea,

they had less of their wits. What must John Paul do but
burst into the hall where the family sat at dinner, and cry
the news to them that " Tam Macmorland was but new
lichtit*at the door, and—wirra, wirra—there were nane to
come behind him " ?

They took the word in silence like folk condemned ;
only Mr. Henry carrying his palm to his face, and Miss
Alison laying her head outright upon her hands. As for
my lord, he was like ashes.

" I have still one son," says he. " And, Henry, I will
do you this justice—it is the kinder that is left."

It was a strange thing to say in such a moment ; but
my lord had never forgotten Mr. Henry's speech, and
he had years of injustice on his conscience. Still it was
a strange thing, and more than Miss Alison could let pass.
She broke out and blamed my lord for his unnatural words,
and Mr. Henry because he was sitting there in safety when
his brother lay dead, and herself because she had given
her sweetheart ill words at his departure, calling him the
flower of the flock, wringing her hands, protesting her love,
and crying on him by his name—so that the servants stood
astonished.

Mr. Henry got to his feet, and stood holding his chair.
It was he that was like ashes now.

" O ! " he burst out suddenly, " I know you loved
him."

" The world knows that, glory be to God ! " cries
she ; and then to Mr. Henry : " There is none but me to
know one thing—that you were a traitor to him in your
heart."

" God knows," groans he, " it was lost love on both
sides."

Time went by in the house after that without much
change ; only they were now three instead of four, which
was a perpetual reminder of their loss. Miss Alison's
money, you are to bear in mind, was highly needful for
the estates ; and the one brother being dead, my old lord

soon set his heart upon her marrying the other. Day in, day out, he would work upon her, sitting by the chimney-side with his finger in his Latin book, and his eyes set upon her face with a kind of pleasant intentness that became the old gentleman very well. If she wept, he would condole with her like an ancient man that has seen worse times and begins to think lightly even of sorrow; if she raged, he would fall to reading again in his Latin book, but always with some civil excuse; if she offered, as she often did, to let them have her money in a gift, he would show her how little it consisted with his honour, and remind her, even if he should consent, that Mr. Henry would certainly refuse. *Non vi sed sæpe cadendo**was a favourite word of his; and no doubt this quiet persecution wore away much of her resolve; no doubt, besides, he had a great influence on the girl, having stood in the place of both her parents; and, for that matter, she was herself filled with the spirit of the Duries, and would have gone a great way for the glory of Durrisdeer; but not so far, I think, as to marry my poor patron, had it not been—strangely enough—for the circumstance of his extreme unpopularity.

This was the work of Tam Macmorland. There was not much harm in Tam; but he had that grievous weakness, a long tongue; and as the only man in that country who had been out—or, rather, who had come in again—he was sure of listeners. Those that have the underhand in any fighting, I have observed, are ever anxious to persuade themselves they were betrayed. By Tam's account of it, the rebels had been betrayed at every turn and by every officer they had; they had been betrayed at Derby, and betrayed at Falkirk; the night march was a step of treachery of my Lord George's; and Culloden was lost by the treachery of the Macdonalds. This habit of imputing treason grew upon the fool, till at last he must have in Mr. Henry also. Mr. Henry (by his account) had betrayed the lads of Durrisdeer; he had promised to follow with more men, and instead of that he had ridden to King George. " Ay, and the next

day ! " Tam would cry.   " The puir bonny Master, and the
puir kind lads that rade wi' him, were hardly ower the
scaur or he was aff—the Judis ! Ay, weel—he has his way
o't : he's to be my lord, nae less, and there's mony a cold
corp amang the Hieland heather ! "   And at this, if Tam
had been drinking, he would begin to weep.

Let any one speak long enough, he will get believers.
This view of Mr. Henry's behaviour crept about the country
by little and little ; it was talked upon by folk that knew
the contrary, but were short of topics ; and it was heard
and believed and given out for gospel by the ignorant and
the ill-willing. Mr. Henry began to be shunned ; yet a
while, and the commons began to murmur as he went by,
and the women (who are always the most bold because they
are the most safe) to cry out their reproaches to his face.
The Master was cried up for a saint. It was remembered
how he had never any hand in pressing the tenants ; as,
indeed, no more he had, except to spend the money. He
was a little wild perhaps, the folk said ; but how much better
was a natural, wild lad that would soon have settled down,
than a skinflint and a sneckdraw,* sitting with his nose in
an account-book to persecute poor tenants ! One trollop,
who had had a child to the Master, and by all accounts
been very badly used, yet made herself a kind of champion
of his memory. She flung a stone one day at Mr. Henry.

" Whaur's the bonny lad that trustit ye ? " she cried.

Mr. Henry reined in his horse and looked upon her,
the blood flowing from his lip. "Ay, Jess, " says he.
" You too ?   And yet ye should ken me better."   For
it was he who had helped her with money.

The woman had another stone ready, which she made
as if she would cast ; and he, to ward himself, threw up
the hand that held his riding-rod.

" What, would ye beat a lassie, ye ugly—— ? " cries
she, and ran away screaming as though he had struck
her.

Next day word went about the country like wildfire

that Mr. Henry had beaten Jessie Broun within an inch
of her life. I give it as one instance of how this snowball
grew, and one calumny brought another ; until my poor
patron was so perished in reputation that he began to keep
the house like my lord. All this while, you may be very
sure, he uttered no complaints at home ; the very ground
of the scandal was too sore a matter to be handled ; and
Mr. Henry was very proud, and strangely obstinate in
silence. My old lord must have heard of it, by John Paul,
if by no one else ; and he must at least have remarked the
altered habits of his son. Yet even he, it is probable,
knew not how high the feeling ran ; and as for Miss Alison,
she was ever the last person to hear news, and the least
interested when she heard them.

In the height of the ill-feeling (for it died away as it
came, no man could say why) there was an election forward
in the town of St. Bride's, which is the next to Durrisdeer,
standing on the Water of Swift ; some grievance was fer-
menting, I forget what, if ever I heard : and it was currently
said there would be broken heads ere night, and that the
sheriff had sent as far as Dumfries for soldiers. My lord
moved that Mr. Henry should be present, assuring him
it was necessary to appear, for the credit of the house.
" It will soon be reported," said he, " that we do not
take the lead in our own country."

" It is a strange lead that I can take," said Mr. Henry ;
and when they had pushed him further, " I tell you the
plain truth," he said : " I dare not show my face."

" You are the first of the house that ever said so," cries
Miss Alison.

" We will go all three," said my lord ; and sure enough
he got into his boots (the first time in four years—a sore
business John Paul had to get them on), and Miss Alison
into her riding-coat, and all three rode together to St.
Bride's.

The streets were full of the riff-raff of all the country-
side, who had no sooner clapped eyes on Mr. Henry than

the hissing began, and the hooting, and the cries of
" Judas ! " and " Where was the Master ? " and " Where
were the poor lads that rode with him ? "   Even a stone
was cast ; but the more part cried shame at that, for my
old lord's sake, and Miss Alison's.   It took not ten minutes
to persuade my lord that Mr. Henry had been right.   He
said never a word, but turned his horse about, and home
again, with his chin upon his bosom.   Never a word said
Miss Alison ; no doubt she thought the more ; no doubt her
pride was stung, for she was a bone-bred Durie ; and no
doubt her heart was touched to see her cousin so unjustly
used.   That night she was never in bed ; I have often
blamed my lady—when I call to mind that night I readily
forgive her all ; and the first thing in the morning she came
to the old lord in his usual seat.

" If Henry still wants me," said she, " he can have me
now."   To himself she had a different speech : " I bring
you no love, Henry ; but God knows, all the pity in the
world."

June the 1st, 1748, was the day of their marriage.
It was December of the same year that first saw me alighting
at the doors of the great house ; and from there I take up
the history of events as they befell under my own observation, like a witness in a court.

CHAPTER II

SUMMARY OF EVENTS (*continued*)

I MADE the last of my journey in the cold end of December, in a mighty dry day of frost, and who should be my guide but Patey Macmorland, brother of Tam! For a tow-headed, bare-legged brat of ten, he had more ill tales upon his tongue than ever I heard the match of; having drunken betimes in his brother's cup. I was still not so old myself; pride had not yet the upper hand of curiosity; and indeed it would have taken any man, that cold morning, to hear all the old clashes of the country, and be shown all the places by the way where strange things had fallen out. I had tales of Claverhouse* as we came through the bogs, and tales of the devil as we came over the top of the scaur.* As we came in by the abbey I heard somewhat of the old monks, and more of the free-traders, who use its ruins for a magazine, landing for that cause within a cannon-shot of Durrisdeer; and along all the road the Duries and poor Mr. Henry were in the first rank of slander. My mind was thus highly prejudiced against the family I was about to serve, so that I was half surprised when I beheld Durrisdeer itself, lying in a pretty, sheltered bay, under the Abbey Hill; the house most commodiously built in the French fashion, or perhaps Italianate, for I have no skill in these arts; and the place the most beautified with gardens, lawns, shrubberies, and trees I had ever seen. The money sunk here unproductively would have quite restored the family; but as it was, it cost a revenue to keep it up.

Mr. Henry came himself to the door to welcome me:

21

a tall dark young gentleman (the Duries are all black men) of a plain and not cheerful face, very strong in body, but not so strong in health ; taking me by the hand without any pride, and putting me at home with plain kind speeches. He led me into the hall, booted as I was, to present me to my lord. It was still daylight ; and the first thing I observed was a lozenge of clear glass in the midst of the shield in the painted window, which I remember thinking a blemish on a room otherwise so handsome, with its family portraits, and the pargeted ceiling with pendants, and the carved chimney, in one corner of which my old lord sat reading in his Livy. He was like Mr. Henry, with much the same plain countenance, only more subtle and pleasant, and his talk a thousand times more entertaining. He had many questions to ask me, I remember, of Edinburgh College, where I had just received my mastership of arts, and of the various professors, with whom and their proficiency he seemed well acquainted ; and thus, talking of things that I knew, I soon got liberty of speech in my new home.

In the midst of this came Mrs. Henry into the room ; she was very far gone, Miss Katharine being due in about six weeks, which made me think less of her beauty at the first sight ; and she used me with more of condescension than the rest ; so that, upon all accounts, I kept her in the third place of my esteem.

It did not take long before all Patey Macmorland's tales were blotted out of my belief, and I was become, what I have ever since remained, a loving servant of the house of Durrisdeer. Mr. Henry had the chief part of my affection. It was with him I worked ; and I found him an exacting master, keeping all his kindness for those hours in which we were unemployed, and in the steward's office not only loading me with work, but viewing me with a shrewd supervision. At length one day he looked up from his paper with a kind of timidness, and says he, " Mr. Mackellar, I think I ought to tell you that you do very well." That was my first word of commendation ; and from that day his jealousy of my performance was relaxed ; soon it was " Mr. Mackellar " here, and " Mr. Mackellar " there, with the whole family ; and for much of my service at Durrisdeer I have transacted everything at my own time, and to my own fancy, and never a farthing challenged. Even while he was driving me, I had begun to find my heart go out to Mr. Henry ; no doubt, partly in pity, he was a man so palpably unhappy. He would fall into a deep muse over our accounts, staring at the page or out of the window ; and at those times the look of his face, and the sigh that would break from him, awoke in me strong feelings of curiosity and commiseration. One day, I remember, we were late upon some business in the steward's room. This room is in the top of the house, and has a view upon the bay, and over a little wooded cape, on the long sands ; and there, right over against the sun, which was then dipping, we saw the free-traders, with a great force of men and horses, scouring on the beach. Mr. Henry had been staring straight west, so that I marvelled he was not blinded by the sun ; suddenly he frowns, rubs his hand upon his brow, and turns to me with a smile.

" You would not guess what I was thinking," says he. " I was thinking I would be a happier man if I could ride and run the danger of my life with these lawless companions."

I told him I had observed he did not enjoy good spirits ; and that it was a common fancy to envy others and think we should be the better of some change ; quoting Horace to the point, like a young man fresh from college.

" Why, just so," said he. " And with that we may get back to our accounts."

It was not long before I began to get wind of the causes that so much depressed him. Indeed, a blind man must have soon discovered there was a shadow on that house, the shadow of the Master of Ballantrae. Dead or alive (and he was then supposed to be dead) that man was his brother's rival : his rival abroad, where there was never a good word for Mr. Henry, and nothing but regret and praise for the Master ; and his rival at home, not only with his father and his wife, but with the very servants.

They were two old serving-men that were the leaders. John Paul, a little, bald, solemn, stomachy man, a great professor of piety and (take him for all in all) a pretty faithful servant, was the chief of the Master's faction. None durst go so far as John. He took a pleasure in disregarding Mr. Henry publicly, often with a slighting comparison. My lord and Mrs. Henry took him up, to be sure, but never so resolutely as they should ; and he had only to pull his weeping face and begin his lamentations for the Master—" his laddie," as he called him—to have the whole condoned. As for Henry, he let these things pass in silence, sometimes with a sad and sometimes with a black look. There was no rivalling the dead, he knew that ; and how to censure an old serving-man for a fault of loyalty was more than he could see. His was not the tongue to do it.

Macconochie was chief upon the other side ; an old, ill-spoken, swearing, ranting, drunken dog ; and I have often thought it an odd circumstance in human nature that these two serving-men should each have been the champion of his contrary, and blackened their own faults, and made light of their own virtues, when they beheld them in a master. Macconochie had soon smelled out my secret inclination, took me much into his confidence, and would rant against the Master by the hour, so that even my work suffered. " They're a' daft here," he would cry, " and be damned to them ! The Master—the deil's in their thrapples that should call him sae ! it's Mr. Henry should be master now ! They were nane sae fond o' the Master when they had him, I'll can tell ye that. Sorrow on his name ! Never a guid word did I hear on his lips, nor naebody else, but just fleering and flyting and profane cursing

—deil hae him ! There's nane kent his wickedness : him
a gentleman ! Did ever ye hear tell, Mr. Mackellar, o'
Wully White the wabster ? No ? Aweel, Wully was an
unco praying kind o' man ; a dreigh body, nane o' my
kind, I never could abide the sight o' him ; onyway he
was a great hand by his way of it, and he up and rebukit
the Master for some of his ongoings. It was a grand thing
for the Master o' Ball'ntrae to tak' up a feud wi' a wabster, wasnae't ? " Macconochie would sneer ; indeed, he
never took the full name upon his lips but with a sort of
a whine of hatred. " But he did ! A fine employ it was :
chapping at the man's door, and crying ' boo ' in his lum,
and puttin' poother in his fire, and pee-oys [1] in his window ; till the man thocht it was Auld Hornie was come
seekin' him. Weel, to mak a lang story short, Wully
gaed gyte. At the hinder end they couldnae get him frae
his knees, but he just roared and prayed and grat straucht
on, till he got his release. It was fair murder, a'body said
that. Ask John Paul—he was brawly ashamed o' that
game, him that's sic a Christian man ! Grand doin's for
the Master o' Ball'ntrae ! " I asked him what the Master
had thought of it himself. " How would I ken ? " says
he ; " He never said naething." * And on again in his
usual manner of banning and swearing, with every now
and again a " Master of Ballantrae " sneered through his
nose. It was in one of these confidences that he showed
me the Carlisle letter, the print of the horse-shoe still
stamped in the paper. Indeed, that was our last confidence ; for he then expressed himself so ill-naturedly
of Mrs. Henry that I had to reprimand him sharply,
and must thenceforth hold him at a distance.

My old lord was uniformly kind to Mr. Henry ; he had
even pretty ways of gratitude, and would sometimes clap
him on the shoulder and say, as if to the world at large :
" This is a very good son to me." And grateful he was,
no doubt, being a man of sense and justice. But I think

[1] A kind of firework made with damp powder.

that was all, and I am sure Mr. Henry thought so. The
love was all for the dead son. Not that this was often
given breath to ; indeed, with me but once. My lord
had asked me one day how I got on with Mr. Henry, and
I had told him the truth.

"Ay," said he, looking sideways on the burning fire,
"Henry is a good lad, a very good lad," said he. "You
have heard, Mr. Mackellar, that I had another son ? I
am afraid he was not so virtuous a lad as Mr. Henry ;
but dear me, he's dead, Mr. Mackellar ! and while he
lived we were all very proud of him, all very proud. If he
was not all he should have been in some ways, well, perhaps we loved him better ! " This last he said looking
musingly in the fire ; and then to me, with a great deal of
briskness, "But I am rejoiced you do so well with Mr.
Henry. You will find him a good master." And with that
he opened his book, which was the customary signal of
dismission. But it would be little that he read, and less
that he understood ; Culloden field and the Master, these
would be the burthen of his thought ; and the burthen of
mine was an unnatural jealousy of the dead man for Mr.
Henry's sake, that had even then begun to grow on me.

I am keeping Mrs. Henry for the last, so that this
expression of my sentiment may seem unwarrantably
strong : the reader shall judge for himself when I have
done. But I must first tell of another matter, which was
the means of bringing me more intimate. I had not yet
been six months at Durrisdeer when it chanced that John
Paul fell sick and must keep his bed ; drink was the root
of his malady, in my poor thought ; but he was tended,
and indeed carried himself, like an afflicted saint ; and
the very minister, who came to visit him, professed himself edified when he went away. The third morning of
his sickness Mr. Henry comes to me with something of a
hang-dog look.

"Mackellar," says he, "I wish I could trouble you
upon a little service. There is a pension we pay ; it is

John's part to carry it, and now that he is sick I know not to whom I should look, unless it was yourself. The matter is very delicate ; I could not carry it with my own hand for a sufficient reason ; I dare not send Macconochie, who is a talker, and I am—I have—I am desirous this should not come to Mrs. Henry's ears," says he, and flushed to his neck as he said it.

To say truth, when I found I was to carry money to one Jessie Broun, who was no better than she should be, I supposed it was some trip of his own that Mr. Henry was dissembling. I was the more impressed when the truth came out.

It was up a wynd off a side street in St. Bride's that Jessie had her lodging. The place was very ill inhabited, mostly by the free-trading sort. There was a man with a broken head at the entry ; half-way up, in a tavern, fellows were roaring and singing, though it was not yet nine in the day. Altogether, I had never seen a worse neighbourhood, even in the great city of Edinburgh, and I was in two minds to go back. Jessie's room was of a piece with her surroundings, and herself no better. She would not give me the receipt (which Mr. Henry had told me to demand, for he was very methodical) until she had sent out for spirits, and I had pledged her in a glass ; and all the time she carried on in a light-headed, reckless way—now aping the manners of a lady, now breaking into unseemly mirth, now making coquettish advances that oppressed me to the ground. Of the money she spoke more tragically.

" It's blood-money ! " said she ; " I take it for that : blood-money for the betrayed ! See what I'm brought down to ! Ah, if the bonny lad were back again, it would be changed days. But he's deid—he's lyin' deid amang the Hieland hills—the bonny lad, the bonny lad ! "

She had a rapt manner of crying on the bonny lad, clasping her hands and casting up her eyes, that I think she must have learned of strolling players ; and I thought her sorrow very much of an affectation, and that she dwelled upon the business because her shame was now all she had to be proud of. I will not say I did not pity her, but it was a loathing pity at the best ; and her last change of manner wiped it out. This was when she had had enough of me for an audience, and had set her name at last to the receipt. " There ! " says she, and, taking the most un-womanly oaths upon her tongue, bade me begone and carry it to the Judas who had sent me. It was the first time I had heard the name applied to Mr. Henry ; I was staggered besides at her sudden vehemence of word and manner, and got forth from the room, under this shower of curses, like a beaten dog. But even then I was not quit, for the vixen threw up her window, and, leaning forth, continued to revile me as I went up the wynd ; the free-traders, coming to the tavern door, joined in the mockery, and one had even the inhumanity to set upon me a very savage small dog, which bit me in the ankle. This was a strong lesson, had I required one, to avoid ill company ; and I rode home in much pain from the bite, and consider-able indignation of mind.

Mr. Henry was in the steward's room, affecting employ-ment, but I could see he was only impatient to hear of my errand.

" Well ? " says he, as soon as I came in ; and when I had told him something of what passed, and that Jessie seemed an undeserving woman, and far from grateful : " She is no friend to me," said he ; " but indeed, Mac-kellar, I have few friends to boast of, and Jessie has some cause to be unjust. I need not dissemble what all the country knows : she was not very well used by one of our family." This was the first time I had heard him refer to the Master, even distantly ; and I think he found his tongue rebellious even for that much, but presently he resumed—" This is why I would have nothing said. It would give pain to Mrs. Henry . . . and to my father," he added, with another flush.

" Mr. Henry," said I, " if you will take a freedom at my hands, I would tell you to let that woman be. What service is your money to the like of her ? She has no sobriety and no economy—as for gratitude, you will as soon get milk from a whinstone ; and if you will pretermit your bounty, it will make no change at all but just to save the ankles of your messengers."

Mr. Henry smiled. " But I am grieved about your ankle," said he the next moment, with a proper gravity.

" And observe," I continued, " I give you this advice upon consideration ; and yet my heart was touched for the woman in the beginning."

" Why, there it is, you see ! " said Mr. Henry. " And you are to remember that I knew her once a very decent lass. Besides which, although I speak little of my family, I think much of its repute."

And with that he broke up the talk, which was the first we had together in such confidence. But the same afternoon I had the proof that his father was perfectly acquainted with the business, and that it was only from his wife that Mr. Henry kept it secret.

" I fear you had a painful errand to-day," says my lord to me, " for which, as it enters in no way among your duties, I wish to thank you, and to remind you at the same time (in case Mr. Henry should have neglected) how very desirable it is that no word of it should reach my daughter. Reflections on the dead, Mr. Mackellar, are doubly painful."

Anger glowed in my heart ; and I could have told my lord to his face how little he had to do, bolstering up the image of the dead in Mrs. Henry's heart, and how much better he were employed to shatter that false idol ; for by this time I saw very well how the land lay between my patron and his wife.

My pen is clear enough to tell a plain tale ; but to render the effect of an infinity of small things, not one

great enough in itself to be narrated ; and to translate
the story of looks, and the message of voices when they
are saying no great matter ; and to put in half a page the
essence of near eighteen months—this is what I despair
to accomplish. The fault, to be very blunt, lay all in
Mrs. Henry. She felt it a merit to have consented to
the marriage, and she took it like a martyrdom ; in which
my old lord, whether he knew it or not, fomented her.
She made a merit, besides, of her constancy to the dead,
though its name, to a nicer conscience, should have seemed
rather disloyalty to the living ; and here also my lord
gave her his countenance. I suppose he was glad to talk
of his loss, and ashamed to dwell on it with Mr. Henry.
Certainly, at least, he made a little coterie apart in that
family of three, and it was the husband who was shut
out. It seems it was an old custom when the family were
alone in Durrisdeer, that my lord should take his wine to
the chimney-side, and Miss Alison, instead of withdrawing, should bring a stool to his knee, and chatter to him
privately ; and after she had become my patron's wife
the same manner of doing was continued. It should have
been pleasant to behold this ancient gentleman so loving
with his daughter, but I was too much a partisan of Mr.
Henry's to be anything but wroth at his exclusion. Many's
the time I have seen him make an obvious resolve, quit
the table, and go and join himself to his wife and my Lord
Durrisdeer ; and on their part, they were never backward to make him welcome, turned to him smilingly as
to an intruding child, and took him into their talk with
an effort so ill-concealed that he was soon back again
beside me at the table, whence (so great is the hall of Durrisdeer) we could but hear the murmur of voices at the
chimney. There he would sit and watch, and I along
with him ; and sometimes by my lord's head-sorrowfully
shaken, or his hand laid on Mrs. Henry's head, or hers
upon his knee as if in consolation, or sometimes by an
exchange of tearful looks, we would draw our conclusion

that the talk had gone to the old subject and the shadow of the dead was in the hall.

I have hours when I blame Mr. Henry for taking all too patiently ; yet we are to remember he was married in pity, and accepted his wife upon that term. And, indeed, he had small encouragement to make a stand. Once, I remember, he announced he had found a man to replace the pane of the stained window, which, as it was he that managed all the business, was a thing clearly within his attributions. But to the Master's fanciers that pane was like a relic ; and on the first word of any change the blood flew to Mrs. Henry's face.

" I wonder at you ! " she cried.

" I wonder at myself," says Mr. Henry, with more of bitterness than I had ever heard him to express.

Thereupon my old lord stepped in with his smooth talk, so that before the meal was at an end all seemed forgotten ; only that, after dinner, when the pair had withdrawn as usual to the chimney-side, we could see her weeping with her head upon his knee. Mr. Henry kept up the talk with me upon some topic of the estates—he could speak of little else but business, and was never the best of company ; but he kept it up that day with more continuity, his eye straying ever and again to the chimney, and his voice changing to another key, but without check of delivery. The pane, however, was not replaced ; and I believe he counted it a great defeat.

Whether he was stout enough or no, God knows he was kind enough. Mrs. Henry had a manner of condescension with him, such as (in a wife) would have pricked my vanity into an ulcer ; he took it like a favour. She held him at the staff's end ; forgot and then remembered and unbent to him, as we do to children ; burthened him with cold kindness ; reproved him with a change of colour and a bitten lip, like one shamed by his disgrace : ordered him with a look of the eye, when she was off her guard ; when she was on the watch, pleaded with him for the most natural attentions, as though they were unheard-of favours. And to all this he replied with the most unwearied service; loving, as folk say, the very ground she trod on, and carrying that love in his eyes as bright as a lamp. When Miss Katharine was to be born, nothing would serve but he must stay in the room behind the head of the bed. There he sat, as white (they tell me) as a sheet, and the sweat dropping from his brow; and the handkerchief he had in his hand was crushed into a little ball no bigger than a musket-bullet. Nor could he bear the sight of Miss Katharine for many a day; indeed, I doubt if he was ever what he should have been to my young lady; for the which want of natural feeling he was loudly blamed.

Such was the state of this family down to the 7th April 1749, when there befell the first of that series of events which were to break so many hearts and lose so many lives.

On that day I was sitting in my room a little before supper, when John Paul burst open the door with no civility of knocking, and told me there was one below that wished to speak with the steward; sneering at the name of my office.

I asked what manner of man, and what his name was; and this disclosed the cause of John's ill-humour; for it appeared the visitor refused to name himself except to me, a sore affront to the major-domo's consequence.

" Well," said I, smiling a little, " I will see what he wants."

I found in the entrance-hall a big man, very plainly habited, and wrapped in a sea-cloak, like one new landed, as indeed he was. Not far off Macconochie was standing, with his tongue out of his mouth and his hand upon his chin, like a dull fellow thinking hard; and the stranger, who had brought his cloak about his face, appeared uneasy. He had no sooner seen me coming than he went to meet me with an effusive manner.

" My dear man," said he, " a thousand apologies for disturbing you, but I'm in the most awkward position. And there's a son of a ramrod there that I should know the looks of, and more, betoken, I believe that he knows mine. Being in this family, sir, and in a place of some responsibility (which was the cause I took the liberty to send for you), you are doubtless of the honest party ? "

" You may be sure at least," says I, " that all of that party are quite safe in Durrisdeer."

" My dear man, it is my very thought," says he. " You see, I have just been set on shore here by a very honest man, whose name I cannot remember, and who is to stand off and on for me till morning, at some danger to himself ; and, to be clear with you, I am a little concerned lest it should be at some to me. I have saved my life so often, Mr. ——, I forget your name, which is a very good one— that, faith, I would be very loth to lose it after all. And the son of a ramrod, whom I believe I saw before Carlisle . . ."

" O, sir," said I, " you can trust Macconochie until to-morrow."

" Well, and it's a delight to hear you say so," says the stranger. " The truth is, that my name is not a very suitable one in this country of Scotland. With a gentleman like you, my dear man, I would have no concealments of course ; and by your leave I'll just breathe it in your ear. They call me Francis Burke—Colonel Francis Burke ; and I am here, at a most damnable risk to myself, to see your masters—if you'll excuse me, my good man, for giving them the name, for I'm sure it's a circumstance I would never have guessed from your appearance. And if you would just be so very obliging as to take my name to them, you might say that I come bearing letters which I am sure they will be very rejoiced to have the reading of."

Colonel Francis Burke was one of the Prince's Irishmen,* that did his cause such an infinity of hurt, and were so much distasted of the Scots at the time of the rebellion ;

and it came at once into my mind how the Master of Ballantrae had astonished all men by going with that party. In the same moment a strong foreboding of the truth possessed my soul.

" If you will step in here," said I, opening a chamber door, " I will let my lord know."

" And I am sure it's very good of you, Mr. What's-your-name," says the Colonel.

Up to the hall I went, slow-footed. There they were, all three—my old lord in his place, Mrs. Henry at work by the window, Mr. Henry (as was much his custom) pacing the low end. In the midst was the table laid for supper. I told them briefly what I had to say. My old lord lay back in his seat. Mrs. Henry sprang up standing with a mechanical motion, and she and her husband stared at each other's eyes across the room ; it was the strangest, challenging look these two exchanged, and as they looked, the colour faded in their faces. Then Mr. Henry turned to me ; not to speak, only to sign with his finger ; but that was enough, and I went down again for the Colonel.

When we returned, these three were in much the same position I had left them in ; I believe no word had passed.

" My Lord Durrisdeer, no doubt ? " says the Colonel, bowing, and my lord bowed in answer. " And this," continues the Colonel, " should be the Master of Ballantrae ? "

" I have never taken that name," said Mr. Henry ; " but I am Henry Durie, at your service."

Then the Colonel turns to Mrs. Henry, bowing with his hat upon his heart and the most killing airs of gallantry. " There can be no mistake about so fine a figure of a lady," says he. " I address the seductive Miss Alison, of whom I have so often heard ? "

Once more husband and wife exchanged a look.

" I am Mrs. Henry Durie," said she ; " but before my marriage my name was Alison Graeme."

Then my lord spoke up. " I am an old man, Colonel Burke," said he, " and a frail one. It will be mercy on

your part to be expeditious. Do you bring me news
of——" he hesitated, and then the words broke from him
with a singular change of voice—"my son?"

" My dear lord, I will be round with you like a soldier,"
said the Colonel. " I do."

My lord held out a wavering hand ; he seemed to wave
a signal, but whether it was to give him time or to speak
on, was more than we could guess. At length he got out
the one word, " Good ? "

"Why, the very best in the creation !" cries the
Colonel. " For my good friend and admired comrade is
at this hour in the fine city of Paris, and as like as not,
if I know anything of his habits, he will be drawing in
his chair to a piece of dinner.—Bedad, I believe the lady's
fainting."

Mrs. Henry was indeed the colour of death, and drooped
against the window-frame. But when Mr. Henry made a
movement as if to run to her, she straightened with
a sort of shiver. " I am well," she said, with her white
lips.

Mr. Henry stopped, and his face had a strong twitch
of anger. The next moment he had turned to the Colonel.
" You must not blame yourself," says he, " for this effect
on Mrs. Durie. It is only natural ; we were all brought
up like brother and sister."

Mrs. Henry looked at her husband with something like
relief, or even gratitude. In my way of thinking, that
speech was the first step he made in her good graces.

" You must try to forgive me, Mrs. Durie, for indeed
and I am just an Irish savage," said the Colonel ; " and
I deserve to be shot for not breaking the matter more
artistically to a lady.—But here are the Master's own
letters ; one for each of the three of you ; and to be sure
(if I know anything of my friend's genius) he will tell his
own story with a better grace."

He brought the three letters forth as he spoke, arranged
them by their superscriptions, presented the first to my

lord, who took it greedily, and advanced towards Mrs. Henry holding out the second.

But the lady waved it back. " To my husband," says she, with a choked voice.

The Colonel was a quick man, but at this he was somewhat nonplussed. " To be sure ! " says he ; " how very dull of me ! To be sure ! " But he still held the letter.

At last Mr. Henry reached forth his hand, and there was nothing to be done but give it up. Mr. Henry took the letters (both hers and his own), and looked upon their outside, with his brows knit hard, as if he were thinking. He had surprised me all through by his excellent behaviour ; but he was to excel himself now.

" Let me give you a hand to your room," said he to his wife. " This has come something of the suddenest ; and, at any rate, you will wish to read your letter by yourself."

Again she looked upon him with the same thought of wonder ; but he gave her no time, coming straight to where she stood. " It will be better so, believe me," said he ; " and Colonel Burke is too considerate not to excuse you." And with that he took her hand by the fingers, and led her from the hall.

Mrs. Henry returned no more that night ; and when Mr. Henry went to visit her next morning, as I heard long afterwards, she gave him the letter again, still unopened.

" O, read it and be done ! " he had cried.

" Spare me that," said she.

And by these two speeches, to my way of thinking, each undid a great part of what they had previously done well. But the letter, sure enough, came into my hands, and by me was burned, unopened.

To be very exact as to the adventures of the Master after Culloden, I wrote not long ago to Colonel Burke, now a Chevalier of the Order of St. Louis, begging him for some notes in writing, since I could scarce depend upon my memory at so great an interval. To confess the truth, I

have been somewhat embarrassed by his response ; for
he sent me the complete memoirs of his life, touching only
in places on the Master ; running to a much greater length
than my whole story, and not everywhere (as it seems to
me) designed for edification. He begged in his letter,
dated from Ettenheim, that I would find a publisher for
the whole, after I had made what use of it I required ; and
I think I shall best answer my own purpose and fulfil his
wishes by giving certain parts of it in full.   In this way
my readers will have a detailed and, I believe, a very
genuine account of some essential matters ; and if any
publisher should take a fancy to the Chevalier's manner of
narration, he knows where to apply for the rest, of which
there is plenty at his service.   I put in my first extract
here, so that it may stand in the place of what the Chevalier
told us over our wine in the hall of Durrisdeer ; but you
are to suppose it was not the brutal fact, but a very varnished
version that he offered to my lord.

CHAPTER III

THE MASTER'S WANDERINGS

From the Memoirs of the Chevalier de Burke

. . . I LEFT Ruthven (it's hardly necessary to remark)
with much greater satisfaction than I had come to it ;
but whether I missed my way in the deserts, or whether
my companions failed me, I soon found myself alone.
This was a predicament very disagreeable ; for I never
understood this horrid country or savage people, and the
last stroke of the Prince's withdrawal had made us of the
Irish more unpopular than ever. I was reflecting on my
poor chances, when I saw another horseman on the hill,
whom I supposed at first to have been a phantom, the news
of his death in the very front at Culloden being current in
the army generally. This was the Master of Ballantrae,
my Lord Durrisdeer's son, a young nobleman of the rarest
gallantry and parts, and equally designed by nature to
adorn a Court and to reap laurels in the field. Our meeting
was the more welcome to both, as he was one of the few
Scots who had used the Irish with consideration, and as
he might now be of very high utility in aiding my escape.
Yet what founded our particular friendship was a circumstance, by itself as romantic as any fable of King Arthur.

This was on the second day of our flight, after we had
slept one night in the rain upon the inclination of a mountain. There was an Appin man, Alan Black Stewart (or
some such name,[1] but I have seen him since in France)

---

[1] *Note by Mr. Mackellar.*—Should not this be Alan *Breck* Stewart,*
afterwards notorious as the Appin murderer ? The Chevalier is
sometimes very weak on names.

who chanced to be passing the same way, and had a jealousy of my companion. Very uncivil expressions were exchanged ; and Stewart calls upon the Master to alight and have it out.

" Why, Mr. Stewart," says the Master, " I think at the present time I would prefer to run a race with you." And with the word claps spurs to his horse.

Stewart ran after us, a childish thing to do, for more than a mile ; and I could not help laughing, as I looked back at last and saw him on a hill, holding his hand to his side, and nearly burst with running.

" But, all the same," I could not help saying to my companion, " I would let no man run after me for any such proper purpose, and not give him his desire. It was a good jest, but it smells a trifle cowardly."

He bent his brows at me. " I do pretty well," says he, " when I saddle myself with the most unpopular man in Scotland, and let that suffice for courage."

" O, bedad," says I, " I could show you a more unpopular with the naked eye. And if you like not my company, you can ' saddle ' yourself on some one else."

" Colonel Burke," says he, " do not let us quarrel ; and, to that effect, let me assure you I am the least patient man in the world."

" I am as little patient as yourself," said I. " I care not who knows that."

" At this rate," says he, reining in, " we shall not go very far. And I propose we do one of two things upon the instant : either quarrel and be done ; or make a sure bargain to bear everything at each other's hands."

" Like a pair of brothers ? " said I.

" I said no such foolishness," he replied. " I have a brother of my own, and I think no more of him than of a colewort. But if we are to have our noses rubbed together in this course of flight, let us each dare to be ourselves like savages, and each swear that he will neither resent nor deprecate the other. I am a pretty bad fellow at bottom, and I find the pretence of virtues very irksome."

" O, I am as bad as yourself," said I. " There is no skim-milk in Francis Burke. But which is it to be ? Fight or make friends ? "

" Why," says he, " I think it will be the best manner to spin a coin for it."

This proposition was too highly chivalrous not to take my fancy ; and, strange as it may seem of two well-born gentlemen of to-day, we span a half-crown (like a pair of ancient paladins) whether we were to cut each other's throats or be sworn friends. A more romantic circumstance can rarely have occurred ; and it is one of those points in my memoirs, by which we may see the old tales of Homer and the poets are equally true to-day—at least, of the noble and genteel. The coin fell for peace, and we shook hands upon our bargain. And then it was that my companion explained to me his thought in running away from Mr. Stewart, which was certainly worthy of his political intellect. The report of his death, he said, was a great guard to him ; Mr. Stewart having recognised him, had become a danger ; and he had taken the briefest road to that gentleman's silence. " For," says he, " Alan Black is too vain a man to narrate any such story of himself."

Towards afternoon we came down to the shores of that loch for which we were heading ; and there was the ship, but newly come to anchor. She was the *Sainte-Marie-des-Anges*, out of the port of Havre-de-Grace. The Master, after we had signalled for a boat, asked me if I knew the captain. I told him he was a countryman of mine, of the most unblemished integrity, but, I was afraid, a rather timorous man.

" No matter," says he. " For all that, he should certainly hear the truth."

I asked him if he meant about the battle ; for if the captain once knew the standard was down, he would certainly put to sea again at once.

"And even then!" said he; "the arms are now of no sort of utility."

"My dear man," said I, "who thinks of the arms? But, to be sure, we must remember our friends. They will be close upon our heels, perhaps the Prince himself, and if the ship be gone, a great number of valuable lives may be imperilled."

"The captain and the crew have lives also, if you come to that," says Ballantrae.

This I declared was but a quibble, and that I would not hear of the captain being told; and then it was that Ballantrae made me a witty answer, for the sake of which (and also because I have been blamed myself in this business of the *Sainte-Marie-des-Anges*) I have related the whole conversation as it passed.

"Frank," says he, "remember our bargain. I must not object to your holding your tongue, which I hereby even encourage you to do; but, by the same terms, you are not to resent my telling."

I could not help laughing at this; though I still fore-warned him what would come of it.

"The devil may come of it for what I care," says the reckless fellow. "I have always done exactly as I felt inclined."

As is well known, my prediction came true. The captain had no sooner heard the news than he cut his cable and to sea again; and before morning broke we were in the Great Minch.

The ship was very old; and the skipper, although the most honest of men (and Irish too), was one of the least capable. The wind blew very boisterous, and the sea raged extremely. All that day we had little heart whether to eat or drink; went early to rest in some concern of mind; and (as if to give us a lesson) in the night the wind chopped suddenly into the north-east, and blew a hurricane. We were awaked by the dreadful thunder of the tempest and the stamping of the mariners on deck; so that I

supposed our last hour was certainly come ; and the terror
of my mind was increased out of all measure by Ballantrae,
who mocked at my devotions.   It is in hours like these that
a man of any piety appears in his true light, and we find
(what we are taught as babes) the small trust that can be
set in worldly friends : I would be unworthy of my religion
if I let this pass without particular remark.   For three days
we lay in the dark in the cabin, and had but a biscuit to
nibble.   On the fourth the wind fell, leaving the ship dismasted and heaving on vast billows.   The captain had not
a guess of whither we were blown ; he was stark ignorant
of his trade, and could do naught but bless the Holy Virgin ;
a very good thing too, but scarce the whole of seamanship.
It seemed, our one hope was to be picked up by another
vessel ; and if that should prove to be an English ship, it
might be no great blessing to the Master and myself.

The fifth and sixth days we tossed there helpless.   The
seventh some sail was got on her, but she was an unwieldy
vessel at the best, and we made little but leeway.   All the
time, indeed, we had been drifting to the south and west,
and during the tempest must have driven in that direction
with unheard-of violence.   The ninth dawn was cold and
black, with a great sea running, and every mark of foul
weather.   In this situation we were overjoyed to sight a
small ship on the horizon, and to perceive her go about and
head for the *Sainte-Marie*.   But our gratification did not
very long endure ; for when she had laid-to and lowered
a boat, it was immediately filled with disorderly fellows,
who sang and shouted as they pulled across to us, and
swarmed in on our deck with bare cutlasses, cursing loudly.
Their leader was a horrible villain, with his face blacked
and his whiskers curled in ringlets ; Teach his name ; a
most notorious pirate.   He stamped about the deck, raving
and crying out that his name was Satan, and his ship was
called Hell.   There was something about him like a wicked
child or a half-witted person, that daunted me beyond expression.   I whispered in the ear of Ballantrae that I would

not be the last to volunteer, and only prayed God they might be short of hands; he approved my purpose with a nod.

"Bedad," said I to Master Teach, "if you are Satan, here is a devil for ye."

The word pleased him; and (not to dwell upon these shocking incidents) Ballantrae and I and two others were taken for recruits, while the skipper and all the rest were cast into the sea by the method of walking the plank. It was the first time I had seen this done; my heart died within me at the spectacle; and Master Teach or one of his acolytes (for my head was too much lost to be precise) remarked upon my pale face in a very alarming manner. I had the strength to cut a step or two of a jig, and cry out some ribaldry, which saved me for that time; but my legs were like water when I must get down into the skiff among these miscreants; and what with my horror of my company and fear of the monstrous billows, it was all I could do to keep an Irish tongue and break a jest or two as we were pulled aboard. By the blessing of God there was a fiddle in the pirate ship, which I had no sooner seen than I fell upon; and in my quality of crowder I had the heavenly good luck to get favour in their eyes. "Crowding Pat" was the name they dubbed me with: and it was little I cared for a name so long as my skin was whole.

What kind of a pandemonium that vessel was I cannot describe, but she was commanded by a lunatic, and might be called a floating Bedlam. Drinking, roaring, singing, quarrelling, dancing, they were never all sober at one time; and there were days together when, if a squall had supervened, it must have sent us to the bottom; or if a King's ship had come along, it would have found us quite helpless for defence. Once or twice we sighted a sail, and, if we were sober enough, overhauled it, God forgive us! and if we were all too drunk, she got away, and I would bless the saints under my breath. Teach ruled, if you can call that rule which brought no order, by the terror he created; and

I observed the man was very vain of his position. I have
known marshals of France—ay, and even Highland chief-
tains—that were less openly puffed up ; which throws a
singular light on the pursuit of honour and glory. Indeed,
the longer we live the more we perceive the sagacity of
Aristotle and the other old philosophers ; and though I
have all my life been eager for legitimate distinctions, I
can lay my hand upon my heart, at the end of my career,
and declare there is not one—no, nor yet life itself—which
is worth acquiring or preserving at the slightest cost of
dignity.

It was long before I got private speech of Ballantrae ;
but at length one night we crept out upon the boltsprit,
when the rest were better employed, and commiserated
our position.

" None can deliver us but the saints," said I.

" My mind is very different," said Ballantrae ; " for
I am going to deliver myself. This Teach is the poorest
creature possible ; we make no profit of him, and lie continually open to capture ; and," says he, " I am not going
to be a tarry pirate for nothing, nor yet to hang in chains
if I can help it."   And he told me what was in his mind to
better the state of the ship in the way of discipline, which
would give us safety for the present, and a sooner hope of
deliverance when they should have gained enough and
should break up their company.

I confessed to him ingenuously that my nerve was
quite shook amid these horrible surroundings, and I durst
scarce tell him to count upon me.

" I am not very easy frightened," said he, " nor very
easy beat."

A few days after there befell an accident which had
nearly hanged us all ; and offers the most extraordinary
picture of the folly that ruled in our concerns. We were
all pretty drunk : and some bedlamite spying a sail, Teach
put the ship about in chase without a glance, and we began
to bustle up the arms and boast of the horrors that should

follow. I observed Ballantrae stood quiet in the bows, looking under the shade of his hand ; but for my part, true to my policy among these savages, I was at work with the busiest, and passing Irish jests for their diversion.

"Run up the colours ! " cries Teach. " Show the ——s the Jolly Roger ! "

It was the merest drunken braggadocio at such a stage, and might have lost us a valuable prize ; but I thought it no part of mine to reason, and I ran up the black flag with my own hand.

Ballantrae steps presently aft with a smile upon his face.

" You may perhaps like to know, you drunken dog," says he, " that you are chasing a King's ship."

Teach roared him the lie ; but he ran at the same time to the bulwarks, and so did they all. I have never seen so many drunken men struck suddenly sober. The cruiser had gone about, upon our impudent display of colours ; she was just then filling on the new tack ; her ensign blew out quite plain to see ; and even as we stared, there came a puff of smoke, and then a report, and a shot plunged in the waves a good way short of us. Some ran to the ropes, and got the *Sarah* round with an incredible swiftness. One fellow fell on the rum-barrel, which stood broached upon the deck, and rolled it promptly overboard. On my part, I made for the Jolly Roger, struck it, tossed it in the sea ; and could have flung myself after, so vexed was I with our mismanagement. As for Teach, he grew as pale as death, and incontinently went down to his cabin. Only twice he came on deck that afternoon ; went to the taffrail ; took a long look at the King's ship, which was still on the horizon heading after us ; and then, without speech, back to his cabin. You may say he deserted us ; and if it had not been for one very capable sailor we had on board, and for the lightness of the airs that blew all day, we must certainly have gone to the yard-arm.

It is to be supposed Teach was humiliated, and perhaps

alarmed for his position with the crew; and the way in which he set about regaining what he had lost was highly characteristic of the man. Early next day we smelled him burning sulphur in his cabin and crying out of "Hell, hell!" which was well understood among the crew, and filled their minds with apprehension. Presently he comes on deck, a perfect figure of fun, his face blacked, his hair and whiskers curled, his belt stuck full of pistols; chewing bits of glass so that the blood ran down his chin, and brandishing a dirk. I do not know if he had taken these manners from the Indians of America, where he was a native; but such was his way, and he would always thus announce that he was wound up to horrid deeds. The first that came near him was the fellow who had sent the rum overboard the day before; him he stabbed to the heart, damning him for a mutineer; and then capered about the body, raving and swearing and daring us to come on. It was the silliest exhibition; and yet dangerous too, for the cowardly fellow was plainly working himself up to another murder.

All of a sudden Ballantrae stepped forth. "Have done with this play-acting," says he. "Do you think to frighten us with making faces? We saw nothing of you yesterday, when you were wanted; and we did well without you, let me tell you that."

There was a murmur and a movement in the crew, of pleasure and alarm, I thought, in nearly equal parts. As for Teach, he gave a barbarous howl, and swung his dirk to fling it, an art in which (like many seamen) he was very expert.

"Knock that out of his hand!" says Ballantrae, so sudden and sharp that my arm obeyed him before my mind had understood.

Teach stood like one stupid, never thinking on his pistols.

"Go down to your cabin," cries Ballantrae, "and come on deck again when you are sober. Do you think we are going to hang for you, you black-faced, half-witted, drunken brute and butcher ? Go down ! " And he stamped his foot at him with such a sudden smartness that Teach fairly ran for it to the companion.

" And now, mates," says Ballantrae, " a word with you. I don't know if you are gentlemen of fortune for the fun of the thing, but I am not. I want to make money, and get ashore again, and spend it like a man. And on one thing my mind is made up : I will not hang if I can help it. Come, give me a hint ; I'm only a beginner ! Is there no way to get a little discipline and common sense about this business ? "

One of the men spoke up : he said by rights they should have a quartermaster ; and no sooner was the word out of his mouth than they were all of that opinion. The thing went by acclamation ; Ballantrae was made quartermaster, the rum was put in his charge, laws were passed in imitation of those of a pirate by the name of Roberts, and the last proposal was to make an end of Teach. But Ballantrae was afraid of a more efficient captain, who might be a counter-weight to himself, and he opposed this stoutly. Teach, he said, was good enough to board ships and frighten fools with his blacked face and swearing ; we could scarce get a better man than Teach for that ; and besides, as the man was now disconsidered, and as good as deposed, we might reduce his proportion of the plunder. This carried it ; Teach's share was cut down to a mere derision, being actually less than mine ; and there remained only two points : whether he would consent, and who was to announce to him this resolution.

" Do not let that stick you," says Ballantrae; " I will do that."

And he stepped to the companion and down alone into the cabin to face that drunken savage.

" This is the man for us," cried one of the hands. " Three cheers for the quartermaster ! " which were given with a will, my own voice among the loudest, and I daresay these plaudits had their effect on Master Teach in the cabin, as we have seen of late days how shouting in the streets may trouble even the minds of legislators.

What passed precisely was never known, though some of the heads of it came to the surface later on ; and we were all amazed, as well as gratified, when Ballantrae came on deck with Teach upon his arm, and announced that all had been consented.

I pass swiftly over those twelve or fifteen months in which we continued to keep the sea in the North Atlantic, getting our food and water from the ships we overhauled, and doing on the whole a pretty fortunate business. Sure, no one could wish to read anything so ungenteel as the memoirs of a pirate, even an unwilling one like me ! Things went extremely better with our designs, and Ballantrae kept his lead, to my admiration, from that day forth. I would be tempted to suppose that a gentleman must every-where be first, even aboard a rover ; but my birth is every whit as good as any Scottish lord's, and I am not ashamed to confess that I stayed Crowding Pat until the end, and was not much better than the crew's buffoon. Indeed, it was no scene to bring out my merits. My health suffered from a variety of reasons ; I was more at home to the last on a horse's back than a ship's deck ; and, to be ingenuous, the fear of the sea was constantly in my mind, battling with the fear of my companions. I need not cry myself up for courage ; I have done well on many fields under the eyes of famous generals, and earned my late advancement by an act of the most distinguished valour before many witnesses. But when we must proceed on one of our abordages, the heart of Francis Burke was in his boots ; the little egg-shell skiff in which we must set forth, the horrible heaving of the vast billows, the height of the ship that we must scale, the thought of how many might be there in garrison upon their legitimate defence, the scowling heavens which (in that climate) so often looked darkly down upon our exploits, and the mere crying of the wind in my ears, were all considerations most unpalatable to my valour. Besides which, as I was always a creature of the nicest sensibility, the scenes that must follow on our success tempted me as little as the chances of defeat. Twice we found women on board; and though I have seen towns sacked, and of late days in France some very horrid public tumults, there was something in the smallness of the numbers engaged, and the bleak dangerous sea-surroundings, that made these acts of piracy far the most revolting. I confess ingenuously I could never proceed unless I was three parts drunk; it was the same even with the crew; Teach himself was fit for no enterprise till he was full of rum; and it was one of the most difficult parts of Ballantrae's performance to serve us with liquor in the proper quantities. Even this he did to admiration; being upon the whole the most capable man I ever met with, and the one of the most natural genius. He did not even scrape favour with the crew, as I did, by continual buffoonery made upon a very anxious heart; but preserved on most occasions a great deal of gravity and distance; so that he was like a parent among a family of young children, or a schoolmaster with his boys. What made his part the harder to perform, the men were most inveterate grumblers; Ballantrae's discipline, little as it was, was yet irksome to their love of licence; and, what was worse, being kept sober they had time to think. Some of them accordingly would fall to repenting their abominable crimes; one in particular, who was a good Catholic, and with whom I would sometimes steal apart for prayer; above all in bad weather, fogs, lashing rain, and the like, when we would be the less observed; and I am sure no two criminals in the cart have ever performed their devotions with more anxious sincerity. But the rest, having no such grounds of hope, fell to another pastime, that of computation. All day long they would be telling up their shares or glooming over the result. I have said we were pretty fortunate. But an observation falls to be made: that in this world, in

no business that I have tried, do the profits rise to a man's
expectations. We found many ships, and took many; yet
few of them contained much money, their goods were usually
nothing to our purpose—what did we want with a cargo
of ploughs, or even of tobacco?—and it is quite a painful
reflection how many whole crews we have made to walk
the plank for no more than a stock of biscuit or an anker
or two of spirits.

In the meanwhile our ship was growing very foul, and
it was high time we should make for our *port de carénage*,
which was in the estuary of a river among swamps. It
was openly understood that we should then break up and
go and squander our proportions of the spoil; and this
made every man greedy of a little more, so that our decision
was delayed from day to day. What finally decided
matters was a trifling accident, such as an ignorant person
might suppose incidental to our way of life. But here I
must explain: on only one of all the ships we boarded, the
first on which we found women, did we meet with any
genuine resistance. On that occasion we had two men
killed and several injured, and if it had not been for the
gallantry of Ballantrae we had surely been beat back at
last. Everywhere else the defence (where there was any
at all) was what the worst troops in Europe would have
laughed at; so that the most dangerous part of our employment
was to clamber up the side of the ship: and I
have even known the poor souls on board to cast us a line,
so eager were they to volunteer instead of walking the
plank. This constant immunity had made our fellows
very soft, so that I understood how Teach had made so
deep a mark upon their minds; for indeed the company
of that lunatic was the chief danger in our way of life.
The accident to which I have referred was this:—We had
sighted a little full-rigged ship very close under our board
in a haze; she sailed near as well as we did—I should be
nearer truth if I said, near as ill; and we cleared the bow-
chaser to see if we could bring a spar or two about their

ears. The swell was exceedingly great ; the motion of
the ship beyond description ; it was little wonder if our
gunners should fire thrice and be still quite broad of what
they aimed at.   But in the meanwhile the chase had cleared
a stern gun, the thickness of the air concealing them ; and
being better marksmen, their first shot struck us in the
bows, knocked our two gunners into mincemeat, so that we
were all sprinkled with the blood, and plunged through the
deck into the forecastle where we slept.   Ballantrae would
have held on ; indeed, there was nothing in this *contretemps*
to affect the mind of any soldier ; but he had a quick
perception of the men's wishes, and it was plain this lucky
shot had given them a sickener of their trade.   In a moment
they were all of one mind : the chase was drawing away
from us, it was needless to hold on, the *Sarah* was too foul
to overhaul a bottle, it was mere foolery to keep the sea
with her ; and on these pretended grounds her head was
incontinently put about and the course laid for the river.
It was strange to see what merriment fell on that ship's
company, and how they stamped about the deck jesting,
and each computing what increase had come to his share
by the death of the two gunners.

We were nine days making our port, so light were the
airs we had to sail on, so foul the ship's bottom ; but early
on the tenth, before dawn, and in a light lifting haze, we
passed the head.   A little after, the haze lifted, and fell
again, showing us a cruiser very close.   This was a sore
blow, happening so near our refuge.   There was a great
debate of whether she had seen us, and if so whether it
was likely they had recognised the *Sarah*.   We were very
careful, by destroying every member of those crews we
overhauled, to leave no evidence as to our own persons ;
but the appearance of the *Sarah* herself we could not keep
so private ; and above all of late, since she had been foul,
and we had pursued many ships without success, it was
plain that her description had been often published.   I
supposed this alert would have made us separate upon the

instant.   But here again that original genius of Ballantrae's
had a surprise in store for me.   He and Teach (and it was
the most remarkable step of his success) had gone hand in
hand since the first day of his appointment.   I often questioned him upon the fact, and never got an answer but
once, when he told me he and Teach had an understanding
" which would very much surprise the crew if they should
hear of it, and would surprise himself a good deal if it was
carried out."   Well, here again he and Teach were of a
mind ; and by their joint procurement the anchor was no
sooner down than the whole crew went off upon a scene of
drunkenness indescribable.   By afternoon we were a mere
shipful of lunatical persons, throwing of things overboard,
howling of different songs at the same time, quarrelling
and falling together, and then forgetting our quarrels to
embrace.   Ballantrae had bidden me drink nothing, and
feign drunkenness, as I valued my life ; and I have never
passed a day so wearisomely, lying the best part of the
time upon the forecastle and watching the swamps and
thickets by which our little basin was entirely surrounded
for the eye.   A little after dusk Ballantrae stumbled up
to my side, feigned to fall, with a drunken laugh, and before
he got to his feet again, whispered me to " reel down into
the cabin and seem to fall asleep upon a locker, for there
would be need of me soon."   I did as I was told, and coming
into the cabin, where it was quite dark, let myself fall on
the first locker.   There was a man there already : by the
way he stirred and threw me off, I could not think he was
much in liquor ; and yet when I had found another place,
he seemed to continue to sleep on.   My heart now beat
very hard, for I saw some desperate matter was in act.
Presently down came Ballantrae, lit the lamp, looked about
the cabin, nodded as if pleased, and on deck again without
a word.   I peered out from between my fingers, and saw
there were three of us slumbering, or feigning to slumber,
on the lockers : myself, one Dutton, and one Grady, both
resolute men.   On deck the rest were got to a pitch of

revelry quite beyond the bounds of what is human ; so that no reasonable name can describe the sounds they were now making. I have heard many a drunken bout in my time, many on board that very *Sarah*, but never anything the least like this, which made me early suppose the liquor had been tampered with. It was a long while before these yells and howls died out into a sort of miserable moaning, and then to silence ; and it seemed a long while after that before Ballantrae came down again, this time with Teach upon his heels. The latter cursed at the sight of us three upon the lockers.

"Tut," says Ballantrae, " you might fire a pistol at their ears. You know what stuff they have been swallowing."

There was a hatch in the cabin floor, and under that the richest part of the booty was stored against the day of division. It fastened with a ring and three padlocks, the keys (for greater security) being divided ; one to Teach, one to Ballantrae, and one to the mate, a man called Hammond. Yet I was amazed to see they were now all in the one hand ; and yet more amazed (still looking through my fingers) to observe Ballantrae and Teach bring up several packets, four of them in all, very carefully made up, and with a loop for carriage.

" And now," says Teach, " let us be going."

" One word," says Ballantrae. " I have discovered there is another man besides yourself who knows a private path across the swamp ; and it seems it is shorter than yours."

Teach cried out, in that case, they were undone.

" I do not know for that," says Ballantrae. " For there are several other circumstances with which I must acquaint you. First of all, there is no bullet in your pistols, which (if you remember) I was kind enough to load for both of us this morning. Secondly, as there is some one else who knows a passage, you must think it highly improbable I should saddle myself with a lunatic like you. Thirdly, these gentlemen (who need no longer pretend to be asleep) are those of my party, and will now proceed to gag and bind you to the mast ; and when your men awaken (if they ever do awake after the drugs we have mingled in their liquor), I am sure they will be so obliging as to deliver you, and you will have no difficulty, I daresay, to explain the business of the keys."

Not a word said Teach, but looked at us like a frightened baby as we gagged and bound him.

"Now you see, you moon-calf," says Ballantrae, " why we made four packets. Heretofore you have been called Captain Teach, but I think you are now rather Captain Learn."

That was our last word on board the *Sarah*. We four, with our four packets, lowered ourselves softly into a skiff, and left that ship behind us as silent as the grave, only for the moaning of some of the drunkards. There was a fog about breast-high on the waters ; so that Dutton, who knew the passage, must stand on his feet to direct our rowing ; and this, as it forced us to row gently, was the means of our deliverance. We were yet but a little way from the ship, when it began to come grey, and the birds to fly abroad upon the water. All of a sudden Dutton clapped down upon his hams, and whispered us to be silent for our lives, and hearken. Sure enough, we heard a little faint creak of oars upon one hand, and then again, and farther off, a creak of oars upon the other. It was clear we had been sighted yesterday in the morning ; here were the cruiser's boats to cut us out ; here were we defenceless in their very midst. Sure, never were poor souls more perilously placed ; and as we lay there on our oars, praying God the mist might hold, the sweat poured from my brow. Presently we heard one of the boats where we might have thrown a biscuit in her. " Softly, men," we heard an officer whisper ; and I marvelled they could not hear the drumming of my heart.

" Never mind the path," says Ballantrae ; " we must

get shelter anyhow; let us pull straight ahead for the sides of the basin."

This we did with the most anxious precaution, rowing, as best we could, upon our hands, and steering at a venture in the fog, which was (for all that) our only safety. But Heaven guided us; we touched ground at a thicket; scrambled ashore with our treasure; and having no other way of concealment, and the mist beginning already to lighten, hove down the skiff and let her sink. We were still but new under cover when the sun rose; and at the same time, from the midst of the basin, a great shouting of seamen sprang up, and we knew the *Sarah* was being boarded. I heard afterwards the officer that took her got great honour; and it's true the approach was creditably managed, but I think he had an easy capture when he came to board.[1]

I was still blessing the saints for my escape, when I became aware we were in trouble of another kind. We were here landed at random in a vast and dangerous swamp; and how to come at the path was a concern of doubt, fatigue, and peril. Dutton, indeed, was of opinion we should wait until the ship was gone, and fish up the skiff; for any delay would be more wise than to go blindly ahead in that morass. One went back accordingly to the basin-side and (peering through the thicket) saw the fog already quite drunk up, and English colours flying on the *Sarah*, but no movement made to get her under way. Our situation was now very doubtful. The swamp was an unhealthful place to linger in; we had been so greedy to bring treasures that we had brought but little food; it was highly desirable, besides, that we should get clear of the neighbourhood and into the settlements before the news

[1] *Note by Mr. Mackellar.*—This Teach of the *Sarah* must not be confused with the celebrated *Blackbeard.** The dates and facts by no means tally. It is possible the second Teach may have at once borrowed the name and imitated the more excessive part of his manners from the first. Even the Master of Ballantrae could make admirers.

of the capture went abroad; and against all these considerations there was only the peril of the passage on the other side. I think it not wonderful we decided on the active part.

It was already blistering hot when we set forth to pass the marsh, or rather to strike the path, by compass. Dutton took the compass, and one or other of us three carried his proportion of the treasure. I promise you he kept a sharp eye to his rear, for it was like the man's soul that he must trust us with. The thicket was as close as a bush; the ground very treacherous, so that we often sank in the most terrifying manner, and must go round about; the heat, besides, was stifling, the air singularly heavy, and the stinging insects abounded in such myriads that each of us walked under his own cloud. It has often been commented on, how much better gentlemen of birth endure fatigue than persons of the rabble; so that walking officers, who must tramp in the dirt beside their men, shame them by their constancy. This was well to be observed in the present instance; for here were Ballantrae and I, two gentlemen of the highest breeding, on the one hand; and on the other, Grady, a common mariner, and a man nearly a giant in physical strength. The case of Dutton is not in point, for I confess he did as well as any of us.[1] But as for Grady, he began early to lament his case, tailed in the rear, refused to carry Dutton's packet when it came his turn, clamoured continually for rum (of which we had too little), and at last even threatened us from behind with a cocked pistol, unless we should allow him rest. Ballantrae would have fought it out, I believe; but I prevailed with him the other way; and we made a stop and ate a meal. It seemed to benefit Grady little; he was in the rear again at once, growling and bemoaning his lot; and at last, by some carelessness, not having followed properly in our

---

[1] *Note by Mr. Mackellar.*—And is not this the whole explanation? since this Dutton, exactly like the officers, enjoyed the stimulus of some responsibility.

tracks, stumbled into a deep part of the slough where it
was mostly water, gave some very dreadful screams, and
before we could come to his aid had sunk along with his
booty. His fate, and above all these screams of his,
appalled us to the soul ; yet it was on the whole a fortunate
circumstance, and the means of our deliverance, for it
moved Dutton to mount into a tree, whence he was able
to perceive and to show me, who had climbed after him, a
high piece of the wood, which was a landmark for the path.
He went forward the more carelessly, I must suppose ; for
presently we saw him sink a little down, draw up his feet
and sink again, and so twice. Then he turned his face to
us, pretty white.

"Lend a hand," said he, "I am in a bad place."

"I don't know about that," says Ballantrae, standing
still.

Dutton broke out into the most violent oaths, sinking
a little lower as he did, so that the mud was nearly to his
waist, and plucking a pistol from his belt, "Help me," he
cries, "or die and be damned to you ! "

"Nay," says Ballantrae, "I did but jest. I am coming." And he set down his own packet and Dutton's,
which he was then carrying. "Do not venture near till
we see if you are needed," said he to me, and went
forward alone to where the man was bogged. He was
quiet now, though he still held the pistol ; and the
marks of terror in his countenance were very moving to
behold.

"For the Lord's sake," says he, "look sharp."

Ballantrae was now got close up. "Keep still," says
he, and seemed to consider ; and then, "Reach out both
your hands ! "

Dutton laid down his pistol, and so watery was the top
surface that it went clear out of sight ; with an oath he
stooped to snatch it ; and as he did so, Ballantrae leaned
forth and stabbed him between the shoulders. Up went
his hands over his head—I know not whether with the pain

or to ward himself ; and the next moment he doubled forward in the mud.

Ballantrae was already over the ankles ; but he plucked himself out, and came back to me, where I stood with my knees smiting one another. " The devil take you, Francis ! " says he. " I believe you are a half-hearted fellow, after all. I have only done justice on a pirate. And here we are quite clear of the *Sarah !* Who shall now say that we have dipped our hands in any irregularities ? "

I assured him he did me injustice ; but my sense of humanity was so much affected by the horridness of the fact that I could scarce find breath to answer with.

" Come," said he, " you must be more resolved. The need for this fellow ceased when he had shown you where the path ran ; and you cannot deny I would have been daft to let slip so fair an opportunity."

I could not deny but he was right in principle ; nor yet could I refrain from shedding tears, of which I think no man of valour need have been ashamed ; and it was not until I had a share of the rum that I was able to proceed. I repeat, I am far from ashamed of my generous emotion ; mercy is honourable in the warrior ; and yet I cannot altogether censure Ballantrae, whose step was really fortunate, as we struck the path without further misadventure, and the same night, about sundown, came to the edge of the morass.

We were too weary to seek far ; on some dry sands, still warm with the day's sun, and close under a wood of pines, we lay down and were instantly plunged in sleep.

We awaked the next morning very early, and began with a sullen spirit a conversation that came near to end in blows. We were now cast on shore in the southern provinces, thousands of miles from any French settlement ; a dreadful journey and a thousand perils lay in front of us ; and sure, if there was ever need for amity, it was in such an hour. I must suppose that Ballantrae had suffered in

his sense of what is truly polite; indeed, and there is
nothing strange in the idea, after the sea-wolves we had
consorted with so long; and as for myself, he fubbed me
off unhandsomely, and any gentleman would have resented
his behaviour.

I told him in what light I saw his conduct; he walked
a little off, I following to upbraid him; and at last he
stopped me with his hand.

"Frank," says he, "you know what we swore; and
yet there is no oath invented would induce me to swallow
such expressions, if I did not regard you with sincere
affection. It is impossible you should doubt me there:
I have given proofs. Dutton I had to take, because he
knew the pass, and Grady because Dutton would not move
without him; but what call was there to carry you along?
You are a perpetual danger to me with your cursed Irish
tongue. By rights you should now be in irons in the cruiser.
And you quarrel with me like a baby for some trinkets!"

I considered this one of the most unhandsome speeches
ever made; and indeed to this day I can scarce reconcile
it to my notion of a gentleman that was my friend. I
retorted upon him with his Scots accent, of which he had
not so much as some, but enough to be very barbarous and
disgusting, as I told him plainly; and the affair would have
gone to a great length, but for an alarming intervention.

We had got some way off upon the sand. The place
where we had slept, with the packets lying undone and the
money scattered openly, was now between us and the pines;
and it was out of these the stranger must have come.
There he was at least, a great hulking fellow of the country,
with a broad axe on his shoulder, looking open-mouthed,
now at the treasure, which was just at his feet, and now
at our disputation, in which we had gone far enough to
have weapons in our hands. We had no sooner observed
him than he found his legs and made off again among the
pines.

This was no scene to put our minds at rest: a couple

of armed men in sea-clothes found quarrelling over a treasure, not many miles from where a pirate had been captured—here was enough to bring the whole country about our ears. The quarrel was not even made up; it was blotted from our minds; and we got our packets together in the twinkling of an eye, and made off, running with the best will in the world. But the trouble was, we did not know in what direction, and must continually return upon our steps. Ballantrae had indeed collected what he could from Dutton; but it's hard to travel upon hearsay; and the estuary, which spreads into a vast irregular harbour, turned us off upon every side with a new stretch of water.

We were near beside ourselves, and already quite spent with running, when, coming to the top of a dune, we saw we were again cut off by another ramification of the bay. This was a creek, however, very different from those that had arrested us before; being set in rocks, and so precipitously deep that a small vessel was able to lie alongside, made fast with a hawser; and her crew had laid a plank to the shore. Here they had lighted a fire, and were sitting at their meal. As for the vessel herself, she was one of those they build in the Bermudas.

The love of gold and the great hatred that everybody has to pirates were motives of the most influential, and would certainly raise the country in our pursuit. Besides, it was now plain we were on some sort of straggling peninsula, like the fingers of a hand; and the wrist, or passage to the mainland, which we should have taken at the first, was by this time not improbably secured. These considerations put us on a bolder counsel. For as long as we dared, looking every moment to hear sounds of the chase, we lay among some bushes on the top of the dune; and having by this means secured a little breath and recomposed our appearance, we strolled down at last, with a great affectation of carelessness, to the party by the fire.

It was a trader and his negroes, belonging to Albany,

in the province of New York, and now on the way home
from the Indies with a cargo ; his name I cannot recall.
We were amazed to learn he had put in here from terror
of the *Sarah ;* for we had no thought our exploits had been
so notorious. As soon as the Albanian heard she had been
taken the day before, he jumped to his feet, gave us a cup
of spirits for our good news, and sent his negroes to get
sail on the Bermudan. On our side, we profited by the
dram to become more confidential, and at last offered ourselves as passengers. He looked askance at our tarry
clothes and pistols, and replied civilly enough that he had
scarce accommodation for himself ; nor could either our
prayers or our offers of money, in which we advanced
pretty far, avail to shake him.

" I see, you think ill of us," says Ballantrae, " but I
will show you how well we think of you by telling you the
truth. We are Jacobite fugitives, and there is a price upon
our heads."

At this the Albanian was plainly moved a little. He
asked us many questions as to the Scots war, which
Ballantrae very patiently answered. And then, with a
wink, in a vulgar manner, " I guess you and your Prince
Charlie got more than you cared about," said he.

" Bedad, and that we did," said I. " And, my dear
man, I wish you would set a new example, and give us just
that much."

This I said in the Irish way, about which there is allowed
to be something very engaging. It's a remarkable thing,
and a testimony to the love with which our nation is regarded, that this address scarce ever fails in a handsome
fellow. I cannot tell how often I have seen a private
soldier escape the horse, or a beggar wheedle out a good
alms, by a touch of the brogue. And, indeed, as soon as
the Albanian had laughed at me I was pretty much at rest.
Even then, however, he made many conditions, and—for
one thing—took away our arms, before he suffered us
aboard ; which was the signal to cast off ; so that in a

moment after we were gliding down the bay with a good breeze, and blessing the name of God for our deliverance. Almost in the mouth of the estuary, we passed the cruiser, and a little after the poor *Sarah* with her prize crew ; and these were both sights to make us tremble. The Bermudan seemed a very safe place to be in, and our bold stroke to have been fortunately played, when we were thus reminded of the case of our companions. For all that, we had only exchanged traps, jumped out of the frying-pan into the fire, run from the yard-arm to the block, and escaped the open hostility of the man-of-war to lie at the mercy of the doubtful faith of our Albanian merchant.

From many circumstances, it chanced we were safer than we could have dared to hope. The town of Albany was at that time much concerned in contraband trade across the desert with the Indians and the French. This, as it was highly illegal, relaxed their loyalty, and as it brought them in relation with the politest people on the earth, divided even their sympathies. In short, they were like all the smugglers in the world, spies and agents ready-made for either party. Our Albanian, besides, was a very honest man indeed, and very greedy ; and, to crown our luck, he conceived a great delight in our society. Before we had reached the town of New York we had come to a full agreement, that he should carry us as far as Albany upon his ship, and thence put us on a way to pass the boundaries and join the French. For all this we were to pay at a high rate ; but beggars cannot be choosers, nor outlaws bargainers.

We sailed, then, up the Hudson River, which, I protest, is a very fine stream, and put up at the " King's Arms " in Albany. The town was full of the militia of the province, breathing slaughter against the French. Governor Clinton* was there himself, a very busy man, and, by what I could learn, very near distracted by the factiousness of his Assembly. The Indians on both sides were on the warpath ; we saw parties of them bringing in prisoners and (what was much worse) scalps, both male and female, for which they were paid at a fixed rate ; and I assure you the sight was not encouraging. Altogether, we could scarce have come at a period more unsuitable for our designs ; our position in the chief inn was dreadfully conspicuous ; our Albanian fubbed us off with a thousand delays, and seemed upon the point of a retreat from his engagements ; nothing but peril appeared to environ the poor fugitives, and for some time we drowned our concern in a very irregular course of living.

This, too, proved to be fortunate ; and it's one of the remarks that fall to be made upon our escape, how providentially our steps were conducted to the very end. What a humiliation to the dignity of man ! My philosophy, the extraordinary genius of Ballantrae, our valour, in which I grant that we were equal—all these might have proved insufficient without the Divine blessing on our efforts. And how true it is, as the Church tells us, that the Truths of Religion are, after all, quite applicable even to daily affairs ! At least, it was in the course of our revelry that we made the acquaintance of a spirited youth by the name of Chew. He was one of the most daring of the Indian traders, very well acquainted with the secret paths of the wilderness, needy, dissolute, and, by a last good fortune, in some disgrace with his family. Him we persuaded to come to our relief ; he privately provided what was needful for our flight, and one day we slipped out of Albany, without a word to our former friend, and embarked, a little above, in a canoe.

To the toils and perils of this journey it would require a pen more elegant than mine to do full justice. The reader must conceive for himself the dreadful wilderness which we had now to thread ; its thickets, swamps, precipitous rocks, impetuous rivers, and amazing waterfalls. Among these barbarous scenes we must toil all day, now paddling, now carrying our canoe upon our shoulders ; and at night we slept about a fire, surrounded by the howling of wolves and other savage animals. It was our design to mount the headwaters of the Hudson, to the neighbourhood of Crown Point, where the French had a strong place in the woods, upon Lake Champlain. But to have done this directly were too perilous; and it was accordingly gone upon by such a labyrinth of rivers, lakes, and portages as makes my head giddy to remember. These paths were in ordinary times entirely desert; but the country was now up, the tribes on the war-path, the woods full of Indian scouts. Again and again we came upon these parties when we least expected them; and one day, in particular, I shall never forget how, as dawn was coming in, we were suddenly surrounded by five or six of these painted devils, uttering a very dreary sort of cry, and brandishing their hatchets. It passed off harmlessly, indeed, as did the rest of our encounters; for Chew was well known and highly valued among the different tribes. Indeed, he was a very gallant, respectable young man; but even with the advantage of his companionship, you must not think these meetings were without sensible peril. To prove friendship on our part, it was needful to draw upon our stock of rum—indeed, under whatever disguise, that is the true business of the Indian trader, to keep a travelling public-house in the forest; and when once the braves had got their bottle of *scaura* (as they call this beastly liquor), it behoved us to set forth and paddle for our scalps. Once they were a little drunk, good-bye to any sense or decency; they had but the one thought, to get more *scaura*. They might easily take it in their heads to give us chase, and had we been overtaken, I had never written these memoirs.

We were come to the most critical portion of our course, where we might equally expect to fall into the hands of French or English, when a terrible calamity befell us. Chew was taken suddenly sick with symptoms like those of poison, and in the course of a few hours expired in the bottom of the canoe. We thus lost at once our guide, our interpreter, our boatman, and our passport, for he was all these in one ; and found ourselves reduced, at a blow, to the most desperate and irremediable distress. Chew, who took a great pride in his knowledge, had indeed often lectured us on the geography ; and Ballantrae, I believe, would listen. But for my part I have always found such information highly tedious ; and beyond the fact that we were now in the country of the Adirondack Indians, and not so distant from our destination, could we but have found the way, I was entirely ignorant. The wisdom of my course was soon the more apparent ; for, with all his pains, Ballantrae was no further advanced than myself. He knew we must continue to go up one stream ; then, by way of a portage, down another ; and then up a third. But you are to consider, in a mountain country, how many streams come rolling in from every hand. And how is a gentleman, who is a perfect stranger in that part of the world, to tell any one of them from any other ? Nor was this our only trouble. We were great novices, besides, in handling a canoe ; the portages were almost beyond our strength, so that I have seen us sit down in despair for half an hour at a time without one word ; and the appearance of a single Indian, since we had now no means of speaking to them, would have been in all probability the means of our destruction. There is altogether some excuse if Ballantrae showed something of a glooming disposition ; his habit of imputing blame to others, quite as capable as himself, was less tolerable, and his language it was not always easy to accept. Indeed, he had contracted on board the pirate ship a manner of address which was in a high degree unusual between gentlemen ; and now, when you might say he was in a fever, it increased upon him hugely.

The third day of these wanderings, as we were carrying the canoe upon a rocky portage, she fell, and was entirely bilged. The portage was between two lakes, both pretty extensive ; the track, such as it was, opened at both ends upon the water, and on both hands was enclosed by the unbroken woods ; and the sides of the lakes were quite impassable with bog : so that we beheld ourselves not only condemned to go without our boat and the greater part of our provisions, but to plunge at once into impenetrable thickets and to desert what little guidance we still had—the course of the river. Each stuck his pistols in his belt, shouldered an axe, made a pack of his treasure and as much food as he could stagger under ; and deserting the rest of our possessions, even to our swords, which would have much embarrassed us among the woods, we set forth on this deplorable adventure. The labours of Hercules, so finely described by Homer, were a trifle to what we now underwent. Some parts of the forest were perfectly dense down to the ground, so that we must cut our way like mites in a cheese. In some the bottom was full of deep swamp, and the whole wood entirely rotten. I have leaped on a great fallen log and sunk to the knees in touchwood ; I have sought to stay myself, in falling, against what looked to be a solid trunk, and the whole thing has whiffed at my touch like a sheet of paper. Stumbling, falling, bogging to the knees, hewing our way, our eyes almost put out with twigs and branches, our clothes plucked from our bodies, we laboured all day, and it is doubtful if we made two miles. What was worse, as we could rarely get a view of the country, and were perpetually justled from our path by obstacles, it was impossible even to have a guess in what direction we were moving.

A little before sundown, in an open place with a stream, and set about with barbarous mountains, Ballantrae threw down his pack. " I will go no further," said he, and bade me light the fire, damning my blood in terms not proper for a chairman.

I told him to try to forget he had ever been a pirate, and to remember he had been a gentleman.

" Are you mad ? " he cried. " Don't cross me here ! " And then, shaking his fist at the hills, " To think," cries he, " that I must leave my bones in this miserable wilderness ! Would God I had died upon the scaffold like a gentleman!" This he said ranting like an actor; and then sat biting his fingers and staring on the ground, a most unchristian object.

I took a certain horror of the man, for I thought a soldier and a gentleman should confront his end with more philosophy. I made him no reply, therefore, in words; and presently the evening fell so chill that I was glad, for my own sake, to kindle a fire. And yet God knows, in such an open spot, and the country alive with savages, the act was little short of lunacy. Ballantrae seemed never to observe me; but at last, as I was about parching a little corn, he looked up.

"Have you ever a brother?" said he.

"By the blessing of Heaven," said I, "not less than five."

"I have the one," said he, with a strange voice; and then presently, "He shall pay me for all this," he added. And when I asked him what was his brother's part in our distress, "What!" he cried, "he sits in my place, he bears my name, he courts my wife; and I am here alone with a damned Irishman in this tooth-chattering desert! O, I have been a common gull!" he cried.

The explosion was in all ways so foreign to my friend's nature that I was daunted out of all my just susceptibility. Sure, an offensive expression, however vivacious, appears a wonderfully small affair in circumstances so extreme! But here there is a strange thing to be noted. He had only once before referred to the lady with whom he was contracted. That was when we came in view of the town of New York, when he had told me, if all had their rights, he was now in sight of his own property, for Miss Graeme enjoyed a large estate in the province. And this was certainly a natural occasion; but now here she was named a second time; and what is surely fit to be observed, in this very month, which was November, 'Forty-seven, and *I believe upon that very day as we sat among these barbarous mountains*, his brother and Miss Graeme were married. I am the least superstitious of men ; but the hand of Providence is here displayed too openly not to be remarked.[1]

The next day, and the next, were passed in similar labours ; Ballantrae often deciding on our course by the spinning of a coin ; and once, when I expostulated on this childishness, he had an odd remark that I never have forgotten. " I know no better way," said he, " to express my scorn of human reason." I think it was the third day that we found the body of a Christian, scalped and most abominably mangled, and lying in a pudder of his blood ; the birds of the desert screaming over him, as thick as flies. I cannot describe how dreadfully this sight affected us ; but it robbed me of all strength and all hope for this world. The same day, and only a little after, we were scrambling over a part of the forest that had been burned, when Ballantrae, who was a little ahead, ducked suddenly behind a fallen trunk. I joined him in this shelter, whence we could look abroad without being seen ourselves ; and in the bottom of the next vale beheld a large war-party of the savages going by across our line. There might be the value of a weak battalion present ; all naked to the waist, blacked with grease and soot, and painted with white lead and vermilion, according to their beastly habits. They went one behind another like a string of geese, and at a quickish trot ; so that they took but a little while to rattle by, and disappear again among the woods. Yet I suppose we endured a greater agony of hesitation and suspense in these few minutes than goes usually to a man's whole life. Whether they were French or English Indians, whether they desired scalps or prisoners, whether we should declare ourselves upon the chance, or lie quiet and continue the heart-breaking business of our journey : sure, I think these were questions to have puzzled the brains of Aristotle himself. Ballantrae turned to me with a face all wrinkled up, and his teeth showing in his mouth, like what I have

---

[1] *Note by Mr. Mackellar.*—A complete blunder : there was at this date no word of the marriage : see above in my own narration.

read of people starving ; he said no word, but his whole appearance was a kind of dreadful question.

" They may be of the English side," I whispered ; " and think ! the best we could then hope is to begin this over again."

" I know—I know," he said. " Yet it must come to a plunge at last." And he suddenly plucked out his coin, shook it in his closed hands, looked at it, and then lay down with his face in the dust.

Addition by Mr. Mackellar.—I drop the Chevalier's narration at this point because the couple quarrelled and separated the same day ; and the Chevalier's account of the quarrel seems to me (I must confess) quite incompatible with the nature of either of the men. Henceforth they wandered alone, undergoing extraordinary sufferings ; until first one and then the other was picked up by a party from Fort St. Frederick. Only two things are to be noted. And first (as most important for my purpose) that the Master, in the course of his miseries, buried his treasure, at a point never since discovered, but of which he took a drawing in his own blood on the lining of his hat. And second, that on his coming thus penniless to the Fort, he was welcomed like a brother by the Chevalier, who thence paid his way to France. The simplicity of Mr. Burke's character leads him at this point to praise the Master exceedingly ; to an eye more worldly-wise, it would seem it was the Chevalier alone that was to be commended. I have the more pleasure in pointing to this really very noble trait of my esteemed correspondent, as I fear I may have wounded him immediately before. I have refrained from comments on any of his extraordinary and (in my eyes) immoral opinions, for I know him to be jealous of respect. But his version of the quarrel is really more than I can reproduce ; for I knew the Master myself, and a man more insusceptible of fear is not conceivable. I regret this oversight of the Chevalier's, and all the more because the tenor of his narrative (set aside a few flourishes) strikes me as highly ingenuous.

CHAPTER IV

PERSECUTIONS ENDURED BY MR. HENRY

You can guess on what part of his adventures the Colonel principally dwelled. Indeed, if we had heard it all, it is to be thought the current of this business had been wholly altered ; but the pirate ship was very gently touched upon. Nor did I hear the Colonel to an end even of that which he was willing to disclose ; for Mr. Henry, having for some while been plunged in a brown study, rose at last from his seat and (reminding the Colonel there were matters that he must attend to) bade me follow him immediately to the office.

Once there, he sought no longer to dissemble his concern, walking to and fro in the room with a contorted face, and passing his hand repeatedly upon his brow.

" We have some business," he began at last ; and there broke off, declared we must have wine, and sent for a magnum of the best. This was extremely foreign to his habitudes ; and, what was still more so, when the wine had come, he gulped down one glass upon another like a man careless of appearances. But the drink steadied him.

" You will scarce be surprised, Mackellar," says he, " when I tell you that my brother—whose safety we are all rejoiced to learn—stands in some need of money."

I told him I had misdoubted as much ; but the time was not very fortunate, as the stock was low.

" Not mine," said he. " There is the money for the mortgage."

I reminded him it was Mrs. Henry's.

70

"I will be answerable to my wife," he cried violently.
"And then," said I, "there is the mortgage."

"I know," said he; "it is on that I would consult you."

I showed him how unfortunate a time it was to divert this money from its destination; and how, by so doing, we must lose the profit of our past economies, and plunge back the estate into the mire. I even took the liberty to plead with him; and when he still opposed me with a shake of the head and a bitter dogged smile, my zeal quite carried me beyond my place. "This is midsummer madness," cried I; "and I for one will be no party to it."

"You speak as though I did it for my pleasure," says he. "But I have a child now; and, besides, I love order; and to say the honest truth, Mackellar, I had begun to take a pride in the estates." He gloomed for a moment. "But what would you have?" he went on. "Nothing is mine, nothing. This day's news has knocked the bottom out of my life. I have only the name and the shadow of things —only the shadow; there is no substance in my rights."

"They will prove substantial enough before a court," said I.

He looked at me with a burning eye, and seemed to repress the word upon his lips; and I repented what I had said, for I saw that while he spoke of the estate he had still a side-thought to his marriage. And then, of a sudden, he twitched the letter from his pocket, where it lay all crumpled, smoothed it violently on the table, and read these words to me with a trembling tongue:—"'My dear Jacob'—This is how he begins!" cries he—"'My dear Jacob, I once called you so, you may remember; and you have now done the business, and flung my heels as high as Criffel.'* What do you think of that, Mackellar," says he, "from an only brother? I declare to God I liked him very well; I was always staunch to him; and this is how he writes! But I will not sit down under the imputation" —walking to and fro—"I am as good as he; I am a better man than he, I call on God to prove it! I cannot give him

all the monstrous sum he asks ; he knows the estate to be
incompetent ; but I will give him what I have, and it is
more than he expects. I have borne all this too long.
See what he writes further on ; read it for yourself : ' I
know you are a niggardly dog.' A niggardly dog ! I
niggardly ? Is that true, Mackellar ? You think it is ? "
I really thought he would have struck me at that. " O,
you all think so ! Well, you shall see, and he shall see, and
God shall see. If I ruin the estate and go barefoot, I shall
stuff this bloodsucker. Let him ask all—all, and he shall
have it ! It is all his by rights. Ah ! " he cried, " and I
foresaw all this, and worse, when he would not let me go."
He poured out another glass of wine, and was about to
carry it to his lips, when I made so bold as to lay a finger
on his arm. He stopped a moment. " You are right," said
he, and flung glass and all in the fireplace. " Come, let
us count the money."

I durst no longer oppose him ; indeed, I was very much
affected by the sight of so much disorder in a man usually
so controlled ; and we sat down together, counted the
money, and made it up in packets for the greater ease of
Colonel Burke, who was to be the bearer. This done, Mr.
Henry returned to the hall, where he and my old lord sat
all night through with their guest.

A little before dawn I was called and set out with the
Colonel. He would scarce have liked a less responsible con-
voy, for he was a man who valued himself ; nor could we
afford him one more dignified, for Mr. Henry must not
appear with the free-traders. It was a very bitter morning
of wind, and as we went down through the long shrubbery
the Colonel held himself muffled in his cloak.

" Sir," said I, " this is a great sum of money that your
friend requires. I must suppose his necessities to be very
great."

" We must suppose so," says he, I thought drily , but
perhaps it was the cloak about his mouth.

" I am only a servant of the family," said I. " You

may deal openly with me. I think we are likely to get little good by him ? "

" My dear man," said the Colonel, " Ballantrae is a gentleman of the most eminent natural abilities, and a man that I admire, and that I revere, to the very ground he treads on." And then he seemed to me to pause like one in a difficulty.

" But for all that," said I, " we are likely to get little good by him ? "

" Sure, and you can have it your own way, my dear man," says the Colonel.

By this time we had come to the side of the creek, where the boat awaited him. " Well," said he, " I am sure I am very much your debtor for all your civility, Mr. Whatever-your-name-is ; and just as a last word, and since you show so much intelligent interest, I will mention a small circumstance that may be of use to the family. For I believe my friend omitted to mention that he has the largest pension on the Scots Fund* of any refugee in Paris ; and it's the more disgraceful, sir," cries the Colonel, warming, " because there's not one dirty penny for myself."

He cocked his hat at me, as if I had been to blame for this partiality ; then changed again into his usual swaggering civility, shook me by the hand, and set off down to the boat, with the money under his arms, and whistling as he went the pathetic air of " Shule Aroon." It was the first time I had heard that tune ; I was to hear it again, words and all, as you shall learn, but I remember how that little stave of it ran in my head after the free-traders had bade him " Wheesht, in the deil's name," and the grating of the oars had taken its place, and I stood and watched the dawn creeping on the sea, and the boat drawing away, and the lugger lying with her foresail backed awaiting it.

The gap made in our money was a sore embarrassment, and, among other consequences, it had this : that I must ride to Edinburgh, and there raise a new loan on very questionable terms to keep the old afloat; and was thus, for close upon three weeks, absent from the house of Durrisdeer.

What passed in the interval I had none to tell me, but I found Mrs. Henry, upon my return, much changed in her demeanour. The old talks with my lord for the most part pretermitted; a certain deprecation visible towards her husband, to whom I thought she addressed herself more often; and, for one thing, she was now greatly wrapped up in Miss Katharine. You would think the change was agreeable to Mr. Henry; no such matter! To the contrary, every circumstance of alteration was a stab to him; he read in each the avowal of her truant fancies. That constancy to the Master of which she was proud while she supposed him dead, she had to blush for now she knew he was alive, and these blushes were the hated spring of her new conduct. I am to conceal no truth; and I will here say plainly, I think this was the period in which Mr. Henry showed the worst. He contained himself, indeed, in public; but there was a deep-seated irritation visible underneath. With me, from whom he had less concealment, he was often grossly unjust, and even for his wife he would sometimes have a sharp retort: perhaps when she had ruffled him with some unwonted kindness; perhaps upon no tangible occasion, the mere habitual tenor of the man's annoyance bursting spontaneously forth. When he would thus forget himself (a thing so strangely out of keeping with the terms of their relation), there went a shock through the whole company, and the pair would look upon each other in a kind of pained amazement.

All the time, too, while he was injuring himself by this defect of temper, he was hurting his position by a silence, of which I scarce know whether to say it was the child of generosity or pride. The free-traders came again and again, bringing messengers from the Master, and none departed empty-handed. I never durst reason with Mr.

Henry ; he gave what was asked of him in a kind of noble
rage. Perhaps because he knew he was by nature inclining
to the parsimonious, he took a backforemost pleasure in
the recklessness with which he supplied his brother's
exigence. Perhaps the falsity of the position would have
spurred a humbler man into the same excess. But the
estate (if I may say so) groaned under it ; our daily expenses
were shorn lower and lower ; the stables were emptied, all
but four roadsters ; servants were discharged, which raised
a dreadful murmuring in the country, and heated up the
old disfavour upon Mr. Henry ; and at last the yearly visit
to Edinburgh must be discontinued.

This was in 1756. You are to suppose that for seven
years this bloodsucker had been drawing the life's blood
from Durrisdeer, and that all this time my patron had held
his peace. It was an effect of devilish malice in the Master
that he addressed Mr. Henry alone upon the matter of his
demands, and there was never a word to my lord. The
family had looked on, wondering at our economies.
They had lamented, I have no doubt, that my patron
had become so great a miser—a fault always despicable,
but in the young abhorrent, and Mr. Henry was not yet
thirty years of age. Still, he had managed the business of
Durrisdeer almost from a boy ; and they bore with these
changes in a silence as proud and bitter as his own, until the
coping-stone of the Edinburgh visit.

At this time I believe my patron and his wife were rarely
together, save at meals. Immediately on the back of
Colonel Burke's announcement Mrs. Henry made palpable
advances ; you might say she had laid a sort of timid court
to her husband, different, indeed, from her former manner
of unconcern and distance. I never had the heart to blame
Mr. Henry because he recoiled from these advances ; nor
yet to censure the wife, when she was cut to the quick by
their rejection. But the result was an entire estrangement,
so that (as I say) they rarely spoke, except at meals. Even
the matter of the Edinburgh visit was first broached at

table, and it chanced that Mrs. Henry was that day ailing and querulous. She had no sooner understood her husband's meaning than the red flew in her face.

"At last," she cried; "this is too much! Heaven knows what pleasure I have in my life, that I should be denied my only consolation. These shameful proclivities must be trod down; we are already a mark and an eye-sore in the neighbourhood. I will not endure this fresh insanity."

"I cannot afford it," says Mr. Henry.

"Afford?" she cried. "For shame! But I have money of my own."

"That is all mine, madam, by marriage," he snarled, and instantly left the room.

My old lord threw up his hands to Heaven, and he and his daughter, withdrawing to the chimney, gave me a broad hint to be gone. I found Mr. Henry in his usual retreat, the steward's room, perched on the end of the table, and plunging his penknife in it with a very ugly counten-ance.

"Mr. Henry," said I, "you do yourself too much in-justice, and it is time this should cease."

"O!" cries he, "nobody minds here. They think it only natural. I have shameful proclivities. I am a niggardly dog," and he drove his knife up to the hilt. "But I will show that fellow," he cried with an oath, "I will show him which is the more generous."

"This is no generosity," said I; "this is only pride."

"Do you think I want morality?" he asked.

I thought he wanted help, and I should give it him, willy-nilly; and no sooner was Mrs. Henry gone to her room than I presented myself at her door and sought admittance.

She openly showed her wonder. "What do you want with me, Mr. Mackellar?" said she.

"The Lord knows, madam," says I, "I have never troubled you before with any freedoms; but this thing lies too hard upon my conscience, and it will out. Is it possible that two people can be so blind as you and my lord ? and have lived all these years with a noble gentleman like Mr. Henry, and understand so little of his nature ? "

" What does this mean ? " she cried.

" Do you not know where his money goes to ? his— and yours—and the money for the very wine he does not drink at table ? " I went on. " To Paris—to that man ! Eight thousand pounds has he had of us in seven years, and my patron fool enough to keep it secret ! "

" Eight thousand pounds ! " she repeated. " It is impossible ; the estate is not sufficient."

" God knows how we have sweated farthings to produce it," said I. " But eight thousand and sixty is the sum, beside odd shillings. And if you can think my patron miserly after that, this shall be my last interference."

" You need say no more, Mr. Mackellar," said she. " You have done most properly in what you too modestly call your interference. I am much to blame ; you must think me indeed a very unobservant wife " (looking upon me with a strange smile), " but I shall put this right at once. The Master was always of a very thoughtless nature ; but his heart is excellent ; he is the soul of generosity. I shall write to him myself. You cannot think how you have pained me by this communication."

" Indeed, madam, I had hoped to have pleased you," said I, for I raged to see her still thinking of the Master.

" And pleased," said she, " and pleased me of course."

That same day (I will not say but what I watched) I had the satisfaction to see Mr. Henry come from his wife's room in a state most unlike himself ; for his face was all bloated with weeping, and yet he seemed to me to walk upon the air. By this, I was sure his wife had made him full amends for once. " Ah," thought I to myself, " I have done a brave stroke this day."

On the morrow, as I was seated at my books, Mr. Henry came in softly behind me, took me by the shoulders

and shook me in a manner of playfulness. " I find you
are a faithless fellow after all," says he, which was his only
reference to my part ; but the tone he spoke in was more
to me than any eloquence of protestation. Nor was this
all I had effected ; for when the next messenger came (as
he did, not long afterwards) from the Master, he got nothing
away with him but a letter. For some while back it had
been I myself who had conducted these affairs ; Mr. Henry
not setting pen to paper, and I only in the driest and most
formal terms. But this letter I did not even see ; it would
scarce be pleasant reading, for Mr. Henry felt he had his
wife behind him for once, and I observed, on the day it
was despatched, he had a very gratified expression.

Things went better now in the family, though it could
scarce be pretended they went well. There was now at
least no misconception ; there was kindness upon all sides ;
and I believe my patron and his wife might again have
drawn together if he could but have pocketed his pride,
and she forgot (what was the ground of all) her brooding
on another man. It is wonderful how a private thought
leaks out ; it is wonderful to me now how we should all
have followed the current of her sentiments ; and though
she bore herself quietly, and had a very even disposition,
yet we should have known whenever her fancy ran to
Paris. And would not any one have thought that my
disclosure must have rooted up that idol ? I think there
is the devil in women : all these years passed, never a
sight of the man, little enough kindness to remember (by
all accounts) even while she had him, the notion of his
death intervening, his heartless rapacity laid bare to her ;
that all should not do, and she must still keep the best
place in her heart for this accursed fellow, is a thing to
make a plain man rage. I had never much natural sympathy for the passion of love ; but this unreason in my
patron's wife disgusted me outright with the whole matter.
I remember checking a maid because she sang some bairnly
kickshaw while my mind was thus engaged ; and my

asperity brought about my ears the enmity of all the petticoats about the house; of which I recked very little, but it amused Mr. Henry, who rallied me much upon our joint unpopularity. It is strange enough (for my own mother was certainly one of the salt of the earth, and my Aunt Dickson, who paid my fees at the University, a very notable woman), but I have never had much toleration for the female sex, possibly not much understanding; and being far from a bold man, I have ever shunned their company. Not only do I see no cause to regret this diffidence in myself, but have invariably remarked the most unhappy consequences follow those who were less wise. So much I thought proper to set down, lest I show myself unjust to Mrs. Henry. And, besides, the remark arose naturally, on a re-perusal of the letter which was the next step in these affairs, and reached me, to my sincere astonishment, by a private hand, some week or so after the departure of the last messenger.

Letter from Colonel BURKE (*afterwards Chevalier*) *to* MR. MACKELLAR.

TROYES IN CHAMPAGNE,
July 12, 1756.

MY DEAR SIR,—You will doubtless be surprised to receive a communication from one so little known to you; but on the occasion I had the good fortune to rencounter you at Durrisdeer, I remarked you for a young man of a solid gravity of character: a qualification which I profess I admire and revere next to natural genius or the bold chivalrous spirit of the soldier. I was, besides, interested in the noble family which you have the honour to serve, or (to speak more by the book) to be the humble and respected friend of; and a conversation I had the pleasure to have with you very early in the morning has remained much upon my mind.

Being the other day in Paris, on a visit from this famous city, where I am in garrison, I took occasion to inquire your name (which I profess I had forgot) at my friend, the Master of B.; and, a fair opportunity occurring, I write to inform you of what's new.

The Master of B. (when we had last some talk of him together) was in receipt, as I think I then told you, of a highly advantageous pension on the Scots Fund. He next received a company, and was soon after advanced to a regiment of his own. My dear sir, I do not offer to explain this circumstance; any more than why I myself, who have rid at the right hand of Princes, should be fubbed off with a pair of colours and sent to rot in a hole at the bottom of the province. Accustomed as I am to Courts, I cannot but feel it is no atmosphere for a plain soldier; and I could never hope to advance by similar means, even could I stoop to the endeavour. But our friend has a particular aptitude to succeed by the means of ladies; and if all be true that I have heard, he enjoyed a remarkable protection. It is like this turned against him; for when I had the honour to shake him by the hand, he was but newly released from the Bastille, where he had been cast on a sealed letter; and, though now released, has both lost his regiment and his pension. My dear sir, the loyalty of a plain Irishman will ultimately succeed in the place of craft; as I am sure a gentleman of your probity will agree.

Now, sir, the Master is a man whose genius I admire beyona expression, and, besides, he is my friend; but I thought a little word of this revolution in his fortunes would not come amiss, for, in my opinion, the man's desperate. He spoke, when I saw him, of an adventure upon India (whither I am myself in some hope of accompanying my illustrious countryman, Mr. Lally); but for this he would require (as I understood) more money than was readily at his command. You may have heard a military proverb: that it is a good thing to make a bridge of gold to a flying enemy? I trust you will take my meaning, and I subscribe myself, with proper respects to my Lord Durrisdeer, to his son, and to the beauteous Mrs. Durie,

My dear Sir,

Your obedient humble Servant,

FRANCIS BURKE. *

This missive I carried at once to Mr. Henry; and I think there was but the one thought between the two of us: that it had come a week too late. I made haste to send an answer to Colonel Burke, in which I begged him, if he should see the Master, to assure him his next messenger would be attended to. But with all my haste I was not in time to avert what was impending: the arrow had been drawn, it must now fly. I could almost doubt the power of Providence (and certainly His will) to stay the issue of events; and it is a strange thought, how many of us had been storing up the elements of this catastrophe, for how long a time, and with how blind an ignorance of what we did.

From the coming of the Colonel's letter, I had a spy-

glass in my room, began to drop questions to the tenant
folk, and as there was no great secrecy observed, and the
free-trade (in our part) went by force as much as stealth,
I had soon got together a knowledge of the signals in use,
and knew pretty well to an hour when any messenger
might be expected. I say, I questioned the tenants ; for
with the traders themselves, desperate blades that went
habitually armed, I could never bring myself to meddle
willingly. Indeed, by what proved in the sequel an
unhappy chance, I was an object of scorn to some of these
braggadocios ; who had not only gratified me with a nickname, but catching me one night upon a by-path, and
being all (as they would have said) somewhat merry, had
caused me to dance for their diversion. The method employed was that of cruelly chipping at my toes with naked
cutlasses, shouting at the same time " Square-toes " ; and
though they did me no bodily mischief, I was none the less
deplorably affected, and was indeed for several days confined to my bed : a scandal on the state of Scotland on
which no comment is required.

It happened on the afternoon of November 7th, in
this same unfortunate year, that I espied, during my walk,
the smoke of a beacon fire upon the Muckleross. It was
drawing near time for my return ; but the uneasiness upon
my spirits was that day so great that I must burst through
the thickets to the edge of what they call the Craig Head.
The sun was already down, but there was still a broad
light in the west, which showed me some of the smugglers
treading out their signal fire upon the Ross, and in the
bay the lugger lying with her sails brailed up. She was
plainly but new come to anchor, and yet the skiff was
already lowered and pulling for the landing-place at the
end of the long shrubbery. And this I knew could signify
but one thing,—the coming of a messenger for Durrisdeer.

I laid aside the remainder of my terrors, clambered
down the brae—a place I had never ventured through
before—and was hid among the shore-side thickets in time

to see the boat touch. Captain Crail himself was steering, a thing not usual ; by his side there sat a passenger ; and the men gave way with difficulty, being hampered with near upon half a dozen portmanteaus, great and small. But the business of landing was briskly carried through ; and presently the baggage was all tumbled on shore, the boat on its return voyage to the lugger, and the passenger standing alone upon the point of rock, a tall slender figure of a gentleman, habited in black, with a sword by his side and a walking-cane upon his wrist. As he so stood, he waved the cane to Captain Crail by way of salutation, with something both of grace and mockery that wrote the gesture deeply on my mind.

No sooner was the boat away with my sworn enemies than I took a sort of half courage, came forth to the margin of the thicket, and there halted again, my mind being greatly pulled about between natural diffidence and a dark foreboding of the truth. Indeed, I might have stood there swithering*all night, had not the stranger turned, spied me through the mists, which were beginning to fall, and waved and cried on me to draw near. I did so with a heart like lead.

" Here, my good man," said he, in the English accent, " here are some things for Durrisdeer."

I was now near enough to see him, a very handsome figure and countenance, swarthy, lean, long, with a quick, alert, black look, as of one who was a fighter, and accustomed to command ; upon one cheek he had a mole, not unbecoming ; a large diamond sparkled on his hand ; his clothes, although of the one hue, were of a French and foppish design ; his ruffles, which he wore longer than common, of exquisite lace ; and I wondered the more to see him in such a guise when he was but newly landed from a dirty smuggling lugger. At the same time he had a better look at me, toised*me a second time sharply, and then smiled.

" I wager, my friend," says he, " that I know both

your name and your nickname. I divined these very clothes upon your hand of writing, Mr. Mackellar."

At these words I fell to shaking.

" O," says he, " you need not be afraid of me. I bear no malice for your tedious letters ; and it is my purpose to employ you a good deal. You may call me Mr. Bally : it is the name I have assumed ; or rather (since I am addressing so great a precisian) it is so I have curtailed my own. Come now, pick up that, and that "—indicating two of the portmanteaus. " That will be as much as you are fit to bear, and the rest can very well wait. Come, lose no more time, if you please."

His tone was so cutting that I managed to do as he bid by a sort of instinct, my mind being all the time quite lost. No sooner had I picked up the portmanteaus than he turned his back and marched off through the long shrubbery, where it began already to be dusk, for the wood is thick and evergreen. I followed behind, loaded almost to the dust, though I profess I was not conscious of the burthen ; being swallowed up in the monstrosity of this return, and my mind flying like a weaver's shuttle.

On a sudden I set the portmanteaus to the ground and halted. He turned and looked back at me.

" Well ? " said he.

" You are the Master of Ballantrae ? "

" You will do me the justice to observe," says he, " that I have made no secret with the astute Mackellar."

" And in the name of God," cries I, " what brings you here ? Go back, while it is yet time."

" I thank you," said he. " Your master has chosen this way, and not I ; but since he has made the choice, he (and you also) must abide by the result.—And now pick up these things of mine, which you have set down in a very boggy place, and attend to that which I have made your business."

But I had no thought now of obedience ; I came straight up to him. " If nothing will move you to go back," said

I ; "though, sure, under all the circumstances, any Christian, or even any gentleman, would scruple to go forward . . ."

"These are gratifying expressions," he threw in.

"If nothing will move you to go back," I continued, "there are still some decencies to be observed. Wait here with your baggage, and I will go forward and prepare your family. Your father is an old man ; and . . . " I stumbled . . . "there are decencies to be observed."

"Truly," said he, "this Mackellar improves upon acquaintance. But look you here, my man, and understand it once for all—you waste your breath upon me, and I go my own way with inevitable motion."

"Ah !" says I. "Is that so ? We shall see then !"

And I turned and took to my heels for Durrisdeer. He clutched at me, and cried out angrily, and then I believe I heard him laugh, and then I am certain he pursued me for a step or two, and (I suppose) desisted. One thing at least is sure, that I came but a few minutes later to the door of the great house, nearly strangled for the lack of breath, but quite alone. Straight up the stair I ran, and burst into the hall, and stopped before the family without the power of speech ; but I must have carried my story in my looks, for they rose out of their places and stared on me like changelings.

"He has come," I panted out at last.

"He ? " said Mr. Henry.

"Himself," said I.

"My son ? " cried my lord. "Imprudent, imprudent boy ! O, could he not stay where he was safe ! "

Never a word says Mrs. Henry ; nor did I look at her, I scarce knew why.

"Well," said Mr. Henry, with a very deep breath, "and where is he ? "

"I left him in the long shrubbery," said I.

"Take me to him," said he.

So we went out together, he and I, without another

word from any one ; and in the midst of the gravelled plot
encountered the Master strolling up, whistling as he came,
and beating the air with his cane. There was still light
enough overhead to recognise, though not to read, a
countenance.

"Ah ! Jacob," says the Master. " So here is Esau
back."

"James," says Mr. Henry, " for God's sake, call me by
my name. I will not pretend that I am glad to see you ;
but I would fain make you as welcome as I can in the
house of our fathers."

" Or in *my* house ? or *yours* ? " says the Master.
" Which were you about to say ?   But this is an old sore,
and we need not rub it. If you would not share with me
in Paris, I hope you will yet scarce deny your elder brother
a corner of the fire at Durrisdeer ? "

" That is very idle speech," replied Mr. Henry.   " And
you understand the power of your position excellently
well."

" Why, I believe I do," said the other, with a little
laugh. And this, though they had never touched hands,
was (as we may say) the end of the brothers' meeting ;
for at this the Master turned to me and bade me fetch his
baggage.

I, on my side, turned to Mr. Henry for a confirmation ;
perhaps with some defiance.

" As long as the Master is here, Mr. Mackellar, you will
very much oblige me by regarding his wishes as you would
my own," says Mr. Henry.   " We are constantly troubling
you : will you be so good as send one of the servants ? "
—with an accent on the word.

If this speech were anything at all, it was surely a well-
deserved reproof upon the stranger ; and yet, so devilish
was his impudence, he twisted it the other way.

" And shall we be common enough to say, ' Sneck
up ' ? "* inquires he softly, looking upon me sideways.

Had a kingdom depended on the act, I could not have

trusted myself in words ; even to call a servant was beyond
me ; I had rather serve the man myself than speak ; and
I turned away in silence and went into the long shrubbery,
with a heart full of anger and despair. It was dark under
the trees, and I walked before me and forgot what business
I was come upon, till I nearly broke my shin on the portmanteaus. Then it was that I remarked a strange particular ; for whereas I had before carried both and scarce
observed it, it was now as much as I could do to manage
one. And this, as it forced me to make two journeys, kept
me the longer from the hall.

When I got there, the business of welcome was over
long ago ; the company was already at supper ; and, by
an oversight that cut me to the quick, my place had been
forgotten. I had seen one side of the Master's return ;
now I was to see the other. It was he who first remarked
my coming in and standing back (as I did) in some annoyance. He jumped from his seat.

" And if I have not got the good Mackellar's place ! "
cries he. " John, lay another for Mr. Bally ; I protest
he will disturb no one, and your table is big enough for
all."

I could scarce credit my ears, nor yet my senses, when
he took me by the shoulders and thrust me, laughing, into
my own place—such an affectionate playfulness was in his
voice. And while John laid the fresh place for him (a
thing on which he still insisted), he went and leaned on
his father's chair and looked down upon him, and the old
man turned about and looked upwards on his son, with such
a pleasant mutual tenderness that I could have carried
my hand to my head in mere amazement.

Yet all was of a piece. Never a harsh word fell from
him, never a sneer showed upon his lip. He had laid aside
even his cutting English accent, and spoke with the kindly
Scots tongue, that set a value on affectionate words ; and
though his manners had a graceful elegance mighty foreign
to our ways in Durrisdeer, it was still a homely courtliness,

that did not shame but flattered us. All that he did throughout the meal, indeed, drinking wine with me with a notable respect, turning about for a pleasant word with John, fondling his father's hand, breaking into little merry tales of his adventures, calling up the past with happy reference—all he did was so becoming, and himself so handsome, that I could scarce wonder if my lord and Mrs. Henry sat about the board with radiant faces, or if John waited behind with dropping tears.

As soon as supper was over, Mrs. Henry rose to withdraw.

" This was never your way, Alison," said he.

" It is my way now," she replied : which was notoriously false, " and I will give you a good-night, James, and a welcome—from the dead," said she, and her voice dropped and trembled.

Poor Mr. Henry, who had made rather a heavy figure through the meal, was more concerned than ever ; pleased to see his wife withdraw, and yet half displeased, as he thought upon the cause of it ; and the next moment altogether dashed by the fervour of her speech.

On my part, I thought I was now one too many ; and was stealing after Mrs. Henry, when the Master saw me.

" Now, Mr. Mackellar," says he, " I take this near on an unfriendliness. I cannot have you go : this is to make a stranger of the prodigal son ; and let me remind you where—in his own father's house ! Come, sit ye down, and drink another glass with Mr. Bally."

" Ay, ay, Mr. Mackellar," says my lord, " we must not make a stranger either of him or you. I have been telling my son," he added, his voice brightening as usual on the word, " how much we valued all your friendly service."

So I sat there, silent, till my usual hour ; and might have been almost deceived in the man's nature but for one passage, in which his perfidy appeared too plain. Here was the passage ; of which, after what he knows of the brothers' meeting, the reader shall consider for himself.

Mr. Henry sitting somewhat dully, in spite of his best endeavours to carry things before my lord, up jumps the Master, passes about the board, and claps his brother on the shoulder.

" Come, come, *Hairry lad*," says he, with a broad accent, such as they must have used together when they were boys, " you must not be downcast because your brother has come home. All's yours, that's sure enough, and little I grudge it you. Neither must you grudge me my place beside my father's fire."

" And that is too true, Henry," says my old lord, with a little frown, a thing rare with him. " You have been the elder brother of the parable in the good sense ; you must be careful of the other."

" I am easily put in the wrong," said Mr. Henry.

" Who puts you in the wrong ? " cried my lord, I thought very tartly for so mild a man. " You have earned my gratitude and your brother's many thousand times : you may count on its endurance ; and let that suffice."

" Ay, Harry, that you may," said the Master ; and I thought Mr. Henry looked at him with a kind of wildness in his eye.

On all the miserable business that now followed, I have four questions that I asked myself often at the time, and ask myself still :—Was the man moved by a particular sentiment against Mr. Henry ? or by what he thought to be his interest ? or by a mere delight in cruelty such as cats display and theologians tell us of the devil ? or by what he would have called love ? My common opinion halts among the three first ; but perhaps there lay at the spring of his behaviour an element of all. As thus :— Animosity to Mr. Henry would explain his hateful usage of him when they were alone ; the interests he came to serve would explain his very different attitude before my lord ; that and some spice of a design of gallantry, his

care to stand well with Mrs. Henry ; and the pleasure of
malice for itself, the pains he was continually at to mingle
and oppose these lines of conduct.

Partly because I was a very open friend to my patron,
partly because in my letters to Paris I had often given
myself some freedom of remonstrance, I was included in
his diabolical amusement. When I was alone with him,
he pursued me with sneers ; before the family he used me
with the extreme of friendly condescension. This was not
only painful in itself ; not only did it put me continually
in the wrong ; but there was in it an element of insult
indescribable. That he should thus leave me out in his
dissimulation, as though even my testimony were too
despicable to be considered, galled me to the blood. But
what it was to me is not worth notice. I make but memorandum of it here ; and chiefly for this reason, that it had
one good result, and gave me the quicker sense of Mr.
Henry's martyrdom.

It was on him the burthen fell. How was he to re-
spond to the public advances of one who never lost a chance
of gibing him in private ? How was he to smile back on
the deceiver and the insulter ? He was condemned to
seem ungracious. He was condemned to silence. Had
he been less proud, had he spoken, who would have credited
the truth ? The acted calumny had done its work ; my
lord and Mrs. Henry were the daily witnesses of what went
on ; they could have sworn in court that the Master was
a model of long-suffering good-nature, and Mr. Henry a
pattern of jealousy and thanklessness. And ugly enough
as these must have appeared in any one, they seemed
tenfold uglier in Mr. Henry ; for who could forget that the
Master lay in peril of his life, and that he had already lost
his mistress, his title, and his fortune ?

" Henry, will you ride with me ? " asks the Master
one day.

And Mr. Henry, who had been goaded by the man all
morning, raps out : " I will not."

" I sometimes wish you would be kinder, Henry," says the other wistfully.

I give this for a specimen ; but such scenes befell continually. Small wonder if Mr. Henry was blamed ; small wonder if I fretted myself into something near upon a bilious fever ; nay, and at the mere recollection feel a bitterness in my blood.

Sure, never in this world was a more diabolical contrivance : so perfidious, so simple, so impossible to combat. And yet I think again, and I think always, Mrs. Henry might have read between the lines ; she might have had more knowledge of her husband's nature ; after all these years of marriage she might have commanded or captured his confidence. And my old lord, too—that very watchful gentleman—where was all his observation ? But, for one thing, the deceit was practised by a master hand, and might have gulled an angel. For another (in the case of Mrs. Henry), I have observed there are no persons so far away as those who are both married and estranged, so that they seem out of earshot, or to have no common tongue. For a third (in the case of both of these spectators) they were blinded by old ingrained predilection. And for a fourth, the risk the Master was supposed to stand in (supposed, I say—you will soon hear why) made it seem the more ungenerous to criticise ; and, keeping them in a perpetual tender solicitude about his life, blinded them the more effectually to his faults.

It was during this time that I perceived most clearly the effect of manner, and was led to lament most deeply the plainness of my own. Mr. Henry had the essence of a gentleman ; when he was moved, when there was any call of circumstance, he could play his part with dignity and spirit ; but in the day's commerce (it is idle to deny it) he fell short of the ornamental. The Master (on the other hand) had never a movement but it commended him. So it befell that when the one appeared gracious and the other ungracious, every trick of their bodies seemed to call out

confirmation. Not that alone : but the more deeply Mr.
Henry floundered in his brother's toils, the more clownish
he grew ; and the more the Master enjoyed his spiteful
entertainment, the more engagingly, the more smilingly,
he went ! So that the plot, by its own scope and progress,
furthered and confirmed itself.

It was one of the man's arts to use the peril in which
(as I say) he was supposed to stand. He spoke of it to
those who loved him with a gentle pleasantry, which made
it the more touching. To Mr. Henry he used it as a cruel
weapon of offence. I remember his laying his finger on the
clean lozenge of the painted window one day when we three
were alone together in the hall. " Here went your lucky
guinea, Jacob," said he. And when Mr. Henry only
looked upon him darkly, " O ! " he added, " you need
not look such impotent malice, my good fly. You can be
rid of your spider when you please. How long, O Lord ?
When are you to be wrought to the point of a denunciation,
scrupulous brother ? It is one of my interests in this dreary
hole. I ever loved experiment." Still Mr. Henry only
stared upon him with a glooming brow, and a changed
colour ; and at last the Master broke out in a laugh and
clapped him on the shoulder, calling him a sulky dog. At
this my patron leaped back with a gesture I thought very
dangerous ; and I must suppose the Master thought so
too, for he looked the least in the world discountenanced,
and I do not remember him again to have laid hands on
Mr. Henry.

But though he had his peril always on his lips in the
one way or the other, I thought his conduct strangely in-
cautious, and began to fancy the Government—who had
set a price upon his head—was gone sound asleep. I will
not deny I was tempted with the wish to denounce him ;
but two thoughts withheld me : one, that if he were thus
to end his life upon an honourable scaffold, the man would
be canonised for good in the minds of his father and my
patron's wife ; the other, that if I was anyway mingled

in the matter, Mr. Henry himself would scarce escape some
glancings of suspicion.   And in the meanwhile our enemy
went in and out more than I could have thought possible,
the fact that he was home again was buzzed about all the
country-side, and yet he was never stirred.   Of all those
so-many and so-different persons who were acquainted
with his presence, none had the least greed— as I used to
say in my annoyance—or the least loyalty ; and the man
rode here and there—fully more welcome, considering the
lees of old unpopularity, than Mr. Henry—and, considering
the free-traders, far safer than myself.

   Not but what he had a trouble of his own ; and this,
as it brought about the gravest consequences, I must now
relate.   The reader will scarce have forgotten Jessie Broun ;
her way of life was much among the smuggling party ;
Captain Crail himself was of her intimates ; and she had
early word of Mr. Bally's presence at the house.   In my
opinion, she had long ceased to care two straws for the
Master's person ; but it was become her habit to connect
herself continually with the Master's name ; that was the
ground of all her play-acting ; and so now, when he was
back, she thought she owed it to herself to grow a haunter
of the neighbourhood of Durrisdeer.   The Master could
scarce go abroad but she was there in wait for him ; a
scandalous figure of a woman, not often sober ; hailing
him wildly as " her bonny laddie," quoting pedlar's poetry,
and, as I receive the story, even seeking to weep upon his
neck.   I own I rubbed my hands over this persecution ;
but the Master, who laid so much upon others, was himself
the least patient of men.   There were strange scenes enacted
in the policies.   Some say he took his cane to her, and
Jessie fell back upon her former weapons—stones.   It is
certain at least that he made a motion to Captain Crail to
have the woman trepanned, and that the Captain refused
the proposition with uncommon vehemence.   And the end
of the matter was victory for Jessie.   Money was got
together ; an interview took place, in which my proud

gentleman must consent to be kissed and wept upon; and the woman was set up in a public of her own, somewhere on Solway side (but I forget where), and, by the only news I ever had of it, extremely ill-frequented.

This is to look forward. After Jessie had been but a little while upon his heels, the Master comes to me one day in the steward's office, and with more civility than usual, "Mackellar," says he, "there is a damned crazy wench comes about here. I cannot well move in the matter myself, which brings me to you. Be so good as to see to it: the men must have a strict injunction to drive the wench away."

"Sir," said I, trembling a little, "you can do your own dirty errands for yourself."

He said not a word to that, and left the room.

Presently came Mr. Henry. "Here is news!" cried he. "It seems all is not enough, and you must add to my wretchedness. It seems you have insulted Mr. Bally."

"Under your kind favour, Mr. Henry," said I, "it was he that insulted me, and, as I think, grossly. But I may have been careless of your position when I spoke; and if you think so when you know all, my dear patron, you have but to say the word. For you I would obey in any point whatever, even to sin, God pardon me!" And thereupon I told him what had passed.

Mr. Henry smiled to himself; a grimmer smile I never witnessed. "You did exactly well," said he. "He shall drink his Jessie Broun to the dregs." And then, spying the Master outside, he opened the window, and, crying to him by the name of Mr. Bally, asked him to step up and have a word.

"James," said he, when our persecutor had come in and closed the door behind him, looking at me with a smile, as if he thought I was to be humbled, "you brought me a complaint against Mr. Mackellar, into which I have inquired. I need not tell you I would always take his word against yours; for we are alone, and I am going to use

something of your own freedom. Mr. Mackellar is a
gentleman I value ; and you must contrive, so long as you
are under this roof, to bring yourself into no more collisions
with one whom I will support at any possible cost to me
or mine. As for the errand upon which you came to him,
you must deliver yourself from the consequences of your
own cruelty, and none of my servants shall be at all employed in such a case."

" My father's servants, I believe," said the Master.

" Go to him with this tale," said Mr. Henry.

The Master grew very white. He pointed at me with
his finger. " I want that man discharged," he said.

" He shall not be," said Mr. Henry.

" You shall pay pretty dear for this," says the
Master.

" I have paid so dear already for a wicked brother,"
said Mr. Henry, " that I am bankrupt even of fears. You
have no place left where you can strike me."

" I will show you about that," says the Master, and
went softly away.

" What will he do next, Mackellar ? " cries Mr. Henry.

" Let me go away," said I. " My dear patron, let me
go away ; I am but the beginning of fresh sorrows."

" Would you leave me quite alone ? " said he.

We were not long in suspense as to the nature of the
new assault. Up to that hour the Master had played a
very close game with Mrs. Henry ; avoiding pointedly to
be alone with her, which I took at the time for an effect
of decency, but now think to have been a most insidious
art ; meeting her, you may say, at meal-time only ; and
behaving, when he did so, like an affectionate brother. Up
to that hour, you may say he had scarce directly interfered
between Mr. Henry and his wife ; except in so far as he
had manœuvred the one quite forth from the good graces
of the other. Now all that was to be changed ; but whether
really in revenge, or because he was wearying of Durrisdeer,

and looked about for some diversion, who but the devil
shall decide ?

From that hour, at least, began the siege of Mrs. Henry ;
a thing so deftly carried on that I scarce know if she was
aware of it herself, and that her husband must look on in
silence. The first parallel was opened (as was made to
appear) by accident. The talk fell, as it did often, on the
exiles in France ; so it glided to the matter of their songs.

" There is one," says the Master, " if you are curious
in these matters, that has always seemed to me very
moving. The poetry is harsh ; and yet, perhaps because
of my situation, it has always found the way to my heart.
It is supposed to be sung, I should tell you, by an exile's
sweetheart ; and represents perhaps not so much the truth
of what she is thinking, as the truth of what he hopes of
her, poor soul ! in these far lands." And here the Master
sighed. " I protest it is a pathetic sight when a score of
rough Irish, all common sentinels, get to this song ; and
you may see, by their falling tears, how it strikes home to
them. It goes thus, father," says he, very adroitly taking
my lord for his listener, " and if I cannot get to the end
of it, you must think it is a common case with us exiles."
And thereupon he struck up the same air as I had heard
the Colonel whistle ; but now to words, rustic indeed, yet
most pathetically setting forth a poor girl's aspirations for
an exiled lover ; of which one verse indeed (or something
like it) still sticks by me :—

> " O, I will dye my petticoat red,
> With my dear boy I'll beg my bread,
> Though all my friends should wish me dead,
> For Willie among the rushes, O ! "

He sang it well, even as a song ; but he did better yet
as a performer. I have heard famous actors, when there
was not a dry eye in the Edinburgh theatre ; a great wonder
to behold ; but no more wonderful than how the Master
played upon that little ballad, and on those who heard him,
like an instrument, and seemed now upon the point of

failing, and now to conquer his distress, so that words and music seemed to pour out of his own heart and his own past, and to be aimed directly at Mrs. Henry. And his art went further yet ; for all was so delicately touched, it seemed impossible to suspect him of the least design ; and so far from making a parade of emotion, you would have sworn he was striving to be calm. When it came to an end, we all sat silent for a time ; he had chosen the dusk of the afternoon, so that none could see his neighbour's face ; but it seemed as if we held our breathing ; only my old lord cleared his throat. The first to move was the singer, who got to his feet suddenly and softly, and went and walked softly to and fro in the low end of the hall, Mr. Henry's customary place. We were to suppose that he there struggled down the last of his emotion ; for he presently returned and launched into a disquisition on the nature of the Irish (always so much miscalled, and whom he defended) in his natural voice ; so that, before the lights were brought, we were in the usual course of talk. But even then, methought Mrs. Henry's face was a shade pale ; and for another thing, she withdrew almost at once.

The next sign was a friendship this insidious devil struck up with innocent Miss Katharine ; so that they were always together, hand in hand, or she climbing on his knee, like a pair of children. Like all his diabolical acts, this cut in several ways. It was the last stroke to Mr. Henry, to see his own babe debauched against him ; it made him harsh with the poor innocent, which brought him still a peg lower in his wife's esteem ; and (to conclude) it was a bond of union between the lady and the Master. Under this influence, their old reserve melted by daily stages. Presently there came walks in the long shrubbery, talks in the Belvedere, and I know not what tender familiarity. I am sure Mrs. Henry was like many a good woman ; she had a whole conscience, but perhaps by the means of a little winking. For even to so dull an observer as myself, it was plain her kindness was of a more moving nature than the sisterly. The tones of her voice appeared more numerous ; she had a light and softness in her eye ; she was more gentle with all of us, even with Mr. Henry, even with myself ; methought she breathed of some quiet melancholy happiness.

To look on at this, what a torment it was for Mr. Henry ! And yet it brought our ultimate deliverance, as I am soon to tell.

The purport of the Master's stay was no more noble (gild it as they might) than to wring money out. He had some design of a fortune in the French Indies,* as the Chevalier wrote me ; and it was the sum required for this that he came seeking. For the rest of the family it spelled ruin ; but my lord, in his incredible partiality, pushed ever for the granting. The family was now so narrowed down (indeed, there were no more of them than just the father and the two sons) that it was possible to break the entail and alienate a piece of land. And to this, at first by hints, and then by open pressure, Mr. Henry was brought to consent. He never would have done so, I am very well assured, but for the weight of the distress under which he laboured. But for his passionate eagerness to see his brother gone, he would not thus have broken with his own sentiment and the traditions of his house. And even so, he sold them his consent at a dear rate, speaking for once openly, and holding the business up in its own shameful colours.

" You will observe," he said, " this is an injustice to my son, if ever I have one."

" But that you are not likely to have," said my lord.

" God knows ! " says Mr. Henry. " And considering the cruel falseness of the position in which I stand to my brother, and that you, my lord, are my father, and have the right to command me, I set my hand to this paper. But one thing I will say first : I have been ungenerously pushed, and when next, my lord, you are tempted to

compare your sons, I call on you to remember what I have
done and what he has done. Acts are the fair test."

My lord was the most uneasy man I ever saw; even
in his old face the blood came up. "I think this is not a
very wisely chosen moment, Henry, for complaints," said
he. "This takes away from the merit of your generosity."

"Do not deceive yourself, my lord," said Mr. Henry.
"This injustice is not done from generosity to him, but
in obedience to yourself."

"Before strangers . . ." begins my lord, still more
unhappily affected.

"There is no one but Mackellar here," said Mr. Henry;
"he is my friend. And, my lord, as you make him no
stranger to your frequent blame, it were hard if I must
keep him one to a thing so rare as my defence."

Almost I believe my lord would have rescinded his
decision; but the Master was on the watch.

"Ah! Henry, Henry," says he, "you are the best of
us still. Rugged and true! Ah! man, I wish I was as
good."

And at that instance of his favourite's generosity my
lord desisted from his hesitation, and the deed was signed.

As soon as it could be brought about, the land of
Ochterhall was sold for much below its value, and the
money paid over to our leech and sent by some private
carriage into France.* And now here was all the man's
business brought to a successful head, and his pockets once
more bulging with our gold; and yet the point for which
we had consented to this sacrifice was still denied us, and
the visitor still lingered on at Durrisdeer. Whether in
malice, or because the time was not yet come for his
adventure to the Indies, or because he had hopes of his
design on Mrs. Henry, or from the orders of the Government, who shall say? but linger he did, and that for weeks.

You will observe I say: "from the orders of the
Government"; for about this time the man's disreput-
able secret trickled out.

The first hint I had was from a tenant, who commented on the Master's stay, and yet more on his security; for this tenant was a Jacobitish sympathiser, and had lost a son at Culloden, which gave him the more critical eye. "There is one thing," said he, "that I cannot but think strange; and that is how he got to Cockermouth."

"To Cockermouth?" said I, with a sudden memory of my first wonder on beholding the man disembark so *point-de-vice* after so long a voyage.

"Why, yes," says the tenant, "it was there he was picked up by Captain Crail. You thought he had come from France by sea? And so we all did."

I turned this news a little in my head, and then carried it to Mr. Henry. "Here is an odd circumstance," said I, and told him.

"What matters how he came, Mackellar, so long as he is here?" groans Mr. Henry.

"No, sir," said I, "but think again! Does not this smack a little of some Government connivance? You know how much we have wondered already at the man's security."

"Stop," said Mr. Henry. "Let me think of this." And as he thought, there came that grim smile upon his face that was a little like the Master's. "Give me paper," said he. And he sat without another word and wrote to a gentleman of his acquaintance—I will name no unnecessary names, but he was one in a high place. This letter I despatched by the only hand I could depend upon in such a case—Macconochie's; and the old man rode hard, for he was back with the reply before even my eagerness had ventured to expect him. Again, as he read it, Mr. Henry had the same grim smile.

"This is the best you have done for me yet, Mackellar," says he. "With this in my hand I will give him a shog.* Watch for us at dinner."

At dinner accordingly Mr. Henry proposed some very

public appearance for the Master; and my lord, as he had
hoped, objected to the danger of the course.

"O!" says Mr. Henry, very easily, "you need no
longer keep this up with me. I am as much in the secret
as yourself."

"In the secret?" says my lord. "What do you
mean, Henry? I give you my word, I am in no secret
from which you are excluded."

The Master had changed countenance, and I saw he
was struck in a joint of his harness.

"How?" says Mr. Henry, turning to him with a huge
appearance of surprise. "I see you serve your masters
very faithfully; but I had thought you would have been
humane enough to set your father's mind at rest."

"What are you talking of? I refuse to have my
business publicly discussed. I order this to cease," cries
the Master very foolishly and passionately, and indeed
more like a child than a man.

"So much discretion was not looked for at your hands,
I can assure you," continued Mr. Henry. "For see what
my correspondent writes"—unfolding the paper—"' It
is, of course, in the interests both of the Government and
the gentleman whom we may perhaps best continue to
call Mr. Bally, to keep this understanding secret; but it
was never meant his own family should continue to endure
the suspense you paint so feelingly; and I am pleased
mine should be the hand to set these fears at rest. Mr.
Bally is as safe in Great Britain as yourself.'"

"Is this possible?" cries my lord, looking at his son,
with a great deal of wonder, and still more of suspicion in
his face.

"My dear father," says the Master, already much recovered. "I am overjoyed that this may be disclosed.
My own instructions, direct from London, bore a very
contrary sense, and I was charged to keep the indulgence
secret from every one, yourself not excepted, and indeed
yourself expressly named—as I can show in black and

white, unless I have destroyed the letter. They must have changed their mind very swiftly, for the whole matter is still quite fresh ; or rather, Henry's correspondent must have misconceived that part, as he seems to have misconceived the rest. To tell you the truth, sir," he continued, getting visibly more easy, " I had supposed this unexplained favour to a rebel was the effect of some application from yourself ; and the injunction to secrecy among my family the result of a desire on your part to conceal your kindness. Hence I was the more careful to obey orders. It remains now to guess by what other channel indulgence can have flowed on so notorious an offender as myself ; for I do not think your son need defend himself from what seems hinted at in Henry's letter. I have never yet heard of a Durrisdeer who was a turncoat or a spy," says he proudly.

And so it seemed he had swum out of this danger unharmed ; but this was to reckon without a blunder he had made, and without the pertinacity of Mr. Henry, who was now to show he had something of his brother's spirit.

" You say the matter is still fresh ? " says Mr. Henry.

" It is recent," says the Master, with a fair show of stoutness, and yet not without a quaver.

" Is it so recent as that ? " asks Mr. Henry, like a man a little puzzled, and spreading his letter forth again.

In all the letter there was no word as to the date ; but how was the Master to know that ?

" It seemed to come late enough for me," says he, with a laugh. And at the sound of that laugh, which rang false, like a cracked bell, my lord looked at him again across the table, and I saw his old lips draw together close.

" No," said Mr. Henry, still glancing on his letter, " but I remember your expression. You said it was very fresh."

And here we had a proof of our victory, and the strongest instance yet of my lord's incredible indulgence ; for what must he do but interfere to save his favourite from exposure !

" I think, Henry," says he, with a kind of pitiful eagerness, " I think we need dispute no more. We are all rejoiced at last to find your brother safe ; we are all at one on that ; and, as grateful subjects, we can do no less than drink to the King's health and bounty."

Thus was the Master extricated ; but at least he had been put to his defence, he had come lamely out, and the attraction of his personal danger was now publicly plucked away from him. My lord, in his heart of hearts, now knew his favourite to be a Government spy ; and Mrs. Henry (however she explained the tale) was notably cold in her behaviour to the discredited hero of romance. Thus in the best fabric of duplicity there is some weak point, if you can strike it, which will loosen all ; and if, by this fortunate stroke, we had not shaken the idol, who can say how it might have gone with us at the catastrophe ?

And yet at the time we seemed to have accomplished nothing. Before a day or two he had wiped off the ill results of his discomfiture, and, to all appearance, stood as high as ever. As for my Lord Durrisdeer, he was sunk in parental partiality ; it was not so much love, which should be an active quality, as an apathy and torpor of his other powers ; and forgiveness (so to misapply a noble word) flowed from him in sheer weakness, like the tears of senility. Mrs. Henry's was a different case ; and Heaven alone knows what he found to say to her, or how he persuaded her from her contempt. It is one of the worst things of sentiment, that the voice grows to be more important than the words, and the speaker than that which is spoken. But some excuse the Master must have found, or perhaps he had even struck upon some art to wrest this exposure to his own advantage ; for after a time of coldness, it seemed as if things went worse than ever between him and Mrs. Henry. They were then constantly together. I would not be thought to cast one shadow of blame, beyond what

is due to a half-wilful blindness, on that unfortunate lady ;
but I do think, in these last days, she was playing very
near the fire ; and whether I be wrong or not in that, one
thing is sure and quite sufficient : Mr. Henry thought so.
The poor gentleman sat for days in my room, so great a
picture of distress that I could never venture to address
him ; yet it is to be thought he found some comfort even
in my presence and the knowledge of my sympathy. There
were times, too, when we talked, and a strange manner of
talk it was ; there was never a person named, nor an
individual circumstance referred to ; yet we had the same
matter in our minds, and we were each aware of it. It is
a strange art that can thus be practised ; to talk for hours
of a thing, and never name nor yet so much as hint at it.
And I remember I wondered if it was by some such natural
skill that the Master made love to Mrs. Henry all day long
(as he manifestly did), yet never startled her into reserve.

To show how far affairs had gone with Mr. Henry, I
will give some words of his, uttered (as I have cause not
to forget) upon the 26th of February 1757. It was unseasonable weather, a cast back into winter : windless,
bitter cold, the world all white with rime, the sky low and
grey : the sea black and silent like a quarry-hole. Mr.
Henry sat close by the fire, and debated (as was now
common with him) whether " a man " should " do things,"
whether " interference was wise," and the like general pro-
positions, which each of us particularly applied. I was by
the window, looking out, when there passed below me the
Master, Mrs. Henry, and Miss Katharine, that now constant
trio. The child was running to and fro, delighted with the
frost ; the Master spoke close in the lady's ear with what
seemed (even from so far) a devilish grace of insinuation ;
and she on her part looked on the ground like a person
lost in listening. I broke out of my reserve.

" If I were you, Mr. Henry," said I, " I would deal
openly with my lord."

" Mackellar, Mackellar," says he, " you do not see the

weakness of my ground.   I can carry no such base thoughts to any one—to my father least of all ; that would be to fall into the bottom of his scorn.   The weakness of my ground," he continued, " lies in myself, that I am not one who engages love.   I have their gratitude, they all tell me that ; I have a rich estate of it !   But I am not present in their minds ; they are moved neither to think with me nor to think for me.   There is my loss ! "   He got to his feet, and trod down the fire.   " But some method must be found, Mackellar," said he, looking at me suddenly over his shoulder ; "some way must be found.   I am a man of a great deal of patience—far too much—far too much. I begin to despise myself.   And yet, sure, never was a man involved in such a toil ! "   He fell back to his brooding.

"Cheer up," said I.   " It will burst of itself."

" I am far past anger now," says he, which had so little coherency with my own observation that I let both fall.

CHAPTER V

ACCOUNT OF ALL THAT PASSED ON THE NIGHT OF FEBRUARY 27TH, 1757

On the evening of the interview referred to, the Master went abroad ; he was abroad a great deal of the next day also, that fatal 27th ; but where he went, or what he did, we never concerned ourselves to ask until next day. If we had done so, and by any chance found out, it might have changed all. But as all we did was done in ignorance, and should be so judged, I shall so narrate these passages as they appeared to us in the moment of their birth, and reserve all that I since discovered for the time of its discovery. For I have now come to one of the dark parts of my narrative, and must engage the reader's indulgence for my patron.

All the 27th that rigorous weather endured : a stifling cold ; the folk passing about like smoking chimneys ; the wide hearth in the hall piled high with fuel ; some of the spring birds that had already blundered north into our neighbourhood besieging the windows of the house or trotting on the frozen turf like things distracted. About noon there came a blink of sunshine ; showing a very pretty, wintry, frosty landscape of white hills and woods, with Crail's lugger waiting for a wind under the Craig Head, and the smoke mounting straight into the air from every farm and cottage. With the coming of night, the haze closed in overhead ; it fell dark and still and starless, and exceeding cold : a night the most unseasonable, fit for strange events.

Mrs. Henry withdrew, as was now her custom, very early. We had set ourselves of late to pass the evening with a game of cards ; another mark that our visitor was wearying mightily of the life at Durrisdeer ; and we had not been long at this when my old lord slipped from his place beside the fire, and was off without a word to seek the warmth of bed. The three thus left together had neither love nor courtesy to share ; not one of us would have sat up one instant to oblige another ; yet from the influence of custom, and as the cards had just been dealt, we continued the form of playing out the round. I should say we were late sitters ; and though my lord had departed earlier than was his custom, twelve was already gone some time upon the clock, and the servants long ago in bed. Another thing I should say, that although I never saw the Master anyway affected with liquor, he had been drinking freely, and was perhaps (although he showed it not) a trifle heated.

Anyway, he now practised one of his transitions ; and so soon as the door closed behind my lord, and without the smallest change of voice, shifted from ordinary civil talk into a stream of insult.

"My dear Henry, it is yours to play," he had been saying, and now continued : " It is a very strange thing how, even in so small a matter as a game of cards, you display your rusticity. You play, Jacob, like a bonnet-laird, or a sailor in a tavern. The same dulness, the same petty greed, *cette lenteur d'hébété qui me fait rager**; it is strange I should have such a brother. Even Square-toes has a certain vivacity when his stake is imperilled ; but the dreariness of a game with you I positively lack language to depict."

Mr. Henry continued to look at his cards, as though very maturely considering some play ; but his mind was elsewhere.

"Dear God, will this never be done ? " cries the Master. " *Quel lourdaud !* But why do I trouble you with French expressions, which are lost on such an ignoramus ? A *lourdaud*, my dear brother, is as we might say a bumpkin, a clown, a clodpole : a fellow without grace, lightness, quickness ; any gift of pleasing, any natural brilliancy : such a one as you shall see, when you desire, by looking in the mirror. I tell you these things for your good, I assure you ; and besides, Square-toes " (looking at me and stifling a yawn), " it is one of my diversions in this very dreary spot to toast you and your master at the fire like chestnuts. I have great pleasure in your case, for I observe the nickname (rustic as it is) has always the power to make you writhe. But sometimes I have more trouble with this dear fellow here, who seems to have gone to sleep upon his cards.—Do you not see the applicability of the epithet I have just explained, dear Henry ? Let me show you. For instance, with all those solid qualities which I delight to recognise in you, I never knew a woman who did not prefer me—nor, I think," he continued, with the most silken deliberation, " I think—who did not continue to prefer me."

Mr. Henry laid down his cards. He rose to his feet very softly, and seemed all the while like a person in deep thought. " You coward ! " he said gently, as if to himself. And then, with neither hurry nor any particular violence, he struck the Master in the mouth.

The Master sprang to his feet like one transfigured ; I had never seen the man so beautiful. " A blow ! " he cried. " I would not take a blow from God Almighty ! "

" Lower your voice," said Mr. Henry. " Do you wish my father to interfere for you again ? "

" Gentlemen, gentlemen," I cried, and sought to come between them.

The Master caught me by the shoulder, held me at arm's length, and still addressing his brother : " Do you know what this means ? " said he.

" It was the most deliberate act of my life," says Mr. Henry.

" I must have blood, I must have blood for this," says the Master.

"Please God it shall be yours," said Mr. Henry; and he went to the wall and took down a pair of swords that hung there with others, naked. These he presented to the Master by the points. "Mackellar shall see us play fair," said Mr. Henry. "I think it very needful."

"You need insult me no more," said the Master, taking one of the swords at random. "I have hated you all my life."

"My father is but newly gone to bed," said Mr. Henry. "We must go somewhere forth of the house."

"There is an excellent place in the long shrubbery," said the Master.

"Gentlemen," said I, "shame upon you both! Sons of the same mother, would you turn against the life she gave you?"

"Even so, Mackellar," said Mr. Henry, with the same perfect quietude of manner he had shown throughout.

"It is what I will prevent," said I.

And now here is a blot upon my life. At these words of mine the Master turned his blade against my bosom; I saw the light run along the steel; and I threw up my arms and fell to my knees before him on the floor. "No, no," I cried, like a baby.

"We shall have no more trouble with him," said the Master. "It is a good thing to have a coward in the house."

"We must have light," said Mr. Henry, as though there had been no interruption.

"This trembler can bring a pair of candles," said the Master.

To my shame be it said, I was still so blinded with the flashing of that bare sword that I volunteered to bring a lantern.

"We do not need a l-l-lantern," says the Master, mocking me. "There is no breath of air. Come, get to your feet, take a pair of lights, and go before. I am close behind with this"—making the blade glitter as he spoke.

I took up the candlesticks and went before them, steps that I would give my hands to recall ; but a coward is a slave at the best ; and even as I went, my teeth smote each other in my mouth. It was as he had said : there was no breath stirring ; a windless stricture of frost had bound the air ; and as we went forth in the shine of the candles, the blackness was like a roof over our heads. Never a word was said ; there was never a sound but the creaking of our steps along the frozen path. The cold of the night fell about me like a bucket of water ; I shook as I went with more than terror ; but my companions, bare-headed like myself, and fresh from the warm hall, appeared not even conscious of the change.

"Here is the place," said the Master. "Set down the candles."

I did as he bid me, and presently the flames went up, as steady as in a chamber, in the midst of the frosted trees, and I beheld these two brothers take their places.

"The light is something in my eyes," said the Master.

"I will give you every advantage," replied Mr. Henry, shifting his ground, "for I think you are about to die." He spoke rather sadly than otherwise, yet there was a ring in his voice.

"Henry Durie," said the Master, "two words before I begin. You are a fencer, you can hold a foil ; you little know what a change it makes to hold a sword ! And by that I know you are to fall. But see how strong is my situation ! If you fall, I shift out of this country to where my money is before me. If I fall, where are you ? My father, your wife—who is in love with me, as you very well know—your child even, who prefers me to yourself :— how will these avenge me ! Had you thought of that, dear Henry ? " He looked at his brother with a smile ; then made a fencing-room salute.

Never a word said Mr. Henry, but saluted too, and the swords rang together.

I am no judge of the play ; my head, besides, was gone

with cold and fear and horror; but it seems that Mr. Henry took and kept the upper hand from the engagement, crowding in upon his foe with a contained and glowing fury. Nearer and nearer he crept upon the man, till of a sudden the Master leaped back with a little sobbing oath; and I believe the movement brought the light once more against his eyes. To it they went again, on the fresh ground; but now methought closer, Mr. Henry pressing more outrageously, the Master beyond doubt with shaken confidence. For it is beyond doubt he now recognised himself for lost, and had some taste of the cold agony of fear; or he had never attempted the foul stroke. I cannot say I followed it, my untrained eye was never quick enough to seize details, but it appears he caught his brother's blade with his left hand, a practice not permitted. Certainly Mr. Henry only saved himself by leaping on one side; as certainly the Master, lungeing in the air, stumbled on his knee, and before he could move, the sword was through his body.

I cried out with a stifled scream, and ran in; but the body was already fallen to the ground, where it writhed a moment like a trodden worm, and then lay motionless.

"Look at his left hand," said Mr. Henry.

"It is all bloody," said I.

"On the inside?" said he.

"It is cut on the inside," said I.

"I thought so," said he, and turned his back.

I opened the man's clothes; the heart was quite still, it gave not a flutter.

"God forgive us, Mr. Henry!" said I. "He is dead."

"Dead?" he repeated, a little stupidly; and then, with a rising tone, "Dead? dead?" says he, and suddenly cast his bloody sword upon the ground.

"What must we do?" said I. "Be yourself, sir. It is too late now: you must be yourself."

He turned and stared at me. "O, Mackellar!" says he, and put his face in his hands.

I plucked him by the coat. " For God's sake, for all our sakes, be more courageous ! " said I. " What must we do ? "

He showed me his face with the same stupid stare. " Do ? " says he. And with that his eye fell on the body, and " O ! " he cries out, with his hand to his brow, as if he had never remembered ; and, turning from me, made off towards the house of Durrisdeer at a strange stumbling run.

I stood a moment mused ; then it seemed to me my duty lay most plain on the side of the living ; and I ran after him, leaving the candles on the frosty ground and the body lying in their light under the trees. But run as I pleased, he had the start of me, and was got into the house, and up to the hall, where I found him standing before the fire with his face once more in his hands, and as he so stood he visibly shuddered.

" Mr. Henry, Mr. Henry," I said, " this will be the ruin of us all."

" What is this that I have done ? " cries he, and then looking upon me with a countenance that I shall never forget, " Who is to tell the old man ? " he said.

The word knocked at my heart ; but it was no time for weakness. I went and poured him out a glass of brandy. " Drink that," said I, " drink it down." I forced him to swallow it like a child ; and, being still perished with the cold of the night, I followed his example.

" It has to be told, Mackellar," said he. " It must be told." And he fell suddenly in a seat—my old lord's seat by the chimney-side—and was shaken with dry sobs.

Dismay came upon my soul ; it was plain there was no help in Mr. Henry. " Well," said I, " sit there, and leave all to me." And taking a candle in my hand, I set forth out of the room in the dark house. There was no movement ; I must suppose that all had gone unobserved ; and I was now to consider how to smuggle through the rest with the like secrecy. It was no hour for scruples ; and

I opened my lady's door without so much as a knock, and passed boldly in.

"There is some calamity happened," she cried, sitting up in bed.

"Madam," said I, "I will go forth again into the passage ; and do you get as quickly as you can into your clothes. There is much to be done."

She troubled me with no questions, nor did she keep me waiting. Ere I had time to prepare a word of that which I must say to her, she was on the threshold signing me to enter.

"Madam," said I, "if you cannot be very brave, I must go elsewhere ; for if no one helps me to-night, there is an end of the house of Durrisdeer."

"I am very courageous," said she ; and she looked at me with a sort of smile, very painful to see, but very brave too.

"It has come to a duel," said I.

"A duel ? " she repeated. "A duel ! Henry and——"

"And the Master," said I. "Things have been borne so long, things of which you know nothing, which you would not believe if I should tell. But to-night it went too far, and when he insulted you——"

"Stop," said she. "He ? Who ? "

"O ! madam," cried I, my bitterness breaking forth, "do you ask me such a question ? Indeed, then, I may go elsewhere for help ; there is none here ! "

"I do not know in what I have offended you," said she. "Forgive me ; put me out of this suspense."

But I dared not tell her yet ; I felt not sure of her ; and at the doubt, and under the sense of impotence it brought with it, I turned on the poor woman with something near to anger.

"Madam," said I, "we are speaking of two men : one of them insulted you, and you ask me which. I will help you to the answer. With one of these men you have spent all your hours : has the other reproached you ? To one you have been always kind ; to the other, as God sees me and judges between us two, I think not always : has his love ever failed you ? To-night one of these two men told the other, in my hearing—the hearing of a hired stranger,—that you were in love with him. Before I say one word, you shall answer your own question : Which was it ? Nay, madam, you shall answer me another : If it has come to this dreadful end, whose fault is it ? "

She stared at me like one dazzled. " Good God ! " she said once, in a kind of bursting exclamation ; and then a second time in a whisper to herself : " Great God !— In the name of mercy, Mackellar, what is wrong ? " she cried. " I am made up ; I can hear all."

" You are not fit to hear," said I. " Whatever it was, you shall say first it was your fault."

" O ! " she cried, with a gesture of wringing her hands, " this man will drive me mad ! Can you not put *me* out of your thoughts ? "

" I think not once of you," I cried. " I think of none but my dear unhappy master."

" Ah ! " she cried, with her hand to her heart, " is Henry dead ? "

" Lower your voice," said I. " The other."

I saw her sway like something stricken by the wind ; and I know not whether in cowardice or misery, turned aside and looked upon the floor. " These are dreadful tidings," said I at length, when her silence began to put me in some fear ; " and you and I behove to be the more bold if the house is to be saved." Still she answered nothing. " There is Miss Katharine, besides," I added : " unless we bring this matter through, her inheritance is like to be of shame."

I do not know if it was the thought of her child or the naked word shame that gave her deliverance ; at least I had no sooner spoken than a sound passed her lips, the like of it I never heard ; it was as though she had lain buried under a hill and sought to move that burthen. And the next moment she had found a sort of voice.

" It was a fight," she whispered. " It was not—— ? " and she paused upon the word.

" It was a fair fight on my dear master's part," said I. " As for the other, he was slain in the very act of a foul stroke."

" Not now ! " she cried.

" Madam," said I, " hatred of that man glows in my bosom like a burning fire ; ay, even now he is dead. God knows, I would have stopped the fighting, had I dared. It is my shame I did not. But when I saw him fall, if I could have spared one thought from pitying of my master, it had been to exult in that deliverance."

I do not know if she marked ; but her next words were, " My lord ? "

" That shall be my part," said I.

" You will not speak to him as you have to me ? " she asked.

" Madam," said I, " have you not some one else to think of ? Leave my lord to me."

" Some one else ? " she repeated.

" Your husband," said I. She looked at me with a countenance illegible. " Are you going to turn your back on him ? " I asked.

Still she looked at me ; then her hand went to her heart again. " No," said she.

" God bless you for that word ! " I said. " Go to him now, where he sits in the hall ; speak to him—it matters not what you say ; give him your hand ; say, ' I know all ' ;—if God gives you grace enough, say, ' Forgive me.' "

" God strengthen you, and make you merciful," said she. " I will go to my husband."

" Let me light you there," said I, taking up the candle.

" I will find my way in the dark," she said, with a shudder, and I think the shudder was at me.

So we separated—she downstairs to where a little light

glimmered in the hall-door, I along the passage to my lord's room. It seems hard to say why, but I could not burst in on the old man as I could on the young woman ; with whatever reluctance, I must knock. But his old slumbers were light, or perhaps he slept not ; and at the first summons I was bidden enter.

He, too, sat up in bed ; very aged and bloodless he looked ; and whereas he had a certain largeness of appearance when dressed for daylight, he now seemed frail and little, and his face (the wig being laid aside) not bigger than a child's. This daunted me ; nor less, the haggard surmise of misfortune in his eye. Yet his voice was even peaceful as he inquired my errand. I set my candle down upon a chair, leaned on the bed-foot, and looked at him.

" Lord Durrisdeer," said I, " it is very well known to you that I am a partisan in your family."

" I hope we are none of us partisans," said he. " That you love my son sincerely, I have always been glad to recognise."

" O ! my lord, we are past the hour of these civilities," I replied. " If we are to save anything out of the fire, we must look the fact in its bare countenance. A partisan I am ; partisans we have all been ; it is as a partisan that I am here in the middle of the night to plead before you. Hear me ; before I go, I will tell you why."

" I would always hear you, Mr. Mackellar," said he, " and that at any hour, whether of the day or night, for I would be always sure you had a reason. You spoke once before to very proper purpose ; I have not forgotten that."

" I am here to plead the cause of my master," I said. " I need not tell you how he acts. You know how he is placed. You know with what generosity he has always met your other—met your wishes," I corrected myself, stumbling at that name of son. " You know—you must know—what he has suffered—what he has suffered about his wife."

"Mr. Mackellar!" cried my lord, rising in bed like a bearded lion.

"You said you would hear me," I continued. "What you do not know, what you should know, one of the things I am here to speak of, is the persecution he must bear in private. Your back is not turned before one whom I dare not name to you falls upon him with the most unfeeling taunts; twits him—pardon me, my lord—twits him with your partiality, calls him Jacob, calls him clown, pursues him with ungenerous raillery, not to be borne by man. And let but one of you appear, instantly he changes; and my master must smile and courtesy to the man who has been feeding him with insults; I know, for I have shared in some of it, and I tell you the life is insupportable. All these months it has endured; it began with the man's landing; it was by the name of Jacob that my master was greeted the first night."

My lord made a movement as if to throw aside the clothes and rise. "If there be any truth in this——" said he.

"Do I look like a man lying?" I interrupted, checking him with my hand.

"You should have told me at first," he said.

"Ah, my lord! indeed I should, and you may well hate the face of this unfaithful servant!" I cried.

"I will take order," said he, "at once," and again made the movement to rise.

Again I checked him. "I have not done," said I. "Would God I had! All this my dear, unfortunate patron has endured without help or countenance. Your own best word, my lord, was only gratitude. O, but he was your son too! He had no other father. He was hated in the country, God knows how unjustly. He had a loveless marriage. He stood on all hands without affection or support—dear, generous, ill-fated, noble heart!"

"Your tears do you much honour and me much shame," says my lord, with a palsied trembling. "But you do me some injustice. Henry has been ever dear to me, very dear. James (I do not deny it, Mr. Mackellar), James is perhaps dearer ; you have not seen my James in quite a favourable light ; he has suffered under his misfortunes ; and we can only remember how great and how unmerited these were. And even now his is the more affectionate nature. But I will not speak of him. All that you say of Henry is most true ; I do not wonder, I know him to be very magnanimous ; you will say I trade upon the knowledge ? It is possible ; there are dangerous virtues : virtues that tempt the encroacher. Mr. Mackellar, I will make it up to him ; I will take order with all this. I have been weak ; and, what is worse, I have been dull."

" I must not hear you blame yourself, my lord, with that which I have yet to tell upon my conscience," I replied. " You have not been weak ; you have been abused by a devilish dissembler. You saw yourself how he had deceived you in the matter of his danger ; he has deceived you throughout in every step of his career. I wish to pluck him from your heart ; I wish to force your eyes upon your other son ; ah, you have a son there ! "

" No, no," said he, " two sons—I have two sons."

I made some gesture of despair that struck him ; he looked at me with a changed face. " There is much worse behind ? " he asked, his voice dying as it rose upon the question.

" Much worse," I answered. " This night he said these words to Mr. Henry : ' I have never known a woman who did not prefer me to you, and I think who did not continue to prefer me.' "

" I will hear nothing against my daughter," he cried ; and from his readiness to stop me in this direction, I conclude his eyes were not so dull as I had fancied, and he had looked not without anxiety upon the siege of Mrs. Henry.

" I think not of blaming her," cried I. " It is not that. These words were said in my hearing to Mr. Henry ; and if you find them not yet plain enough, these others but a little after : ' Your wife, who is in love with me.' "

" They have quarrelled ? " he said.

I nodded.

" I must fly to them," he said, beginning once again to leave his bed.

" No, no ! " I cried, holding forth my hands.

" You do not know," said he. " These are dangerous words."

" Will nothing make you understand, my lord ? " said I.

His eyes besought me for the truth.

I flung myself on my knees by the bedside. " O, my lord," cried I, " think on him you have left ; think of this poor sinner whom you begot, whom your wife bore to you, whom we have none of us strengthened as we could ; think of him, not of yourself ; he is the other sufferer— think of him ! That is the door for sorrow—Christ's door, God's door : O ! it stands open. Think of him, even as he thought of you. ' *Who is to tell the old man ?* '—these were his words. It was for that I came ; that is why I am here pleading at your feet."

" Let me get up," he cried, thrusting me aside, and was on his feet before myself. His voice shook like a sail in the wind, yet he spoke with a good loudness ; his face was like the snow, but his eyes were steady and dry. " Here is too much speech," said he. " Where was it ? "

" In the shrubbery," said I.

" And Mr. Henry ? " he asked. And when I had told him he knotted his old face in thought.

" And Mr. James ? " says he.

" I have left him lying," said I, " beside the candles."

" Candles ? " he cried. And with that he ran to the window, opened it, and looked abroad. " It might be spied from the road."

" Where none goes by at such an hour," I objected.

" It makes no matter," he said. " One might.—Hark !"
cries he. " What is that ? "

It was the sound of men very guardedly rowing in the
bay ; and I told him so.

" The free-traders," said my lord. " Run at once,
Mackellar ; put these candles out. I will dress in the meanwhile ; and when you return we can debate on what is
wisest."

I groped my way downstairs, and out at the door.
From quite a far way off a sheen was visible, making points
of brightness in the shrubbery ; in so black a night it
might have been remarked for miles ; and I blamed myself
bitterly for my incaution. How much more sharply when
I reached the place ! One of the candlesticks was overthrown, and that taper quenched. The other burned
steadily by itself, and made a broad space of light upon the
frosted ground. All within that circle seemed, by the
force of contrast and the overhanging blackness, brighter
than by day. And there was the blood-stain in the midst ;
and a little farther off Mr. Henry's sword, the pommel of
which was of silver ; but of the body, not a trace. My
heart thumped upon my ribs, the hair stirred upon my
scalp, as I stood there staring—so strange was the sight, so
dire the fears it wakened. I looked right and left ; the
ground was so hard, it told no story. I stood and listened
till my ears ached, but the night was hollow about me like
an empty church ; not even a ripple stirred upon the shore ;
it seemed you might have heard a pin drop in the county.

I put the candle out, and the blackness fell about me
groping dark ; it was like a crowd surrounding me ; and
I went back to the house of Durrisdeer, with my chin upon
my shoulder, startling, as I went, with craven suppositions.
In the door a figure moved to meet me, and I had near
screamed with terror ere I recognised Mrs. Henry.

" Have you told him ? " says she.

" It was he who sent me," said I. " It is gone.—But
why are you here ? "

"It is gone!" she repeated. "What is gone?"

"The body," said I. "Why are you not with your husband?"

"Gone?" said she. "You cannot have looked. Come back."

"There is no light now," said I. "I dare not."

"I can see in the dark. I have been standing here so long—so long," said she. "Come, give me your hand."

We returned to the shrubbery hand in hand, and to the fatal place.

"Take care of the blood," said I.

"Blood?" she cried, and started violently back.

"I suppose it will be," said I. "I am like a blind man."

"No," said she, "nothing! Have you not dreamed?"

"Ah, would to God we had!" cried I.

She spied the sword, picked it up, and seeing the blood, let it fall again with her hands thrown wide. "Ah!" she cried, and then, with an instant courage, handled it the second time.* "I will take it back and clean it properly," says she, and again looked about her on all sides. "It cannot be that he was dead?" she added.

"There was no flutter of his heart," said I, and then remembering: "Why are you not with your husband?"

"It is no use," said she; "he will not speak to me."

"Not speak to you?" I repeated. "Oh! you have not tried."

"You have a right to doubt me," she replied, with a gentle dignity.

At this, for the first time, I was seized with sorrow for her. "God knows, madam," I cried, "God knows I am not so hard as I appear; on this dreadful night who can veneer his words? But I am a friend to all who are not Henry Durie's enemies."

"It is hard, then, you should hesitate about his wife," said she.

I saw all at once, like the rending of a veil, how nobly she had borne this unnatural calamity, and how generously my reproaches.

"We must go back and tell this to my lord," said I.

"Him I cannot face," she cried.

"You will find him the least moved of all of us," said I.

"And yet I cannot face him," said she.

"Well," said I, "you can return to Mr. Henry; I will see my lord."

As we walked back, I bearing the candlesticks, she the sword—a strange burthen for that woman—she had another thought. "Should we tell Henry?" she asked.

"Let my lord decide," said I.

My lord was nearly dressed when I came to his chamber. He heard me with a frown. "The free-traders," said he. "But whether dead or alive?"

"I thought him——" said I, and paused, ashamed of the word.

"I know; but you may very well have been in error. Why should they remove him if not living?" he asked. "O! here is a great door of hope. It must be given out that he departed—as he came—without any note of preparation. We must save all scandal."

I saw he had fallen, like the rest of us, to think mainly of the house. Now that all the living members of the family were plunged in irremediable sorrow, it was strange how we turned to that conjoint abstraction of the family itself, and sought to bolster up the airy nothing of its reputation: not the Duries only, but the hired steward himself.

"Are we to tell Mr. Henry?" I asked him.

"I will see," said he. "I am going first to visit him; then I go forth with you to view the shrubbery and consider."

We went downstairs into the hall. Mr. Henry sat by the table with his head upon his hand, like a man of stone.

His wife stood a little back from him, her hand at her mouth; it was plain she could not move him. My old lord walked very steadily to where his son was sitting; he had a steady countenance, too, but methought a little cold. When he was come quite up, he held out both his hands and said, " My son ! "

With a broken, strangled cry, Mr. Henry leaped up and fell on his father's neck, crying and weeping, the most pitiful sight that ever a man witnessed. " O ! father," he cried, " you know I loved him ; you know I loved him in the beginning ; I could have died for him—you know that ! I would have given my life for him and you. O ! say you know that. O ! say you can forgive me. O, father, father, what have I done—what have I done ? And we used to be bairns together ! " and wept and sobbed, and fondled the old man, and clutched him about the neck, with a passion of a child in terror.

And then he caught sight of his wife (you would have thought for the first time), where she stood weeping to hear him, and in a moment had fallen at her knees. " And O my lass," he cried, " you must forgive me, too ! Not your husband—I have only been the ruin of your life. But you knew me when I was a lad ; there was no harm in Henry Durie then ; he meant aye to be a friend to you. It's him—it's the old bairn that played with you—O, can ye never, never forgive him ? "

Throughout all this my lord was like a cold, kind spectator with his wits about him. At the first cry, which was indeed enough to call the house about us, he had said to me over his shoulder, " Close the door." And now he nodded to himself.

" We may leave him to his wife now," says he. " Bring a light, Mr. Mackellar."

Upon my going forth again with my lord, I was aware of a strange phenomenon ; for though it was quite dark, and the night not yet old, methought I smelt the morning. At the same time there went a tossing through the branches of the evergreens, so that they sounded like a quiet sea, and the air puffed at times against our faces, and the flame of the candle shook. We made the more speed, I believe, being surrounded by this bustle; visited the scene of the duel, where my lord looked upon the blood with stoicism; and passing farther on toward the landing-place, came at last upon some evidences of the truth. For, first of all, where was a pool across the path, the ice had been trodden in, plainly by more than one man's weight; next, and but a little farther, a young tree was broken, and down by the landing-place, where the traders' boats were usually beached, another stain of blood marked where the body must have been infallibly set down to rest the bearers.

The stain we set ourselves to wash away with the sea-water, carrying it in my lord's hat; and as we were thus engaged there came up a sudden moaning gust and left us instantly benighted.

"It will come to snow," says my lord; "and the best thing that we could hope. Let us go back now; we can do nothing in the dark."

As we went houseward, the wind being again subsided, we were aware of a strong pattering noise about us in the night; and when we issued from the shelter of the trees, we found it raining smartly.

Throughout the whole of this, my lord's clearness of mind, no less than his activity of body, had not ceased to minister to my amazement. He set the crown upon it in the council we held on our return. The free-traders had certainly secured the Master, though whether dead or alive we were still left to our conjectures; the rain would, long before day, wipe out all marks of the transaction; by this we must profit. The Master had unexpectedly come after the fall of night; it must now be given out he had as suddenly departed before the break of day; and, to make all this plausible, it now only remained for me to mount into the man's chamber, and pack and conceal his

baggage.   True, we still lay at the discretion of the traders ;
but that was the incurable weakness of our guilt.

I heard him, as I said, with wonder, and hastened to
obey.   Mr. and Mrs. Henry were gone from the hall ; my
lord, for warmth's sake, hurried to his bed ; there was still
no sign of stir among the servants, and as I went up the
tower stair, and entered the dead man's room, a horror
of solitude weighed upon my mind.   To my extreme surprise, it was all in the disorder of departure.   Of his three
portmanteaus, two were already locked ; a third lay open
and near full.   At once there flashed upon me some suspicion
of the truth.   The man had been going, after all ; he had
but waited upon Crail, as Crail waited upon the wind ;
early in the night the seamen had perceived the weather
changing ; the boat had come to give notice of the change
and call the passenger aboard, and the boat's crew had
stumbled on him lying in his blood.   Nay, and there was
more behind.   This pre-arranged departure shed some
light upon his inconceivable insult of the night before ;
it was a parting shot, hatred being no longer checked by
policy.   And, for another thing, the nature of that insult,
and the conduct of Mrs. Henry, pointed to one conclusion,
which I have never verified, and can now never verify until
the great assize—the conclusion that he had at last forgotten himself, had gone too far in his advances, and had
been rebuffed.   It can never be verified, as I say ; but
as I thought of it that morning among his baggage, the
thought was sweet to me like honey.

Into the open portmanteau I dipped a little ere I closed
it.   The most beautiful lace and linen, many suits of those
fine plain clothes in which he loved to appear ; a book or
two, and those of the best, Cæsar's " Commentaries," a
volume of Mr. Hobbes, the " Henriade " of M. de Voltaire,
a book upon the Indies, one on the mathematics, far beyond
where I have studied : these were what I observed with
very mingled feelings.   But in the open portmanteau, no
papers of any description.   This set me musing.   It was

possible the man was dead; but, since the traders had carried him away, not likely. It was possible he might still die of his wound; but it was also possible he might not. And in this latter case I was determined to have the means of some defence.

One after another I carried his portmanteaus to a loft in the top of the house which we kept locked; went to my own room for my keys, and, returning to the loft, had the gratification to find two that fitted pretty well. In one of the portmanteaus there was a shagreen letter-case, which I cut open with my knife; and thenceforth (so far as any credit went) the man was at my mercy. Here was a vast deal of gallant correspondence, chiefly of his Paris days; and, what was more to the purpose, here were the copies of his own reports to the English Secretary, and the originals of the Secretary's answers: a most damning series: such as to publish would be to wreck the Master's honour and to set a price upon his life. I chuckled to myself as I ran through the documents; I rubbed my hands, I sang aloud in my glee. Day found me at the pleasing task; nor did I then remit my diligence, except in so far as I went to the window—looked out for a moment, to see the frost quite gone, the world turned black again, and the rain and the wind driving in the bay—and to assure myself that the lugger was gone from its anchorage, and the Master (whether dead or alive) now tumbling on the Irish Sea.

It is proper I should add in this place the very little I have subsequently angled out upon the doings of that night. It took me a long while to gather it; for we dared not openly ask, and the free-traders regarded me with enmity, if not with scorn. It was near six months before we even knew for certain that the man survived; and it was years before I learned from one of Crail's men, turned publican on his ill-gotten gain, some particulars which smack to me of truth. It seems the traders found the Master struggled on one elbow, and now staring round him, and now gazing

at the candle, or at his hand, which was all bloodied, like
a man stupid. Upon their coming, he would seem to have
found his mind, bade them carry him aboard, and hold
their tongues ; and on the captain asking how he had
come in such a pickle, replied with a burst of passionate
swearing and incontinently fainted. They held some
debate, but they were momently looking for a wind, they
were highly paid to smuggle him to France, and did not
care to delay. Besides which, he was well enough liked
by these abominable wretches : they supposed him under
capital sentence, knew not in what mischief he might have
got his wound, and judged it a piece of good-nature to
remove him out of the way of danger. So he was taken
aboard, recovered on the passage over, and was set
ashore a convalescent at the Havre de Grace. What is
truly notable : he said not a word to any one of the duel,
and not a trader knows to this day in what quarrel, or by
the hand of what adversary, he fell. With any other man
I should have set this down to natural decency ; with him,
to pride. He could not bear to avow, perhaps even to
himself, that he had been vanquished by one whom he had
so much insulted and whom he so cruelly despised.

CHAPTER VI

SUMMARY OF EVENTS DURING THE MASTER'S
SECOND ABSENCE

OF the heavy sickness which declared itself next morning
I can think with equanimity, as of the last unmingled
trouble that befell my master ; and even that was perhaps
a mercy in disguise ; for what pains of the body could
equal the miseries of his mind ? Mrs. Henry and I had
the watching by the bed. My old lord called from time
to time to take the news, but would not usually pass the
door. Once, I remember, when hope was nigh gone, he
stepped to the bedside, looked a while in his son's face, and
turned away with a singular gesture of the head and hand
thrown up, that remains upon my mind as something
tragic ; such grief and such a scorn of sublunary things
were there expressed. But the most of the time Mrs.
Henry and I had the room to ourselves, taking turns by
night, and bearing each other company by day, for it was
dreary watching. Mr. Henry, his shaven head bound in
a napkin, tossed to and fro without remission, beating the
bed with his hands. His tongue never lay ; his voice ran
continuously like a river, so that my heart was weary with
the sound of it. It was notable, and to me inexpressibly
mortifying, that he spoke all the while on matters of no
import : comings and goings, horses—which he was ever
calling to have saddled, thinking perhaps (the poor soul !)
that he might ride away from his discomfort—matters of
the garden, the salmon nets, and (what I particularly raged
to hear) continually of his affairs, ciphering figures and
holding disputation with the tenantry. Never a word of

127

his father or his wife, nor of the Master, save only for a day or two, when his mind dwelled entirely in the past, and he supposed himself a boy again and upon some innocent child's play with his brother. What made this the more affecting : it appeared the Master had then run some peril of his life, for there was a cry—" O ! Jamie will be drowned—O, save Jamie ! " which he came over and over with a great deal of passion.

This, I say, was affecting, both to Mrs. Henry and myself ; but the balance of my master's wanderings did him little justice. It seemed he had set out to justify his brother's calumnies ; as though he was bent to prove himself a man of a dry nature, immersed in money-getting. Had I been there alone, I would not have troubled my thumb ; but all the while, as I listened, I was estimating the effect on the man's wife, and telling myself that he fell lower every day. I was the one person on the surface of the globe that comprehended him, and I was bound there should be yet another. Whether he was to die there and his virtues perish : or whether he should save his days and come back to that inheritance of sorrows, his right memory : I was bound he should be heartily lamented in the one case, and unaffectedly welcomed in the other, by the person he loved the most, his wife.

Finding no occasion of free speech, I bethought me at last of a kind of documentary disclosure ; and for some nights, when I was off duty, and should have been asleep, I gave my time to the preparation of that which I may call my budget. But this I found to be the easiest portion of my task, and that which remained—namely, the presentation to my lady—almost more than I had fortitude to overtake. Several days I went about with my papers under my arm, spying for some juncture of talk to serve as introduction. I will not deny but that some offered ; only when they did my tongue clove to the roof of my mouth ; and I think I might have been carrying about my packet till this day, had not a fortunate accident delivered me from all my hesitations. This was at night, when I was once more leaving the room, the thing not yet done, and myself in despair at my own cowardice.

" What do you carry about with you, Mr. Mackellar ? " she asked. " These last days, I see you always coming in and out with the same armful."

I returned upon my steps without a word, laid the papers before her on the table, and left her to her reading. Of what that was, I am now to give you some idea ; and the best will be to reproduce a letter of my own which came first in the budget, and of which (according to an excellent habitude) I have preserved the scroll. It will show, too, the moderation of my part in these affairs, a thing which some have called recklessly in question.

Durrisdeer,
1757.

HONOURED MADAM,

I trust I would not step out of my place without occasion ; but I see how much evil has flowed in the past to all of your noble house from that unhappy and secretive fault of reticency, and the papers on which I venture to call your attention are family papers, and all highly worthy your acquaintance.

I append a schedule with some necessary observations,
And am,
Honoured Madam,
Your ladyship's obliged, obedient servant,
EPHRAIM MACKELLAR.

Schedule of Papers.

A.   Scroll of ten letters from Ephraim Mackellar to the Hon. James Durie, Esq., by courtesy Master of Ballantrae, during the latter's residence in Paris : under dates . . . *(follow the dates)* . . . *Nota :* to be read in connection with B and C.

B.   Seven original letters from the said M^r of Ballantrae to the said E. Mackellar, under dates . . . *(follow the dates).*

C.   Three original letters from the said M^r of Ballantrae to the Hon. Henry Durie, Esq., under dates . . . *(follow the dates)* . . . *Nota :* given me by Mr. Henry to answer : copies of my answers A 4, A 5, and A 9 of these productions. The purport of Mr. Henry's communications, of which I can find no scroll, may be gathered from those of his unnatural brother.

D.   A correspondence, original and scroll, extending over a period of three years till January of the current year, between the said M^r of Ballantrae and —— ——, Under Secretary of State ; twenty-seven in all. *Nota :* found among the Master's papers.

Weary as I was with watching and distress of mind, it was impossible for me to sleep. All night long I walked in my chamber, revolving what should be the issue, and sometimes repenting the temerity of my immixture in affairs so private ; and with the first peep of the morning I was at the sick-room door. Mrs. Henry had thrown open the shutters, and even the window, for the temperature was mild. She looked steadfastly before her ; where was nothing to see, or only the blue of the morning creeping among woods. Upon the stir of my entrance she did not so much as turn about her face : a circumstance from which I augured very ill.

"Madam," I began ; and then again, " Madam " ; but could make no more of it. Nor yet did Mrs. Henry come to my assistance with a word. In this pass I began gathering up the papers where they lay scattered on the table ; and the first thing that struck me, their bulk appeared to have diminished. Once I ran them through, and twice ; but the correspondence with the Secretary of State, on which I had reckoned so much against the future, was nowhere to be found. I looked in the chimney ; amid the smouldering embers, black ashes of paper fluttered in the draught ; and at that my timidity vanished.

"Good God, madam," cried I, in a voice not fitting for a sick-room, " Good God, madam, what have you done with my papers ? "

" I have burned them," said Mrs. Henry, turning about. " It is enough, it is too much, that you and I have seen them."

"This is a fine night's work that you have done ! " cried I. " And all to save the reputation of a man that ate bread by the shedding of his comrades' blood, as I do by the shedding of ink."

"To save the reputation of that family in which you are a servant, Mr. Mackellar," she returned, " and for which you have already done so much."

"It is a family I will not serve much longer," I cried,

" for I am driven desperate. You have stricken the sword out of my hands ; you have left us all defenceless. I had always these letters I could shake over his head ; and now —what is to do ? We are so falsely situate we dare not show the man the door ; the country would fly on fire against us ; and I had this one hold upon him—and now it is gone—now he may come back to-morrow, and we must all sit down with him to dinner, go for a stroll with him on the terrace, or take a hand at cards, of all things, to divert his leisure ! No, madam ! God forgive you, if He can find it in His heart ; for I cannot find it in mine."

" I wonder to find you so simple, Mr. Mackellar," said Mrs. Henry. " What does this man value reputation ? But he knows how high we prize it ; he knows we would rather die than make these letters public ; and do you suppose he would not trade upon the knowledge ? What you call your sword, Mr. Mackellar, and which had been one indeed against a man of any remnant of propriety, would have been but a sword of paper against him. He would smile in your face at such a threat. He stands upon his degradation, he makes that his strength ; it is in vain to struggle with such characters." She cried out this last a little desperately, and then with more quiet : " No, Mr. Mackellar ; I have thought upon this matter all night, and there is no way out of it. Papers or no papers, the door of this house stands open for him ; he is the rightful heir, forsooth ! If we sought to exclude him, all would redound against poor Henry, and I should see him stoned again upon the streets. Ah ! if Henry dies, it is a different matter ! They have broke the entail for their own good purposes ; the estate goes to my daughter ; and I shall see who sets a foot upon it. But if Henry lives, my poor Mr. Mackellar, and that man returns, we must suffer : only this time it will be together."

On the whole I was well pleased with Mrs. Henry's attitude of mind ; nor could I even deny there was some cogency in that which she advanced about the papers.

"Let us say no more about it," said I. "I can only be sorry I trusted a lady with the originals, which was an unbusinesslike proceeding at the best. As for what I said of leaving the service of the family, it was spoken with the tongue only; and you may set your mind at rest. I belong to Durrisdeer, Mrs. Henry, as if I had been born there."

I must do her the justice to say she seemed perfectly relieved; so that we began this morning, as we were to continue for so many years, on a proper ground of mutual indulgence and respect.

The same day, which was certainly prededicate to joy, we observed the first signal of recovery in Mr. Henry; and about three of the following afternoon he found his mind again, recognising me by name with the strongest evidences of affection. Mrs. Henry was also in the room, at the bed-foot; but it did not appear that he observed her. And indeed (the fever being gone) he was so weak that he made but the one effort and sank again into a lethargy. The course of his restoration was now slow, but equal; every day his appetite improved; every week we were able to remark an increase both of strength and flesh; and before the end of the month he was out of bed and had even begun to be carried in his chair upon the terrace.

It was perhaps at this time that Mrs. Henry and I were the most uneasy in mind. Apprehension for his days was at an end; and a worse fear succeeded. Every day we drew consciously nearer to a day of reckoning; and the days passed on, and still there was nothing. Mr. Henry bettered in strength, he held long talks with us on a great diversity of subjects, his father came and sat with him and went again; and still there was no reference to the late tragedy or to the former troubles which had brought it on. Did he remember, and conceal his dreadful knowledge? or was the whole blotted from his mind? This was the problem that kept us watching and trembling all day when we were in his company, and held us awake at night when we were in our lonely beds. We knew not even which alternative to hope for, both appearing so unnatural, and pointing so directly to an unsound brain. Once this fear offered, I observed his conduct with sedulous particularity. Something of the child he exhibited : a cheerfulness quite foreign to his previous character, an interest readily aroused, and then very tenacious, in small matters which he had heretofore despised. When he was stricken down, I was his only confidant, and I may say his only friend, and he was on terms of division with his wife ; upon his recovery, all was changed, the past forgotten, the wife first and even single in his thoughts. He turned to her with all his emotions, like a child to its mother, and seemed secure of sympathy ; called her in all his needs with something of that querulous familiarity that marks a certainty of indulgence ; and I must say, in justice to the woman, he was never disappointed. To her, indeed, this changed behaviour was inexpressibly affecting ; and I think she felt it secretly as a reproach ; so that I have seen her, in early days, escape out of the room that she might indulge herself in weeping. But to me the change appeared not natural ; and viewing it along with all the rest, I began to wonder, with many head-shakings, whether his reason were perfectly erect.

As this doubt stretched over many years, endured indeed until my master's death, and clouded all our subsequent relations, I may well consider of it more at large. When he was able to resume some charge of his affairs, I had many opportunities to try him with precision. There was no lack of understanding, nor yet of authority ; but the old continuous interest had quite departed ; he grew readily fatigued, and fell to yawning ; and he carried into money relations, where it is certainly out of place, a facility that bordered upon slackness. True, since we had no longer the exactions of the Master to contend against,

there was the less occasion to raise strictness into principle
or do battle for a farthing. True, again, there was nothing
excessive in these relaxations, or I would have been no
party to them. But the whole thing marked a change,
very slight yet very perceptible ; and though no man
could say my master had gone at all out of his mind, no
man could deny that he had drifted from his character.
It was the same to the end, with his manner and appearance. Some of the heat of the fever lingered in his veins :
his movements a little hurried, his speech notably more
voluble, yet neither truly amiss. His whole mind stood
open to happy impressions, welcoming these and making
much of them ; but the smallest suggestion of trouble or
sorrow he received with visible impatience, and dismissed
again with immediate relief. It was to this temper that
he owed the felicity of his later days ; and yet here it was,
if anywhere, that you could call the man insane. A great
part of this life consists in contemplating what we cannot
cure ; but Mr. Henry, if he could not dismiss solicitude by
an effort of the mind, must instantly and at whatever cost
annihilate the cause of it ; so that he played alternately
the ostrich and the bull. It is to this strenuous cowardice
of pain that I have to set down all the unfortunate and
excessive steps of his subsequent career. Certainly this
was the reason of his beating M'Manus, the groom, a thing
so much out of all his former practice, and which awakened
so much comment at the time. It is to this, again, that
I must lay the total loss of near upon two hundred pounds,
more than the half of which I could have saved if his
impatience would have suffered me. But he preferred loss
or any desperate extreme to a continuance of mental
suffering.

All this has led me far from our immediate trouble :
whether he remembered or had forgotten his late dreadful
act ; and if he remembered, in what light he viewed it.
The truth burst upon us suddenly, and was indeed one of
the chief surprises of my life. He had been several times

abroad, and was now beginning to walk a little with an arm, when it chanced I should be left alone with him upon the terrace. He turned to me with a singular furtive smile, such as schoolboys use when in fault ; and says he, in a private whisper, and without the least preface : "Where have you buried him ? "

I could not make one sound in answer.

"Where have you buried him ? " he repeated. " I want to see his grave."

I conceived I had best take the bull by the horns. "Mr. Henry," said I, " I have news to give that will rejoice you exceedingly. In all human likelihood, your hands are clear of blood. I reason from certain indices ; and by these it should appear your brother was not dead, but was carried in a swound on board the lugger. But now he may be perfectly recovered."

What there was in his countenance I could not read. "James ? " he asked.

"Your brother James," I answered. " I would not raise a hope that may be found deceptive, but in my heart I think it very probable he is alive."

"Ah ! " says Mr. Henry ; and suddenly rising from his seat with more alacrity than he had yet discovered, set one finger on my breast, and cried at me in a kind of screaming whisper, " Mackellar "—these were his words— "nothing can kill that man. He is not mortal. He is bound upon my back to all eternity—to all God's eternity ! " says he, and, sitting down again, fell upon a stubborn silence.

A day or two after, with the same secret smile, and first looking about as if to be sure we were alone, " Mackellar," said he, " when you have any intelligence, be sure and let me know. We must keep an eye upon him, or he will take us when we least expect."

"He will not show face here again," said I.

"O yes, he will," said Mr. Henry. " Wherever I am, there will he be." And again he looked all about him.

" You must not dwell upon this thought, Mr. Henry,"
said I.

" No," said he, " that is a very good advice. We will
never think of it, except when you have news. And we
do not know yet," he added ; " he may be dead."

The manner of his saying this convinced me thoroughly
of what I had scarce ventured to suspect : that, so far
from suffering any penitence for the attempt, he did but
lament his failure. This was a discovery I kept to myself,
fearing it might do him a prejudice with his wife. But I
might have saved myself the trouble ; she had divined it
for herself, and found the sentiment quite natural. Indeed,
I could not but say that there were three of us, all of the
same mind ; nor could any news have reached Durrisdeer
more generally welcome than tidings of the Master's death.

This brings me to speak of the exception, my old lord.
As soon as my anxiety for my own master began to be
relaxed, I was aware of a change in the old gentleman,
his father, that seemed to threaten mortal consequences.
His face was pale and swollen ; as he sat in the chimney-
side with his Latin, he would drop off sleeping and the book
roll in the ashes ; some days he would drag his foot, others
stumble in speaking. The amenity of his behaviour
appeared more extreme ; full of excuses for the least trouble,
very thoughtful for all ; to myself, of a most flattering
civility. One day, that he had sent for his lawyer, and
remained a long while private, he met me as he was crossing
the hall with painful footsteps, and took me kindly by the
hand. " Mr. Mackellar," said he, " I have had many occasions to set a proper value on your services ; and to-day,
when I re-cast my will, I have taken the freedom to name
you for one of my executors. I believe you bear love
enough to our house to render me this service." At that
very time he passed the greater portion of his days in
slumber, from which it was often difficult to rouse him ;
seemed to have lost all count of years, and had several
times (particularly on waking) called for his wife and for

an old servant whose very gravestone was now green with moss.   If I had been put to my oath, I must have declared he was incapable of testing ; and yet there was never a will drawn more sensible in every trait, or showing a more excellent judgment both of persons and affairs.

His dissolution, though it took not very long, proceeded by infinitesimal gradations.   His faculties decayed together steadily ; the power of his limbs was almost gone, he was extremely deaf, his speech had sunk into mere mumblings ; and yet to the end he managed to discover something of his former courtesy and kindness, pressing the hand of any that helped him, presenting me with one of his Latin books, in which he had laboriously traced my name, and in a thousand ways reminding us of the greatness of that loss which it might almost be said we had already suffered. To the end, the power of articulation returned to him in flashes ; it seemed he had only forgotten the art of speech as a child forgets his lesson, and at times he would call some part of it to mind.   On the last night of his life he suddenly broke silence with these words from Virgil : " Gnatique patrisque, alma, precor, miserere,"* perfectly uttered, and with a fitting accent.   At the sudden clear sound of it we started from our several occupations ; but it was in vain we turned to him ; he sat there silent, and, to all appearance, fatuous.   A little later he was had to bed with more difficulty than ever before ; and some time in the night, without any mortal violence, his spirit fled.

At a far later period I chanced to speak of these particulars with a doctor of medicine, a man of so high a reputation that I scruple to adduce his name.   By his view of it, father and son both suffered from the same affection : the father from the strain of his unnatural sorrows —the son, perhaps in the excitation of the fever ; each had ruptured a vessel in the brain, and there was probably (my doctor added) some predisposition in the family to accidents of that description.   The father sank, the son recovered all the externals of a healthy man ; but it is like there was some destruction in those delicate tissues where the soul resides and does her earthly business ; her heavenly, I would fain hope, cannot be thus obstructed by material accidents. And yet, upon a more mature opinion, it matters not one jot; for He who shall pass judgment on the records of our life is the same that formed us in frailty.

The death of my old lord was the occasion of a fresh surprise to us who watched the behaviour of his successor. To any considering mind, the two sons had between them slain their father, and he who took the sword might be even said to have slain him with his hand ; but no such thought appeared to trouble my new lord. He was becomingly grave ; I could scarce say sorrowful, or only with a pleasant sorrow ; talking of the dead with a regretful cheerfulness, relating old examples of his character, smiling at them with a good conscience ; and when the day of the funeral came round, doing the honours with exact propriety. I could perceive, besides, that he found a solid gratification in his accession to the title ; the which he was punctilious in exacting.

And now there came upon the scene a new character, and one that played his part, too, in the story ; I mean the present lord, Alexander, whose birth (17th July 1757) filled the cup of my poor master's happiness. There was nothing then left him to wish for ; nor yet leisure to wish for it. Indeed, there never was a parent so fond and doting as he showed himself. He was continually uneasy in his son's absence. Was the child abroad ? the father would be watching the clouds in case it rained. Was it night ? he would rise out of his bed to observe its slumbers. His conversation grew even wearyful to strangers, since he talked of little but his son. In matters relating to the estate, all was designed with a particular eye to Alexander ; and it would be :—" Let us put it in hand at once, that the wood may be grown against Alex-

ander's majority "; or, " This will fall in again handsomely for Alexander's marriage." Every day this ab-
sorption of the man's nature became more observable, with
many touching and some very blameworthy particulars.
Soon the child could walk abroad with him, at first on the
terrace, hand in hand, and afterward at large about the
policies ; and this grew to be my lord's chief occupation.
The sound of their two voices (audible a great way off, for
they spoke loud) became familiar in the neighbourhood ;
and for my part I found it more agreeable than the sound
of birds. It was pretty to see the pair returning full of
briers, and the father as flushed and sometimes as be-
muddied as the child, for they were equal sharers in all
sorts of boyish entertainment, digging in the beach,
damming of streams, and what not ; and I have seen them
gaze through a fence at cattle with the same childish con-
templation.

The mention of these rambles brings me to a strange
scene of which I was a witness. There was one walk I
never followed myself without emotion, so often had I
gone there upon miserable errands, so much had there
befallen against the house of Durrisdeer. But the path
lay handy from all points beyond the Muckle Ross ; and
I was driven, although much against my will, to take my
use of it perhaps once in the two months. It befell when
Mr. Alexander was of the age of six or seven, I had some
business on the far side in the morning, and entered the
shrubbery, on my homeward way, about nine of a bright
forenoon. It was that time of year when the woods are
all in their spring colours, the thorns all in flower, and the
birds in the high season of their singing. In contrast to
this merriment, the shrubbery was only the more sad, and
I the more oppressed by its associations. In this situation
of spirit it struck me disagreeably to hear voices a little
way in front, and to recognise the tones of my lord and
Mr. Alexander. I pushed ahead, and came presently into
their view. They stood together in the open space where

the duel was, my lord with his hand on his son's shoulder, and speaking with some gravity. At least, as he raised his head upon my coming, I thought I could perceive his countenance to lighten.

"Ah!" says he, "here comes the good Mackellar. I have just been telling Sandie the story of this place, and how there was a man whom the devil tried to kill, and how near he came to kill the devil instead."

I had thought it strange enough he should bring the child into that scene; that he should actually be discoursing of his act, passed measure. But the worst was yet to come : for he added, turning to his son—"You can ask Mackellar; he was here and saw it."

"Did you really see the devil?"* asked the child.

"I have not heard the tale," I replied; "and I am in a press of business." So far I said, sourly, fencing with the embarrassment of the position; and suddenly the bitterness of the past, and the terror of that scene by candlelight, rushed in upon my mind. I bethought me that, for a difference of a second's quickness in parade, the child before me might have never seen the day; and the emotion that always fluttered round my heart in that dark shrubbery burst forth in words. "But so much is true," I cried, "that I have met the devil in these woods, and seen him foiled here. Blessed be God that we escaped with life— blessed be God that one stone yet stands upon another in the walls of Durrisdeer! And, O! Mr. Alexander, if ever you come by this spot, though it was a hundred years hence, and you came with the gayest and the highest in the land, I would step aside and remember a bit prayer."

My lord bowed his head gravely. "Ah!" says he, "Mackellar is always in the right. Come, Alexander, take your bonnet off." And with that he uncovered, and held out his hand. "O Lord," said he, "I thank Thee and my son thanks Thee, for Thy manifold great mercies. Let us have peace for a little; defend us from the evil man. Smite him, O Lord, upon the lying mouth!" The last broke out of him like a cry ; and at that, whether remembered anger choked his utterance, or whether he perceived this was a singular sort of prayer, at least he suddenly came to a full stop ; and, after a moment, set back his hat upon his head.

" I think you have forgot a word, my lord," said I. " ' Forgive us our trespasses, as we forgive them that trespass against us. For Thine is the kingdom, and the power, and the glory, for ever and ever. Amen.' "

" Ah ! that is easy saying," said my lord. " That is very easy saying, Mackellar. But for me to forgive !— I think I would cut a very silly figure if I had the affectation to pretend it."

" The bairn, my lord ! " said I, with some severity, for I thought his expressions little fitted for the ears of children.

" Why, very true," said he. " This is dull work for a bairn. Let's go nesting."

I forget if it was the same day, but it was soon after, my lord, finding me alone, opened himself a little more on the same head.

" Mackellar," he said, " I am now a very happy man."

" I think so indeed, my lord," said I, " and the sight of it gives me a light heart."

" There is an obligation in happiness—do you not think so ? " says he musingly.

" I think so indeed," says I, " and one in sorrow too. If we are not here to try to do the best, in my humble opinion the sooner we are away the better for all parties."

" Ay, but if you were in my shoes, would you forgive him ? " asks my lord.

The suddenness of the attack a little gravelled me. " It is a duty laid upon us strictly," said I.

" Hut ! " said he. " These are expressions ! Do you forgive the man yourself ? "

" Well—no ! " said I. " God forgive me, I do not."

"Shake hands upon that!" cries my lord, with a kind of joviality.

"It is an ill sentiment to shake hands upon," said I, "for Christian people. I think I will give you mine on some more evangelical occasion."

This I said, smiling a little; but as for my lord, he went from the room laughing aloud.

For my lord's slavery to the child I can find no expression adequate. He lost himself in that continual thought: business, friends, and wife being all alike forgotten, or only remembered with a painful effort, like that of one struggling with a posset. It was most notable in the matter of his wife. Since I had known Durrisdeer, she had been the burthen of his thought and the loadstone of his eyes; and now she was quite cast out. I have seen him come to the door of a room, look round, and pass my lady over as though she were a dog before the fire. It would be Alexander he was seeking, and my lady knew it well. I have heard him speak to her so ruggedly that I nearly found it in my heart to intervene: the cause would still be the same, that she had in some way thwarted Alexander. Without doubt this was in the nature of a judgment on my lady; without doubt she had the tables turned upon her, as only Providence can do it; she who had been cold so many years to every mark of tenderness, it was her part now to be neglected.*

An odd situation resulted: that we had once more two parties in the house, and that now I was of my lady's. Not that ever I lost the love I bore my master. But, for one thing, he had the less use for my society. For another, I could not but compare the case of Mr. Alexander with that of Miss Katharine; for whom my lord had never found the least attention. And for a third, I was wounded by the change he discovered to his wife, which struck me in the nature of an infidelity. I could not but admire, besides, the constancy and kindness she displayed. Perhaps her sentiment to my lord, as it had been founded from the first in pity, was that rather of a mother than a wife ; perhaps it pleased her—if I may say so—to behold her two children so happy in each other ; the more as one had suffered so unjustly in the past. But, for all that, and though I could never trace in her one spark of jealousy, she must fall back for society on poor neglected Miss Katharine ; and I, on my part, came to pass my spare hours more and more with the mother and daughter. It would be easy to make too much of this division, for it was a pleasant family, as families go ; still the thing existed ; whether my lord knew it or not, I am in doubt. I do not think he did ; he was bound up so entirely in his son ; but the rest of us knew it, and in a manner suffered from the knowledge.

What troubled us most, however, was the great and growing danger to the child. My lord was his father over again ; it was to be feared the son would prove a second Master. Time has proved these fears to have been quite exaggerate. Certainly there is no more worthy gentleman to-day in Scotland than the seventh Lord Durrisdeer. Of my own exodus from his employment it does not become me to speak, above all in a memorandum written only to justify his father. . . .

[EDITOR'S NOTE.—*Five pages of Mr. Mackellar's MS. are here omitted. I have gathered from their perusal an impression that Mr. Mackellar, in his old age, was rather an exacting servant. Against the seventh Lord Durrisdeer (with whom, at any rate, we have no concern) nothing material is alleged.*—R. L. S.]

. . . But our fear at the time was lest he should turn out, in the person of his son, a second edition of his brother. My lady had tried to interject some wholesome discipline ; she had been glad to give that up, and now looked on with secret dismay ; sometimes she even spoke of it by hints ; and sometimes, when there was brought to her knowledge some monstrous instance of my lord's indulgence, she would betray herself in a gesture or perhaps an exclamation. As for myself, I was haunted by the thought both day and night : not so much for the child's sake as for the father's. The man had gone to sleep, he was dreaming a dream, and any rough awakening must infallibly prove mortal. That he should survive the child's death was inconceivable ; and the fear of its dishonour made me cover my face.

It was this continual preoccupation that screwed me up at last to a remonstrance : a matter worthy to be narrated in detail. My lord and I sat one day at the same table upon some tedious business of detail ; I have said that he had lost his former interest in such occupations ; he was plainly itching to be gone, and he looked fretful, weary, and methought older than I had ever previously observed. I suppose it was the haggard face that put me suddenly upon my enterprise.

"My lord," said I, with my head down, and feigning to continue my occupation—" or, rather, let me call you again by the name of Mr. Henry, for I fear your anger, and want you to think upon old times——"

"My good Mackellar !" said he ; and that in tones so kindly that I had near forsook my purpose. But I called to mind that I was speaking for his good, and stuck to my colours.

"Has it never come in upon your mind what you are doing ? " I asked.

"What I am doing ? " he repeated ; "I was never good at guessing riddles."

"What you are doing with your son ? " said I.

"Well," said he, with some defiance in his tone, "and what am I doing with my son ? "

"Your father was a very good man," says I, straying from the direct path. "But do you think he was a wise father ? "

There was a pause before he spoke, and then : "I say nothing against him," he replied. "I had the most cause perhaps ; but I say nothing."

"Why, there it is," said I. "You had the cause at least. And yet your father was a good man ; I never knew a better, save on the one point, nor yet a wiser. Where he stumbled, it is highly possible another man should fall. He had the two sons——"

My lord rapped suddenly and violently on the table. "What is this?" cried he. "Speak out!"

"I will, then," said I, my voice almost strangled with the thumping of my heart. "If you continue to indulge Mr. Alexander, you are following in your father's footsteps. Beware, my lord, lest (when he grows up) your son should follow in the Master's."

I had never meant to put the thing so crudely; but in the extreme of fear there comes a brutal kind of courage, the most brutal indeed of all; and I burnt my ships with that plain word. I never had the answer. When I lifted my head my lord had risen to his feet, and the next moment he fell heavily on the floor. The fit or seizure endured not very long; he came to himself vacantly, put his hand to his head, which I was then supporting, and says he, in a broken voice: "I have been ill," and a little after: "Help me." I got him to his feet, and he stood pretty well, though he kept hold of the table. "I have been ill, Mackellar," he said again. "Something broke, Mackellar— or was going to break, and then all swam away. I think I was very angry. Never you mind, Mackellar; never you mind, my man. I wouldnae*hurt a hair upon your head. Too much has come and gone. It's a certain thing between us two. But I think, Mackellar, I will go to Mrs. Henry —I think I will go to Mrs. Henry," said he, and got pretty steadily from the room, leaving me overcome with penitence.

Presently the door flew open, and my lady swept in with flashing eyes. "What is all this?" she cried. "What have you done to my husband? Will nothing teach you your position in this house? Will you never cease from making and meddling?"

"My lady," said I, "since I have been in this house I have had plenty of hard words. For a while they were my daily diet, and I swallowed them all. As for to-day, you may call me what you please ; you will never find the name hard enough for such a blunder. And yet I meant it for the best."

I told her all with ingenuity, even as it is written here ; and when she had heard me out, she pondered, and I could see her animosity fall. " Yes," she said, " you meant well indeed. I have had the same thought myself, or the same temptation rather, which makes me pardon you. But, dear God, can you not understand that he can bear no more ? He can bear no more ! " she cried. " The cord is stretched to snapping. What matters the future if he have one or two good days ? "

" Amen," said I. " I will meddle no more. I am pleased enough that you should recognise the kindness of my meaning."

" Yes," said my lady ; " but when it came to the point, I have to suppose your courage failed you ; for what you said was said cruelly." She paused, looking at me ; then suddenly smiled a little, and said a singular thing : " Do you know what you are, Mr. Mackellar ? You are an old maid."

No more incident of any note occurred in the family until the return of that ill-starred man, the Master. But I have to place here a second extract from the memoirs of Chevalier Burke, interesting in itself, and highly necessary for my purpose. It is our only sight of the Master on his Indian travels ; and the first word in these pages of Secundra Dass. One fact, it is to observe, appears here very clearly, which if we had known some twenty years ago, how many calamities and sorrows had been spared !—that Secundra Dass spoke English.

CHAPTER VII

ADVENTURE OF CHEVALIER BURKE IN INDIA

Extracted from his Memoirs

. . . Here was I, therefore, on the streets of that city, the name of which I cannot call to mind, while even then I was so ill acquainted with its situation that I knew not whether to go south or north. The alert being sudden, I had run forth without shoes or stockings; my hat had been struck from my head in the mellay; my kit was in the hands of the English; I had no companion but the cipaye, no weapon but my sword, and the devil a coin in my pocket. In short, I was for all the world like one of those calendars* with whom Mr. Galland* has made us acquainted in his elegant tales. These gentlemen, you will remember, were for ever falling in with extraordinary incidents; and I was myself upon the brink of one so astonishing that I protest I cannot explain it to this day.

The cipaye was a very honest man; he had served many years with the French colours, and would have let himself be cut to pieces for any of the brave countrymen of Mr. Lally.* It is the same fellow (his name has quite escaped me) of whom I have narrated already a surprising instance of generosity of mind—when he found Mr. de Fessac and myself upon the ramparts, entirely overcome with liquor, and covered us with straw while the commandant was passing by. I consulted him, therefore, with perfect freedom. It was a fine question what to do; but we decided at last to escalade a garden wall, where we could certainly sleep in the shadow of the trees,

147

and might perhaps find an occasion to get hold of a pair
of slippers and a turban. In that part of the city we had
only the difficulty of the choice, for it was a quarter consisting entirely of walled gardens, and the lanes which
divided them were at that hour of the night deserted.
I gave the cipaye a back, and we had soon dropped into
a large enclosure full of trees. The place was soaking
with the dew, which, in that country, is exceedingly un-
wholesome, above all to whites ; yet my fatigue was so
extreme that I was already half asleep, when the cipaye
recalled me to my senses. In the far end of the enclosure
a bright light had suddenly shone out, and continued to
burn steadily among the leaves. It was a circumstance
highly unusual in such a place and hour ; and, in our
situation, it behoved us to proceed with some timidity.
The cipaye was sent to reconnoitre, and pretty soon returned with the intelligence that we had fallen extremely
amiss, for the house belonged to a white man, who was in
all likelihood English.

"Faith," says I, "if there is a white man to be seen,
I will have a look at him ; for, the Lord be praised ! there
are more sorts than the one ! "

The cipaye led me forward accordingly to a place from
which I had a clear view upon the house. It was surrounded with a wide verandah ; a lamp, very well trimmed,
stood upon the floor of it, and on either side of the lamp
there sat a man, cross-legged, after the Oriental manner.
Both, besides, were bundled up in muslin like two natives ;
and yet one of them was not only a white man, but a man
very well known to me and the reader, being indeed that
very Master of Ballantrae of whose gallantry and genius
I have had to speak so often. Word had reached me that
he was come to the Indies, though we had never met
and I heard little of his occupations. But, sure, I had
no sooner recognised him, and found myself in the arms
of so old a comrade, than I supposed my tribulations
were quite done. I stepped plainly forth into the light of

the moon, which shone exceeding strong, and hailing
Ballantrae by name, made him in a few words master of
my grievous situation. He turned, started the least thing
in the world, looked me fair in the face while I was speaking,
and when I had done addressed himself to his companion
in the barbarous native dialect. The second person, who
was of an extraordinary delicate appearance, with legs
like walking canes and fingers like the stalk of a tobacco-
pipe,[1] now rose to his feet.

"The Sahib," says he, "understands no English
language. I understand it myself, and I see you make
some small mistake—O! which may happen very often.
But the Sahib would be glad to know how you come in a
garden?"

"Ballantrae!" I cried, "have you the damned impudence to deny me to my face?"

Ballantrae never moved a muscle, staring at me like
an image in a pagoda.

"The Sahib understands no English language," says
the native, as glib as before. "He be glad to know how
you come in a garden?"

"O! the divil* fetch him," says I. "He would be
glad to know how I come in a garden, would he? Well,
now, my dear man, just have the civility to tell the Sahib,
with my kind love, that we are two soliders here whom he
never met and never heard of, but the cipaye is a broth of
a boy, and I am a broth of a boy* myself; and if we don't
get a full meal of meat, and a turban, and slippers, and
the value of a gold mohur in small change as a matter of
convenience, bedad, my friend, I could lay my finger on
a garden where there is going to be trouble."

They carried their comedy so far as to converse a
while in Hindustanee; and then says the Hindu, with the
same smile, but sighing as if he were tired of the repetition,
"The Sahib would be glad to know how you come in a
garden?"

[1] *Note by Mr. Mackellar.*—Plainly Secundra Dass.—E. McK.

" Is that the way of it ? " says I, and laying my hand on my sword-hilt I bade the cipaye draw.

Ballantrae's Hindu, still smiling, pulled out a pistol from his bosom, and though Ballantrae himself never moved a muscle I knew him well enough to be sure he was prepared.

" The Sahib thinks you better go away," says the Hindu.

Well, to be plain, it was what I was thinking myself ; for the report of a pistol would have been, under Providence, the means of hanging the pair of us.

" Tell the Sahib I consider him no gentleman," says I, and turned away with a gesture of contempt.

I was not gone three steps when the voice of the Hindu called me back. " The Sahib would be glad to know if you are a dam low Irishman," says he ; and at the words Ballantrae smiled and bowed very low.

" What is that ? " says I.

" The Sahib say you ask your friend Mackellar," says the Hindu. " The Sahib he cry quits."

" Tell the Sahib I will give him a cure for the Scots fiddle when next we meet," cried I.

The pair were still smiling as I left.

There is little doubt some flaws may be picked in my own behaviour ; and when a man, however gallant, appeals to posterity with an account of his exploits, he must almost certainly expect to share the fate of Cæsar and Alexander, and to meet with some detractors. But there is one thing that can never be laid at the door of Francis Burke : he never turned his back on a friend. . . .

(Here follows a passage which the Chevalier Burke has been at the pains to delete before sending me his manuscript. Doubtless it was some very natural complaint of what he supposed to be an indiscretion on my part ; though, indeed, I can call none to mind. Perhaps Mr. Henry was less guarded ; or it is just possible the Master found the means to examine my correspondence, and himself read the letter from Troyes : in revenge for which this cruel jest was perpetrated on Mr. Burke in his extreme necessity. The Master, for all his wickedness, was not without some natural affection ; I believe he was sincerely attached to Mr. Burke in the beginning ; but the thought of treachery dried up the springs of his very shallow friendship, and his detestable nature appeared naked.—E.McK.)

CHAPTER VIII

THE ENEMY IN THE HOUSE

It is a strange thing that I should be at a stick for a date
—the date, besides, of an incident that changed the very
nature of my life, and sent us all into foreign lands. But
the truth is, I was stricken out of all my habitudes, and find
my journals very ill redd-up,[1] the day not indicated sometimes for a week or two together, and the whole fashion of
the thing like that of a man near desperate. It was late
in March at least, or early in April, 1764. I had slept
heavily, and wakened with a premonition of some evil to
befall. So strong was this upon my spirit that I hurried
downstairs in my shirt and breeches, and my hand (I
remember) shook upon the rail. It was a cold, sunny
morning, with a thick white frost ; the blackbirds sang
exceeding sweet and loud about the house of Durrisdeer,
and there was a noise of the sea in all the chambers. As I
came by the doors of the hall, another sound arrested me
—of voices talking. I drew nearer, and stood like a man
dreaming. Here was certainly a human voice, and that
in my own master's house, and yet I knew it not ; certainly
human speech, and that in my native land ; and yet, listen
as I pleased, I could not catch one syllable. An old tale
started up in my mind of a fairy wife (or perhaps only a
wandering stranger), that came to the place of my fathers
some generations back, and stayed the matter of a week,
talking often in a tongue that signified nothing to the
hearers ; and went again, as she had come, under cloud of

[1] Ordered.

night, leaving not so much as a name behind her. A
little fear I had, but more curiosity ; and I opened the
hall-door, and entered.

The supper-things still lay upon the table ; the shutters
were still closed, although day peeped in the divisions ;
and the great room was lighted only with a single taper
and the shining of the fire.* Close in the chimney sat two
men. The one that was wrapped in a cloak and wore
boots, I knew at once : it was the bird of ill omen back
again. Of the other, who was set close to the red embers,
and made up into a bundle like a mummy, I could but
see that he was an alien, of a darker hue than any man
of Europe, very frailly built, with a singular tall forehead,
and a secret eye. Several packets and a small valise were
on the floor ; and to judge by the smallness of this luggage,
and by the condition of the Master's boots, grossly patched
by some unscrupulous country cobbler, evil had not
prospered.

He rose upon my entrance ; our eyes crossed ; and I
know not why it should have been, but my courage rose
like a lark on a May morning.

" Ha ! " said I, " is this you ? "—and I was pleased
with the unconcern of my own voice.

" It is even myself, worthy Mackellar," says the Master.

" This time you have brought the black dog visibly
upon your back," I continued.

" Referring to Secundra Dass ? " asked the Master.
" Let me present you. He is a native gentleman of India."

" Hum ! " said I. " I am no great lover either of you
or your friends, Mr. Bally. But I will let a little daylight
in, and have a look at you." And so saying, I undid the
shutters of the eastern window.

By the light of the morning I could perceive the man
was changed. Later, when we were all together, I was
more struck to see how lightly time had dealt with him ;
but the first glance was otherwise.

" You are getting an old man," said I.

A shade came upon his face. " If you could see yourself," said he, " you would perhaps not dwell upon the topic."

" Hut ! " I returned, " old age is nothing to me. I think I have been always old ; and I am now, I thank God, better known and more respected. It is not every one that can say that, Mr. Bally ! The lines in *your* brow are calamities ; your life begins to close in upon you like a prison ; death will soon be rapping at the door ; and I see not from what source you are to draw your consolations."

Here the Master addressed himself to Secundra Dass in Hindustanee, from which I gathered (I freely confess, with a high degree of pleasure) that my remarks annoyed him. All this while, you may be sure, my mind had been busy upon other matters, even while I rallied my enemy ; and chiefly as to how I should communicate secretly and quickly with my lord. To this, in the breathing-space now given me, I turned all the forces of my mind ; when, suddenly shifting my eyes, I was aware of the man himself standing in the doorway, and, to all appearance, quite composed. He had no sooner met my looks than he stepped across the threshold. The Master heard him coming, and advanced upon the other side ; about four feet apart, these brothers came to a full pause, and stood exchanging steady looks, and then my lord smiled, bowed a little forward, and turned briskly away.

" Mackellar," says he, " we must see to breakfast for these travellers."

It was plain the Master was a trifle disconcerted ; but he assumed the more impudence of speech and manner. " I am as hungry as a hawk," says he. " Let it be something good, Henry."

My lord turned to him with the same hard smile. " Lord Durrisdeer," says he.

" O ! never in the family," returned the Master.

" Every one in this house renders me my proper title,"

says my lord. " If it please you to make an exception, I will leave you to consider what appearance it will bear to strangers, and whether it may not be translated as an effect of impotent jealousy."

I could have clapped my hands together with delight : the more so as my lord left no time for any answer, but, bidding me with a sign to follow him, went straight out of the hall.

" Come quick," says he ; " we have to sweep vermin from the house." And he sped through the passages, with so swift a step that I could scarce keep up with him, straight to the door of John Paul, the which he opened without summons and walked in. John was, to all appearance, sound asleep, but my lord made no pretence of waking him.

" John Paul," said he, speaking as quietly as ever I heard him, " you served my father long, or I would pack you from the house like a dog. If in half an hour's time I find you gone, you shall continue to receive your wages in Edinburgh. If you linger here or in St. Bride's—old man, old servant, and altogether—I shall find some very astonishing way to make you smart for your disloyalty. Up and begone. The door you let them in by will serve for your departure. I do not choose my son shall see your face again."

" I am rejoiced to find you bear the thing so quietly," said I, when we were forth again by ourselves.

" Quietly ! " cries he, and put my hand suddenly against his heart, which struck upon his bosom like a sledge.

At this revelation I was filled with wonder and fear. There was no constitution could bear so violent a strain— his least of all, that was unhinged already ; and I decided in my mind that we must bring this monstrous situation to an end.

" It would be well, I think, if I took word to my lady," said I. Indeed, he should have gone himself, but I counted —not in vain—on his indifference.

" Ay," says he, " do. I will hurry breakfast : we must all appear at the table, even Alexander ; it must appear we are untroubled."

I ran to my lady's room, and with no preparatory cruelty disclosed my news.

" My mind was long ago made up," said she. " We must make our packets secretly to-day, and leave secretly to-night. Thank Heaven, we have another house ! The first ship that sails shall bear us to New York."

" And what of him ? " I asked.

" We leave him Durrisdeer," she cried. " Let him work his pleasure upon that."

" Not so, by your leave," said I. " There shall be a dog at his heels that can hold fast. Bed he shall have, and board, and a horse to ride upon, if he behave himself ; but the keys—if you think well of it, my lady—shall be left in the hands of one Mackellar. There will be good care taken ; trust him for that."

" Mr. Mackellar," she cried, " I thank you for that thought. All shall be left in your hands. If we must go into a savage country, I bequeath it to you to take our vengeance. Send Macconochie to St. Bride's, to arrange privately for horses and to call the lawyer. My lord must leave procuration."

At that moment my lord came to the door, and we opened our plan to him.

" I will never hear of it," he cried ; " he would think I feared him. I will stay in my own house, please God, until I die. There lives not the man can beard me out of it. Once and for all, here I am, and here I stay, in spite of all the devils in hell." I can give no idea of the vehemency of his words and utterance ; but we both stood aghast, and I in particular, who had been a witness of his former self-restraint.

My lady looked at me with an appeal that went to my heart and recalled me to my wits. I made her a private sign to go, and when my lord and I were alone, went up to him where he was racing to and fro in one end of the room like a half-lunatic, and set my hand firmly on his shoulder.

" My lord," says I, " I am going to be the plain-dealer once more ; if for the last time, so much the better, for I am grown weary of the part."

" Nothing will change me," he answered.   " God forbid I should refuse to hear you ; but nothing will change me." This he said firmly, with no signal of the former violence, which already raised my hopes.

" Very well," said I.   " I can afford to waste my breath."   I pointed to a chair, and he sat down and looked at me.   " I can remember a time when my lady very much neglected you," said I.

" I never spoke of it while it lasted," returned my lord, with a high flush of colour ; " and it is all changed now."

" Do you know how much ? " I said.   " Do you know how much it is all changed ?   The tables are turned, my lord !   It is my lady that now courts you for a word, a look—ay, and courts you in vain.   Do you know with whom she passes her days while you are out gallivanting in the policies ?   My lord, she is glad to pass them with a certain dry old grieve[1] of the name of Ephraim Mackellar ; and I think you may be able to remember what that means, for I am the more in a mistake or you were once driven to the same company yourself."

" Mackellar ! " cries my lord, getting to his feet.   " O my God, Mackellar ! "

" It is neither the name of Mackellar nor the name of God that can change the truth," said I ; " and I am telling you the fact.   Now for you, that suffered so much, to deal out the same suffering to another, is that the part of any Christian ?   But you are so swallowed up in your new friend that the old are all forgotten.   They are all clean vanished from your memory.   And yet they stood by you at the darkest ; my lady not the least.   And does my lady

[1] Land steward.

ever cross your mind ?   Does it ever cross your mind what
she went through that night ?—or what manner of a wife
she has been to you thenceforward ?—or in what kind of
a position she finds herself to-day ?   Never.   It is your
pride to stay and face him out, and she must stay along
with you.   O ! my lord's pride—that's the great affair !
And yet she is the woman, and you are a great hulking
man !   She is the woman that you swore to protect ; and,
more betoken, the own mother of that son of yours ! "

" You are speaking very bitterly, Mackellar," said he ;
" but, the Lord knows, I fear you are speaking very true.
I have not proved worthy of my happiness.   Bring my
lady back."

My lady was waiting near at hand to learn the issue.
When I brought her in, my lord took a hand of each of us,
and laid them both upon his bosom.   " I have had two
friends in my life," said he.   " All the comfort ever I had,
it came from one or other.   When you two are in a mind,
I think I would be an ungrateful dog——"   He shut his
mouth very hard, and looked on us with swimming eyes.
" Do what ye like with me," says he, " only don't think——"
He stopped again.   " Do what you please with me : God
knows I love and honour you."   And dropping our two
hands, he turned his back and went and gazed out of the
window.   But my lady ran after, calling his name, and
threw herself upon his neck in a passion of weeping.

I went out and shut the door behind me, and stood and
thanked God from the bottom of my heart.

At the breakfast-board, according to my lord's design,
we were all met.   The Master had by that time plucked
off his patched boots and made a toilet suitable to the hour ;
Secundra Dass was no longer bundled up in wrappers, but
wore a decent plain black suit, which misbecame him
strangely ; and the pair were at the great window, looking
forth, when the family entered.   They turned ; and the
black man (as they had already named him in the house)

bowed almost to his knees, but the Master was for running
forward like one of the family. My lady stopped him,
curtsying low from the far end of the hall, and keeping her
children at her back. My lord was a little in front : so
there were the three cousins of Durrisdeer face to face.
The hand of time was very legible on all ; I seemed to
read in their changed faces a *memento mori ;* and what
affected me still more, it was the wicked man that bore
his years the handsomest. My lady was quite transfigured
into the matron, a becoming woman for the head of a great
tableful of children and dependants. My lord was grown
slack in his limbs ; he stooped ; he walked with a running
motion, as though he had learned again from Mr. Alexander ;
his face was drawn ; it seemed a trifle longer than of old ;
and it wore at times a smile very singularly mingled, and
which (in my eyes) appeared both bitter and pathetic.
But the Master still bore himself erect, although perhaps
with effort ; his brow barred about the centre with imperious lines, his mouth set as for command. He had all
the gravity and something of the splendour of Satan in
the " Paradise Lost." I could not help but see the man with
admiration, and was only surprised that I saw him with so
little fear.

But indeed (as long as we were at the table) it seemed
as if his authority were quite vanished and his teeth all
drawn. We had known him a magician that controlled
the elements ; and here he was, transformed into an
ordinary gentleman, chatting like his neighbours at the
breakfast-board. For now the father was dead, and my
lord and lady reconciled, in what ear was he to pour his
calumnies ? It came upon me in a kind of vision how
hugely I had overrated the man's subtlety. He had his
malice still ; he was false as ever ; and, the occasion being
gone that made his strength, he sat there impotent ; he
was still the viper, but now spent his venom on a file.
Two more thoughts occurred to me while yet we sat at
breakfast : the first, that he was abashed—I had almost

said, distressed—to find his wickedness quite unavailing ; the second, that perhaps my lord was in the right, and we did amiss to fly from our dismasted enemy. But my poor master's leaping heart came in my mind, and I remembered it was for his life we played the coward.

When the meal was over, the Master followed me to my room, and, taking a chair (which I had never offered him), asked me what was to be done with him.

" Why, Mr. Bally," said I, " the house will still be open to you for a time."

" For a time ? " says he. " I do not know if I quite take your meaning."

" It is plain enough," said I. " We keep you for our reputation ; as soon as you shall have publicly disgraced yourself by some of your misconduct, we shall pack you forth again."

" You are become an impudent rogue," said the Master, bending his brows at me dangerously.

" I learned in a good school," I returned. " And you must have perceived yourself that with my old lord's death your power is quite departed. I do not fear you now, Mr. Bally ; I think even—God forgive me—that I take a certain pleasure in your company."

He broke out in a burst of laughter, which I clearly saw to be assumed.

" I have come with empty pockets," says he, after a pause.

" I do not think there will be any money going," I replied. " I would advise you not to build on that."

" I shall have something to say on the point," he returned.

" Indeed ? " said I. " I have not a guess what it will be, then."

" O ! you affect confidence," said the Master. " I have still one strong position—that you people fear a scandal, and I enjoy it."

" Pardon me, Mr. Bally," says I. " We do not in the least fear a scandal against you."

He laughed again. " You have been studying repartee," he said. " But speech is very easy, and sometimes very deceptive. I warn you fairly : you will find me vitriol in the house. You would do wiser to pay money down and see my back." And with that he waved his hand to me and left the room.

A little after, my lord came with the lawyer, Mr. Carlyle ; a bottle of old wine was brought, and we all had a glass before we fell to business. The necessary deeds were then prepared and executed, and the Scots estates made over in trust to Mr. Carlyle and myself.

" There is one point, Mr. Carlyle," said my lord, when these affairs had been adjusted, " on which I wish that you would do us justice. This sudden departure coinciding with my brother's return will be certainly commented on. I wish you would discourage any conjunction of the two."

" I will make a point of it, my lord," said Mr. Carlyle. " The Mas—Mr. Bally does not, then, accompany you ? "

" It is a point I must approach," said my lord. " Mr. Bally remains at Durrisdeer, under the care of Mr. Mackellar ; and I do not mean that he shall even know our destination."

" Common report, however——" began the lawyer.

" Ah ! but, Mr. Carlyle, this is to be a secret quite among ourselves," interrupted my lord. " None but you and Mackellar are to be made acquainted with my movements."

" And Mr. Bally stays here ? Quite so," said Mr. Carlyle. " The powers you leave——" Then he broke off again. " Mr. Mackellar, we have a rather heavy weight upon us."

" No doubt, sir," said I.

" No doubt," said he. " Mr. Bally will have no voice ? "

" He will have no voice," said my lord ; " and, I hope, no influence. Mr. Bally is not a good adviser."

" I see," said the lawyer.—" By the way, has Mr. Bally means ? "

" I understand him to have nothing," replied my lord. " I give him table, fire, and candle in this house."

" And in the matter of an allowance ? If I am to share the responsibility, you will see how highly desirable it is that I should understand your views," said the laywer. " On the question of an allowance ? "

" There will be no allowance," said my lord. " I wish Mr. Bally to live very private. We have not always been gratified with his behaviour."

" And in the matter of money," I added, " he has shown himself an infamous bad husband. Glance your eye upon that docket, Mr. Carlyle, where I have brought together the different sums the man has drawn from the estate in the last fifteen or twenty years. The total is pretty."

Mr. Carlyle made the motion of whistling. " I had no guess of this," said he. " Excuse me once more, my lord, if I appear to push you ; but it is really desirable I should penetrate your intentions. Mr. Mackellar might die, when I should find myself alone upon this trust. Would it not be rather your lordship's preference that Mr. Bally should—ahem—should leave the country ? "

My lord looked at Mr. Carlyle. " Why do you ask that ? " said he.

" I gather, my lord, that Mr. Bally is not a comfort to his family," says the lawyer, with a smile.

My lord's face became suddenly knotted. " I wish he was in hell ! " cried he, and filled himself a glass of wine, but with a hand so tottering that he spilled the half into his bosom. This was the second time that, in the midst of the most regular and wise behaviour, his animosity had spurted out. It startled Mr. Carlyle, who observed my lord thenceforth with covert curiosity ; and to me it re-stored the certainty that we were acting for the best in view of my lord's health and reason.

Except for this explosion the interview was very
successfully conducted. No doubt Mr. Carlyle would talk,
as lawyers do, little by little. We could thus feel we had
laid the foundations of a better feeling in the country, and
the man's own misconduct would certainly complete what
we had begun. Indeed, before his departure, the lawyer
showed us there had already gone abroad some glimmerings
of the truth.

"I should perhaps explain to you, my lord," said he,
pausing, with his hat in his hand, "that I have not been
altogether surprised with your lordship's dispositions in
the case of Mr. Bally. Something of this nature oozed
out when he was last in Durrisdeer. There was some talk
of a woman at St. Bride's, to whom you had behaved extremely handsome, and Mr. Bally with no small degree of
cruelty. There was the entail, again, which was much
controverted. In short, there was no want of talk, back
and forward; and some of our wiseacres took up a strong
opinion. I remained in suspense, as became one of my
cloth; but Mr. Mackellar's docket here has finally opened
my eyes.—I do not think, Mr. Mackellar, that you and I
will give him that much rope."

The rest of that important day passed prosperously
through. It was our policy to keep the enemy in view,
and I took my turn to be his watchman with the rest.
I think his spirits rose as he perceived us to be so attentive,
and I know that mine insensibly declined. What chiefly
daunted me was the man's singular dexterity to worm
himself into our troubles. You may have felt (after a
horse accident) the hand of a bone-setter artfully divide
and interrogate the muscles, and settle strongly on the
injured place? It was so with the Master's tongue, that
was so cunning to question; and his eyes, that were so
quick to observe. I seemed to have said nothing, and yet
to have let all out. Before I knew where I was the man
was condoling with me on my lord's neglect of my lady

and myself, and his hurtful indulgence to his son. On this
last point I perceived him (with panic fear) to return
repeatedly. The boy had displayed a certain shrinking
from his uncle ; it was strong in my mind his father had
been fool enough to indoctrinate the same, which was no
wise beginning : and when I looked upon the man before
me, still so handsome, so apt a speaker, with so great a
variety of fortunes to relate, I saw he was the very personage
to captivate a boyish fancy. John Paul had left only that
morning ; it was not to be supposed he had been altogether
dumb upon his favourite subject : so that here would be
Mr. Alexander in the part of Dido, with a curiosity inflamed
to hear ; and there would be the Master, like a diabolical
Æneas, full of matter the most pleasing in the world to any
youthful ear, such as battles, sea-disasters, flights, the
forests of the West, and (since his later voyage) the ancient
cities of the Indies. How cunningly these baits might be
employed, and what an empire might be so founded, little
by little, in the mind of any boy, stood obviously clear to
me. There was no inhibition, so long as the man was in
the house, that would be strong enough to hold these two
apart ; for if it be hard to charm serpents, it is no very
difficult thing to cast a glamour on a little chip of manhood
not very long in breeches. I recalled an ancient sailor-
man who dwelt in a lone house beyond the Figgate Whins
(I believe, he called it after Portobello), and how the boys
would troop out of Leith on a Saturday, and sit and listen
to his swearing tales, as thick as crows about a carrion : a
thing I often remarked as I went by, a young student, on
my own more meditative holiday diversion. Many of these
boys went, no doubt, in the face of an express command ;
many feared, and even hated, the old brute of whom they
made their hero ; and I have seen them flee from him when
he was tipsy, and stone him when he was drunk. And yet
there they came each Saturday ! How much more easily
would a boy like Mr. Alexander fall under the influence of
a high-looking, high-spoken gentleman-adventurer, who

should conceive the fancy to entrap him; and the influence gained, how easy to employ it for the child's perversion!

I doubt if our enemy had named Mr. Alexander three times before I perceived which way his mind was aiming—all this train of thought and memory passed in one pulsation through my own—and you may say I started back as though an open hole had gaped across a pathway. Mr. Alexander: there was the weak point, there was the Eve in our perishable paradise; and the serpent was already hissing on the trail.

I promise you, I went the more heartily about the preparations; my last scruple gone, the danger of delay written before me in huge characters. From that moment forth I seem not to have sat down or breathed. Now I would be at my post with the Master and his Indian; now in the garret buckling a valise; now sending forth Macconochie by the side postern and the wood-path to bear it to the trysting-place; and, again, snatching some words of counsel with my lady. This was the *verso* of our life in Durrisdeer that day; but on the *recto* all appeared quite settled, as of a family at home in its paternal seat; and what perturbation may have been observable, the Master would set down to the blow of his unlooked-for coming, and the fear he was accustomed to inspire.

Supper went creditably off, cold salutations passed, and the company trooped to their respective chambers. I attended the Master to the last. We had put him next door to his Indian, in the north wing; because that was the most distant and could be severed from the body of the house with doors. I saw he was a kind friend or a good master (whichever it was) to his Secundra Dass—seeing to his comfort; mending the fire with his own hand, for the Indian complained of cold; inquiring as to the rice on which the stranger made his diet; talking with him pleasantly in the Hindustanee, while I stood by, my candle in my hand, and affected to be overcome with slumber.

At length the Master observed my signals of distress. " I perceive," says he, " that you have all your ancient habits : early to bed and early to rise. Yawn yourself away ! "

Once in my own room, I made the customary motions of undressing, so that I might time myself ; and when the cycle was complete, set my tinder-box ready, and blew out my taper. The matter of an hour afterward I made a light again, put on my shoes of list that I had worn by my lord's sick-bed, and set forth into the house to call the voyagers. All were dressed and waiting—my lord, my lady, Miss Katharine, Mr. Alexander, my lady's woman Christie ; and I observed the effect of secrecy even upon quite innocent persons, that one after another showed in the chink of the door a face as white as paper. We slipped out of the side postern into a night of darkness, scarce broken by a star or two ; so that at first we groped and stumbled and fell among the bushes. A few hundred yards up the wood-path Macconochie was waiting us with a great lantern ; so the rest of the way we went easy enough, but still in a kind of guilty silence. A little beyond the abbey the path debouched on the main road ; and some quarter of a mile farther, at the place called Eagles, where the moors begin, we saw the lights of the two carriages stand shining by the wayside. Scarce a word or two was uttered at our parting, and these regarded business : a silent grasping of hands, a turning of faces aside, and the thing was over ; the horses broke into a trot, the lamplight sped like Will-o'-the-Wisp upon the broken moorland, it dipped beyond Stony Brae ; and there were Macconochie and I alone with our lantern on the road. There was one thing more to wait for, and that was the reappearance of the coach upon Cartmore. It seems they must have pulled up upon the summit, looked back for a last time, and seen our lantern not yet moved away from the place of separation. For a lamp was taken from a carriage, and waved three times up and down by way of a farewell. And then they were gone indeed, having looked their last on the kind roof of Durrisdeer, their faces toward a barbarous country. I never knew before the greatness of that vault of night in which we two poor serving-men—the one old, and the one elderly —stood for the first time deserted ; I had never felt before my own dependency upon the countenance of others. The sense of isolation burned in my bowels like a fire. It seemed that we who remained at home were the true exiles, and that Durrisdeer and Solwayside, and all that made my country native, its air good to me, and its language welcome, had gone forth and was far over the sea with my old masters.

The remainder of that night I paced to and fro on the smooth highway, reflecting on the future and the past. My thoughts, which at first dwelled tenderly on those who were just gone, took a more manly temper as I considered what remained for me to do. Day came upon the inland mountain-tops, and the fowls began to cry, and the smoke of homesteads to arise in the brown bosom of the moors, before I turned my face homeward, and went down the path to where the roof of Durrisdeer shone in the morning by the sea.

At the customary hour I had the Master called, and awaited his coming in the hall with a quiet mind. He looked about him at the empty room and the three covers set.

" We are a small party," said he.   " How comes that ? "

" This is the party to which we must grow accustomed," I replied.

He looked at me with a sudden sharpness. " What is all this ? " said he.

" You and I and your friend Mr. Dass are now all the company," I replied.   " My lord, my lady, and the children are gone upon a voyage."

" Upon my word ! " said he.   " Can this be possible ? I have indeed fluttered your Volscians in Corioli ! But this is no reason why our breakfast should go cold. Sit

down, Mr. Mackellar, if you please "—taking, as he spoke,
the head of the table, which I had designed to occupy
myself—" and as we eat, you can give me the details of
this evasion."

I could see he was more affected than his language
carried, and I determined to equal him in coolness. " I
was about to ask you to take the head of the table," said
I ; " for though I am now thrust into the position of your
host, I could never forget that you were, after all, a member
of the family."

For a while he played the part of entertainer, giving
directions to Macconochie, who received them with an
evil grace, and attending specially upon Secundra. " And
where has my good family withdrawn to ? " he asked
carelessly.

" Ah ! Mr. Bally, that is another point," said I. " I
have no orders to communicate their destination."

" To me," he corrected.

" To any one," said I.

" It is the less pointed," said the Master ; " *c'est de bon
ton :* my brother improves as he continues. And I, dear
Mr. Mackellar ? "

" You will have bed and board, Mr. Bally," said I.
" I am permitted to give you the run of the cellar, which
is pretty reasonably stocked. You have only to keep well
with me, which is no very difficult matter, and you shall
want neither for wine nor a saddle-horse."

He made an excuse to send Macconochie from the
room.

" And for money ? " he inquired. " Have I to keep
well with my good friend Mackellar for my pocket-money
also ? This is a pleasing return to the principles of boy-
hood."

" There was no allowance made," said I ; " but I will
take it on myself to see you are supplied in moderation."

" In moderation ? " he repeated. " And you will take
it on yourself ? " He drew himself up, and looked about

the hall at the dark rows of portraits. " In the name of my ancestors, I thank you," says he ; and then, with a return to irony, " But there must certainly be an allowance for Secundra Dass ? " he said. " It is not possible they have omitted that ? "

" I will make a note of it, and ask instructions when I write," said I.

And he, with a sudden change of manner, and leaning forward with an elbow on the table—" Do you think this entirely wise ? "

" I execute my orders, Mr. Bally," said I.

" Profoundly modest," said the Master ; " perhaps not equally ingenuous. You told me yesterday my power was fallen with my father's death. How comes it, then, that a peer of the realm flees under cloud of night out of a house in which his fathers have stood several sieges ? that he conceals his address, which must be a matter of concern to his Gracious Majesty and to the whole republic ? and that he should leave me in possession, and under the paternal charge of his invaluable Mackellar ? This smacks to me of a very considerable and genuine apprehension."

I sought to interrupt him with some not very truthful denegation ; but he waved me down, and pursued his speech.

" I say, it smacks of it," he said ; " but I will go beyond that, for I think the apprehension grounded. I came to this house with some reluctancy. In view of the manner of my last departure, nothing but necessity could have induced me to return. Money, however, is that which I must have. You will not give with a good grace ; well, I have the power to force it from you. Inside of a week, without leaving Durrisdeer, I will find out where these fools are fled to. I will follow ; and when I have run my quarry down, I will drive a wedge into that family that shall once more burst it into shivers. I shall see then whether my Lord Durrisdeer " (said with indescribable scorn and rage) " will choose to buy my absence ; and you will all see whether, by that time, I decide for profit or revenge."

I was amazed to hear the man so open. The truth is, he was consumed with anger at my lord's successful flight, felt himself to figure as a dupe, and was in no humour to weigh language.

" Do you consider *this* entirely wise ? " said I, copying his words.

" These twenty years I have lived by my poor wisdom," he answered with a smile that seemed almost foolish in its vanity.

" And come out a beggar in the end," said I, " if beggar be a strong enough word for it."

" I would have you to observe, Mr. Mackellar," cried he, with a sudden imperious heat, in which I could not but admire him, " that I am scrupulously civil ; copy me in that, and we shall be the better friends."

Throughout this dialogue I had been incommoded by the observation of Secundra Dass. Not one of us, since the first word, had made a feint of eating : our eyes were in each other's faces—you might say, in each other's bosoms ; and those of the Indian troubled me with a certain changing brightness, as of comprehension. But I brushed the fancy aside, telling myself once more he understood no English ; only, from the gravity of both voices, and the occasional scorn and anger in the Master's, smelled out there was something of import in the wind.

For the matter of three weeks we continued to live together in the house of Durrisdeer : the beginning of that most singular chapter of my life—what I must call my intimacy with the Master. At first he was somewhat changeable in his behaviour : now civil, now returning to his old manner of flouting me to my face ; and in both I met him half-way. Thanks be to Providence, I had now no measure to keep with the man ; and I was never afraid of black brows, only of naked swords. So that I found a

certain entertainment in these bouts of incivility, and was
not always ill inspired in my rejoinders. At last (it was
at supper) I had a droll expression that entirely vanquished
him. He laughed again and again ; and " Who would
have guessed," he cried, " that this old wife had any wit
under his petticoats ? "

" It is no wit, Mr. Bally," said I : " a dry Scots humour,
and something of the driest." And, indeed, I never had
the least pretension to be thought a wit.

From that hour he was never rude with me, but all
passed between us in a manner of pleasantry. One of our
chief times of daffing [1] was when he required a horse,
another bottle, or some money. He would approach me
then after the manner of a schoolboy, and I would carry
it on by way of being his father : on both sides, with an
infinity of mirth. I could not but perceive that he thought
more of me, which tickled that poor part of mankind, the
vanity. He dropped, besides (I must suppose unconsciously), into a manner that was not only familiar, but
even friendly ; and this, on the part of one who had so
long detested me, I found the more insidious. He went
little abroad ; sometimes even refusing invitations. " No,"
he would say, " what do I care for these thick-headed
bonnet-lairds ? I will stay at home, Mackellar ; and we
shall share a bottle quietly, and have one of our good
talks." And, indeed, meal-time at Durrisdeer must have
been a delight to any one, by reason of the brilliancy of
the discourse. He would often express wonder at his
former indifference to my society. " But, you see," he
would add, " we were upon opposite sides. And so we
are to-day ; but let us never speak of that. I would think
much less of you if you were not staunch to your employer."
You are to consider he seemed to me quite impotent for
any evil ; and how it is a most engaging form of flattery
when (after many years) tardy justice is done to a man's
character and parts. But I have no thought to excuse

[1] Fooling.

myself. I was to blame; I let him cajole me, and, in short, I think the watch-dog was gone sound asleep, when he was suddenly aroused.

I should say the Indian was continually travelling to and fro in the house. He never spoke, save in his own dialect and with the Master; walked without sound; and was always turning up where you would least expect him, fallen into a deep abstraction, from which he would start (upon your coming) to mock you with one of his grovelling obeisances. He seemed so quiet, so frail, and so wrapped in his own fancies, that I came to pass him over without much regard, or even to pity him for a harmless exile from his country. And yet without doubt the creature was still eavesdropping; and without doubt it was through his stealth and my security that our secret reached the Master.

It was one very wild night, after supper, and when we had been making more than usually merry, that the blow fell on me.

" This is all very fine," says the Master, " but we should do better to be buckling our valise."

" Why so ? " I cried. " Are you leaving ? "

" We are all leaving to-morrow in the morning," said he. " For the port of Glascow first, thence for the province of New York."

I suppose I must have groaned aloud.

" Yes," he continued, " I boasted; I said a week, and it has taken me near twenty days. But never mind; I shall make it up; I will go the faster."

" Have you the money for this voyage ? " I asked.

" Dear and ingenuous personage, I have," said he. " Blame me, if you choose, for my duplicity; but while I have been wringing shillings from my daddy, I had a stock of my own put by against a rainy day. You will pay for your own passage, if you choose to accompany us on our flank march; I have enough for Secundra and myself, but not more—enough to be dangerous, not enough to be generous. There is, however, an outside seat upon the chaise which I will let you have upon a moderate commutation; so that the whole menagerie can go together—the house-dog, the monkey, and the tiger."

" I go with you," said I.

" I count upon it," said the Master. " You have seen me foiled; I mean you shall see me victorious. To gain that I will risk wetting you like a sop in this wild weather."

" And at least," I added, " you know very well you could not throw me off."

" Not easily," said he. " You put your finger on the point with your usual excellent good sense. I never fight with the inevitable."

" I suppose it is useless to appeal to you ? " said I.

" Believe me, perfectly," said he.

" And yet, if you would give me time, I could write——" I began.

" And what would be my Lord Durrisdeer's answer ? " asks he.

" Ay," said I, " that is the rub."

" And, at any rate, how much more expeditious that I should go myself! " says he. " But all this is quite a waste of breath. At seven to-morrow the chaise will be at the door. For I start from the door, Mackellar; I do not skulk through woods and take my chaise upon the wayside—shall we say, at Eagles ? "

My mind was now thoroughly made up. " Can you spare me quarter of an hour at St. Bride's ? " said I. " I have a little necessary business with Carlyle."

" An hour, if you prefer," said he. " I do not seek to deny that the money for your seat is an object to me; and you could always get the first to Glascow with saddle-horses."

" Well," said I, " I never thought to leave old Scotland."

" It will brisken you up," says he.

" This will be an ill journey for someone," I said. " I

think, sir, for you. Something speaks in my bosom; and so much it says plain—that this is an ill-omened journey."

"If you take to prophecy," says he, "listen to that."

There came up a violent squall off the open Solway, and the rain was dashed on the great windows.

"Do ye ken what that bodes, warlock?" said he, in a broad accent: "that there'll be a man Mackellar unco sick at sea."

When I got to my chamber, I sat there under a painful excitation, hearkening to the turmoil of the gale, which struck full upon that gable of the house. What with the pressure on my spirits, the eldritch cries of the wind among the turret-tops, and the perpetual trepidation of the masoned house, sleep fled my eyelids utterly. I sat by my taper, looking on the black panes of the window, where the storm appeared continually on the point of bursting in its entrance; and upon that empty field I beheld a perspective of consequences that made the hair to rise upon my scalp. The child corrupted, the home broken up, my master dead, or worse than dead, my mistress plunged in desolation—all these I saw before me painted brightly on the darkness; and the outcry of the wind appeared to mock at my inaction.

CHAPTER IX

MR. MACKELLAR'S JOURNEY WITH THE MASTER

THE chaise came to the door in a strong drenching mist. We took our leave in silence : the house of Durrisdeer standing with drooping gutters and windows closed, like a place dedicate to melancholy. I observed the Master kept his head out, looking back on these splashed walls and glimmering roofs, till they were suddenly swallowed in the mist ; and I must suppose some natural sadness fell upon the man at this departure ; or was it some prevision of the end ? At least, upon our mounting the long brae from Durrisdeer, as we walked side by side in the wet, he began first to whistle and then to sing the saddest of our country tunes, which sets folk weeping in a tavern, " Wandering Willie." The set of words he used with it I have not heard elsewhere, and could never come by any copy ; but some of them which were the most appropriate to our departure linger in my memory. One verse began—

" Home was home then, my dear, full of kindly faces ;
　Home was home then, my dear, happy for the child."

And ended somewhat thus—

" Now, when day dawns on the brow of the moorland,
　Lone stands the house, and the chimney-stone is cold,
Lone let it stand, now the folks are all departed,
　The kind hearts, the true hearts, that loved the place of old.'

I could never be a judge of the merit of these verses ; they were so hallowed by the melancholy of the air, and were sung (or rather " soothed ") to me by a master-singer at a time so fitting. He looked in my face when he had done, and saw that my eyes watered.

"Ah! Mackellar," said he, "do you think I have never a regret?"

"I do not think you could be so bad a man," said I, "if you had not all the machinery to be a good one."

"No, not all," says he: "not all. You are there in error. The malady of not wanting, my evangelist." But methought he sighed as he mounted again into the chaise.

All day long we journeyed in the same miserable weather: the mist besetting us closely, the heavens incessantly weeping on my head. The road lay over moorish hills, where was no sound but the crying of moor-fowl in the wet heather and the pouring of the swollen burns. Sometimes I would doze off in slumber, when I would find myself plunged at once in some foul and ominous nightmare, from the which I would awake strangling. Sometimes, if the way was steep and the wheels turning slowly, I would overhear the voices from within, talking in that tropical tongue which was to me as inarticulate as the piping of the fowls. Sometimes, at a longer ascent, the Master would set foot to ground and walk by my side, mostly without speech. And all the time, sleeping or waking, I beheld the same black perspective of approaching ruin; and the same pictures rose in my view, only they were now painted upon hill-side mist. One, I remember, stood before me with the colours of a true illusion. It showed me my lord seated at a table in a small room; his head, which was at first buried in his hands, he slowly raised, and turned upon me a countenance from which hope had fled. I saw it first on the black window-panes, my last night in Durrisdeer; it haunted and returned upon me half the voyage through; and yet it was no effect of lunacy, for I have come to a ripe old age with no decay of my intelligence; nor yet (as I was then tempted to suppose) a heaven-sent warning of the future, for all manner of calamities befell, not that calamity—and I saw many pitiful sights, but never that one.

It was decided we should travel on all night; and it was singular, once the dusk had fallen, my spirits some-what rose. The bright lamps, shining forth into the mist and on the smoking horses and the hodding post-boy, gave me perhaps an outlook intrinsically more cheerful than what day had shown; or perhaps my mind had become wearied of its melancholy. At least I spent some waking hours, not without satisfaction in my thoughts, although wet and weary in my body; and fell at last into a natural slumber without dreams. Yet I must have been at work even in the deepest of my sleep; and at work with at least a measure of intelligence. For I started broad awake, in the very act of crying out to myself

" Home was home then, my dear, happy for the child,"

stricken to find in it an appropriateness, which I had not yesterday observed, to the Master's detestable purpose in the present journey.

We were then close upon the city of Glascow, where we were soon breakfasting together at an inn, and where (as the devil would have it) we found a ship in the very article of sailing. We took our places in the cabin; and, two days after, carried our effects on board. Her name was the *Nonesuch*, a very ancient ship, and very happily named. By all accounts this should be her last voyage; people shook their heads upon the quays, and I had several warnings offered me by strangers in the street to the effect that she was rotten as a cheese, too deeply loaden, and must infallibly founder if we met a gale. From this it fell out we were the only passengers; the Captain, M'Murtrie, was a silent, absorbed man, with the Glascow or Gaelic accent; the mates ignorant rough seafarers, come in through the hawsehole; and the Master and I were cast upon each other's company.

The *Nonesuch* carried a fair wind out of the Clyde, and

for near upon a week we enjoyed bright weather and a sense of progress. I found myself (to my wonder) a born seaman, in so far at least as I was never sick ; yet I was far from tasting the usual serenity of my health. Whether it was the motion of the ship on the billows, the confinement, the salted food, or all of these together, I suffered from a blackness of spirit and a painful strain upon my temper. The nature of my errand on that ship perhaps contributed ; I think it did no more ; the malady (whatever it was) sprang from my environment ; and if the ship were not to blame, then it was the Master. Hatred and fear are ill bedfellows ; but (to my shame be it spoken) I have tasted those in other places, lain down and got up with them, and eaten and drunk with them, and yet never before, nor after, have I been so poisoned through and through, in soul and body, as I was on board the *Nonesuch.* I freely confess my enemy set me a fair example of forbearance ; in our worst days displayed the most patient geniality, holding me in conversation as long as I would suffer, and when I had rebuffed his civility, stretching himself on deck to read. The book he had on board with him was Mr. Richardson's famous " Clarissa," and among other small attentions he would read me passages aloud ; nor could any elocutionist have given with greater potency the pathetic portions of that work. I would retort upon him with passages out of the Bible, which was all my library—and very fresh to me, my religious duties (I grieve to say it) being always and even to this day extremely neglected. He tasted the merits of the work like the connoisseur he was ; and would sometimes take it from my hand, turn the leaves over like a man that knew his way, and give me, with his fine declamation, a Roland for my Oliver. But it was singular how little he applied his reading to himself ; it passed high above his head like summer thunder ; Lovelace and Clarissa, the tales of David's generosity, the psalms of his penitence, the solemn questions of the Book of Job, the touching poetry of

Isaiah—they were to him a source of entertainment only, like the scraping of a fiddle in a change-house. This outer sensibility and inner toughness set me against him; it seemed of a piece with that impudent grossness which I knew to underlie the veneer of his fine manners; and sometimes my gorge rose against him as though he were deformed—and sometimes I would draw away as though from something partly spectral. I had moments when I thought of him as of a man of pasteboard—as though, if one should strike smartly through the buckram of his countenance, there would be found a mere vacuity within. This horror (not merely fanciful, I think) vastly increased my detestation of his neighbourhood; I began to feel something shiver within me on his drawing near; I had at times a longing to cry out; there were days when I thought I could have struck him. This frame of mind was doubtless helped by shame, because I had dropped during our last days at Durrisdeer into a certain toleration of the man; and if any one had then told me I should drop into it again, I must have laughed in his face. It is possible he remained unconscious of this extreme fever of my resentment; yet I think he was too quick; and rather that he had fallen, in a long life of idleness, into a positive need of company, which obliged him to confront and tolerate my unconcealed aversion. Certain, at least, that he loved the note of his own tongue, as, indeed, he entirely loved all the parts and properties of himself; a sort of imbecility which almost necessarily attends on wickedness. I have seen him driven, when I proved recalcitrant, to long discourses with the skipper; and this, although the man plainly testified his weariness, fiddling miserably with both hand and foot, and replying only with a grunt.

After the first week out we fell in with foul winds and heavy weather. The sea was high. The *Nonesuch* being an old-fashioned ship, and badly loaden, rolled beyond belief; so that the skipper trembled for his masts, and

I for my life. We made no progress on our course. An unbearable ill-humour settled on the ship : men, mates, and master, girding at one another all day long. A saucy word on the one hand, and a blow on the other, made a daily incident. There were times when the whole crew refused their duty ; and we of the afterguard were twice got under arms—being the first time that ever I bore weapons—in the fear of mutiny.

In the midst of our evil season sprang up a hurricane of wind ; so that all supposed she must go down. I was shut in the cabin from noon of one day till sundown of the next. The Master was somewhere lashed on deck ; Secundra had eaten of some drug and lay insensible ; so you may say I passed these hours in an unbroken solitude. At first I was terrified beyond motion, and almost beyond thought, my mind appearing to be frozen. Presently there stole in on me a ray of comfort. If the *Nonesuch* foundered, she would carry down with her into the deeps of that unsounded sea the creature whom we all so feared and hated ; there would be no more Master of Ballantrae, the fish would sport among his ribs ; his schemes all brought to nothing, his harmless enemies at peace. At first, I have said, it was but a ray of comfort ; but it had soon grown to be broad sunshine. The thought of the man's death, of his deletion from this world, which he embittered for so many, took possession of my mind. I hugged it ; I found it sweet in my belly. I conceived the ship's last plunge, the sea bursting upon all sides into the cabin, the brief mortal conflict there, all by myself, in that closed place ; I numbered the horrors, I had almost said with satisfaction ; I felt I could bear all and more, if the *Nonesuch* carried down with her, overtook by the same ruin, the enemy of my poor master's house. Towards noon of the second day the screaming of the wind abated ; the ship lay not so perilously over, and it began to be clear to me that we were past the height of the tempest. As I hope for mercy, I was singly disappointed. In the

selfishness of that vile, absorbing passion of hatred, I
forgot the case of our innocent shipmates, and thought
but of myself and my enemy. For myself, I was already
old ; I had never been young, I was not formed for the
world's pleasures, I had few affections ; it mattered not
the toss of a silver tester whether I was drowned there and
then in the Atlantic, or dribbled out a few more years, to
die, perhaps no less terribly, in a deserted sick-bed. Down
I went upon my knees—holding on by the locker, or else
I had been instantly dashed across the tossing cabin—and,
lifting up my voice in the midst of that clamour of the
abating hurricane, impiously prayed for my own death.
" O God ! " I cried, " I would be liker a man if I rose
and struck this creature down ; but Thou madest me a
coward from my mother's womb. O Lord, Thou madest
me so, Thou knowest my weakness, Thou knowest that
any face of death will set me shaking in my shoes. But,
lo ! here is Thy servant ready, his mortal weakness laid
aside. Let me give my life for this creature's ; take the
two of them, Lord ! take the two, and have mercy on the
innocent ! " In some such words as these, only yet more
irreverent and with more sacred adjurations, I continued
to pour forth my spirit. God heard me not, I must suppose
in mercy ; and I was still absorbed in my agony of suppli-
cation when some one, removing the tarpaulin cover, let
the light of the sunset pour into the cabin. I stumbled
to my feet ashamed, and was seized with surprise to find
myself totter and ache like one that had been stretched
upon the rack. Secundra Dass, who had slept off the effects
of his drug, stood in a corner not far off, gazing at me with
wild eyes ; and from the open skylight the captain thanked
me for my supplications.

" It's you that saved the ship, Mr. Mackellar," says he.
" There is no craft of seamanship that could have kept her
floating : well may we say, ' Except the Lord the city
keep, the watchmen watch in vain ' ! "

I was abashed by the captain's error ; abashed, also,

by the surprise and fear with which the Indian regarded me at first, and the obsequious civilities with which he soon began to cumber me. I know now that he must have overheard and comprehended the peculiar nature of my prayers. It is certain, of course, that he at once disclosed the matter to his patron; and looking back with greater knowledge, I can now understand what so much puzzled me at the moment, those singular and (so to speak) approving smiles with which the Master honoured me. Similarly, I can understand a word that I remember to have fallen from him in conversation that same night; when, holding up his hand and smiling, " Ah! Mackellar," said he, " not every man is so great a coward as he thinks he is—nor yet so good a Christian." He did not guess how true he spoke! For the fact is, the thoughts which had come to me in the violence of the storm retained their hold upon my spirit; and the words that rose to my lips unbidden in the instancy of prayer continued to sound in my ears: with what shameful consequences it is fitting I should honestly relate; for I could not support a part of such disloyalty as to describe the sins of others and conceal my own.

The wind fell, but the sea hove ever the higher. All night the *Nonesuch* rolled outrageously; the next day dawned, and the next, and brought no change. To cross the cabin was scarce possible; old experienced seamen were cast down upon the deck, and one cruelly mauled in the concussion; every board and block in the old ship cried out aloud; and the great bell by the anchor-bitts continually and dolefully rang. One of these days the Master and I sate alone together at the break of the poop. I should say the *Nonesuch* carried a high, raised poop. About the top of it ran considerable bulwarks, which made the ship unweatherly: and these, as they approached the front on each side, ran down in a fine, old-fashioned, carven scroll to join the bulwarks of the waist. From this disposition, which seems designed rather for ornament than use, it followed there was a discontinuance of protection:

and that, besides, at the very margin of the elevated part
where (in certain movements of the ship) it might be the
most needful. It was here we were sitting : our feet
hanging down, the Master betwixt me and the side, and I
holding on with both hands to the grating of the cabin
skylight ; for it struck me it was a dangerous position, the
more so as I had continually before my eyes a measure of
our evolutions in the person of the Master, which stood
out in the break of the bulwarks against the sun. Now
his head would be in the zenith and his shadow fall quite
beyond the *Nonesuch* on the farther side ; and now he
would swing down till he was underneath my feet, and the
line of the sea leaped high above him like the ceiling of
a room. I looked on upon this with a growing fascination,
as birds are said to look on snakes. My mind, besides, was
troubled with an astonishing diversity of noises ; for now
that we had all sails spread in the vain hope to bring her
to the sea, the ship sounded like a factory with their rever-
berations. We spoke first of the mutiny with which we
had been threatened ; this led us on to the topic of assassination ; and that offered a temptation to the Master
more strong than he was able to resist. He must tell me
a tale, and show me at the same time how clever he was,
and how wicked. It was a thing he did always with affectation and display ; generally with a good effect. But
this tale, told in a high key in the midst of so great a tumult,
and by a narrator who was one moment looking down at
me from the skies and the next peering up from under the
soles of my feet—this particular tale, I say, took hold upon
me in a degree quite singular.

" My friend the count," it was thus that he began his
story, " had for an enemy a certain German baron, a
stranger in Rome. It matters not what was the ground of
the count's enmity ; but as he had a firm design to be
revenged, and that with safety to himself, he kept it secret
even from the baron. Indeed, that is the first principle of
vengeance ; and hatred betrayed is hatred impotent. The

count was a man of a curious, searching mind ; he had
something of the artist ; if anything fell for him to do, it
must always be done with an exact perfection, not only
as to the result, but in the very means and instruments,
or he thought the thing miscarried. It chanced he was
one day riding in the outer suburbs, when he came to a
disused by-road branching off into the moor which lies
about Rome. On the one hand was an ancient Roman
tomb ; on the other a deserted house in a garden of evergreen trees. This road brought him presently into a field
of ruins, in the midst of which, in the side of a hill, he saw
an open door, and, not far off, a single stunted pine no
greater than a currant-bush. The place was desert and
very secret ; a voice spoke in the count's bosom that there
was something here to his advantage. He tied his horse
to the pine-tree, took his flint and steel in his hand to make
a light, and entered into the hill. The doorway opened on
a passage of old Roman masonry, which shortly after
branched in two. The count took the turning to the right,
and followed it, groping forward in the dark, till he was
brought up by a kind of fence, about elbow-high, which
extended quite across the passage. Sounding forward
with his foot, he found an edge of polished stone, and then
vacancy. All his curiosity was now awakened, and, getting
some rotten sticks that lay about the floor, he made a fire.
In front of him was a profound well ; doubtless some neigh-
bouring peasant had once used it for his water, and it was
he that had set up the fence. A long while the count
stood leaning on the rail and looking down into the pit.
It was of Roman foundation, and, like all that nation set
their hands to, built as for eternity ; the sides were still
straight, and the joints smooth ; to a man who should
fall in, no escape was possible. 'Now,' the count was
thinking, ' a strong impulsion brought me to this place.
What for ? what have I gained ? why should I be sent
to gaze into this well ? ' when the rail of the fence gave
suddenly under his weight, and he came within an ace of

falling headlong in. Leaping back to save himself, he trod out the last flicker of his fire, which gave him thenceforward no more light, only an incommoding smoke. ' Was I sent here to my death ? ' says he, and shook from head to foot. And then a thought flashed in his mind. He crept forth on hands and knees to the brink of the pit, and felt above him in the air. The rail had been fast to a pair of uprights ; it had only broken from the one, and still depended from the other. The count set it back again as he had found it, so that the place meant death to the first comer, and groped out of the catacomb like a sick man. The next day, riding in the Corso with the baron, he purposely betrayed a strong preoccupation. The other (as he had designed) inquired into the cause ; and he, after some fencing, admitted that his spirits had been dashed by an unusual dream. This was calculated to draw on the baron—a superstitious man, who affected the scorn of superstition. Some rallying followed, and then the count, as if suddenly carried away, called on his friend to beware, for it was of him that he had dreamed. You know enough of human nature, my excellent Mackellar, to be certain of one thing : I mean that the baron did not rest till he had heard the dream. The count, sure that he would never desist, kept him in play till his curiosity was highly inflamed, and then suffered himself, with seeming reluctance, to be overborne. ' I warn you,' says he, ' evil will come of it ; something tells me so. But since there is to be no peace either for you or me except on this condition, the blame be on your own head ! This was the dream :—I beheld you riding, I know not where, yet I think it must have been near Rome, for on your one hand was an ancient tomb, and on the other a garden of evergreen trees. Methought I cried and cried upon you to come back in a very agony of terror ; whether you heard me I know not, but you went doggedly on. The road brought you to a desert place among ruins, where was a door in a hill-side, and hard by the door a misbegotten pine. Here you dis-

mounted (I still crying on you to beware), tied your horse
to the pine-tree, and entered resolutely in by the door.
Within, it was dark; but in my dream I could still see
you, and still besought you to hold back. You felt your
way along the right-hand wall, took a branching passage
to the right, and came to a little chamber, where was a
well with a railing. At this—I know not why—my alarm
for you increased a thousandfold, so that I seemed to
scream myself hoarse with warnings, crying it was still
time, and bidding you begone at once from that vestibule.
Such was the word I used in my dream, and it seemed
then to have a clear significancy; but to-day, and awake,
I profess I know not what it means. To all my outcry
you rendered not the least attention, leaning the while
upon the rail and looking down intently in the water.
And then there was made to you a communication; I do
not think I even gathered what it was, but the fear of it
plucked me clean out of my slumber, and I awoke shaking
and sobbing. And now,' continues the count, ' I thank
you from my heart for your insistency. This dream lay
on me like a load; and now I have told it in plain words
and in the broad daylight, it seems no great matter.'—
' I do not know,' says the baron. ' It is in some points
strange. A communication, did you say! O! it is an
odd dream. It will make a story to amuse our friends.'
—' I am not so sure,' says the count. ' I am sensible of
some reluctancy. Let us rather forget it.'—' By all
means,' says the baron. And (in fact) the dream was not
again referred to. Some days after, the count proposed a
ride in the fields, which the baron (since they were daily
growing faster friends) very readily accepted. On the way
back to Rome, the count led them insensibly by a particular
route. Presently he reined in his horse, clapped his hand
before his eyes, and cried out aloud. Then he showed his
face again (which was now quite white, for he was a con-
summate actor), and stared upon the baron. ' What ails
you?' cries the baron. ' What is wrong with you?'—

'Nothing,' cries the count. 'It is nothing. A seizure, I know not what. Let us hurry back to Rome.' But in the meanwhile the baron had looked about him; and there, on the left-hand side of the way as they went back to Rome, he saw a dusty by-road with a tomb upon the one hand and a garden of evergreen trees upon the other. —'Yes,' says he, with a changed voice. 'Let us by all means hurry back to Rome. I fear you are not well in health.'—'O, for God's sake!' cried the count, shuddering; 'back to Rome and let me get to bed.' They made their return with scarce a word; and the count, who should by rights have gone into society, took to his bed and gave out he had a touch of country fever. The next day the baron's horse was found tied to the pine, but himself was never heard of from that hour.—And now, was that a murder?" says the Master, breaking sharply off.

"Are you sure he was a count?" I asked.

"I am not certain of the title," said he, "but he was a gentleman of family: and the Lord deliver you, Mackellar, from an enemy so subtile!"

These last words he spoke down at me, smiling from high above; the next, he was under my feet. I continued to follow his evolutions with a childish fixity: they made me giddy and vacant, and I spoke as in a dream.

"He hated the baron with a great hatred?" I asked.

"His belly moved when the man came near him," said the Master.

"I have felt that same," said I.

"Verily!" cries the Master. "Here is news indeed! I wonder—do I flatter myself? or am I the cause of these ventral perturbations?"

He was quite capable of choosing out a graceful posture, even with no one to behold him but myself, and all the more if there were any element of peril. He sat now with one knee flung across the other, his arms on his bosom, fitting the swing of the ship with an exquisite balance, such as a featherweight might overthrow. All at once I

had the vision of my lord at the table, with his head upon
his hands ; only now, when he showed me his countenance,
it was heavy with reproach. The words of my own prayer
—*I were liker a man if I struck this creature down*—shot at
the same time into my memory. I called my energies
together, and (the ship then heeling downward toward my
enemy) thrust at him swiftly with my foot. It was written
I should have the guilt of this attempt without the profit.
Whether from my own uncertainty or his incredible quickness, he escaped the thrust, leaping to his feet and catching
hold at the same moment of a stay.

I do not know how long a time passed by : I lying
where I was upon the deck, overcome with terror and remorse and shame : he standing with the stay in his hand,
backed against the bulwarks, and regarding me with an
expression singularly mingled. At last he spoke.

" Mackellar," said he, " I make no reproaches, but I
offer you a bargain. On your side, I do not suppose you
desire to have this exploit made public ; on mine, I own
to you freely I do not care to draw my breath in a perpetual
terror of assassination by the man I sit at meat with.
Promise me—but no," says he, breaking off, " you are not
yet in the quiet possession of your mind ; you might think
I had extorted the promise from your weakness ; and I
would leave no door open for casuistry to come in—
that dishonesty of the conscientious. Take time to
meditate."

With that he made off up the sliding deck like a squirrel,
and plunged into the cabin. About half an hour later he
returned—I still lying as he had left me.

" Now," says he, " will you give me your troth as a
Christian, and a faithful servant of my brother's, that I
shall have no more to fear from your attempts ? "

" I give it you," said I.

" I shall require your hand upon it," says he.

" You have the right to make conditions," I replied,
and we shook hands.

He sat down at once in the same place and the old perilous attitude.

"Hold on!" cried I, covering my eyes. "I cannot bear to see you in that posture. The least irregularity of the sea might plunge you overboard."

"You are highly inconsistent," he replied, smiling, but doing as I asked. "For all that, Mackellar, I would have you to know you have risen forty feet in my esteem. You think I cannot set a price upon fidelity? But why do you suppose I carry that Secundra Dass about the world with me? Because he would die or do murder for me to-morrow; and I love him for it. Well, you may think it odd, but I like you the better since this afternoon. I thought you were magnetised with the Ten Commandments; but no——God damn my soul!"—he cries, "the old wife has blood in his body after all! Which does not change the fact," he continued, smiling again, "that you have done well to give your promise; for I doubt if you would ever shine in your new trade."

"I suppose," said I, "I should ask your pardon and God's for my attempt. At any rate, I have passed my word, which I will keep faithfully. But when I think of those you persecute——" I paused.

"Life is a singular thing," said he, "and mankind a very singular people. You suppose yourself to love my brother. I assure you, it is merely custom. Interrogate your memory; and when first you came to Durrisdeer, you will find you considered him a dull, ordinary youth. He is as dull and ordinary now, though not so young. Had you instead fallen in with me, you would to-day be as strong upon my side."

"I would never say you were ordinary, Mr. Bally," I returned; "but here you prove yourself dull. You have just shown your reliance on my word—in other terms, that is, my conscience—the same which starts instinctively back from you, like the eye from a strong light."

"Ah!" says he, "but I mean otherwise. I mean had

I met you in my youth. You are to consider I was not
always as I am to-day ; nor (had I met in with a friend of
your description) should I have ever been so."

"Hut, Mr. Bally," says I, "you would have made a
mock of me ; you would never have spent ten civil words
on such a Square-toes."

But he was now fairly started on his new course of
justification, with which he wearied me throughout the
remainder of the passage. No doubt in the past he had
taken pleasure to paint himself unnecessarily black, and
made a vaunt of his wickedness, bearing it for a coat-of-arms.
Nor was he so illogical as to abate one item of his old confessions. "But now that I know you are a human being,"
he would say, " I can take the trouble to explain myself.
For I assure you I am human too, and have my virtues
like my neighbours." I say, he wearied me, for I had only
the one word to say in answer : twenty times I must have
said it : "Give up your present purpose and return with me
to Durrisdeer : then I will believe you."

Thereupon he would shake his head at me. "Ah !
Mackellar, you might live a thousand years and never
understand my nature," he would say. "This battle is
now committed, the hour of reflection quite past, the hour
for mercy not yet come. It began between us when we
span a coin in the hall of Durrisdeer, now twenty years
ago ; we have had our ups and downs, but never either
of us dreamed of giving in ; and as for me, when my glove
is cast, life and honour go with it."

"A fig for your honour !" I would say. "And by
your leave, these warlike similitudes are something too
high-sounding for the matter in hand. You want some
dirty money ; there is the bottom of your contention ;
and as for your means, what are they ? to stir up sorrow
in a family that never harmed you, to debauch (if you
can) your own nephew, and to wring the heart of your
born brother ! A footpad that kills an old granny in
a woollen mutch with a dirty bludgeon, and that for a

shilling piece and a paper of snuff—there is all the warrior that you are."

When I would attack him thus (or somewhat thus) he would smile, and sigh like a man misunderstood. Once, I remember, he defended himself more at large, and had some curious sophistries, worth repeating, for a light upon his character.

" You are very like a civilian to think war consists in drums and banners," said he. " War (as the ancients said very wisely) is *ultima ratio*. When we take our advantage unrelentingly, then we make war. Ah! Mackellar, you are a devil of a soldier in the steward's room at Durrisdeer, or the tenants do you sad injustice!"

" I think little of what war is or is not," I replied. " But you weary me with claiming my respect. Your brother is a good man, and you are a bad one—neither more nor less."

" Had I been Alexander——" he began.

" It is so we all dupe ourselves," I cried. " Had I been St. Paul, it would have been all one; I would have made the same hash of that career that you now see me making of my own."

" I tell you," he cried, bearing down my interruption, " had I been the least petty chieftain in the Highlands, had I been the least king of naked negroes in the African desert, my people would have adored me. A bad man, am I? Ah! but I was born for a good tyrant! Ask Secundra Dass; he will tell you I treat him like a son. Cast in your lot with me to-morrow, become my slave, my chattel, a thing I can command as I command the powers of my own limbs and spirit—you will see no more that dark side that I turn upon the world in anger. I must have all or none. But where all is given I give it back with usury. I have a kingly nature: there is my loss!"

" It has been hitherto rather the loss of others," I remarked, " which seems a little on the hither side of royalty."

"Tilly-vally!" cried he. "Even now, I tell you, I would spare that family in which you take so great an interest: yes, even now—to-morrow I would leave them to their petty welfare, and disappear in that forest of cut-throats and thimble-riggers that we call the world. I would do it to-morrow!" says he. "Only—only——"

"Only what?" I asked.

"Only they must beg it on their bended knees. I think in public, too," he added, smiling. "Indeed, Mackellar, I doubt if there be a hall big enough to serve my purpose for that act of reparation."

"Vanity, vanity!" I moralised. "To think that this great force for evil should be swayed by the same sentiment that sets a lassie mincing to her glass!"

"O! there are double words for everything: the word that swells, the word that belittles; you cannot fight me with a word!" said he. "You said the other day that I relied on your conscience: were I in your humour of detraction, I might say I built upon your vanity. It is your pretension to be *un homme de parole;* 'tis mine not to accept defeat. Call it vanity, call it virtue, call it great-ness of soul—what signifies the expression? But recognise in each of us a common strain: that we both live for an idea."

It will be gathered from so much familiar talk, and so much patience on both sides, that we now lived together upon excellent terms. Such was again the fact, and this time more seriously than before. Apart from disputations such as that which I have tried to reproduce, not only consideration reigned, but, I am tempted to say, even kindness. When I fell sick (as I did shortly after our great storm), he sat by my berth to entertain me with his conversation, and treated me with excellent remedies, which I accepted with security. Himself commented on the circumstance. "You see," says he, "you begin to know me better. A very little while ago, upon this lonely ship, where no one but myself has any smattering of science, you would have made sure I had designs upon your life. And, observe, it is since I found you had designs upon my own that I have shown you most respect. You will tell me if this speaks of a small mind." I found little to reply. In so far as regarded myself, I believed him to mean well ; I am, perhaps, the more a dupe of his dissimulation, but I believed (and I still believe) that he regarded me with genuine kindness. Singular and sad fact! so soon as this change began, my animosity abated, and these haunting visions of my master passed utterly away. So that, perhaps, there was truth in the man's last vaunting word to me, uttered on the twenty-second day of July,* when our long voyage was at last brought almost to an end, and we lay becalmed at the sea end of the vast harbour of New York, in a gasping heat, which was presently exchanged for a surprising waterfall of rain. I stood on the poop, regarding the green shores near at hand, and now and then the light smoke of the little town, our destination. And as I was even then devising how to steal a march on my familiar enemy, I was conscious of a shade of embarrassment when he approached me with his hand extended.

" I am now to bid you farewell," said he, " and that for ever. For now you go among my enemies, where all your former prejudices will revive. I never yet failed to charm a person when I wanted ; even you, my good friend— to call you so for once—even you have now a very different portrait of me in your memory, and one that you will never quite forget. The voyage has not lasted long enough, or I should have wrote the impression deeper. But now all is at an end, and we are again at war. Judge by this little interlude how dangerous I am ; and tell those fools "— pointing with his finger to the town—" to think twice and thrice before they set me at defiance."

CHAPTER X

PASSAGES AT NEW YORK

I HAVE mentioned I was resolved to steal a march upon the Master; and this, with the complicity of Captain M'Murtrie, was mighty easily effected: a boat being partly loaded on the one side of our ship, and the Master placed on board of it, the while a skiff put off from the other, carrying me alone. I had no more trouble in finding a direction to my lord's house, whither I went at top speed, and which I found to be on the outskirts of the place, a very suitable mansion, in a fine garden, with an extraordinary large barn, byre, and stable, all in one. It was here my lord was walking when I arrived; indeed, it had become his chief place of frequentation, and his mind was now filled with farming. I burst in upon him breathless, and gave him my news: which was indeed no news at all, several ships having outsailed the *Nonesuch* in the interval.

"We have been expecting you long," said my lord; "and indeed, of late days, ceased to expect you any more. I am glad to take your hand again, Mackellar. I thought you had been at the bottom of the sea."

"Ah! my lord, would God I had!" cried I. "Things would have been better for yourself."

"Not in the least," says he grimly. "I could not ask better. There is a long score to pay, and now—at last— I can begin to pay it."

I cried out against his security.

"O!" says he, "this is not Durrisdeer, and I have taken my precautions. His reputation awaits him; I have prepared a welcome for my brother. Indeed, fortune has

194

served me ; for I found here a merchant of Albany who knew him after the 'Forty-five, and had mighty convenient suspicions of a murder : some one of the name of Chew it was, another Albanian.* No one here will be surprised if I deny him my door ; he will not be suffered to address my children, nor even to salute my wife : as for myself, I make so much exception for a brother that he may speak to me. I should lose my pleasure else," says my lord, rubbing his palms.

Presently he bethought himself, and set men off running, with billets, to summon the magnates of the province. I cannot recall what pretext he employed ; at least, it was successful ; and when our ancient enemy appeared upon the scene, he found my lord pacing in front of his house under some trees of shade, with the Governor upon one hand and various notables upon the other. My lady, who was seated in the verandah, rose with a very pinched expression and carried her children into the house.

The Master, well dressed, and with an elegant walking-sword, bowed to the company in a handsome manner, and nodded to my lord with familiarity. My lord did not accept the salutation, but looked upon his brother with bended brows.

" Well, sir," says he at last, " what ill wind brings you hither of all places, where (to our common disgrace) your reputation has preceded you ? "

" Your lordship is pleased to be civil," cries the Master, with a fine start.

" I am pleased to be very plain," returned my lord ; " because it is needful you should clearly understand your situation. At home, where you were so little known, it was still possible to keep appearances ; that would be quite vain in this province ; and I have to tell you that I am quite resolved to wash my hands of you. You have already ruined me almost to the door, as you ruined my father before me ;—whose heart you also broke. Your crimes escape the law ; but my friend the Governor has

promised protection to my family. Have a care, sir ! "
cries my lord, shaking his cane at him : " if you are observed
to utter two words to any of my innocent household, the
law shall be stretched to make you smart for it."

" Ah ! " says the Master, very slowly. " And so this
is the advantage of a foreign land ! These gentlemen are
unacquainted with our story, I perceive. They do not
know that I am the true Lord Durrisdeer ; they do not
know you are my younger brother, sitting in my place
under a sworn family compact ; they do not know (or they
would not be seen with you in familiar correspondence)
that every acre is mine before God Almighty—and every
doit of the money you withhold from me, you do it as a
thief, a perjurer, and a disloyal brother ! "

" General Clinton,"*I cried, " do not listen to his lies.
I am the steward of the estate, and there is not one word
of truth in it. The man is a forfeited rebel turned into a
hired spy : there is his story in two words."

It was thus (in the heat of the moment) I let slip his
infamy.

" Fellow," said the Governor, turning his face sternly
on the Master, " I know more of you than you think for.
We have some broken ends of your adventures in the
provinces, which you will do very well not to drive me to
investigate. There is the disappearance of Mr. Jacob
Chew with all his merchandise ; there is the matter of where
you came ashore from with so much money and jewels,
when you were picked up by a Bermudan out of Albany.
Believe me, if I let these matters lie, it is in commiseration
for your family, and out of respect for my valued friend,
Lord Durrisdeer."

There was a murmur of applause from the provincials.

" I should have remembered how a title would shine
out in such a hole as this," says the Master, white as a
sheet : " no matter how unjustly come by. It remains
for me, then, to die at my lord's door, where my dead
body will form a very cheerful ornament."

" Away with your affections ! " cries my lord. " You know very well I have no such meaning ; only to protect myself from calumny, and my home from your intrusion. I offer you a choice. Either I shall pay your passage home on the first ship, when you may perhaps be able to resume your occupations under Government, although God knows I would rather see you on the highway ! Or, if that likes you not, stay here and welcome ! I have inquired the least sum on which body and soul can be decently kept together in New York ; so much you shall have, paid weekly ; and if you cannot labour with your hands to better it, high time you should betake yourself to learn. The condition is—that you speak with no member of my family except myself," he added.

I do not think I have ever seen any man so pale as was the Master ; but he was erect and his mouth firm.

" I have been met here with some very unmerited insults," said he, " from which I have certainly no idea to take refuge by flight. Give me your pittance ; I take it without shame, for it is mine already—like the shirt upon your back ; and I choose to stay until these gentlemen shall understand me better. Already they must spy the cloven hoof, since with all your pretended eagerness for the family honour, you take a pleasure to degrade it in my person."

" This is all very fine," says my lord ; " but to us who know you of old, you must be sure it signifies nothing. You take that alternative out of which you think that you can make the most. Take it, if you can, in silence ; it will serve you better in the long-run, you may believe me, than this ostentation of ingratitude."

" O, gratitude, my lord ! " cries the Master, with a mounting intonation, and his forefinger very conspicuously lifted up. " Be at rest : it will not fail you. It now remains that I should salute these gentlemen whom we have wearied with our family affairs."

And he bowed to each in succession, settled his walking-sword, and took himself off, leaving every one amazed at his behaviour, and me not less so at my lord's.

We were now to enter on a changed phase of this family division. The Master was by no manner of means so helpless as my lord supposed, having at his hand, and entirely devoted to his service, an excellent artist in all sorts of goldsmith work. With my lord's allowance, which was not so scanty as he had described it, the pair could support life ; and all the earnings of Secundra Dass might be laid upon one side for any future purpose. That this was done, I have no doubt. It was in all likelihood the Master's design to gather a sufficiency, and then proceed in quest of that treasure which he had buried long before among the mountains ; to which, if he had confined himself, he would have been more happily inspired. But unfortunately for himself and all of us, he took counsel of his anger. The public disgrace of his arrival—which I sometimes wonder he could manage to survive—rankled in his bones ; he was in that humour when a man—in the words of the old adage—will cut off his nose to spite his face ; and he must make himself a public spectacle in the hopes that some of the disgrace might spatter on my lord.

He chose, in a poor quarter of the town, a lonely, small house of boards, overhung with some acacias. It was furnished in front with a sort of hutch opening, like that of a dog's kennel, but about as high as a table from the ground, in which the poor man that built it had formerly displayed some wares ; and it was this which took the Master's fancy and possibly suggested his proceedings. It appears, on board the pirate ship he had acquired some quickness with the needle—enough, at least, to play the part of tailor in the public eye; which was all that was required by the nature of his vengeance. A placard was hung above the hutch, bearing these words in something of the following disposition :

JAMES DURIE,

FORMERLY MASTER OF BALLANTRAE.

CLOTHES NEATLY CLOUTED.

SECUNDRA DASS,

DECAYED GENTLEMAN OF INDIA.

FINE GOLDSMITH WORK.

Underneath this, when he had a job, my gentleman sat withinside tailor-wise and busily stitching. I say, when he had a job; but such customers as came were rather for Secundra, and the Master's sewing would be more in the manner of Penelope's. He could never have designed to gain even butter to his bread by such a means of livelihood : enough for him that there was the name of Durie dragged in the dirt on the placard, and the sometime heir of that proud family set up cross-legged in public for a reproach upon his brother's meanness. And in so far his device succeeded that there was murmuring in the town and a party formed highly inimical to my lord. My lord's favour with the Governor laid him more open on the other side ; my lady (who was never so well received in the colony) met with painful innuendoes ; in a party of women, where it would be the topic most natural to introduce, she was almost debarred from the naming of needle-work ; and I have seen her return with a flushed countenance, and vow that she would go abroad no more.

In the meanwhile my lord dwelled in his decent mansion, immersed in farming ; a popular man with his intimates, and careless or unconscious of the rest. He laid on flesh ; had a bright, busy face ; even the heat seemed to prosper with him ; and my lady—in despite of her own annoyances —daily blessed Heaven her father should have left her such a paradise. She had looked on from a window upon the Master's humiliation ; and from that hour appeared to feel at ease. I was not so sure myself ; as time went on, there seemed to me a something not quite wholesome in my lord's condition.   Happy he was, beyond a doubt, but the grounds of this felicity were secret ; even in the bosom of his family he brooded with manifest delight upon some private thought; and I conceived at last the suspicion (quite unworthy of us both) that he kept a mistress somewhere in the town. Yet he went little abroad, and his day was very fully occupied ; indeed, there was but a single period, and that pretty early in the morning, while Mr. Alexander was at his lesson-book, of which I was not certain of the disposition. It should be borne in mind, in the defence of that which I now did, that I was always in some fear my lord was not quite justly in his reason ; and with our enemy sitting so still in the same town with us, I did well to be upon my guard.   Accordingly I made a pretext, had the hour changed at which I taught Mr. Alexander the foundation of ciphering and the mathematic, and set myself instead to dog my master's footsteps.

Every morning, fair or foul, he took his gold-headed cane, set his hat on the back of his head—a recent habitude, which I thought to indicate a burning brow—and betook himself to make a certain circuit.   At the first his way was among pleasant trees and beside a graveyard, where he would sit a while, if the day were fine, in meditation. Presently the path turned down to the water-side, and came back along the harbour-front and past the Master's booth.   As he approached this second part of his circuit, my Lord Durrisdeer began to pace more leisurely, like a man delighted with the air and scene ; and before the booth, half-way between that and the water's edge, would pause a little, leaning on his staff.   It was the hour when the Master sate within upon his board and plied his needle. So these two brothers would gaze upon each other with hard faces ; and then my lord move on again, smiling to himself.

It was but twice that I must stoop to that ungrateful necessity of playing spy.   I was then certain of my lord's

purpose in his rambles and of the secret source of his
delight. Here was his mistress : it was hatred and not
love that gave him healthful colours. Some moralists
might have been relieved by the discovery ; I confess that
I was dismayed. I found this situation of two brethren
not only odious in itself, but big with possibilities of further
evil ; and I made it my practice, in so far as many occupations would allow, to go by a shorter path and be secretly
present at their meeting. Coming down one day a little
late, after I had been near a week prevented, I was struck
with surprise to find a new development. I should say
there was a bench against the Master's house, where
customers might sit to parley with the shopman ; and here
I found my lord seated, nursing his cane and looking pleasantly forth upon the bay. Not three feet from him sate
the Master, stitching. Neither spoke ; nor (in this new
situation) did my lord so much as cast a glance upon his
enemy. He tasted his neighbourhood, I must suppose,
less indirectly in the bare proximity of person ; and,
without doubt, drank deep of hateful pleasures.

He had no sooner come away than I openly joined
him.

"My lord, my lord," said I, "this is no manner of
behaviour."

"I grow fat upon it," he replied : and not merely the
words, which were strange enough, but the whole character
of his expression, shocked me.

"I warn you, my lord, against this indulgency of evil
feeling," said I. "I know not to which it is more perilous,
the soul or the reason ; but you go the way to murder
both."

"You cannot understand," said he. "You had never
such mountains of bitterness upon your heart."

"And if it were no more," I added, "you will surely
goad the man to some extremity."

"To the contrary ; I am breaking his spirit," says
my lord.

Every morning for hard upon a week my lord took his same place upon the bench. It was a pleasant place, under the green acacias, with a sight upon the bay and shipping, and a sound (from some way off) of mariners singing at their employ. Here the two sate without speech or any external movement, beyond that of the needle, or the Master biting off a thread, for he still clung to his pretence of industry; and here I made a point to join them, wondering at myself and my companions. If any of my lord's friends went by, he would hail them cheerfully, and cry out he was there to give some good advice to his brother, who was now (to his delight) grown quite industrious. And even this the Master accepted with a steady countenance; what was in his mind, God knows, or perhaps Satan only.

All of a sudden, on a still day of what they call the Indian Summer, when the woods were changed into gold and pink and scarlet, the Master laid down his needle and burst into a fit of merriment. I think he must have been preparing it a long while in silence, for the note in itself was pretty naturally pitched; but breaking suddenly from so extreme a silence, and in circumstances so averse from mirth, it sounded ominously on my ear.

"Henry," said he, "I have for once made a false step, and for once you have had the wit to profit by it. The farce of the cobbler ends to-day; and I confess to you (with my compliments) that you have had the best of it. Blood will out; and you have certainly a choice idea of how to make yourself unpleasant."

Never a word said my lord; it was just as though the Master had not broken silence.

"Come," resumed the Master, "do not be sulky; it will spoil your attitude. You can now afford (believe me) to be a little gracious; for I have not merely a defeat to accept. I had meant to continue this performance till I had gathered enough money for a certain purpose; I confess ingenuously I have not the courage. You naturally

desire my absence from this town ; I have come round by
another way to the same idea. And I have a proposition to make ; or, if your lordship prefers, a favour to
ask."

" Ask it," says my lord.

" You may have heard that I had once in this country
a considerable treasure," returned the Master ; " it matters
not whether or no—such is the fact ; and I was obliged to
bury it in a spot of which I have sufficient indications.
To the recovery of this has my ambition now come down ;
and, as it is my own, you will not grudge it me."

" Go and get it," says my lord. " I make no op-
position."

" Yes," said the Master ; " but to do so I must find
men and carriage. The way is long and rough, and the
country infested with wild Indians. Advance me only so
much as shall be needful : either as a lump sum, in lieu of
my allowance ; or, if you prefer it, as a loan, which I
shall repay on my return. And then, if you so decide,
you may have seen the last of me."

My lord stared him steadily in the eyes ; there was a
hard smile upon his face, but he uttered nothing.

" Henry," said the Master, with a formidable quietness,
and drawing at the same time somewhat back—" Henry,
I had the honour to address you."

" Let us be stepping homeward," says my lord to me,
who was plucking at his sleeve ; and with that he rose,
stretched himself, settled his hat, and, still without a
syllable of response, began to walk steadily along the
shore.

I hesitated a while between the two brothers, so serious
a climax did we seem to have reached. But the Master
had resumed his occupation, his eyes lowered, his hand
seemingly as deft as ever ; and I decided to pursue my
lord.

" Are you mad ? " I cried, so soon as I had overtook
him. " Would you cast away so fair an opportunity ? "

" Is it possible you should still believe in him ? " inquired my lord, almost with a sneer.

" I wish him forth of this town ! " I cried. " I wish him anywhere and anyhow but as he is."

" I have said my say," returned my lord, " and you have said yours. There let it rest."

But I was bent on dislodging the Master. That sight of him patiently returning to his needlework was more than my imagination could digest. There was never a man made, and the Master the least of any, that could accept so long a series of insults. The air smelt blood to me. And I vowed there should be no neglect of mine if, through any chink of possibility, crime could be yet turned aside. That same day, therefore, I came to my lord in his business room, where he sat upon some trivial occupation.

" My lord," said I, " I have found a suitable investment for my small economies. But these are unhappily in Scotland ; it will take some time to lift them, and the affair presses. Could your lordship see his way to advance me the amount against my note ? "

He read me a while with keen eyes. " I have never inquired into the state of your affairs, Mackellar," says he. " Beyond the amount of your caution, you may not be worth a farthing, for what I know."

" I have been a long while in your service, and never told a lie, nor yet asked a favour for myself," said I, " until to-day."

" A favour for the Master," he returned quietly. " Do you take me for a fool, Mackellar ? Understand it once and for all, I treat this beast in my own way ; fear nor favour shall not move me ; and before I am hoodwinked, it will require a trickster less transparent than yourself. I ask service, loyal service ; not that you should make and mar behind my back, and steal my own money to defeat me."

" My lord," said I, " these are very unpardonable expressions."

" Think once more, Mackellar," he replied ; " and you will see they fit the fact. It is your own subterfuge that is unpardonable. Deny (if you can) that you designed this money to evade my orders with, and I will ask your pardon freely. If you cannot, you must have the resolution to hear your conduct go by its own name."

" If you think I had any design but to save you——" I began.

" O ! my old friend," said he, " you know very well what I think ! Here is my hand to you with all my heart ; but of money, not one rap."

Defeated upon this side, I went straight to my room, wrote a letter, ran with it to the harbour, for I knew a ship was on the point of sailing ; and came to the Master's door a little before dusk. Entering without the form of any knock, I found him sitting with his Indian at a simple meal of maize porridge with some milk. The house within was clean and poor ; only a few books upon a shelf distinguished it, and (in one corner) Secundra's little bench.

" Mr. Bally," said I, " I have near five hundred pounds laid by in Scotland, the economies of a hard life. A letter goes by yon ship to have it lifted. Have so much patience till the return ship comes in, and it is all yours, upon the same condition you offered to my lord this morning."

He rose from the table, came forward, took me by the shoulders, and looked me in the face, smiling.

" And yet you are very fond of money ! " said he. " And yet you love money beyond all things else, except my brother ! "

" I fear old age and poverty," said I, " which is another matter."

" I will never quarrel for a name. Call it so," he replied.—" Ah ! Mackellar, Mackellar, if this were done from any love to me, how gladly would I close upon your offer ! "

" And yet," I eagerly answered—" I say it to my shame, but I cannot see you in this poor place without

compunction. It is not my single thought, nor my first ;
and yet it's there ! I would gladly see you delivered.
I do not offer it in love, and far from that ; but, as God
judges me—and I wonder at it too !—quite without
enmity."

"Ah ! " says he, still holding my shoulders, and now
gently shaking me, " you think of me more than you
suppose. ' And I wonder at it too,' " he added, repeating
my expression and, I suppose, something of my voice.
" You are an honest man, and for that cause I spare you."

" Spare me ? " I cried.

" Spare you," he repeated, letting me go and turning
away. And then, fronting me once more : " You little
know what I would do with it, Mackellar ! Did you think
I had swallowed my defeat indeed ? Listen : my life has
been a series of unmerited cast-backs. That fool, Prince
Charlie, mismanaged a most promising affair : there fell
my first fortune. In Paris I had my foot once more high
up on the ladder : that time it was an accident ; a letter
came to the wrong hand, and I was bare again. A third
time I found my opportunity ; I built up a place for myself
in India with an infinite patience ; and then Clive* came,
my rajah was swallowed up, and I escaped out of the con-
vulsion, like another Æneas, with Secundra Dass upon my
back. Three times I have had my hand upon the highest
station : and I am not yet three-and-forty. I know the
world as few men know it when they come to die—Court
and camp, the East and the West ; I know where to go,
I see a thousand openings. I am now at the height of my
resources, sound of health, of inordinate ambition. Well,
all this I resign ; I care not if I die, and the world never
hear of me ; I care only for one thing, and that I will have.
Mind yourself ; lest, when the roof falls, you, too, should
be crushed under the ruins."

As I came out of his house, all hope of intervention
quite destroyed, I was aware of a stir on the harbour-side,

and, raising my eyes, there was a great ship newly come
to anchor. It seems strange I could have looked upon her
with so much indifference, for she brought death to the
brothers of Durrisdeer. After all the desperate episodes
of this contention, the insults, the opposing interests, the
fraternal duel in the shrubbery, it was reserved for some
poor devil in Grub Street, scribbling for his dinner, and
not caring what he scribbled, to cast a spell across four
thousand miles of the salt sea, and send forth both these
brothers into savage and wintry deserts, there to die.
But such a thought was distant from my mind ; and while
all the provincials were fluttered about me by the unusual
animation of their port, I passed throughout their midst
on my return homeward, quite absorbed in the recollection
of my visit and the Master's speech.

The same night there was brought to us from the ship
a little packet of pamphlets. The next day my lord was
under engagement to go with the Governor upon some
party of pleasure ; the time was nearly due, and I left him
for a moment alone in his room and skimming through the
pamphlets. When I returned, his head had fallen upon
the table, his arms lying abroad amongst the crumpled
papers.

" My lord, my lord ! " I cried as I ran forward, for I
supposed he was in some fit.

He sprang up like a figure upon wires, his countenance
deformed with fury, so that in a strange place I should
scarce have known him. His hand at the same time flew
above his head, as though to strike me down. " Leave
me alone ! " he screeched, and I fled, as fast as my shaking
legs would bear me, for my lady. She, too, lost no time ;
but when we returned, he had the door locked within, and
only cried to us from the other side to leave him be. We
looked in each other's faces, very white—each supposing the
blow had come at last.

" I will write to the Governor to excuse him," says she.
" We must keep our strong friends." But when she took

up the pen it flew out of her fingers. " I cannot write,"
said she. " Can you ? "

" I will make a shift, my lady," said I.

She looked over me as I wrote. " That will do," she
said, when I had done. " Thank God, Mackellar, I have
you to lean upon ! But what can it be now ? What, what
can it be ? "

In my own mind I believed there was no explanation
possible, and none required ; it was my fear that the
man's madness had now simply burst forth its way, like
the long-smothered flames of a volcano ; but to this (in
mere mercy to my lady) I durst not give expression.

" It is more to the purpose to consider our own behaviour," said I. " Must we leave him there alone ? "

" I do not dare disturb him," she replied. " Nature
may know best ; it may be Nature that cries to be alone ;
and we grope in the dark. O yes, I would leave him as
he is."

" I will, then, despatch this letter, my lady, and return
here, if you please, to sit with you," said I.

" Pray do," cries my lady.

All afternoon we sat together, mostly in silence, watching my lord's door. My own mind was busy with the
scene that had just passed, and its singular resemblance
to my vision. I must say a word upon this, for the story
has gone abroad with great exaggeration, and I have even
seen it printed, and my own name referred to for particulars.
So much was the same : here was my lord in a room, with
his head upon the table, and when he raised his face, it
wore such an expression as distressed me to the soul. But
the room was different, my lord's attitude at the table
not at all the same, and his face, when he disclosed it,
expressed a painful degree of fury instead of that haunting
despair which had always (except once, already referred
to) characterised it in the vision. There is the whole
truth at last before the public ; and if the differences be
great, the coincidence was yet enough to fill me with

uneasiness. All afternoon, as I say, I sat and pondered upon this quite to myself; for my lady had trouble of her own, and it was my last thought to vex her with fancies. About the midst of our time of waiting, she conceived an ingenious scheme, had Mr. Alexander fetched, and bid him knock at his father's door. My lord sent the boy about his business, but without the least violence, whether of manner or expression; so that I began to entertain a hope the fit was over.

At last, as the night fell and I was lighting a lamp that stood there trimmed, the door opened and my lord stood within upon the threshold. The light was not so strong that we could read his countenance; when he spoke, methought his voice a little altered, but yet perfectly steady.

"Mackellar," said he, "carry this note to its destination with your own hand. It is highly private. Find the person alone when you deliver it."

"Henry," says my lady, "you are not ill?"

"No, no," says he querulously, "I am occupied. Not at all; I am only occupied. It is a singular thing a man must be supposed to be ill when he has any business! Send me supper to this room, and a basket of wine: I expect the visit of a friend. Otherwise I am not to be disturbed."

And with that he once more shut himself in.

The note was addressed to one Captain Harris, at a tavern on the port-side. I knew Harris (by reputation) for a dangerous adventurer, highly suspected of piracy in the past, and now following the rude business of an Indian trader. What my lord should have to say to him, or he to my lord, it passed my imagination to conceive: or yet how my lord had heard of him, unless by a disgraceful trial from which the man was recently escaped. Altogether I went upon the errand with reluctance, and from the little I saw of the captain, returned from it with sorrow. I found him in a foul-smelling chamber, sitting by a guttering

candle and an empty bottle ; he had the remains of a
military carriage, or rather perhaps it was an affectation,
for his manners were low.

" Tell my lord, with my service, that I will wait upon
his lordship in the inside of half an hour," says he when
he had read the note ; and then had the servility, pointing
to his empty bottle, to propose that I should buy him
liquor.

Although I returned with my best speed, the captain
followed close upon my heels, and he stayed late into the
night. The cock was crowing a second time when I saw
(from my chamber window) my lord lighting him to the
gate, both men very much affected with their potations,
and sometimes leaning one upon the other to confabulate.
Yet the next morning my lord was abroad again early with
a hundred pounds of money in his pocket. I never supposed
that he returned with it ; and yet I was quite sure it did
not find its way to the Master, for I lingered all morning
within view of the booth. That was the last time my Lord
Durrisdeer passed his own enclosure till we left New York ;
he walked in his barn, or sat and talked with his family, all
much as usual ; but the town saw nothing of him, and
his daily visits to the Master seemed forgotten. Nor yet
did Harris reappear ; or not until the end.

I was now much oppressed with a sense of the mysteries
in which we had begun to move. It was plain, if only
from his change of habitude, my lord had something on
his mind of a grave nature ; but what it was, whence it
sprang, or why he should now keep the house and garden,
I could make no guess at. It was clear, even to probation,
the pamphlets had some share in this revolution ; I read
all I could find, and they were all extremely insignificant,
and of the usual kind of party scurrility ; even to a high
politician, I could spy out no particular matter of offence,
and my lord was a man rather indifferent on public questions. The truth is, the pamphlet which was the spring
of this affair lay all the time on my lord's bosom. There it

was that I found it at last, after he was dead, in the midst
of the north wilderness : in such a place, in such dismal
circumstances, I was to read for the first time these idle,
lying words of a Whig pamphleteer declaiming against
indulgency to Jacobites :—" Another notorious Rebel, the
M——r of B——e, is to have his Title restored," the passage
ran. " This Business has been long in hand, since he
rendered some very disgraceful Services in Scotland and
France. His Brother, L——d D——r, is known to be no
better than himself in Inclination ; and the supposed Heir,
who is now to be set aside, was bred up in the most detestable Principles. In the old Phrase, it is *six of the one and
half a dozen of the other ;* but the Favour of such a Reposi-
tion is too extreme to be passed over." A man in his right
wits could not have cared two straws for a tale so manifestly
false ; that Government should ever entertain the notion
was inconceivable to any reasoning creature, unless possibly
the fool that penned it ; and my lord, though never brilliant,
was ever remarkable for sense. That he should credit such
a rodomontade, and carry the pamphlet on his bosom and
the words in his heart, is the clear proof of the man's lunacy.
Doubtless the mere mention of Mr. Alexander, and the
threat directly held out against the child's succession,
precipitated that which had so long impended. Or else
my master had been truly mad for a long time, and we were
too dull or too much used to him, and did not perceive the
extent of his infirmity.

About a week after the day of the pamphlets I was late
upon the harbour-side, and took a turn towards the Master's,
as I often did. The door opened, a flood of light came
forth upon the road, and I beheld a man taking his departure
with friendly salutations. I cannot say how singularly I
was shaken to recognise the adventurer Harris. I could
not but conclude it was the hand of my lord that had brought
him there ; and prolonged my walk in very serious and
apprehensive thought. It was late when I came home, and
there was my lord making up his portmanteau for a voyage.

" Why do you come so late ? " he cried. " We leave to-morrow for Albany, you and I together ; and it is high time you were about your preparations."

" For Albany, my lord ? " I cried. " And for what earthly purpose ? "

" Change of scene," said he.

And my lady, who appeared to have been weeping, gave me the signal to obey without more parley. She told me a little later (when we found occasion to exchange some words) that he had suddenly announced his intention after a visit from Captain Harris, and her best endeavours, whether to dissuade him from the journey, or to elicit some explanation of its purpose, had alike proved unavailing.

CHAPTER XI

THE JOURNEY IN THE WILDERNESS

We made a prosperous voyage up that fine river of the Hudson, the weather grateful, the hills singularly beautified with the colours of the autumn. At Albany we had our residence at an inn, where I was not so blind and my lord not so cunning but what I could see he had some design to hold me prisoner. The work he found for me to do was not so pressing that we should transact it apart from necessary papers in the chamber of an inn ; nor was it of such importance that I should be set upon as many as four or five scrolls of the same document. I submitted in appearance ; but I took private measures on my own side, and had the news of the town communicated to me daily by the politeness of our host. In this way I received at last a piece of intelligence for which, I may say, I had been waiting. Captain Harris (I was told) with " Mr. Mountain, the trader," had gone by up the river in a boat. I would have feared the landlord's eye, so strong the sense of some complicity upon my master's part oppressed me. But I made out to say I had some knowledge of the captain, although none of Mr. Mountain, and to inquire who else was of the party. My informant knew not ; Mr. Mountain had come ashore upon some needful purchases ; had gone round the town buying, drinking, and prating ; and it seemed the party went upon some likely venture, for he had spoken much of great things he would do when he returned. No more was known, for none of the rest had come ashore, and it seemed they were pressed for time to reach a certain spot before the snow should fall.

And sure enough, the next day there fell a sprinkle even in Albany ; but it passed as it came, and was but a reminder of what lay before us. I thought of it lightly then, knowing so little as I did of that inclement province : the retrospect is different ; and I wonder at times if some of the horror of these events which I must now rehearse flowed not from the foul skies and savage winds to which we were exposed, and the agony of cold that we must suffer.

The boat having passed by, I thought at first we should have left the town. But no such matter. My lord continued his stay in Albany, where he had no ostensible affairs, and kept me by him, far from my due employment, and making a pretence of occupation. It is upon this passage I expect, and perhaps deserve, censure. I was not so dull but what I had my own thoughts. I could not see the Master entrust himself into the hands of Harris, and not suspect some underhand contrivance. Harris bore a villainous reputation, and he had been tampered with in private by my lord ; Mountain, the trader, proved, upon inquiry, to be another of the same kidney ; the errand they were all gone upon being the recovery of ill-gotten treasures, offered in itself a very strong incentive to foul play ; and the character of the country where they journeyed promised impunity to deeds of blood. Well : it is true I had all these thoughts and fears, and guesses of the Master's fate. But you are to consider I was the same man that sought to dash him from the bulwarks of a ship in the mid-sea ; the same that, a little before, very impiously but sincerely offered God a bargain, seeking to hire God to be my bravo. It is true again that I had a good deal melted towards our enemy. But this I always thought of as a weakness of the flesh, and even culpable ; my mind remaining steady and quite bent against him. True, yet again, that it was one thing to assume on my own shoulders the guilt and danger of a criminal attempt, and another to stand by and see my lord imperil and besmirch himself.

But this was the very ground of my inaction. For (should
I anyway stir in the business) I might fail indeed to save
the Master, but I could not miss to make a byword of
my lord.

Thus it was that I did nothing ; and upon the same
reasons, I am still strong to justify my course.* My lord
had carried with him several introductions to chief people
of the town and neighbourhood ; others he had before
encountered in New York : with this consequence, that
he went much abroad, and I am sorry to say was altogether
too convivial in his habits. I was often in bed, but never
asleep, when he returned ; and there was scarce a night
when he did not betray the influence of liquor. By day
he would still lay upon me endless tasks, which he showed
considerable ingenuity to fish up and renew, in the manner
of Penelope's web. I never refused, as I say, for I was
hired to do his bidding ; but I took no pains to keep my
penetration under a bushel, and would sometimes smile in
his face.

" I think I must be the devil and you Michael Scott,"*
I said to him one day. " I have bridged Tweed and split
the Eildons ; and now you set me to the rope of sand."

He looked at me with shining eyes, and looked away
again, his jaw chewing, but without words.

" Well, well, my lord," said I, " your will is my pleasure.
I will do this thing for the fourth time ; but I would beg
of you to invent another task against to-morrow, for by
my troth, I am weary of this one."

" You do not know what you are saying," returned my
lord, putting on his hat and turning his back to me. " It
is a strange thing you should take a pleasure to annoy me.
A friend—but that is a different affair. It is a strange
thing. I am a man that has had ill-fortune all my life
through. I am still surrounded by contrivances. I am
always treading in plots," he burst out. " The whole
world is banded against me."

" I would not talk wicked nonsense if I were you,"

said I ; " but I will tell you what I *would* do—I would put
my head in cold water, for you had more last night than
you could carry."

" Do ye think that ? " said he, with a manner of interest
highly awakened. " Would that be good for me ? It's
a thing I never tried."

" I mind the days when you had no call to try, and
I wish, my lord, that they were back again," said I. " But
the plain truth is, if you continue to exceed, you will do
yourself a mischief."

" I don't appear to carry drink the way I used to,"
said my lord. " I get overtaken, Mackellar. But I will
be more upon my guard."

" That is what I would ask of you," I replied. " You
are to bear in mind that you are Mr. Alexander's father :
give the bairn a chance to carry his name with some responsibility."

" Ay, ay," said he. " Ye're a very sensible man, Mackellar, and have been long in my employ. But I think,
if you have nothing more to say to me I will be stepping.
If you have nothing more to say ? " he added, with that
burning, childish eagerness that was now so common with
the man.

" No, my lord, I have nothing more," said I, drily
enough.

" Then I think I will be stepping," says my lord, and
stood and looked at me, fidgeting with his hat, which he
had taken off again. " I suppose you will have no errands ?
No ? I am to meet Sir William Johnson,* but I will be
more upon my guard." He was silent for a time, and then,
smiling : " Do you call to mind a place, Mackellar—it's a
little below Eagles—where the burn runs very deep under
a wood of rowans ? I mind being there when I was a lad
—dear, it comes over me like an old song !—I was after
the fishing, and I made a bonny cast. Eh, but I was
happy. I wonder, Mackellar, why I am never happy
now ? "

" My lord," said I, " if you would drink with more moderation you would have the better chance. It is an old byword that the bottle is a false consoler."

" No doubt," said he, " no doubt. Well, I think I will be going."

" Good-morning, my lord," said I.

" Good-morning, good-morning," said he, and so got himself at last from the apartment.

I give that for a fair specimen of my lord in the morning ; and I must have described my patron very ill if the reader does not perceive a notable falling off. To behold the man thus fallen : to know him accepted among his companions for a poor, muddled toper, welcome (if he were welcome at all) for the bare consideration of his title ; and to recall the virtues he had once displayed against such odds of fortune ; was not this a thing at once to rage and to be humbled at ?

In his cups, he was more excessive. I will give but the one scene, close upon the end, which is strongly marked upon my memory to this day, and at the time affected me almost with horror.

I was in bed, lying there awake, when I heard him stumbling on the stair and singing. My lord had no gift of music, his brother had all the graces of the family, so that when I say singing, you are to understand a manner of high, carolling utterance, which was truly neither speech nor song. Something not unlike is to be heard upon the lips of children, ere they learn shame ; from those of a man grown elderly it had a strange effect. He opened the door with noisy precaution ; peered in, shading his candle ; conceived me to slumber ; entered, set his light upon the table, and took off his hat. I saw him very plain ; a high, feverish exultation appeared to boil in his veins, and he stood and smiled and smirked upon the candle. Presently he lifted up his arm, snapped his fingers, and fell to undress. As he did so, having once more forgot my presence, he took back to his singing ; and now I could hear the words, which were these from the old song of the " Twa Corbies " endlessly repeated :

> " And over his banes when they are bare
> The wind sall blaw for evermair ! "

I have said there was no music in the man. His strains had no logical succession except in so far as they inclined a little to the minor mode ; but they exercised a rude potency upon the feelings, and followed the words, and signified the feelings of the singer with barbaric fitness. He took it first in the time and manner of a rant ; presently this ill-favoured gleefulness abated, he began to dwell upon the notes more feelingly, and sank at last into a degree of maudlin pathos that was to me scarce bearable. By equal steps, the original briskness of his acts declined ; and when he was stripped to his breeches, he sat on the bedside and fell to whimpering. I know nothing less respectable than the tears of drunkenness, and turned my back impatiently on this poor sight.

But he had started himself (I am to suppose) on that slippery descent of self-pity ; on the which, to a man un-strung by old sorrows and recent potations, there is no arrest except exhaustion. His tears continued to flow, and the man to sit there, three parts naked, in the cold air of the chamber. I twitted myself alternately with in-humanity and sentimental weakness, now half rising in my bed to interfere, now reading myself lessons of in-difference and courting slumber, until, upon a sudden, the *quantum mutatus ab illo**shot into my mind ; and calling to remembrance his old wisdom, constancy, and patience, I was overborne with a pity almost approaching the passionate, not for my master alone, but for the sons of man.

At this I leaped from my place, went over to his side and laid a hand on his bare shoulder, which was cold as stone. He uncovered his face and showed it me all swollen and begrutten [1] like a child's ; and at the sight my impatience partially revived.

" Think shame to yourself," said I. " This is bairnly conduct. I might have been snivelling myself, if I had cared to swill my belly with wine. But I went to my bed sober like a man. Come : get into yours, and have done with this pitiable exhibition."

" O, Mackellar," said he, " my heart is wae ! "

" Wae ? " cried I. " For a good cause, I think. What words were these you sang as you came in ? Show pity to others, we then can talk of pity to yourself. You can be the one thing or the other, but I will be no party to half-way houses. If you're a striker, strike, and if you're a bleater, bleat ! "

" Ay ! " cries he, with a burst, " that's it—strike ! that's talking ! Man, I've stood it all too long. But when they laid a hand upon the child, when the child's threatened "—his momentary vigour whimpering off—" my child, my Alexander ! "—and he was at his tears again.

I took him by the shoulders and shook him. " Alexander ! " said I. " Do you even think of him ? Not you ! Look yourself in the face like a brave man, and you'll find you're but a self-deceiver. The wife, the friend, the child, they're all equally forgot, and you sunk in a mere bog of selfishness."

" Mackellar," said he, with a wonderful return to his old manner and appearance, " you may say what you will of me, but one thing I never was—I was never selfish."

" I will open your eyes in your despite," said I. " How long have we been here ? and how often have you written to your family ? I think this is the first time you were ever separate : have you written at all ? Do they know if you are dead or living ? "

I had caught him here too openly ; it braced his better nature ; there was no more weeping, he thanked me very penitently, got to bed, and was soon fast asleep ; and the

---

[1] Tear-marked.

first thing he did the next morning was to sit down and
begin a letter to my lady : a very tender letter it was too,
though it was never finished. Indeed, all communication
with New York was transacted by myself ; and it will be
judged I had a thankless task of it. What to tell my lady,
and in what words, and how far to be false and how far
cruel, was a thing that kept me often from my slumber.

All this while, no doubt, my lord waited with growing
impatiency for news of his accomplices. Harris, it is to be
thought, had promised a high degree of expedition ; the
time was already overpast when word was to be looked for ;
and suspense was a very evil counsellor to a man of an
impaired intelligence. My lord's mind throughout this
interval dwelled almost wholly in the Wilderness, following
that party with whose deeds he had so much concern. He
continually conjured up their camps and progresses, the
fashion of the country, the perpetration in a thousand
different manners of the same horrid fact, and that con-
sequent spectacle of the Master's bones lying scattered in
the wind. These private, guilty considerations I would
continually observe to peep forth in the man's talk, like
rabbits from a hill. And it is the less wonder if the scene
of his meditations began to draw him bodily.

It is well known what pretext he took. Sir William
Johnson had a diplomatic errand in these parts ; and my
lord and I (from curiosity, as was given out) went in his
company. Sir William was well attended and liberally
supplied. Hunters brought us venison, fish was taken for
us daily in the streams, and brandy ran like water. We
proceeded by day and encamped by night in the military
style ; sentinels were set and changed ; every man had
his named duty ; and Sir William was the spring of all.
There was much in this that might at times have entertained me ; but, for our misfortune, the weather was
extremely harsh, the days were in the beginning open, but
the nights frosty from the first. A painful keen wind blew

most of the time, so that we sat in the boat with blue fingers, and at night, as we scorched our faces at the fire, the clothes upon our back appeared to be of paper. A dreadful solitude surrounded our steps ; the land was quite dispeopled, there was no smoke of fires , and save for a single boat of merchants on the second day, we met no travellers. The season was indeed late, but this desertion of the waterways impressed Sir William himself ; and I have heard him more than once express a sense of intimidation. " I have come too late, I fear ; they must have dug up the hatchet"; he said ; and the future proved how justly he had reasoned.

I could never depict the blackness of my soul upon this journey. I have none of those minds that are in love with the unusual : to see the winter coming and to lie in the field so far from any house, oppressed me like a nightmare ; it seemed, indeed, a kind of awful braving of God's power ; and this thought, which I daresay only writes me down a coward, was greatly exaggerated by my private knowledge of the errand we were come upon. I was besides encumbered by my duties to Sir William, whom it fell upon me to entertain ; for my lord was quite sunk into a state bordering on *pervigilium*, watching the woods with a rapt eye, sleeping scarce at all, and speaking sometimes not twenty words in a whole day. That which he said was still coherent ; but it turned almost invariably upon the party for whom he kept his crazy look-out. He would tell Sir William often, and always as if it were a new communication, that he had " a brother somewhere in the woods," and beg that the sentinels should be directed " to inquire for him." " I am anxious for news of my brother," he would say. And sometimes, when we were under way, he would fancy he spied a canoe far off upon the water or a camp on the shore, and exhibit painful agitation. It was impossible but Sir William should be struck with these singularities ; and at last he led me aside, and hinted his uneasiness. I touched my head and shook it ; quite rejoiced to prepare a little testimony against possible disclosures.

"But in that case," cries Sir William, "is it wise to let him go at large?"

"Those that know him best," said I, "are persuaded that he should be humoured."

"Well, well," replied Sir William, "it is none of my affairs. But if I had understood, you would never have been here."

Our advance into this savage country had thus un-eventfully proceeded for about a week, when we encamped for a night at a place where the river ran among considerable mountains clothed in wood. The fires were lighted on a level space at the water's edge; and we supped and lay down to sleep in the customary fashion. It chanced the night fell murderously cold; the stringency of the frost seized and bit me through my coverings, so that pain kept me wakeful; and I was afoot again before the peep of day, crouching by the fires or trotting to and fro at the stream's edge, to combat the aching of my limbs. At last dawn began to break upon hoar woods and mountains, the sleepers rolled in their robes, and the boisterous river dashing among spears of ice. I stood looking about me, swaddled in my stiff coat of a bull's fur, and the breath smoking from my scorched nostrils, when, upon a sudden, a singular, eager cry rang from the borders of the wood. The sentries answered it, the sleepers sprang to their feet; one pointed, the rest followed his direction with their eyes, and there, upon the edge of the forest, and betwixt two trees, we beheld the figure of a man reaching forth his hands like one in ecstasy. The next moment he ran forward, fell on his knees at the side of the camp, and burst in tears.

This was John Mountain, the trader, escaped from the most horrid perils; and his first word, when he got speech, was to ask if we had seen Secundra Dass.

"Seen what?" cries Sir William.

"No," said I, "we have seen nothing of him. Why?"

"Nothing?" says Mountain. "Then I was right after all." With that he struck his palm upon his brow.

" But what takes him back ? " he cried. " What takes the man back among dead bodies ?   There is some damned mystery here."

This was a word which highly aroused our curiosity, but I shall be more perspicacious if I narrate these incidents in their true order.   Here follows a narrative which I have compiled out of three sources, not very consistent in all points :

First, a written statement by Mountain, in which everything criminal is cleverly smuggled out of view ;

Second, two conversations with Secundra Dass ;   and

Third, many conversations with Mountain himself, in which he was pleased to be entirely plain ;   for the truth is he regarded me as an accomplice.

NARRATIVE OF THE TRADER, MOUNTAIN

The crew that went up the river under the joint command of Captain Harris and the Master numbered in all nine persons, of whom (if I except Secundra Dass) there was not one that had not merited the gallows.   From Harris downward the voyagers were notorious in that colony for desperate, bloody-minded miscreants ;   some were reputed pirates, the most hawkers of rum ;   all ranters and drinkers ;   all fit associates, embarking together without remorse, upon this treacherous and murderous design.   I could not hear there was much discipline or any set captain in the gang ; but Harris and four others, Mountain himself, two Scotsmen—Pinkerton and Hastie—and a man of the name of Hicks, a drunken shoemaker, put their heads together and agreed upon the course.   In a material sense, they were well provided ;   and the Master in particular brought with him a tent where he might enjoy some privacy and shelter.

Even this small indulgence told against him in the minds of his companions.   But indeed he was in a position so entirely false (and even ridiculous) that all his habit of command and arts of pleasing were here thrown away.

In the eyes of all, except Secundra Dass, he figured as a common gull and designated victim ; going unconsciously to death ; yet he could not but suppose himself the contriver and the leader of the expedition ; he could scarce help but so conduct himself ; and at the least hint of authority or condescension, his deceivers would be laughing in their sleeves. I was so used to see and to conceive him in a high, authoritative attitude, that when I had conceived his position on this journey, I was pained and could have blushed. How soon he may have entertained a first surmise, we cannot know ; but it was long, and the party had advanced into the Wilderness beyond the reach of any help, ere he was fully awakened to the truth.

It fell thus. Harris and some others had drawn apart into the woods for consultation, when they were startled by a rustling in the brush. They were all accustomed to the arts of Indian warfare, and Mountain had not only lived and hunted, but fought and earned some reputation, with the savages. He could move in the woods without noise, and follow a trail like a hound ; and upon the emergence of this alert, he was deputed by the rest to plunge into the thicket for intelligence. He was soon convinced there was a man in his close neighbourhood, moving with precaution but without art among the leaves and branches ; and coming shortly to a place of advantage, he was able to observe Secundra Dass crawling briskly off with many backward glances. At this he knew not whether to laugh or cry ; and his accomplices, when he had returned and reported, were in much the same dubiety. There was now no danger of an Indian onslaught ; but on the other hand, since Secundra Dass was at the pains to spy upon them, it was highly probable he knew English, and if he knew English it was certain the whole of their design was in the Master's knowledge. There was one singularity in the position. If Secundra Dass knew and concealed his knowledge of English, Harris was a proficient in several of the tongues of India, and as his career in that part of the world had been a great deal worse than profligate, he had not thought proper to remark upon the circumstance. Each side had thus a spy-hole on the counsels of the other. The plotters, so soon as this advantage was explained, returned to camp ; Harris, hearing the Hindustani was once more closeted with his master, crept to the side of the tent ; and the rest, sitting about the fire with their tobacco, awaited his report with impatience. When he came at last, his face was very black. He had overheard enough to confirm the worst of his suspicions. Secundra Dass was a good English scholar ; he had been some days creeping and listening, the Master was now fully informed of the conspiracy, and the pair proposed on the morrow to fall out of line at a carrying place and plunge at a venture in the woods : preferring the full risk of famine, savage beasts, and savage men to their position in the midst of traitors.

What, then, was to be done ? Some were for killing the Master on the spot ; but Harris assured them that would be a crime without profit, since the secret of the treasure must die along with him that buried it. Others were for desisting at once from the whole enterprise and making for New York ; but the appetising name of treasure, and the thought of the long way they had already travelled, dissuaded the majority. I imagine they were dull fellows for the most part. Harris, indeed, had some acquirements, Mountain was no fool, Hastie was an educated man ; but even these had manifestly failed in life, and the rest were the dregs of colonial rascality. The conclusion they reached, at least, was more the offspring of greed and hope than reason. It was to temporise, to be wary and watch the Master, to be silent and supply no further aliment to his suspicions, and to depend entirely (as well as I make out) on the chance that their victim was as greedy, hopeful, and irrational as themselves, and might, after all, betray his life and treasure.

Twice in the course of the next day Secundra and the

Master must have appeared to themselves to have escaped ; and twice they were circumvented. The Master, save that the second time he grew a little pale, displayed no sign of disappointment, apologised for the stupidity with which he had fallen aside, thanked his recapturers as for a service, and rejoined the caravan with all his usual gallantry and cheerfulness of mien and bearing. But it is certain he had smelled a rat ; for from thenceforth he and Secundra spoke only in each other's ear, and Harris listened and shivered by the tent in vain. The same night it was announced they were to leave the boats and proceed by foot, a circumstance which (as it put an end to the confusion of the portages) greatly lessened the chances of escape.

And now there began between the two sides a silent contest, for life on the one hand, for riches on the other. They were now near that quarter of the desert in which the Master himself must begin to play the part of guide ; and using this for a pretext of persecution, Harris and his men sat with him every night about the fire, and laboured to entrap him into some admission. If he let slip his secret, he knew well it was the warrant for his death ; on the other hand, he durst not refuse their questions, and must appear to help them to the best of his capacity, or he practically published his mistrust. And yet Mountain assures me the man's brow was never ruffled. He sat in the midst of these jackals, his life depending by a thread, like some easy, witty householder at home by his own fire ; an answer he had for everything—as often as not, a jesting answer ; avoided threats, evaded insults ; talked, laughed, and listened with an open countenance ; and, in short, conducted himself in such a manner as must have disarmed suspicion, and went near to stagger knowledge. Indeed, Mountain confessed to me they would soon have disbelieved the captain's story, and supposed their designated victim still quite innocent of their designs ; but for the fact that he continued (however ingeniously) to give the slip to questions, and the yet stronger confirmation of his repeated

efforts to escape. The last of these, which brought things
to a head, I am now to relate. And first I should say that
by this time the temper of Harris's companions was utterly
worn out ; civility was scarce pretended ; and, for one very
significant circumstance, the Master and Secundra had been
(on some pretext) deprived of weapons. On their side,
however, the threatened pair kept up the parade of friendship handsomely ; Secundra was all bows, the Master
all smiles ; and on the last night of the truce he had even
gone so far as to sing for the diversion of the company.
It was observed that he had also eaten with unusual hearti-
ness, and drank deep, doubtless from design.

At least, about three in the morning, he came out of
the tent into the open air, audibly mourning and complain-
ing, with all the manner of a sufferer from surfeit. For some
while, Secundra publicly attended on his patron, who at
last became more easy, and fell asleep on the frosty ground
behind the tent, the Indian returning within. Some time
after, the sentry was changed ; had the Master pointed out
to him, where he lay in what is called a robe of buffalo : and
thenceforth kept an eye upon him (he declared) without
remission. With the first of the dawn, a draught of wind
came suddenly and blew open one side of the corner of the
robe ; and with the same puff the Master's hat whirled in
the air and fell some yards away. The sentry thinking it
remarkable the sleeper should not awaken, thereupon drew
near ; and the next moment, with a great shout, informed
the camp their prisoner was escaped. He had left behind
his Indian, who (in the first vivacity of the surprise) came
near to pay the forfeit of his life, and was, in fact, inhumanly
mishandled ; but Secundra, in the midst of threats and
cruelties, stuck to it with extraordinary loyalty, that he
was quite ignorant of his master's plans, which might
indeed be true, and of the manner of his escape, which was
demonstrably false. Nothing was therefore left to the
conspirators but to rely entirely on the skill of Mountain.
The night had been frosty, the ground quite hard ; and

the sun was no sooner up than a strong thaw set in. It was Mountain's boast that few men could have followed that trail, and still fewer (even of the native Indians) found it. The Master had thus a long start before his pursuers had the scent, and he must have travelled with surprising energy for a pedestrian so unused, since it was near noon before Mountain had a view of him. At this conjuncture the trader was alone, all his companions following, at his own request, several hundred yards in the rear ; he knew the Master was unarmed ; his heart was besides heated with the exercise and lust of hunting ; and seeing the quarry so close, so defenceless, and seeming so fatigued, he vaingloriously determined to effect the capture with his single hand. A step or two farther brought him to one margin of a little clearing ; on the other, with his arms folded and his back to a huge stone, the Master sat. It is possible Mountain may have made a rustle, it is certain, at least, the Master raised his head and gazed directly at that quarter of the thicket where his hunter lay ; " I could not be sure he saw me," Mountain said ; " he just looked my way like a man with his mind made up, and all the courage ran out of me like rum out of a bottle." And presently, when the Master looked away again, and appeared to resume those meditations in which he had sat immersed before the trader's coming, Mountain slunk stealthily back and returned to seek the help of his companions.

And now began the chapter of surprises, for the scout had scarce informed the others of his discovery, and they were yet preparing their weapons for a rush upon the fugitive, when the man himself appeared in their midst, walking openly and quietly, with his hands behind his back.

" Ah, men ! " says he, on his beholding them. " Here is a fortunate encounter. Let us get back to camp."

Mountain had not mentioned his own weakness or the Master's disconcerting gaze upon the thicket, so that (with all the rest) his return appeared spontaneous. For all that, a hubbub arose; oaths flew, fists were shaken, and guns pointed.

"Let us get back to camp," said the Master. "I have an explanation to make, but it must be laid before you all. And in the meanwhile I would put up these weapons, one of which might very easily go off and blow away your hopes of treasure. I would not kill," says he, smiling, "the goose with the golden eggs."

The charm of his superiority once more triumphed; and the party, in no particular order, set off on their return. By the way, he found occasion to get a word or two apart with Mountain.

"You are a clever fellow and a bold," says he, "but I am not so sure that you are doing yourself justice. I would have you to consider whether you would not do better, ay, and safer, to serve me instead of serving so commonplace a rascal as Mr. Harris. Consider of it," he concluded, dealing the man a gentle tap upon the shoulder, "and don't be in haste. Dead or alive, you will find me an ill man to quarrel with."

When they were come back to the camp, where Harris and Pinkerton stood guard over Secundra, these two ran upon the Master like viragoes, and were amazed out of measure when they were bidden by their comrades to "stand back and hear what the gentleman had to say." The Master had not flinched before their onslaught; nor, at this proof of the ground he had gained, did he betray the least sufficiency.

"Do not let us be in haste," says he. "Meat first and public speaking after."

With that they made a hasty meal: and as soon as it was done, the Master, leaning on one elbow, began his speech. He spoke long, addressing himself to each except Harris, finding for each (with the same exception) some particular flattery. He called them "bold, honest blades," declared he had never seen a more jovial company, work better done, or pains more merrily supported. "Well, then," says he, " some one asks me,'Why the devil I ran away?' But that is scarce worth answer, for I think you all know pretty well. But you know only pretty well: that is a point I shall arrive at presently, and be you ready to remark it when it comes. There is a traitor here: a double traitor: I will give you his name before I am done; and let that suffice for now. But here comes some other gentleman and asks me, ' Why, in the devil, I came back?' Well, before I answer that question, I have one to put to you. It was this cur here, this Harris, that speaks Hindustani?" cries he, rising on one knee and pointing fair at the man's face, with a gesture indescribably menacing; and when he had been answered in the affirmative, " Ah!" says he, " then are all my suspicions verified, and I did rightly to come back. Now, men, hear the truth for the first time." Thereupon he launched forth in a long story, told with extraordinary skill, how he had all along suspected Harris, how he had found the confirmation of his fears, and how Harris must have misrepresented what passed between Secundra and himself. At this point he made a bold stroke with excellent effect. " I suppose," says he, " you think you are going shares with Harris, I suppose you think you will see to that yourselves; you would naturally not think so flat a rogue could cozen you. But have a care! These half-idiots have a sort of cunning, as the skunk has its stench; and it may be news to you that Harris has taken care of himself already. Yes, for him the treasure is all money in the bargain. You must find it or go starve. But he has been paid beforehand; my brother paid him to destroy me; look at him, if you doubt—look at him, grinning and gulping, a detected thief!" Thence, having made this happy impression, he explained how he had escaped, and thought better of it, and at last concluded to come back, lay the truth before the company, and take his chance with them once more: persuaded as he was, they would instantly depose Harris and elect some other leader. " There is the whole truth," said he : " and, with one exception, I put myself entirely in your hands. What is the exception ? There he sits," he cried, pointing once more to Harris ; " a man that has to die ! Weapons and conditions are all one to me ; put me face to face with him, and if you give me nothing but a stick, in five minutes I will show you a sop of broken carrion, fit for dogs to roll in."

It was dark night when he made an end ; they had listened in almost perfect silence ; but the firelight scarce permitted any one to judge, from the look of his neighbours, with what result of persuasion or conviction. Indeed, the Master had set himself in the brightest place, and kept his face there, to be the centre of men's eyes : doubtless on a profound calculation. Silence followed for a while, and presently the whole party became involved in disputation : the Master lying on his back, with his hands knit under his head and one knee flung across the other, like a person unconcerned in the result. And here, I daresay, his bravado carried him too far and prejudiced his case. At least, after a cast or two back and forward, opinion settled finally against him. It's possible he hoped to repeat the business of the pirate ship, and be himself, perhaps, on hard enough conditions, elected leader ; and things went so far that way that Mountain actually threw out the proposition. But the rock he split upon was Hastie. This fellow was not well liked, being sour and slow, with an ugly, glowering disposition, but he had studied some time for the Church at Edinburgh College, before ill-conduct had destroyed his prospects, and he now remembered and applied what he had learned. Indeed, he had not proceeded very far, when the Master rolled carelessly upon one side, which was done (in Mountain's opinion) to conceal the beginnings of despair upon his countenance. Hastie dismissed the most of what they had heard as nothing to the matter : what they wanted was the treasure. All that was said of Harris might be true, and they would have to see to that in time. But what had that to do with the treasure ? They had heard a vast of words ; but the truth was just this, that Mr. Durie was damnably frightened and had several times run off. Here he was—whether caught or come back was all one to Hastie : the point was to make an end of the business. As for the talk of deposing and electing captains, he hoped they were all free men and could attend their own affairs. That was dust flung in their eyes, and so was the proposal to fight Harris. " He shall fight no one in this camp, I can tell him that," said Hastie. " We had trouble enough to get his arms away from him, and we should look pretty fools to give them back again. But if it's excitement the gentleman is after, I can supply him with more than perhaps he cares about. For I have no intention to spend the remainder of my life in these mountains ; already I have been too long ; and I propose that he should immediately tell us where that treasure is, or else immediately be shot. And there," says he, producing his weapon, " there is the pistol that I mean to use."

" Come, I call you a man," cries the Master, sitting up and looking at the speaker with an air of admiration.

" I didn't ask you to call me anything," returned Hastie ; " which is it to be ? "

" That's an idle question," said the Master. " Needs must when the devil drives. The truth is we are within easy walk of the place, and I will show it you to-morrow."

With that, as if all were quite settled, and settled exactly to his mind, he walked off to his tent, whither Secundra had preceded him.

I cannot think of these last turns and wriggles of my old enemy, except with admiration ; scarce even pity is mingled with the sentiment, so strongly the man supported, so boldly resisted his misfortunes. Even at that hour, when he perceived himself quite lost, when he saw he had but effected an exchange of enemies, and overthrown

Harris to set Hastie up, no sign of weakness appeared in his behaviour, and he withdrew to his tent, already determined (I must suppose) upon affronting the incredible hazard of his last expedient, with the same easy, assured, genteel expression and demeanour as he might have left a theatre withal to join a supper of the wits. But doubtless within, if we could see there, his soul trembled.

Early in the night word went about the camp that he was sick ; and the first thing the next morning he called Hastie to his side, and inquired most anxiously if he had any skill in medicine. As a matter of fact, this was a vanity of that fallen divinity student's, to which he had cunningly addressed himself. Hastie examined him ; and being flattered, ignorant, and highly suspicious, knew not in the least whether the man was sick or malingering. In this state he went forth again to his companions ; and (as the thing which would give himself most consequence either way) announced that the patient was in a fair way to die.

" For all that," he added, with an oath, " and if he bursts by the wayside, he must bring us this morning to the treasure."

But there were several in the camp (Mountain among the number) whom this brutality revolted. They would have seen the Master pistolled, or pistolled him themselves, without the smallest sentiment of pity ; but they seemed to have been touched by his gallant fight and unequivocal defeat the night before ; perhaps, too, they were even already beginning to oppose themselves to their new leader : at least, they now declared that (if the man was sick) he should have a day's rest in spite of Hastie's teeth.

The next morning he was manifestly worse, and Hastie himself began to display something of humane concern, so easily does even the pretence of doctoring awaken sympathy. The third the Master called Mountain and Hastie to the tent, announced himself to be dying, gave them full

particulars as to the position of the cache, and begged them
to set out incontinently on the quest, so that they might
see if he deceived them, and (if they were at first unsuccess-
ful) he should be able to correct their error.

But here arose a difficulty on which he doubtless counted.
None of these men would trust another, none would consent
to stay behind. On the other hand, although the Master
seemed extremely low, spoke scarce above a whisper, and
lay much of the time insensible, it was still possible it was
a fraudulent sickness ; and if all went treasure-hunting,
it might prove they had gone upon a wild-goose chase, and
return to find their prisoner flown. They concluded, therefore, to hang idling round the camp, alleging sympathy to
their reason ; and certainly, so mingled are our dispositions,
several were sincerely (if not very deeply) affected by the
natural peril of the man whom they callously designed to
murder. In the afternoon, Hastie was called to the bedside
to pray : the which (incredible as it must appear) he did
with unction ; about eight at night the wailing of Secundra
announced that all was over ; and before ten, the Indian,
with a link stuck in the ground, was toiling at the grave.
Sunrise of next day beheld the Master's burial, all hands
attending with great decency of demeanour ; and the body
was laid in the earth, wrapped in a fur robe, with only
the face uncovered , which last was of a waxy whiteness,
and had the nostrils plugged according to some Oriental
habit of Secundra's. No sooner was the grave filled than
the lamentations of the Indian once more struck concern
to every heart ; and it appears this gang of murderers, so
far from resenting his outcries, although both distressful
and (in such a country) perilous to their own safety, roughly
but kindly endeavoured to console him.

But if human nature is even in the worst of men occasionally kind, it is still, and before all things, greedy ;
and they soon turned from the mourner to their own concerns. The cache of the treasure being hard by, although
yet unidentified, it was concluded not to break camp ; and

the day passed, on the part of the voyagers, in unavailing exploration of the woods, Secundra the while lying on his master's grave. That night they placed no sentinel, but lay altogether about the fire, in the customary woodman fashion, the heads outward, like the spokes of a wheel. Morning found them in the same disposition ; only Pinkerton, who lay on Mountain's right, between him and Hastie, had (in the hours of darkness) been secretly butchered, and there lay, still wrapped as to his body in his mantle, but offering above that ungodly and horrific spectacle of the scalped head. The gang were that morning as pale as a company of phantoms, for the pertinacity of Indian war (or, to speak more correctly, Indian murder) was well known to all. But they laid the chief blame on their unsentinelled posture ; and, fired with the neighbourhood of the treasure, determined to continue where they were. Pinkerton was buried hard by the Master ; the survivors again passed the day in exploration, and returned in a mingled humour of anxiety and hope, being partly certain they were now close on the discovery of what they sought, and on the other hand (with the return of darkness) infected with the fear of Indians. Mountain was the first sentry ; he declares he neither slept nor yet sat down, but kept his watch with a perpetual and straining vigilance, and it was even with unconcern that (when he saw by the stars his time was up) he drew near the fire to awaken his successor. This man (it was Hicks the shoemaker) slept on the lee side of the circle, something farther off in consequence than those to windward, and in a place darkened by the blowing smoke. Mountain stooped and took him by the shoulder ; his hand was at once smeared by some adhesive wetness ; and (the wind at the moment veering) the firelight shone upon the sleeper, and showed him, like Pinkerton, dead and scalped.

It was clear they had fallen in the hands of one of those matchless Indian bravos, that will sometimes follow a party for days, and in spite of indefatigable travel, and unsleeping watch, continue to keep up with their advance, and steal a scalp at every resting-place. Upon this discovery, the treasure-seekers, already reduced to a poor half-dozen, fell into mere dismay, seized a few necessaries, and, deserting the remainder of their goods, fled outright into the forest. Their fire they left still burning, and their dead comrade unburied. All day they ceased not to flee, eating by the way, from hand to mouth ; and since they feared to sleep, continued to advance at random even in the hours of darkness. But the limit of man's endurance is soon reached ; when they rested at last it was to sleep profoundly ; and when they woke, it was to find that the enemy was still upon their heels, and death and mutilation had once more lessened and deformed their company.

By this they had become light-headed, they had quite missed their path in the Wilderness, their stores were already running low. With the further horrors it is superfluous that I should swell this narrative, already too prolonged. Suffice it to say that when at length a night passed by innocuous, and they might breathe again in the hope that the murderer had at last desisted from pursuit, Mountain and Secundra were alone. The trader is firmly persuaded their unseen enemy was some warrior of his own acquaintance, and that he himself was spared by favour. The mercy extended to Secundra he explains on the ground that the East Indian was thought to be insane ; partly from the fact that, through all the horrors of the flight, and while others were casting away their very food and weapons, Secundra continued to stagger forward with a mattock on his shoulder, and partly because, in the last days, and with a great degree of heat and fluency, he perpetually spoke with himself in his own language. But he was sane enough when it came to English.

" You think he will be gone quite away ? " he asked, upon their blest awakening in safety.

" I pray God so, I believe so, I dare to believe so,"

Mountain had replied almost with incoherence, as he described the scene to me.

And indeed he was so much distempered that until he met us, the next morning, he could scarce be certain whether he had dreamed, or whether it was a fact, that Secundra had thereupon turned directly about and returned without a word upon their footprints, setting his face for these wintry and hungry solitudes along a path whose every stage was mile-stoned with a mutilated corpse.

CHAPTER XII

THE JOURNEY IN THE WILDERNESS (*continued*)

MOUNTAIN's story, as it was laid before Sir William Johnson and my lord, was shorn, of course, of all the earlier particulars, and the expedition described to have proceeded uneventfully, until the Master sickened. But the latter part was very forcibly related, the speaker visibly thrilling to his recollections; and our then situation, on the fringe of the same desert, and the private interests of each, gave him an audience prepared to share in his emotions. For Mountain's intelligence not only changed the world for my Lord Durrisdeer, but materially affected the designs of Sir William Johnson.

These I find I must lay more at length before the reader. Word had reached Albany of dubious import; it had been rumoured some hostility was to be put in act; and the Indian diplomatist had, thereupon, sped into the Wilderness, even at the approach of winter, to nip that mischief in the bud. Here, on the borders, he learned that he was come too late; and a difficult choice was thus presented to a man (upon the whole) not any more bold than prudent. His standing with the painted braves may be compared to that of my Lord President Culloden* among the chiefs of our own Highlanders at the 'Forty-five; that is as much as to say, he was, to these men, reason's only speaking-trumpet, and counsels of peace and moderation, if they were to prevail at all, must prevail singly through his influence. If, then, he should return, the province must lie open to all the abominable tragedies of Indian war —the houses blaze, the wayfarer be cut off, and the men of

238

the woods collect their usual disgusting spoil of human scalps. On the other side, to go farther forth, to risk so small a party deeper in the desert, to carry words of peace among warlike savages already rejoicing to return to war : here was an extremity from which it was easy to perceive his mind revolted.

"I have come too late," he said more than once, and would fall into a deep consideration, his head bowed in his hands, his foot patting the ground.

At length he raised his face and looked upon us, that is to say, upon my lord, Mountain, and myself, sitting close round a small fire, which had been made for privacy in one corner of the camp.

"My lord, to be quite frank with you, I find myself in two minds," said he. "I think it very needful I should go on, but not at all proper I should any longer enjoy the pleasure of your company. We are here still upon the water-side ; and I think the risk to southward no great matter. Will not yourself and Mr. Mackellar take a single boat's crew and return to Albany ? "

My lord, I should say, had listened to Mountain's narrative, regarding him throughout with a painful intensity of gaze ; and, since the tale concluded, had sat as in a dream. There was something very daunting in his look ; something to my eyes not rightly human ; the face, lean, and dark, and aged, the mouth painful, the teeth disclosed in a perpetual rictus ; the eyeball swimming clear of the lids upon a field of blood-shot white. I could not behold him myself without a jarring irritation, such as, I believe, is too frequently the uppermost feeling on the sickness of those dear to us. Others, I could not but remark, were scarce able to support his neighbourhood—Sir William eviting to be near him, Mountain dodging his eye, and, when he met it, blenching and halting in his story. At this appeal, however, my lord appeared to recover his command upon himself.

"To Albany ? " said he, with a good voice.

"Not short of it, at least," replied Sir William.   "There is no safety nearer hand."

"I would be very sweir[1] to return," says my lord. "I am not afraid—of Indians," he added, with a jerk.

"I wish that I could say so much," returned Sir William, smiling; "although, if any man durst say it, it should be myself. But you are to keep in view my responsibility, and that as the voyage has now become highly dangerous, and your business—if you ever had any," says he,— "brought quite to a conclusion by the distressing family intelligence you have received, I should be hardly justified if I even suffered you to proceed, and run the risk of some obloquy if anything regrettable should follow."

My lord turned to Mountain. "What did he pretend he died of?" he asked.

"I don't think I understand your honour," said the trader, pausing, like a man very much affected, in the dressing of some cruel frost-bites.

For a moment my lord seemed at a full stop; and then, with some irritation, "I ask you what he died of. Surely that's a plain question," said he.

"O! I don't know," said Mountain. "Hastie even never knew. He seemed to sicken natural, and just pass away."

"There it is, you see!" concluded my lord, turning to Sir William.

"Your lordship is too deep for me," replied Sir William.

"Why," says my lord, "this is a matter of succession; my son's title may be called in doubt; and the man being supposed to be dead of nobody can tell what, a great deal of suspicion would be naturally roused."

"But, God damn me, the man's buried!" cried Sir William.

"I will never believe that," returned my lord, painfully trembling. "I'll never believe it!" he cried again, and

[1] Unwilling.

jumped to his feet. " Did he *look* dead ? " he asked of Mountain.

" Look dead ? " repeated the trader. " He looked white. Why, what would he be at ? I tell you, I put the sods upon him."

My lord caught Sir William by the coat with a hooked hand. " This man has the name of my brother," says he, " but it's well understood that he was never canny."

" Canny ? " says Sir William. " What is that ? "

" He's not of this world," whispered my lord, " neither him nor the black deil that serves him. I have struck my sword throughout his vitals," he cried ; " I have felt the hilt dirl [1] on his breastbone, and the hot blood spirt in my very face, time and again, time and again ! " he repeated, with a gesture indescribable. " But he was never dead for that," said he, and sighed aloud. " Why should I think he was dead now ? No, not till I see him rotting," says he.

Sir William looked across at me with a long face. Mountain forgot his wounds, staring and gaping.

" My lord," said I, " I wish you would collect your spirits." But my throat was so dry, and my own wits so scattered, I could add no more.

" No," says my lord, " it's not to be supposed that he would understand me. Mackellar does, for he kens all, and has seen him buried before now. This is a very good servant to me, Sir William, this man Mackellar ; he buried him with his own hands—he and my father—by the light of two siller candlesticks. The other man is a familiar spirit ; he brought him from Coromandel. I would have told ye this long syne, Sir William, only it was in the family." These last remarks he made with a kind of melancholy composure, and his time of aberration seemed to pass away. " You can ask yourself what it all means," he proceeded. " My brother falls sick, and dies, and is buried, or so they say ; and all seems very plain. But

[1] Ring.

why did the familiar go back ? I think ye must see for yourself it's a point that wants some clearing."

" I will be at your service, my lord, in half a minute," said Sir William, rising.—" Mr. Mackellar, two words with you " ; and he led me without the camp, the frost crunching in our steps, the trees standing at our elbow, hoar with frost, even as on that night in the long shrubbery. " Of course, this is midsummer madness," said Sir William, as soon as we were gotten out of hearing.

" Why, certainly," said I. " The man is mad. I think that manifest."

" Shall I seize and bind him ? " asked Sir William. " I will upon your authority. If these are all ravings, that should certainly be done."

I looked down upon the ground, back at the camp, with its bright fires and the folk watching us, and about me on the woods and mountains ; there was just the one way that I could not look, and that was in Sir William's face.

" Sir William," said I at last, " I think my lord not sane, and have long thought him so. But there are degrees in madness ; and whether he should be brought under restraint—Sir William, I am no fit judge," I concluded.

" I will be the judge," said he. " I ask for facts. Was there, in all that jargon, any word of truth or sanity ? Do you hesitate ? " he asked. " Am I to understand you have buried this gentleman before ? "

" Not buried," said I ; and then, taking up courage at last, " Sir William," said I, " unless I were to tell you a long story, which much concerns a noble family (and myself not in the least), it would be impossible to make this matter clear to you. Say the word, and I will do it, right or wrong. And, at any rate, I will say so much, that my lord is not so crazy as he seems. This is a strange matter, into the tail of which you are unhappily drifted."

" I desire none of your secrets," replied Sir William ;

" but I will be plain, at the risk of incivility, and confess that I take little pleasure in my present company."

" I would be the last to blame you," said I, " for that."

" I have not asked either for your censure or your praise, sir," returned Sir William. " I desire simply to be quit of you ; and to that effect, I put a boat and complement of men at your disposal."

" This is fairly offered," said I, after reflection. " But you must suffer me to say a word upon the other side. We have a natural curiosity to learn the truth of this affair ; I have some of it myself ; my lord (it is very plain) has but too much. The matter of the Indian's return is enigmatical."

" I think so myself," Sir William interrupted, " and I propose (since I go in that direction) to probe it to the bottom. Whether or not the man has gone like a dog to die upon his master's grave, his life, at least, is in great danger, and I propose, if I can, to save it.—There is nothing against his character ? "

" Nothing, Sir William," I replied.

" And the other ? " he said. " I have heard my lord, of course ; but, from the circumstances of his servant's loyalty, I must suppose he had some noble qualities."

" You must not ask me that ! " I cried. " Hell may have noble flames. I have known him a score of years, and always hated, and always admired, and always slavishly feared him."

" I appear to intrude again upon your secrets," said Sir William, " believe me, inadvertently. Enough that I will see the grave, and (if possible) rescue the Indian. Upon these terms, can you persuade your master to return to Albany ? "

" Sir William," said I, " I will tell you how it is. You do not see my lord to advantage ; it will seem even strange to you that I should love him ; but I do, and I am not alone. If he goes back to Albany, it must be by force, and it will be the death-warrant of his reason, and perhaps his life. That is my sincere belief ; but I am in your hands, and ready to obey, if you will assume so much responsibility as to command.''

" I will have no shred of responsibility ; it is my single endeavour to avoid the same," cried Sir William. " You insist upon following this journey up ; and be it so ! I wash my hands of the whole matter."

With which word he turned upon his heel and gave the order to break camp ; and my lord, who had been hovering near by, came instantly to my side.

" Which is it to be ? " said he.

" You are to have your way," I answered. " You shall see the grave."

The situation of the Master's grave was, between guides, easily described ; it lay, indeed, beside a chief landmark of the Wilderness, a certain range of peaks, conspicuous by their design and altitude, and the source of many brawling tributaries to that inland sea, Lake Champlain. It was therefore possible to strike for it direct, instead of following back the blood-stained trail of the fugitives, and to cover, in some sixteen hours of march, a distance which their perturbed wanderings had extended over more than sixty. Our boats we left under a guard upon the river ; it was, indeed, probable we should return to find them frozen fast ; and the small equipment with which we set forth upon the expedition included not only an infinity of furs to protect us from the cold, but an arsenal of snow-shoes to render travel possible, when the inevitable snow should fall. Considerable alarm was manifested at our departure ; the march was conducted with soldierly pre-caution, the camp at night sedulously chosen and patrolled ; and it was a consideration of this sort that arrested us, the second day, within not many hundred yards of our destina-tion—the night being already imminent, the spot in which we stood well qualified to be a strong camp for a party of our numbers ; and Sir William, therefore, on a sudden thought, arresting our advance.

Before us was the high range of mountains toward which we had been all day deviously drawing near. From the first light of the dawn, their silver peaks had been the goal of our advance across a tumbled lowland forest, thrid with rough streams, and strewn with monstrous boulders ; the peaks (as I say) silver, for already at the higher altitudes the snow fell nightly ; but the woods and the low ground only breathed upon with frost. All day heaven had been charged with ugly vapours, in the which the sun swam and glimmered like a shilling-piece ; all day the wind blew on our left cheek barbarous cold, but very pure to breathe. With the end of the afternoon, however, the wind fell ; the clouds, being no longer reinforced, were scattered or drunk up ; the sun set behind us with some wintry splendour, and the white brow of the mountains shared its dying glow.

It was dark ere we had supper ; we ate in silence, and the meal was scarce despatched before my lord slunk from the fireside to the margin of the camp ; whither I made haste to follow him. The camp was on high ground, overlooking a frozen lake, perhaps a mile in its longest measurement ; all about us the forest lay in heights and hollows ; above rose the white mountains ; and higher yet, the moon rode in a fair sky. There was no breath of air ; nowhere a twig creaked ; and the sounds of our own camp were hushed and swallowed up in the surrounding stillness. Now that the sun and the wind were both gone down, it appeared almost warm, like a night of July : a singular illusion of the sense, when earth, air, and water were strained to bursting with the extremity of frost.

My lord (or what I still continued to call by his loved name) stood with his elbow in one hand, and his chin sunk in the other, gazing before him on the surface of the wood. My eyes followed his, and rested almost pleasantly upon the frosted contexture of the pines, rising in moonlit

hillocks, or sinking in the shadow of small glens.   Hard by,
I told myself, was the grave of our enemy, now gone where
the wicked cease from troubling, the earth heaped for ever
on his once so active limbs.   I could not but think of him
as somehow fortunate to be thus done with man's anxiety
and weariness, the daily expense of spirit, and that daily
river of circumstance to be swum through, at any hazard,
under the penalty of shame or death.   I could not but
think how good was the end of that long travel ; and with
that, my mind swung at a tangent to my lord.   For was
not my lord dead also ?   a maimed soldier, looking vainly
for discharge, lingering derided in the line of battle ?   A
kind man, I remembered him ; wise, with a decent pride,
a son perhaps too dutiful, a husband only too loving,
one that could suffer and be silent, one whose hand I loved
to press.   Of a sudden, pity caught in my wind-pipe with
a sob ; I could have wept aloud to remember and behold
him ; and standing thus by his elbow, under the broad
moon, I prayed fervently either that he should be released,
or I strengthened to persist in my affection.

" O God," said I, " this was the best man to me and
to himself, and now I shrink from him.   He did no wrong,
or not till he was broke with sorrows ; these are but his
honourable wounds that we begin to shrink from.   O
cover them up, O take him away, before we hate him ! "

I was still so engaged in my own bosom, when a sound
broke suddenly upon the night.   It was neither very loud
nor very near ; yet, bursting as it did from so profound
and so prolonged a silence, it startled the camp like an
alarm of trumpets.   Ere I had taken breath, Sir William
was beside me, the main part of the voyagers clustered at
his back, intently giving ear.   Methought, as I glanced at
them across my shoulder, there was a whiteness, other than
moonlight, on their cheeks ; and the rays of the moon
reflected with a sparkle on the eyes of some, and the
shadows lying black under the brows of others (according
as they raised or bowed the head to listen) gave to the

group a strange air of animation and anxiety. My lord was to the front, crouching a little forth, his hand raised as for silence : a man turned to stone. And still the sounds continued, breathlessly renewed with a precipitate rhythm.

Suddenly Mountain spoke in a loud, broken whisper, as of a man relieved. " I have it now," he said ; and, as we all turned to hear him, " the Indian must have known the cache," he added. " That is he—he is digging out the treasure."

" Why, to be sure ! " exclaimed Sir William. " We were geese not to have supposed so much."

" The only thing is," Mountain resumed, " the sound is very close to our old camp. And, again, I do not see how he is there before us, unless the man had wings ! "

" Greed and fear are wings," remarked Sir William. " But this rogue has given us an alert, and I have a notion to return the compliment.—What say you, gentlemen, shall we have a moonlight hunt ? "

It was so agreed ; dispositions were made to surround Secundra at his task ; some of Sir William's Indians hastened in advance ; and a strong guard being left at our headquarters, we set forth along the uneven bottom of the forest ; frost crackling, ice sometimes loudly splitting under foot ; and overhead the blackness of pine-woods and the broken brightness of the moon. Our way led down into a hollow of the land ; and as we descended, the sounds diminished and had almost died away. Upon the other slope it was more open, only dotted with a few pines, and several vast and scattered rocks that made inky shadows in the moonlight. Here the sounds began to reach us more distinctly ; we could now perceive the ring of iron, and more exactly estimate the furious degree of haste with which the digger plied his instrument. As we neared the top of the ascent, a bird or two winged aloft and hovered darkly in the moonlight ; and the next moment we were gazing through a fringe of trees upon a singular picture.

A narrow plateau, overlooked by the white mountains, and encompassed nearer hand by woods, lay bare to the strong radiance of the moon. Rough goods, such as make the wealth of foresters, were sprinkled here and there upon the ground in meaningless disarray. About the midst, a tent stood, silvered with frost : the door open, gaping on the black interior. At the one end of this small stage lay what seemed the tattered remnants of a man. Without doubt we had arrived upon the scene of Harris's encampment ; there were the goods scattered in the panic of flight ; it was in yon tent the Master breathed his last ; and the frozen carrion that lay before us was the body of the drunken shoemaker. It was always moving to come upon the theatre of any tragic incident ; to come upon it after so many days, and to find it (in the seclusion of a desert) still unchanged, must have impressed the mind of the most careless. And yet it was not that which struck us into pillars of stone ; but the sight (which yet we had been half expecting) of Secundra ankle-deep in the grave of his late master. He had cast the main part of his raiment by, yet his frail arms and shoulders glistered in the moonlight with a copious sweat ; his face was contracted with anxiety and expectation ; his blows resounded on the grave, as thick as sobs ; and behind him, strangely deformed and ink-black upon the frosty ground, the creature's shadow repeated and parodied his swift gesticulations. Some night-birds arose from the boughs upon our coming, and then settled back ; but Secundra, absorbed in his toil, heard or heeded not at all.

I heard Mountain whisper to Sir William, " Good God ! it's the grave ! He's digging him up ! " It was what we had all guessed, and yet to hear it put in language thrilled me. Sir William violently started.

" You damned sacrilegious hound ! " he cried. " What's this ? "

Secundra leaped in the air, a little breathless cry escaped him, the tool flew from his grasp, and he stood one instant staring at the speaker. The next, swift as an arrow, he sped for the woods upon the farther side ; and the next again, throwing up his hands with a violent gesture of resolution, he had begun already to retrace his steps.

" Well, then, you come, you help——" he was saying. But by now my lord had stepped beside Sir William ; the moon shone fair upon his face, and the words were still upon Secundra's lips, when he beheld and recognised his master's enemy. " Him ! " he screamed, clasping his hands, and shrinking on himself.

" Come, come ! " said Sir William. " There is none here to do you harm, if you be innocent ; and if you be guilty, your escape is quite cut off. Speak, what do you here among the graves of the dead and the remains of the unburied ? "

" You no murderer ? " inquired Secundra. " You true man ? You see me safe ? "

" I will see you safe, if you be innocent," returned Sir William. " I have said the thing, and I see not wherefore you should doubt it."

" These all murderers," cried Secundra, " that is why ! He kill—murderer," pointing to Mountain ; " these two hire-murderers," pointing to my lord and myself—" all gallows-murderers ! Ah ! I see you all swing in a rope. Now I go save the Sahib ; he see you swing in a rope. The Sahib," he continued, pointing to the grave, " he not dead. He bury, he not dead."*

My lord uttered a little noise, moved nearer to the grave, and stood and stared in it.

" Buried and not dead ? " exclaimed Sir William. " What kind of rant is this ? "

" See, Sahib," said Secundra. " The Sahib and I alone with murderers ; try all way to escape, no way good. Then try this way : good way in warm climate, good way in India ; here, in this dam cold place, who can tell ? I tell you pretty good hurry : you help, you light a fire, help rub."

" What is the creature talking of ? " cried Sir William. " My head goes round."

" I tell you I bury him alive," said Secundra. " I teach him swallow his tongue. Now dig him up pretty good hurry, and he not much worse. You light a fire."

Sir William turned to the nearest of his men. " Light a fire," said he. " My lot seems to be cast with the insane."

" You good man," returned Secundra. " Now I go dig the Sahib up."

He returned as he spoke to the grave, and resumed his former toil. My lord stood rooted, and I at my lord's side, fearing I knew not what.

The frost was not yet very deep, and presently the Indian threw aside his tool, and began to scoop the dirt by handfuls. Then he disengaged a corner of a buffalo robe ; and then I saw hair catch among his fingers : yet a moment more, and the moon shone on something white. A while Secundra crouched upon his knees, scraping with delicate fingers, breathing with puffed lips ; and when he moved aside, I beheld the face of the Master wholly disengaged. It was deadly white, the eyes closed, the ears and nostrils plugged, the cheeks fallen, the nose sharp as if in death ; but for all he had lain so many days under the sod, corruption had not approached him, and (what strangely affected all of us) his lips and chin were mantled with a swarthy beard.

" My God ! " cried Mountain, " he was as smooth as a baby when we laid him there ! "

" They say hair grows upon the dead," observed Sir William ; but his voice was thick and weak.

Secundra paid no heed to our remarks, digging swift as a terrier in the loose earth. Every moment the form of the Master, swathed in his buffalo robe, grew more distinct in the bottom of that shallow trough ; the moon shining strong, and the shadows of the standers-by, as they drew forward and back, falling and flitting over his

emergent countenance. The sight held us with a horror
not before experienced. I dared not look my lord in the
face ; but for as long as it lasted, I never observed him to
draw breath ; and a little in the background one of the
men (I know not whom) burst into a kind of sobbing.

" Now," said Secundra, " you help me lift him out."

Of the flight of time I have no idea ; it may have been
three hours, and it may have been five, that the Indian
laboured to reanimate his master's body. One thing only
I know, that it was still night, and the moon was not yet
set, although it had sunk low, and now barred the plateau
with long shadows, when Secundra uttered a small cry of
satisfaction : and, leaning swiftly forth, I thought I could
myself perceive a change upon that icy countenance of the
unburied. The next moment I beheld his eyelids flutter ;
the next they rose entirely, and the week-old corpse looked
me for a moment in the face.

So much display of life I can myself swear to. I have
heard from others that he visibly strove to speak, that his
teeth showed in his beard, and that his brow was contorted
as with an agony of pain and effort. And this may have
been ; I know not, I was otherwise engaged. For at that
first disclosure of the dead man's eyes my Lord Durrisdeer
fell to the ground, and when I raised him up he was a corpse.

Day came, and still Secundra could not be persuaded
to desist from his unavailing efforts. Sir William, leaving
a small party under my command, proceeded on his
embassy with the first light ; and still the Indian rubbed
the limbs and breathed in the mouth of the dead body.
You would think such labours might have vitalised a
stone ; but, except for that one moment (which was my
lord's death), the black spirit of the Master held aloof from
its discarded clay ; and by about the hour of noon, even
the faithful servant was at length convinced. He took it
with unshaken quietude.

" Too cold," said he, " good way in India, no good

here." And, asking for some food, which he ravenously devoured as soon as it was set before him, he drew near to the fire and took his place at my elbow. In the same spot, as soon as he had eaten, he stretched himself out, and fell into a childlike slumber, from which I must arouse him, some hours afterwards, to take his part as one of the mourners at the double funeral. It was the same throughout ; he seemed to have outlived at once, and with the same effort, his grief for his master and his terror of myself and Mountain.

One of the men left with me was skilled in stone-cutting ; and before Sir William returned to pick us up, I had chiselled on a boulder this inscription, with a copy of which I may fitly bring my narrative to a close :

J. D.

HEIR TO A SCOTTISH TITLE,
A MASTER OF THE ARTS AND GRACES,
ADMIRED IN EUROPE, ASIA, AMERICA,
IN WAR AND PEACE,
IN THE TENTS OF SAVAGE HUNTERS AND THE
CITADELS OF KINGS, AFTER SO MUCH
ACQUIRED, ACCOMPLISHED, AND
ENDURED, LIES HERE FOR-
GOTTEN.

———

H. D.

HIS BROTHER,
AFTER A LIFE OF UNMERITED DISTRESS,
BRAVELY SUPPORTED,
DIED ALMOST IN THE SAME HOUR,
AND SLEEPS IN THE SAME GRAVE
WITH HIS FRATERNAL ENEMY.

———

THE PIETY OF HIS WIFE AND ONE OLD
SERVANT RAISED THIS STONE
TO BOTH.

EXPLANATORY NOTES

PREFACE

7 *In 1783*: there is some inconsistency here: the brothers in *The Master* died in the winter of 1764–5.

8 In a letter to his friend, Charles Baxter, of May 1894, Stevenson writes:

> I must tell you, what I just remembered in a flash as I was walking about dictating this letter—there was in the original plan of the *Master of Ballantrae* a sort of introduction describing my arrival in Edinburgh on a visit to yourself and your placing in my hands the papers of the story. I actually wrote it, and then condemned the idea—as being a little too like Scott, I suppose. Now I must really find the MS. and try to finish it for the E.E. [Edinburgh Edition] It will give you, what I should so much like you to have, another corner of your own in that lofty monument. (*Letters*, XXV, pp. 395–6.)

Note: unless otherwise stated *Letters*, and volume numbers, refer to the Swanston Edition of the Works of R. L. Stevenson.

CHAPTER I

9 *David First*: King of Scots (c. 1084–53), youngest son of Malcolm III and St. Margaret.

11 *Prince Charlie's landing*: Charles Edward, the Young Pretender, son of "James VIII", the Old Pretender, and Clementina Sobieski, sailed from France to Scotland in June 1745. With seven companions, he landed on 23 July at Eriskay in the Outer Hebrides; on 19 August he raised his standard at Glenfinnan in Inverness-shire. With the support of an army drawn mainly from the central and western Highlands, and the north-east Lowlands, the Jacobites were successful in taking Perth on 4 September

and Edinburgh on 17 September. They were again victorious at Prestonpans; but, in the south, anticipated
support from the English Jacobites was not forthcoming
and, on 6 December, Prince Charlie's army made an unwilling retreat from Derby. Despite another victory at
Falkirk on 17 January 1746, the Young Pretender was
finally defeated at Culloden on 16 April 1746. See William
Ferguson, *Scotland 1689 to the Present*, Edinburgh,
1968, ch. V.

In May 1892, in the last years of his life, and at a time
when he was much preoccupied with Scottish themes,
R.L.S. planned a novel, *The Young Chevalier*, based on the
Young Pretender's adventures in France from 1749 on-
wards. This exists only as a fragment, consisting of a
Prologue and part of chapter one: the Master appears in
the latter in the company of his friend, Balmile. The two
men are seen as potential rivals for the love of a French
wine-seller's wife. Her attraction to the Master causes a
brawl between her husband and an innocent onlooker and
partly recalls James Durie's attempts in *The Master* to
win again his brother's wife's affections (chapter IV); and
cf. "An Old Song" and note 11 in Introduction.

12 *King James . . . King George*: for a discussion of James and
Henry Durie as Jacobite and Whig respectively, and the
historical implications of this division, see Joseph J. Egan,
"From History to Myth: A Symbolic Reading of *The
Master of Ballantrae*", *Studies in English Literature, 1500–
1900*, VIII, 1968, pp. 699–710.

13 *I could not love you, dear, so well, loved I not honour more*:
from Richard Lovelace's "To Lucasta on going to the
Wars".

15 *my Lord George*: Lord George Murray (*c.* 1700–1760), a
Jacobite General who, together with his brother, the
Marquis of Tullibardine, took part in the 1715 rising.
Murray was pardoned in 1726 but his brother remained in
exile. When Prince Charles Edward returned to Scotland
in 1745, accompanied by Tullibardine, Murray joined the
Jacobite Rebellion. He was unpopular amongst some of the
Prince's Irish followers and aroused Charles Edward's
jealousy. It was his decision to retire from Derby and he

advised against fighting at Culloden. After the '45 he escaped to France and died in Holland.

16 *lichtit*: Sc., arrived, alighted.

17 *Non vi sed saepe cadendo*: not by force but by frequent falling. (Perseverance is essential.)

18 *sneckdraw*: Sc., a crafty, deceitful person, a sneak-thief, cf. *sneck up*, p. 85 and note.

CHAPTER II

21 (1) *Claverhouse*: John Graham of Claverhouse, Viscount Dundee (1648–89); in 1687 he was commissioned to act against the Covenanting conventicles then meeting in south-western Scotland. Famed for his cruelty during this "Killing Time", John Graham lives in Scots memory as "Bloody Clavers" or, more occasionally, as "Bonnie Dundee". Scots writers of the nineteenth century are divided as to his true part in the Covenanting troubles: see Walter Scott's *Old Mortality* (1816), James Hogg's *The Brownie of Bodsbeck* (1818) and John Galt's *Ringan Gilhaize* (1823). Scott's novel is biased towards Claverhouse and against the "beastly Covenanters"; Hogg's and Galt's novels are more emphatically pro-Covenanter. In 1893, Stevenson considers a novel of the "Killing Time". *Letters*, XXV, p. 361. This survives only as the fragment named *Heathercat*, Swanston, XXI.

(2) *scaur*: Sc., crag, cliff; a steep hill from which the soil has been washed away.

25 In this passage, readings of the Scots words of the First Edition have been restored. Stevenson's letters show that Sidney Colvin, editor of the E.E., was, on occasion, unsure about Scots words and that Stevenson sometimes had to insist that these were "good Scots" and not errors. Cf. *R.L.S.: Stevenson's Letters to Charles Baxter*, ed. De Lancey Ferguson and Marshall Waingrow, 1956, p. viii; and see, e.g., *Letters*, XXV, p. 294.

thrapples: Sc., throats; *fleering*: Sc., jeering; *chapping*: Sc., knocking; *lum*: Sc., chimney; *poother*: Sc., gunpowder; *Auld Hornie*: Sc., Satan.

33 *the Prince's Irishmen*: R.L.S. has made Francis Burke, his

second narrator in *The Master*, one of the army of exiled Irish Jacobites who supported the Young Pretender.

CHAPTER III

38 *Alan Breck*: the romantic Jacobite hero of Stevenson's *Kidnapped* (1886) who appears also in its sequel, *Catriona* (1893). Mackellar's comment on the Chevalier's "weakness" on names suggests his own trustworthiness on details (albeit minor ones) and also casts doubt on Burke's reliability.

55 *Blackbeard*. Edward Teach (d. 1718), an English pirate famed for many robberies and atrocities in the Spanish Main, the West Indies and off the coasts of Carolina and Virginia. He was finally killed by a Lieutenant Maynard, on the instructions of the Governor of Virginia, on 22 November 1718. His nickname derives from his habit of tying the ends of his long, black beard with ribbon and curling them around his ears. In view of the dates (Burke's narrative here covers the period immediately following Culloden, 1746), Mackellar's comment is just: the Teach of *The Master* could not be the notorious Blackbeard.

62 *Governor Clinton*: George Clinton (1686–1761), British colonial administrator, Governor of New York, 1743–53.

CHAPTER IV

71 *Criffel*: a mountain peak in the Grampians.

73 *Scots Fund*: money collected for the support of any Scot who had been forced to leave his country for his part in the Jacobite Rising of 1745.

80 This is the letter which Mackellar later suggests may have contributed to Ballantrae's change of heart towards Francis Burke when they meet in India (see pp. 150–1).

82 (1) *swithering*: Sc., dithering.
    (2) *toised:* eyed from head to foot.

85 *sneck up*: Sc., lock up.

97 *French Indies*: although by the early eighteenth century, the British had gained the major share of European trade with India, the French developed into serious rivals at the

time of the conflict over the Austrian Succession. In 1746, under the direction of Joseph Francois Dupleix, they took Madras in addition to Pondicherry which they had previously acquired. In 1748, Dupleix embarked on a policy of intervention in internal Indian affairs, supporting claimants to Hyderabad and the Carnatic. Britain followed with counter-intervention. Although peace was made in 1754, the Seven Years' War (1756) brought further conflict and disaster to the French. By 1761, their influence in the Indian states was greatly undermined and their presence in India very much reduced. The Master's plans to make his fortune in French India begin about the time of the "Troyes letter" (pp. 79–80), that is in July, 1756, and they are still in his mind on his return in November of that year. The dates suggest that his plans are connected with Mr. Lally's expedition to India (see note to p. 147). The Master later states, when reviewing his life, that the arrival of Clive defeated his plans (p. 206 and note).

98 *into France*: First Edition reads, ". . . into France. Or so he said; though I have suspected since it did not go so far."

99 *shog*: Sc., shock, jolt. Here Henry adopts a comparable use of Scots to the Master's to coincide with a somewhat ignominious scheme to discountenance his brother.

CHAPTER V

106 *cette . . . rager*: "this dull-witted passivity which infuriates me". The Master's use of French in private with Henry contrasts with his affectionate Scots accent when he speaks in public to his brother (p. 88).

120 *she spied . . . second time*: in the First Edition, this reads:

She spied the sword, picked it up, and seeing the blood, let it fall again with her hands thrown wide. "Ah!" she cried. And then, with an instant courage, handled it the second time, and thrust it to the hilt into the frozen ground.

Writing to the French translator, Marcel Schwob, Stevenson recommends either *Kidnapped* or *The Master* for French editions, and says:

Should you choose the latter, pray do not let Mrs. Henry thrust the sword up to the hilt in the frozen ground—one of my inconceivable blunders, an exaggeration to stagger Hugo. Say "she sought to thrust it in the ground." *Letters*, XXV, p. 52.

CHAPTER VI

137 *Gnatique . . . miserere*: "Have mercy, O dear one, on a son and a father, I pray." Virgil, *Aeneid*, VI, 116–17.

140 *Did you . . . devil*: First Edition reads, " 'Is it true, Mr. Mackellar?' asked the child. 'And did you really see the devil?' "

142 *neglected*: First Edition reads, ". . . neglected: the more praise to her that she played it well."

145 *wouldnae*: "wouldna" has here been amended to "wouldnae" to follow the First Edition.

CHAPTER VII

147 (1) *calendars*: the sense suggests that Burke means "calenders", members of an order of mendicant dervishes in Turkey and Persia.

(2) *Mr. Galland*: Antoine Galland (1646–1715), French orientalist and archaeologist and the first European translator of the *Arabian Nights*. These tales appeared as *Les mille et une nuits* (1704–17): the first English translation of some of Galland's tales was published in 1713.

(3) *Mr. Lally*: Thomas Arthur Lally, Comte de, Baron de Tollendal (1702–66), the son of a French noblewoman and an Irish Jacobite. Lally served in the French army, commanded the *regiment de Lally* at Fontenoy and was made a brigadier by Louis XV; previously involved in various Jacobite plots, he was one of the Irishmen who supported the Young Pretender in the 1745 Rising. After Culloden, he escaped to France and served with Marshal Saxe. With the outbreak of war with England in 1756, he commanded a French expedition to India (see note to p. 97). Arriving at Pondicherry in April 1758, Lally had, at first, some military success but, with the arrival of the British Fleet in 1758, he was forced to retreat from Madras. After further defeats, he was sent, in 1761, as prisoner of war to London where he discovered that he had been accused of treachery in France. He insisted on returning to France to stand trial

and, after many delays, was sentenced to death, and be-
headed on 9 May 1766. His sentence is generally considered
a political gesture and Lally himself a scapegoat for
Louis XV's more unpopular policies. Despite Francis
Burke's assured statement that the cipaye would have
"let himself be cut to pieces for any of the brave countrymen of Mr. Lally", Lally is said to have been disliked by
the native Indians, to have disregarded their caste traditions and refused their assistance.

149 *divil; broth of a boy*: Burke's Irishisms (*broth of a boy*: a
good, brave boy) contrast with Mackellar's Scots in *his*
narratives. Some contemporary reviewers objected to the
diversity of styles in *The Master*, singling out, for instance,
Burke's and Secundra Dass's linguistic mannerisms as not
adding "either to the intelligibility or symmetry of the
narrative"; *Glasgow Herald*, 17 October 1889. For a representative selection of contemporary reviews, see *Robert
Louis Stevenson, The Critical Heritage*, ed. Paul Maixner,
1981.

CHAPTER VIII

153 *taper . . . fire*: First Edition reads, "taper and some lurching
reverberation of the fire".

CHAPTER IX

193 *twenty-second day of July*: First Edition reads, "second day
of July". Presumably R.L.S. amended this in view of the
length of the sea voyage to New York.

CHAPTER X

195 *another Albanian*: the suspicion that the Master murdered
Chew would, if we are to believe Burke's account of the
matter (p. 64), seem unjustified.

196 *General Clinton*: there is a minor error here: in a letter to
E. L. Burlingame, Stevenson writes, "Please see that I
haven't the name of the Governor of New York wrong
(1764 is the date) in part ten." *Letters*, XXIV, p. 320. However, George Clinton's first period of office as Governor
(1777–95) is too late to coincide with the events narrated
in this chapter.

206 *Clive*: Robert Clive (1725–74), the statesman and General famous for his part in the founding of the empire of British India. In 1751, when the French hold was at its strongest in southern India, Clive lead an expedition against Arcot, capital of the Carnatic, in order to relieve the British in Trichinopoly. He held Arcot for 53 days and the French surrendered in June 1752. After three years in England, Clive returned to India and, in 1756, was in charge of re-establishing the British position in Bengal where he successfully marched on Calcutta in January 1757. Clive left India in 1760 but returned, in 1764, to Bengal for his second governorship.

CHAPTER XI

215 (1) *course*: First Edition adds here, "We lived meanwhile in Albany, but though alone together in a strange place, had little traffic beyond formal salutations."

(2) *Michael Scott*: (c. 1160–c. 1235); philosopher, astrologer and mathematician. In Scots legend, he lives as a wizard and a confederate of the devil. Stevenson's allusions here are explained by Walter Scott's note to Canto II, st.xiii, of *The Lay of the Last Minstrel* (1805):

Michael Scott was, once upon a time, much embarrassed by a spirit, for whom he was under the necessity of finding constant employment. He commanded him to build a *cauld* or dam-head, across the Tweed at Kelso: it was accomplished in one night, and still does honour to the infernal architect. Michael next ordered that Eildon hill, which was then a uniform cone, should be divided into the three picturesque peaks which it now bears. At length the enchanter conquered this indefatigable daemon, by employing him in the hopeless and endless task of making ropes out of sea sand.

Michael Scott also appears in Canto XX of Dante's *Inferno* in the company of magicians and sooth-sayers. See also Rev. J. Wood Brown, *Life and Legend of Michael Scott*, 1897. Perhaps Mackellar's suggestion supports the idea that Henry now shares something of the Master's diabolic nature and that Mackellar is *his* familiar spirit just as Secundra Dass is the Master's. Cf. Gifford, op. cit., Intro.

216 *Sir William Johnson*: (1715–74); British soldier and

American pioneer, Johnson is mainly known for his part in the affairs of the Six Nations (a confederacy of eastern North American Indian tribes). Governor George Clinton (see note to p. 62) appointed him to take charge of their affairs in 1744, and, in 1746, he was engaged in preparing them for war with French Canada. He later became a life-member of the Governor's Council, and resigned his Indian responsibilities until 1754. As Major-General, Johnson commanded the expedition against Crown Point in 1755; at the Battle of Lake George, he defeated the French and Indian armies. He was created a baronet in this struggle. In 1756, he became "Sole Superintendent of the Six Nations and Other Northern Indians". It is said to be due to his influence that the Iroquois (Six Nations) refused to join Pontiac's conspiracy (1763; peace treaty concluded with Sir William in 1766). In terms of his influence over the Indian tribes Stevenson compares him to Scotland's Lord President at the time of the 'Forty-five (p. 238 and note).

218 *quantum mutatus ab illo*: "how changed from what he once was".

CHAPTER XII

238 *Lord President Culloden*: Duncan Forbes (1685–1747), lawyer, laird of Culloden from 1734. In the period of the 1745 Rising, he persuaded many of the northern clans of Scotland not to join the Jacobite forces. In this, lies the comparison with Sir William Johnson as the voice of reason in the face, respectively, of rebellious Highlanders and unruly Indians.

249 *He bury, he not dead*: in "The Genesis of *The Master of Ballantrae*", Stevenson writes of his effort to find "some similar belief" to that of Marryat's *Phantom Ship* (i.e. the Flying Dutchman legends), to be the "centre-piece" of *The Master*:

In the course of this vain search there cropped up in my memory a singular case of a buried and resuscitated fakir, which I had been often told by an uncle of mine, then lately dead, Inspector-General John Balfour. (*Tusitala*, X, xxiii.)

THE WORLD'S CLASSICS

A Select List

BEN JONSON: Five Plays
Edited by G. A. Wilkes

LEONARDO DA VINCI: Notebooks
Edited by Irma A. Richter

HERMAN MELVILLE: The Confidence-Man
Edited by Tony Tanner

PROSPER MÉRIMÉE: Carmen and Other Stories
Translated by Nicholas Jotcham

EDGAR ALLAN POE: Selected Tales
Edited by Julian Symons

MARY SHELLEY: Frankenstein
Edited by M. K. Joseph

BRAM STOKER: Dracula
Edited by A. N. Wilson

ANTHONY TROLLOPE: The American Senator
Edited by John Halperin

OSCAR WILDE: Complete Shorter Fiction
Edited by Isobel Murray

A complete list of Oxford Paperbacks, including The World's
Classics, OPUS, Past Masters, Oxford Authors, Oxford
Shakespeare, and Oxford Paperback Reference, is available in the
UK from the Arts and Reference Publicity Department (RS),
Oxford University Press, Walton Street, Oxford OX2 6DP.

In the USA, complete lists are available from the Paperbacks
Marketing Manager, Oxford University Press, 200 Madison
Avenue, New York, NY 10016.

Oxford Paperbacks are available from all good bookshops. In case
of difficulty, customers in the UK can order direct from Oxford
University Press Bookshop, Freepost, 116 High Street, Oxford
OX1 4BR, enclosing full payment. Please add 10 per cent of
published price for postage and packing.